Searching For Sunrise

by

Lyndsey Jeminson

Copyright © 2023 Lyndsey Jeminson

All rights reserved.

ISBN:
ISBN-13:

Warning: This book deals with confronting subjects including depression and suicide.

More than eight Australians die every day from suicide and seventy-five per cent of those are male. (Abs.gov.au)

The impact of this is far reaching. Besides the tragic loss of the person, suicide deeply affects family, friends, colleagues, first-responders and whole communities.

The characters and events in this book are entirely fictional and any similarities to people living or dead are purely coincidental. However, the research involved in creating this story delved through the very real thoughts and feelings of people both suffering from depression and/or at risk of suicide. It must be said that experiences of depression and suicide are different for everyone, as is recovery from mental illness, and I must stress that this is a story of just one woman's method of coping with tragedy and loss.

I would like to thank the brave people who kindly opened up to me about their experiences of depression and suicide and gave permission for me to draw from their insights into mental health to create this story.

If you are affected by depression and/or have thoughts of suicide, help is available.

Contacts

In Australia contact lifeline.org.au or beyondblue.org.au

In the UK contact mind.org.uk or supportline.org.uk

In the USA contact 988lifeline.org

If your country is not listed, please refer to your national mental health crisis helpline/website for help.

Your life matters.

For Bruce, with love

Steph

Dear Steph,

It has tormented me for many years that I could not find the courage to speak these words aloud. Maybe if I had, I wouldn't be in the position I've found myself in. Before I begin, please believe me when I say I love you and I'm so very sorry.

You are everything I ever wanted, and I need you to understand that my decision has nothing to do with you, or our boys, but entirely on me.

As you know, my upbringing was traumatic. I was raised in a household where fear of my father was far worse than the fear of God I had drilled into me every waking hour. The physical abuse and mental torture he inflicted on me throughout my teenage years took its toll on me. I thought escaping him would be the end of my nightmares. You introduced me to a whole new life, one of love and compassion, and I suppressed the darkness in me.

When Caleb was born and I held him in my arms, I vowed to be the father I never had, but as he grew older, the praise and encouragement turned into criticism and pressure. I wanted him to succeed where I had failed, but instead of supporting him in his goals, I allowed my father's toxic traits to seep through.

I see a lot of myself in Caleb, his strive for perfection and constant need of approval, that I live in perpetual fear of passing on my damaging behaviour. I can hand on heart say I never laid a finger on my sons, but from my experience, the emotional trauma runs deeper than the physical abuse ever has.

I'm stuck in the cycle, Steph, and it must end with me. I have never spoken of the desolation that overwhelms me every day. The fear, the desperation, and the despair have taken over my life. I can no longer see a future. It's been a constant fight, just trying to keep my head above water, but I'm done. I've lost the battle.

You will be better off without me. You are strong, Steph, and you will get through this and raise our boys to be fine young men. They can't turn out like me. I want them to be happy and know they are loved beyond measure.

Steph, you are a wonderful mother, and the best wife I could have wished for. I'm sorry I failed you. I'm sorry I couldn't be the husband you deserve, and I hope that in time you will find true happiness with a man worthy of your love.

I have left my affairs in order as much as possible.

I hope one day you'll find it in your heart to forgive me.

Chris

Angry tears stain my cheeks as I clutch the letter in

my sweaty grip. I'm furious that he's put me in this position. A kaleidoscope of thoughts swarms my mind, but I'm numb to them all. The police knocked on my door last Friday with the news my husband's BMW had been involved in a head on collision with a tree, killing my husband on impact, and my light went out. Chris was my light, my love, the father of my children. How did I miss he was so unhappy?

The black midi dress hugs my curves and my mass of curls has been tamed and scraped into an elegant bun, my neat appearance belying the turmoil within. I glare at my husband's handwriting as it scowls back at me.

A knock sounds on my bedroom door and I stuff the letter back into the envelope, swiping my hand across my face to hide any evidence.

'Mum?' Caleb calls.

'Come in Cale,' I dig deep to find levity in my voice that is lacking.

Caleb pushes the door and stands in the open doorway, looking at me for approval. At sixteen, he's tall and broad, athletically built from all his football training. Dressed in smart black pants and a long-sleeved shirt, he looks unsure of more than just his appearance.

'Is this okay?' he asks, nodding his head at his attire.

'You look lovely, Cale. Is Levi ready?'

Caleb shrugs, his eyes raking over my face, taking in my tear stains.

'Are you okay, Mum?'

I stand and deposit the envelope back in the drawer to deal with later, putting on my game face to get myself and my two boys through this upcoming ordeal.

'Yes, I'm okay, love,' I lie, again wiping at the residual staining across my cheeks. 'We'll get through this, I promise.'

Caleb nods. His relationship with his father has been fractious; a constant pattern of hard work and commitment, striving for his approval, but falling short of his unattainable standards. My view of their relationship has become much clearer, a beacon of light shed on the reasons Chris pushed him so hard. The cycle of abuse that Chris had fought hard to escape was so entrenched in his own psyche, it had literally killed him. He died to save his own son from the hurt and pain he'd suffered all his life. My mind can't decide whether that's honourable or just plain tragic.

I shake my head to clear my thoughts, unable to reconcile myself with the fact I hadn't known the depth of his suffering. I refuse to believe my entire marriage has been a fraud, but what else could it have been if I was unaware of something so intrinsic about my husband?

'Mum?' Levi hesitates, lingering in the doorway. 'What's going on?'

'Nothing sweetheart, I was just thinking of your dad, that's all.'

I hold my arms out wide to both of my boys and pull them towards me, squeezing them tight. They're all I have left of him. I breathe them in, dropping a kiss to each of their heads, their sweet baby smell long since replaced by the scent of adolescence.

'Whatever happens today, I'll be here for you, okay? Take a breath and we'll get through it together. I love you both.'

'We love you too, Mum,' Levi says.

The crunch of tyres on the gravel driveway alerts me to the time. I swing my bag over my shoulder and take a deep breath before ushering my boys outside under the clear blue sky, the weather a sharp contrast to the sombre occasion.

'Good morning Mrs Wilson, Caleb, Levi,' the funeral director speaks to the three of us. 'We'll get through today as seamlessly as we can. Please speak up if there's anything I can do for you.' He bows his head and opens the rear door of the Mercedes limousine. The boys sit shoulder to shoulder, their faces stoic in expression. As the car approaches the end of our tree-lined driveway, I recognise the moment Caleb catches sight of the hearse, its engine idling on the road outside our property, the coffin containing his father visible through the tinted windows. His gasp is audible, sending Levi's hand to grip his brother's. Whether in support or need, it isn't clear. Watching the solidarity between my sons as they shoulder their shared trauma, my head is besieged with thoughts of my new discovery. I've cycled through all five stages of grief in the short time since I found the letter earlier this morning. I'm unsure what led me to open that drawer, but now that I've unleashed this can of worms, my brain is struggling to comprehend what this means for us all for the future. The biggest dilemma I'm facing is whether to show it to the boys or continue to let them believe their father's death was a tragic accident. Chris had named Caleb in the letter and even though his rationale was about protecting his son from entering the same spiralling vortex of pain that had consumed him, just knowing that their relationship was a significant factor in his father's death could trigger a multitude of emotions for Caleb with devastating consequences. I don't want to cause my children unnecessary pain, but to conceal something so significant may do more harm than good. As my emotions once again flicker through the stages of grief in rapid succession, I settle back on anger.

'Mum, we're here,' Levi's voice coaxes me from my absence. I snap back to the present and beseech myself to get a grip.

'Are you ready for this?' I reach for their hands. They both shake their heads in a solemn nod and climb out of the door being held open by the funeral director. Dazed by the sunshine, the remaining members of our little family huddle together outside the crematorium. Mourners arrive, paying their respects as they pass us by, and the three of us make our way inside the building.

I absent-mindedly tune out of most of the service; I have no specific religious alignment, but my husband was raised in a God-fearing family. Even though he hadn't attended church for many years, a Christian funeral service would have been important to him. My eyes glaze over as the manager from Chris's dental practice delivers a bible reading and his oldest friend reads the eulogy. Neither speech occupies my mind.

I'm only aware the service is over when Levi grasps my arm and ushers me to stand. My lifeless expression can be forgiven today of all days. Clutching my sons' hands, I bow my head and walk back down the aisle to the awaiting car. I don't have the mental capacity to speak to the other mourners, but I need to prepare myself for when they descend on my house for the wake. I haven't been involved in the plans. My closest friend, Terri, has taken over with profound consideration for my loss.

I expect a large turnout back at the house. Chris was popular in both his personal and professional life, and the crematorium bursts at the seams. The three of us settle in for the car journey home; Caleb plugged into his earphones and Levi scrolling through his phone. I sit and contemplate the future and the impending gloom of life as a single mother of teenage boys. And worse, the long and lonely times ahead when my boys no longer need me.

I thank the funeral director for his kindness, and I'm greeted at my back door by the caterer. Terri booked a local company, run by a family from the boys' school, and the kind eyes and a glass of red are welcomed.

'Thank you, Josie, that's very thoughtful.' I flash the most genuine smile I've conveyed all day.

'You're welcome, Steph.' Josie's tone is compassionate. 'We have everything set up and ready to go. We'll circle around with the food as and when your guests arrive, along with champagne. Beer, wine and soft drinks are in the bar fridges on the veranda.'

'I appreciate it, thank you.'

'That's what I'm here for. Why don't you take a breather outside before everyone arrives?'

I nod, grateful for her warmth, and make my way to the veranda, taking in the comfort of my surroundings. Chris and I bought the property many years ago, and it's been an ongoing labour of love. We restored the original house and had the garden and pool area landscaped and manicured. We're surrounded by ten acres of bushland, which incorporates a small paddock where Levi keeps his sheep, and another area for his chicken coop. It's a beautiful place to live, and I always assumed Chris and I were happy here together. I sense a shadow cloud my face as my thoughts turn dark and I'm reminded once again of the reason for today.

A rumble of cars makes its way down the driveway, doors slamming as people exit their vehicles. I mask my face with that of the perfect hostess and welcome our family and friends, thanking them for their kindness. Some are close, others I barely know, but I treat them all with the same reserve.

I've never wished more that I could fast forward time. Or go back. I'm not sure how long I can keep my current mood under wraps. In fact, I don't think I would've got through the day if it hadn't been for Terri, who has remained close by my side throughout.

'Hey Steph, how are you holding up?' Alison sidles up beside me. Chris's practice manager for over twenty years, Alison and I have become friendly over the years.

'I'll be glad when today's over.'

'I'm sure you will. I can round people up if that'll help.' Alison's eyes glance at the hordes of well-wishers making no effort to leave.

'Yeah, maybe, if they don't start making a move

soon. Listen, Ali, I'm sorry I've not spoken to you about the future of the practice, but I promise to get the very best outcome for you and the other staff.'

The expression that meets mine is one of bewilderment.

'What do you mean?'

'Well, I'll have to sell, but I'll need to speak to the other dentists first to get their input.'

'Steph, the sale's already gone through. It settled last month. I've signed my contract with the new owner.' She's confused why I'm only hearing of this now.

My stomach turns. I'm blindsided by my friend's words.

'What sale?' The tremor in my voice is clear as my full awareness of what this means hits me.

'You weren't aware he sold the practice?' Alison's mouth hangs open at the downright deceit of her ex-employer. Chris had asked for her discretion regarding the sale, but she'd never imagined he would have kept it from his wife.

'N-no.' I'm rendered unable to form a coherent sentence, aghast at the sheer number of secrets I've stumbled across in one day.

Alison bites her lip, her thought process obvious, trying not to say something she might regret.

'It surprised me when he told me he was selling up, but…' she pauses, a dark cloud settling over her face.

'Christ, Steph, it's almost like he knew he didn't have long left.' She clasps her hand to her mouth, unconcealed shock flooding her face.

I close my eyes, blinking away the impending tears.

'Ali.' I lower my voice. 'This is between you and me…'

'Steph, what is it?'

'I found a suicide note this morning.'

Nick

Nick Salvatore pounded the pavement, his breathing heavy, his thoughts concentrated on the news his best friend had just shared. It had rocked him. He remembered Steph. It was difficult not to. They'd only met a handful of times over the years at events hosted by Paul and his husband, Gerry, but she'd left an impression. She was beautiful, but also intelligent and quick-witted. She had certainly charmed him. The news of her husband's tragic demise evoked powerful memories of his own past trauma, and his heart went out to her. It was a devastating blow to anyone, being widowed, with two children to raise. He felt compelled to offer both support and comfort, but debated whether he knew her well enough to encroach on her grief.

Nick and Paul's friendship went way back. The two psychologists had taken on the heavy burden of guilt together when Nick's first wife, and Paul's best friend Lee, had died many years earlier. Neither man had seen the signs of post-natal depression until it was too late and their lives were shattered. Nick buried his grief, focusing only on his two young daughters, ensuring life for them continued as smoothly as possible under the tragic circumstances. It wasn't until his second marriage began to unravel that Nick finally allowed himself to grieve fully, and Paul was with him every step of the way, stitching back together the empty fabric of his life, and loving Nick's girls like they were his own.

Nick's second marriage stumbled from the beginning. He never loved Sarah, not the way she loved him. She was besotted from the outset. He was desperate to find a replacement mother for his girls. By the time he realised he wasn't in love with her, Millie had come along and entrenched herself in his heart the same way Hannah and Lucy had. Nick's three daughters meant everything to him, and he didn't want to de-stabilise their lives. The marriage fell apart anyway. Sarah's love for Millie visibly outshone any feelings she had for her stepdaughters, and Hannah became jealous of the attention her youngest sister received. The effects of seeing his eldest daughter suffer sent Nick spiralling into an unexpected and intense form of delayed grief. With Paul's help, he managed to climb from the pit of despair to dissolve his marriage and give his daughters the love and attention they needed. He worked hard to re-establish his relationship with his two grown-up daughters and had finally found happiness within himself.

Nick wiped the sweat from his brow with the bottom of his t-shirt and unlocked his front door. He'd bought the house following his divorce; it was compact, but big enough for his needs. There were two bedrooms on the top floor, with a shared bathroom. One belonged to Millie, and the other had been Lucy's room before she moved out. Hannah had left home before the divorce, the strained relationship with her step-mum and her dad's spiralling delayed grief becoming too much to bear. Hannah and Lucy now shared an apartment, and although Millie technically lived with her mum, she stayed with her dad often.

He made his way to the kitchen and switched on his coffee machine. The motor whirred as it ground the beans, spitting the dark roast into the basket. Nick picked up his phone as he waited for the espresso to extract into his mug. He didn't have Steph's number. They didn't know each other well enough, but a quick search on Facebook messenger found her almost immediately. He structured his thoughts as he stretched his milk, swirling it around the metal jug to create the perfect blend to add to his coffee.

Nick sat on his tiny deck, savouring the smooth warmth of his drink while his fingers tapped away on his phone, deleting and re-writing his message.

Dear Stephanie,

You may not remember me, but we've met several times at Paul and Gerry's. I've just heard about your devastating news and wanted to reach out to offer my deepest condolences for your loss. I appreciate you have lots of resources at your fingertips, and many people wishing to help, but I've been where you are, and I understand what you are going through. If you ever need a friendly ear or a shoulder to cry on, please pick up the

phone.
 I mean that sincerely.
 Nick Salvatore

Nick pressed send. She probably wouldn't call, but the offer was there.

Steph

I run my fingers over the letter. Backwards and forwards, trying to glean any scrap of guidance in figuring out my next move. Alison knew Chris almost as well as I did and I'm reassured that she, too, had missed any signs of his depression. The fact that Chris sold his dental practice without my knowledge has me most perturbed. His death appears to have been one calculated move after another and the sheer notion of that sends a cool shiver through my body. I'm hoping our lawyer will provide clarity.

'Mum?' Caleb startles me and I slip the letter back into the drawer. I can't face answering questions about its contents right now, if ever.

'Hey sweetheart, how are you holding up after today?'

'I'm okay,' he mumbles. 'I was thinking I'd go back to school tomorrow.'

'If you're ready, I think the distraction will be good for you.' Routine will be beneficial for moving forward.

'What were you looking at?' he queries.

The cool prickle of dread rushes my body, creeping inwards from the tips of my fingers.

'What was what?' I splutter.

'That piece of paper you just had.' He's nothing if not persistent.

'Oh, nothing, just something for Dad's practice.' The lie is unconvincing. I know it and he knows it.

There's a split second when Cale locks his eyes on mine, challenging. He blinks and the moment is gone.

'What'll happen to the practice?' Caleb asks, changing tack.

'I'm not sure, Cale. I need to speak to our lawyer.' The heaviness of that particular meeting weighs on me. 'You don't need to worry about it. Just concentrate on yourself. I'm here for you if you need to talk, Caleb. Don't forget that.'

'I'm fine, Mum.'

'It's okay not to be fine, Cale. You've lost your dad. I'm just saying, if you need to talk about it, I will always make the time to listen,' I reiterate, concern mounting at the thought of one of my boys heading down the same road as their father. My biggest worry now is how to navigate them through the next few weeks and months in the least disruptive way possible.

Caleb mutters and turns to leave. 'I'm off to bed, night.'

'Night, Cale, I'll see you in the morning.'

My phone blows up with a string of notifications, drawing my attention from my present unease. Most are messages of condolence. One is from Terri, her nightly check-in, and another from my colleague, Paul, offering his love and support in whatever way I may need it. I'm surrounded by good people and I know I can count on any one of them in my hour of need, but they all have lives of their own and families to take care of. I can only request so much of their time. I continue the listless scroll until one message captures my attention. Nick Salvatore. The name strikes me with a certain familiarity.

Upon opening the message, it becomes clear who he is. If my recollection is accurate, Paul's friend is tall, with dark hair and a swarthy complexion. Easy on the eye if a little miserable is my immediate judgement. I recall his wife making a scene and storming out of Paul's wedding ceremony several years ago, leaving her husband seething. We've spoken several times over the years at various events we've attended, but I wouldn't profess to knowing him well. If my memory serves me correctly, Nick and his wife divorced soon after the whole wedding fiasco. The message feels personal. He's telling me he understands how I feel because he's experienced the same trauma. He can't be comparing his divorce to my husband's death. The concept makes me feel nauseous and I close the message and scroll on.

After such a trying day, I thought sleep would engulf me. I toss and turn, my mind buzzing with all the new knowledge the day has brought. My thoughts soon wander from this new, unrecognisable version of Chris to the loving man to whom I was married. I miss him. I miss his presence, his touch, his funny little ways. It's difficult to visualise my life without him. Nothing feels familiar anymore. I need that. I need to engage in a familiar routine. Whenever I'd had a bad day, Chris would make me a hot chocolate before bed, complete with marshmallows and whipped cream. He once told me it was a routine his mum had started with him when he was young, when his dad had made him feel worthless. I think it's what I need right now.

'Hey, Mum.' Levi appears beside me in the kitchen. 'You making hot chocolate?'

'I am. Do you want one?' I ask.

'Please.'

'You can't sleep either?'

'I thought I would after today,' Levi says, 'but my brain's still wired.'

My heart breaks to see my boys having to process the loss of their father. I can't even begin to think about how they'll deal with the full truth.

'It's a lot to take in, hey sweetheart?'

'Yeah, it is. I still can't believe he's gone. I keep thinking about what happened. Did he lose control or did he hit a roo? I just can't get my head around it.'

Adrenalin surges through my body. My heart pounds in my chest and my tongue feels rough in my mouth when I try to speak. I cannot keep the truth from them, but I need to get more answers.

'I know, sweetheart. It's difficult to make sense of, but I think it might help if we try not to dwell on how it happened and just try to work on processing the fact it did happen,' I say. 'Like I said to your brother earlier, don't bottle up your feelings. I'm always here to listen if you need to talk.'

'Same goes for you, Mum.'

I whisk the chocolate powder into the warmed

milk and pour the thickened mixture between two mugs. After adding the marshmallows and a quick squirt of cream, I slide one across the bench to Levi. I smile and watch as he takes a sip. Although he's a couple of years younger than Caleb, he often appears older. Things don't come as easily for Levi as they do for his brother, yet he has a wisdom and maturity well beyond his years. He's thoughtful and charming and is determined to do things his own way. Chris didn't put the same pressure on Levi as he did on Caleb. As with everything since his death, I question the reasoning behind that. Had he not thought him good enough? Or had he just known he wouldn't reach his desired outcome that way? Levi is very much his own person and never seeks validation from anyone else. I know it's pointless analysing something I'll never get clarification on, so I snap myself out of this wasted thought process.

This evening is surprisingly warm, and Levi and I sit outside with the dogs snuggled close by, the gentle sounds of nature providing a welcome moment of peace. I open a packet of Tim Tam biscuits and we begin to devour them.

'You didn't buy the double coat ones,' Levi muses as he dunks his third one.

'I know, disappointing, hey?' The ordinary conversation makes me smile. 'What was I thinking?'

Levi laughs, but catches himself. Guilt torments his face.

'It's okay to laugh, Levi,' I assure him, craving that same levity for myself. 'Just because Dad's gone, it doesn't mean our lives have ended too. We have to make the best of what we have left. He would want that for us.'

'I know, it just feels too soon.'

'I understand that. The grieving process is unique for everyone and there's no set time period.' I've reverted to doctor mode. 'We'll all have good days and bad days, so if something makes you laugh, go with it because some days you won't feel like laughing at all.'

Not sure where this strength has come from, I dig deep, trying to provide every shred of guidance and support I can muster, no matter my own feelings. My boys must take priority. Working as a GP I've witnessed numerous patients dealing with grief firsthand and it's one of the most difficult times for people to navigate, but what I have learnt over the years is that having support, in whatever form, is key to traversing the journey.

We hug our mugs in contemplative silence, whilst demolishing the packet of biscuits. Sometimes, chocolate fixes everything, if only for a few moments.

My fingers drum on the sculpted arm of the antique chair. I look around at the wood panelled waiting room of Hartley, Tate & Jones and feel the anger stage recommence with a vengeance. My lawyer, Jason Tate, has been with both Chris and me since the start, and has dealt with both businesses along with our personal affairs.

The receptionist interrupts my restlessness.

'Mrs Wilson, you can go through. Jason's expecting you.'

I gather my bag and jacket from the adjacent chair and knock on Jason's office door before entering. He stands from behind his desk, his arms wide in sympathetic greeting. We hug briefly before he ushers me towards the informal lounge area in the corner of his office. Jason's a damn good lawyer, but as a man, I've never taken to him in the way Chris did. I find he lacks integrity; his manner is a little too flirty, his hands a little too friendly, and his track record with women is something I have little respect for.

'I'm so sorry for your loss, Steph.' His brows furrow with unease.

I nod, sinking into the leather couch.

'Coffee?' Jason asks, and again I only offer a nod.

He pops his head out of the door and puts an order in with his receptionist before slumping into the chair opposite me, his fingers loosening his tie.

'How are you holding up, Steph? How are the boys?'

'Let's cut to the chase, Jason. What the fuck has been going on?' I want answers.

Jason is taken aback by my forthright statement.

'I'm not sure what you mean, Steph.'

'Then let me make myself clear.' My tone is snarky and I don't hold back. 'First, my husband crashes his car into a tree and dies. Second, I find a suicide note.' Jason gasps at the obvious surprise. 'And third, I discover Chris sold his practice. How much do you know?'

'Steph, I had no idea… I mean, I knew about the sale, but the other… fuck. I'm so sorry to hear that. God, if I'd known that was what he was planning…' Jason's eyes are brimming with tears, and I realise I could have handled that a little more compassionately. Chris and Jason weren't friends per se, more long term acquaintances and occasional golf partners. I adjust my tone, silently admitting I may have come across as a little aggressive.

'When did he sell? And why? He never even discussed it with me, Jason.' My voice catches. Our coffee arrives, allowing me a momentary reprieve.

The receptionist puts the tray on the coffee table, arranged with a coffee pot, cream, and a selection of miniature muffins.

'The sale went through around four or five weeks ago. He sold to one of the other dentists at his practice. He made some changes to his will, too. It all makes sense to me now.'

Jason pauses, scrubbing his hand over his jaw, unsure how to proceed.

'What did the note say? Did it give you any clarification?' He squirms at his own question, realising his insensitivity.

'It's fine, Jason. There's no easy way to talk about all this. The letter didn't help, to be honest. I think I'd have preferred to keep thinking it was an accident. He was depressed, and I had no idea. What kind of GP am I if I never picked up on the signs?' I shake my head. 'Now I see it. It's clear as day.'

Jason pulls up Chris's file, laying all the details out before me. Chris has crossed every 't' and dotted every single 'i'. There's a trust for each of the boys and enough life insurance to keep me financially comfortable for the rest of my life, even if I gave up my career tomorrow.

'I'll get everything moving, Steph. If you need me for anything, call me.' His eyes zero in on mine with a suggestive gaze, sparking an awkward vibe.

I force a smile, nodding before leaving the office,

feeling somehow tainted.

My X5 rolls to a halt under the car port beside my home and I sigh as I switch off the engine. I allow a vacant expression to mask my face as I sit for a few moments in the safety of my own little bubble. I need to speak to the boys about this unravelling situation, but I need a moment. There's no easy way to tell your children their father took his own life.

A flurry of activity captures my attention and I watch in horror as my boys fly out of the back door and on to the lawn, fists flying. They've never been the closest of siblings, but I've never seen them get physical with each other before. I fling open the car door and rush towards the battle scene to find Levi pinned to the floor, Caleb pummelling him hard with his fists.

'Caleb!' I grab the back of his shirt. 'Get off him.'

Levi lies still, his hands covering his face in protection. He doesn't stand a chance against his much bigger, stronger, older brother.

'Caleb!' I scream at him a second time, shoving harder to get him off his brother. He rolls onto the grass before pushing himself up to stand, glaring at me with what I can only describe as loathing.

'Fuck you!' He storms back into the house and leaves me stunned in his wake. I turn my attention to my youngest son laid out before me with tears in his eyes.

'Hey, sweetheart. Are you okay?' I'm wary of whatever caused them to come to blows.

Levi nods, sitting up, his finger running across his lip.

'It's split, and it looks like he got your eye, too.

That's going to be a shiner. Do you mind telling me what's going on?'

Levi's tears spill over, and he hangs his head.

'What is it?' I ask.

Levi falls into my arms, sobbing on my shoulder.

'Levi, why were you fighting?' I ask again once his tears have subsided.

'He found the letter.'

I feel the colour leave my face as I think through the repercussions of what this means.

'Oh, Levi, I only found it myself on the morning of the funeral. I was going to talk to you both once I'd got my head around it. I'm sorry you had to find out this way.'

'It's okay, Mum, that's what I tried to tell Cale, but he wouldn't listen. He just went off.' Levi lifts the hem of his t-shirt and wipes away the tear stains on his cheeks, blotting his runny nose to stem the drips.

'We'll get you cleaned up and have a chat.'

Caleb

Dear Dad

I hate you for this.

You made me feel like I'm not good enough, like I could never live up to your ridiculously high standards.

Well, fuck you. Fuck you and your rules.

You put so much pressure on me, but gave Levi a pass to do whatever the hell he wanted with no consequences.

Fuck you for not having the balls to fight.

But most of all, fuck you for leaving me. I'll never forgive you for what you've done to our family.

I wish I'd never found your stupid letter. You've made me question my whole life.

What's the point of anything?

Why do I even play football? Has it always been for you?

I don't even know anymore.

You think I'm like you, but you're wrong. I'm stronger than you because I would never ruin my family like you just have.

Caleb

Nick

'Dad!' Millie gunned for her father's attention.

Nick snapped out of his reverie and brought his mind back to the present. His youngest daughter was walking towards him across the edge of the oval after celebrating their first win of the season. He blinked, trying to shake off the preoccupation that he'd succumbed to over the last few days. A team talk with the girls was where he needed to focus his attention. Coaching Millie's dismal team had been something he'd volunteered for several years earlier, and it had become the single best part of his week. Millie's talent far outshone the rest of the girls, but she adored the team and loved the time she spent with her dad. Nick would love Millie to move on to a better team, but he cherished the time he got to spend with her.

'Okay girls, huddle up,' he said, as they all made their way over to him, jubilant smiles on their faces. 'Good effort this week. You deserved that win.'

He kept it short and sweet, knowing they were all itching to get away, and after wishing them a good weekend, he threw an arm around Millie's shoulders as they made their way back to his car.

'Are you okay, Dad?' Millie asked, climbing into the passenger seat after throwing her bag in the back. 'You seem a little distracted.'

Nick shook his head at his wise daughter. 'You know me too well, Mills.'

'Come on then, out with it, a problem shared and all that.'

'Are you turning the tables on me?'

'What can I say? If there's one thing I've learnt from having a psychologist for a dad, it's that talking out your problems really does help,' Millie said, 'even when you're reluctant.' She glared at her dad, not allowing him to avoid her question.

Nick sighed. 'It's Paul's friend, Steph. Her husband died last week.'

Millie frowned. 'That's so sad. Are you concerned about Paul, or has it brought back difficult memories for you?'

Nick turned to his daughter; his forehead crinkled in thought.

'I'm not sure, to be honest, but it's had me feeling all jittery.' Nick screwed his eyes up tightly, considering his feelings. 'I've met Steph and her husband several times and I reached out to her, thinking that maybe I could help. She hasn't replied and now I feel like I might have overstepped. She probably doesn't even remember me.'

Millie watched her dad as he berated himself, overthinking his actions.

'Dad, don't beat yourself up. It was nice of you to reach out, but she probably has a lot going on right now. Don't take it personally that she hasn't replied,' Millie counselled.

'I know. I don't know what's wrong with me. You're probably right, it's probably just stirred up emotions I haven't experienced in a while.'

'You sure that's all it is?'

Nick started the ignition and put the car in reverse. As he looked over his shoulder, he caught Millie's guarded gaze and carefully considered her question.

Nick hoped Paul would be able to offer some perspective on his recent musings. He considered his friend to be a voice of reason whenever something weighed on his mind.

'Hey mate, you look like shit,' Gerry said in greeting, opening the door further to allow Nick access.

'Cheers, man,' Nick huffed.

Gerry grinned. 'Come on through. Coffee or something stronger?'

'Coffee's fine. Is Paul around?' Nick asked.

'Through here, Nick,' Paul's voice sounded from the kitchen.

Paul frowned when his husband appeared with Nick in tow.

'You okay? You look like shit,' Paul emulated Gerry's concern.

Nick glared at his friends. 'Do I really look that bad?'

'You look like you have something on your mind and judging by the fact you rarely turn up unannounced I'd say I'm right,' Paul guessed, guiding his friend towards a stool at the kitchen island while his husband got to work on the coffee.

Nick sighed, something he had done a lot over the last few days.

'You're right, I do, but you'll think it's weird.'

'Try me,' Paul said, reaching out to give Nick's hand a supportive squeeze.

'It's your friend, Steph. I can't stop thinking about her situation.' Nick frowned. 'I sent her a message to offer my support, not that she'll have any idea who I am. I don't know, I guess it's just brought all my memories to the surface, and I felt I needed to do something.'

'Nick, of course she knows who you are. You two are my closest friends. You've met numerous times.' Paul frowned at Nick's lack of certainty. 'It was thoughtful of you to reach out.'

Nick's eyes glazed, a lump forming in his throat, rendering him voiceless.

Gerry carefully put three mugs on the granite island, then squeezed Nick's shoulder gently before taking a seat.

'Losing a spouse will affect you for the rest of your life, Nick. It's normal to feel emotional when you hear of someone else's loss. You have an affinity with Steph, you know what she's going through, and it will be reigniting memories and emotions of your own,' Paul gently counselled.

'You're right, I know,' Nick said. 'I guess I just feel helpless. I don't even know her that well.'

'It's been a huge shock, but she has a great support network. She'll get through it. I know she'll appreciate your message.'

Nick nodded. 'Let her know that I've been there if she ever wants to talk. The circumstances are different, but the grief is the same.'

'I will,' Paul assured him.

Nick's mood lifted after unloading to his friends. Paul was right, the situation had brought back memories and emotions surrounding his own wife's death. It had been over twenty years, but the full extent of grief hadn't truly hit him until the breakdown of his second marriage. His focus on making sure his girls were okay followed closely by a new wife and a new baby had forced him to keep a lid on his grief until it became too strong to constrain any longer and it had bubbled up slowly from deep within him and spilled over, drowning every aspect of his life. Paul had been there to guide him through, and the love of his girls had helped heal his wounds.

He unlocked his front door and walked inside the quiet walls of his house. It rarely felt like a home unless his girls were there. Nick looked around sadly at the sparse furnishings and minimal decor. It was comfortable and clean, but it lacked warmth. Maybe a woman's touch. Admittedly, he missed a woman's touch, too. After the divorce, he was glad to be alone; the drama Sarah had brought to his life was heavy, and he didn't have the strength to carry it. Now he was stronger, and the loneliness had begun to creep in. Feeling a readiness to move forward, he wondered if that's why he was so caught up in Steph's situation. Maybe he just didn't want anyone else to feel the loneliness that he'd been feeling of late.

Steph

Caleb skulks into the lounge room and flops onto the couch, refusing to make eye contact. I perch on the edge of the coffee table facing the boys and take a deep breath before addressing the difficult situation we've found ourselves in.

'I'm sorry you found out the way you did, Caleb, but you shouldn't have been snooping. I had planned to talk to you both today now that I've spoken to our lawyer. I was hoping he might be able to shed more light on the matter.'

'That's bullshit and you know it, Jason has nothing to do with this.' Caleb's combative attitude is like a red rag to a bull and I fight to keep my rage under wraps. I take another breath to centre myself before addressing them again.

'This is difficult for all of us, but can you please listen to what I have to say?'

A barely perceptible nod of the head from both boys gives me the go ahead to continue.

'I found the letter the morning of the funeral. I knew nothing of Dad's illness. And that's what this was, boys, a mental illness.'

Levi's lower lip quivers as Caleb glares at me with eyes of steel.

'I was speaking to Alison afterwards, and she told me that Dad had sold the practice recently. She was shocked that I didn't know. I was hoping to get clarity from Jason as to why he'd sold without telling me.'

Levi's head jerks up in surprise.

'Dad sold the practice without telling you?' I can only nod in response.

'So, what did Jason say?' Caleb asks, his tone still contentious.

'Not a lot, really.' I don't want to discuss this with my children, but I don't think I have a choice. 'He hadn't known that Dad sold without my knowledge, and when I told him about the note, he said his actions and requests over the last few months made much more sense to him.'

'What do you mean? What made more sense?' Levi asks.

'Well, not only did Dad sell the practice, he also upped his life insurance and set up trust funds for both of you.'

'So he's been planning to off himself for a while then?' Caleb spits.

'Caleb!' I struggle to stay calm and keep the tears at bay.

'Cale, stop being a dick. This isn't Mum's fault,' Levi fires at his brother.

'She's a fucking doctor, Levi. How could she not know he needed help?' Caleb turns to me and asks me the one question that I have no answer to. 'Why didn't you know?'

'Caleb, I've been asking myself that question since the moment I read the letter, but depression isn't always cut and dried. He obviously didn't want me to know. You read the letter. He said he wished he could talk to me, but he just couldn't find the strength within himself. Your dad had a tough relationship with his father and after his mother died, he never saw him again. He told me fragments of what happened to him when he was younger, but when we got married he was determined to put his past behind him. He didn't want that part of his life to overshadow his life with us. If I'd had any idea that he'd been harbouring such desolate thoughts, I would've arranged for some help.' As angry as I still feel towards Chris, I don't want my boys feeding on resentment. It's important they have compassion for their father's illness.

'Mental illness still has such a stigma attached to it, but it's just like having a physical illness and often can be treated successfully. I want you to understand that his death had nothing to do with us and everything to do with his illness.' I hope like hell neither one of them takes on any guilt.

'But if I'd got better grades, or played better footy, he wouldn't have done it,' Caleb shrugs, torment weighing heavy in his eyes.

'Caleb, listen to me. That's not what this is about. Please don't think like that. Dad's illness had nothing to do with you.' My heart breaks for Caleb, understanding exactly what he'd derived from his father's words.

'That's not true, Mum, and you know it. He said so himself in the letter. He killed himself because of me. Because he didn't want to follow in his dad's footsteps. If I hadn't given him a reason to be disappointed in me all the time he wouldn't have done it and he'd still be here,' Caleb's physical frame folds in on himself and his hands fist his eyes, shamefully trying to eradicate the tears flooding down his cheeks.

I leap forward, pulling him into my arms. He stiffens before finally giving in and allowing himself to break. Sobs wrack his body and I hold him firmly until the anger and devastation drain from him.

'Caleb, sweetheart,' I pull back and take his face in my hands. 'That's not true. It wouldn't have mattered if you'd scored a hundred per cent in every test or if you'd won the Brownlow Medal. It was never about you. Your dad suffered from past trauma, which managed to consume him and manifest itself in ways that might not make sense to us. He didn't want to put pressure on you, but he didn't know any other way. He didn't know how to ask for help. There's nothing you could've done differently, Cale. Please don't blame yourself.'

Caleb sniffs and wipes his face on his sleeve.

'Promise me,' I reiterate, needing to know he understands. I accept the slight nod of his head as confirmation and continue on the subject.

'It's important we talk about how we feel in the wake of all this. It doesn't matter if you talk to me, your friends, or the school counsellor, but please don't bottle things up, okay?'

I watch them both as my words sink in.

'I'm serious boys.'

Both Caleb and Levi are a little taken aback by the vehemence in my voice and I'm starting to feel like my words may have got through.

'Right, now let's talk about what happened outside.'

Caleb turns to look at Levi for the first time since he sat down, and when he realises the damage he's done, his eyes widen in shock.

'Shit, I'm sorry, bro.'

'It's okay, but don't do it again. It fucking hurt.' Levi grins at his brother.

'Boys! Stop with the language. I've heard enough.'

'Sorry, Mum,' Levi says. Caleb's cheeks flush.

'Thank you for apologising to your brother. Now do you mind telling me why you took your anger out on Levi?'

Caleb knows I won't drop the subject until I've got to the bottom of it

'I found the letter, and I was pissed at you for not telling us. He tried to tell me you would've had your reasons, but I guess I just lost it. I was mad. I didn't mean to hurt him.'

'Thank you for being honest, but next time you feel that way, please talk to me first instead of using violence. That's not okay, Caleb, you could've done some serious damage.'

Caleb hangs his head in defeat.

'I'm not going to punish you this time due to the circumstances, but you won't get a second chance. Grief doesn't excuse violence.'

Caleb's eyes meet mine, a complex confusion of grief, shame, anger, and guilt, and I know in my heart it's time to buckle up for the long ride ahead.

'Mum?' Levi asks, brushing his blonde curls from his face. 'Can I ask you something?'

My hand pauses on the vegetable knife. I need to return to some semblance of normal after a week of not cooking. Admittedly, cooking is baby steps in the grand scheme of things, but it's a start.

'Of course. What is it?'

Levi leans his elbows on the wooden bench top,

worrying his lip between his teeth. It's unusual for Levi not to be forthright, his mind is generally an open book. I don't rush him. I wait patiently while he orders his thoughts.

'Why did Dad only pick on Caleb?'

I'm stumped by his question. The issue has already run deeper than I'd originally thought.

'I'm not sure that he picked on him, Levi. Is that what you saw?'

Levi eyes me like I'm crazy.

'Are you kidding? He picked on him all the time and put so much pressure on him to do well. I'm not gonna lie. I'm grateful I never got that kind of attention, but I always felt bad for Cale. I also kind of wondered whether it was just because I'm not clever like Cale and he never expected much from me,' Levi shrugs.

I suddenly feel like I don't know my own children. I had no idea Levi felt this way.

'Levi, that's not true. You're clever in different ways. Just look at the money you've made from your little business, buying your own chooks and selling their eggs. Just because you might not get A's in English and Maths doesn't mean you won't amount to anything. Where's this coming from? It's not like you.' I'm completely floored by the sentiments my usually confident and carefree son is conveying.

'I know that, Mum, that's not what I mean.' Levi rolls his eyes. 'I guess I'm just thinking a lot about Dad and why he was like he was. Some things make more sense now, but other things, I don't know, it's just a lot to get my head around.'

'It is a lot, Levi, and we have to try to accept that

we might never fully understand. I think maybe Dad saw himself in Caleb and he wanted him to succeed in ways that he hadn't. From what he said in the letter and reading between the lines, I guess what started out as encouragement and support of Cale turned into pressure and criticism. He didn't have a good role model.'

'Did you know his dad?' Levi asks.

'I met him several times when we first started dating; he wasn't a nice man, Levi. He made your dad's life a misery, and everyone around him. Once your dad left home, he kept his distance as much as possible, and after your grandmother passed away, he never saw his dad again. He died not long after. I honestly thought he'd closed that chapter and never looked back,' I muse, realising with hindsight that's not how the mind works.

'Trauma runs deep, and can affect survivors in so many ways, which is why I'm encouraging you and Caleb to talk about how you feel. If you ever feel like you're struggling, I need to know. You read your dad's letter. The cycle has to stop with you guys. It's not a sign of weakness or failure to get the help we need. It's just like getting a cast on a broken arm.'

Levi nods slowly, taking in everything I've said, and we fall comfortably into a pensive silence. I've never worried about Levi in the way I have with Caleb, but I'm beginning to see a few little chinks in his armour. Cale has always been desperate for acceptance, from me, from his dad, his football coaches, friends, and even his teachers. That's always given him the drive to be his best, but relying on other people's views and opinions has the power to bring someone down as quickly as it builds them up. Thinking about that now, it's blatantly obvious to me that was what Chris used to control Cale. Anger was Chris's presiding emotion whenever Caleb didn't meet his high standards. Being told to "man up" when he hadn't played well or done badly in a test only fuelled Cale to push himself harder, even though his father's demands often made him miserable. I berate myself for not seeing those toxic patterns before. I'd always worried about the amount of pressure Cale put on himself, but I'd completely missed the control his father had over him. Now, it seems I not only have Cale to worry about, but his brother too. If Levi's been harbouring feelings that he was unworthy of his father's love and attention, who knows what damage has already been done? I don't want to feel anger towards Chris. He was a good husband, and his issues obviously ran deep, but right now I'm struggling to feel the compassion I ought to.

'Do you need help with dinner?' Levi asks, breaking the silence with a lighter subject.

'No, I'm fine thanks, love, you go out and sort your animals.' I'm proud of my entrepreneurial son. I'm proud of both of my boys. Even more so now that I have a deeper understanding of what they've been dealing with.

'Speaking of…' Levi draws out his words, a sure sign he's after something.

'Oh no, what now?' His face tells me he has another crazy idea up his sleeve.

'I was thinking of buying a goat.' Levi flashes the cheeky grin he knows I can't say no to.

I laugh again, grateful he still seems well adjusted, despite his earlier comments.

'As long as you know what you're doing and take on all the extra responsibilities that will bring,' I warn, knowing it will be his top priority, along with his chooks and his sheep.

'Awesome. I'll call my guy later,' he says, heading out of the door with a spring in his step.

I shake my head, smiling as I watch him go. The fact that he has "a guy" is not even a surprise to me at this stage.

'Boys, dinner's ready.'

I heap three plates with food. Levi's at the table within seconds, always ready to get his fill. I pour myself a glass of wine and sit down to join him. I welcome the first few sips as the buzz brings a much needed relief after today's stress. As we tuck into our meal, there's no sign of Caleb and I frown at Levi, wondering where he is.

'I'll go see if he's coming,' Levi says, pushing back his chair.

While he's gone, I savour the strong flavour of the wine and mentally remind myself that this is becoming a daily practice. I vow to myself that this will be my last midweek glass. I certainly don't want to fall into that trap with everything else I have to deal with.

'He's not coming.' Levi shrugs and returns to his seat.

'Why not?' A sense of unease surges through my stomach.

'He said he's not hungry. He was just laid on his bed with his headphones on.'

It's not like Caleb to miss a meal and the possible reasons for that troubles me more than I'd like to admit.

Steph

'Morning, Steph.' My receptionist welcomes me back to work. Her glazed eyes crinkle at the corners. 'I've not booked you up too much, just like you asked, but if you need me to fill more of your time, let me know, won't you?'

'Thanks, Jayne, I appreciate that.'

I walk through to the kitchen to find my colleague, Jonathan, at the coffee machine preparing for his day.

'Usual?' He turns as I enter, his eyes sympathetic to my situation.

'I'd love one, thanks Jon.' I sink into a chair at the kitchen table.

'How're you holding up since the funeral?' Jon asks. 'And the boys, how are they coping?'

I shake my head, thinking of everything I've learnt since I last saw my work colleagues at Chris's funeral.

'Jon, you wouldn't believe me if I told you.' I say and laugh without humour. 'It's just gone from bad to worse.'

'Try me.' Jon is visibly concerned by my comment. 'Do you have some time?'

I glance at the wall clock and nod as I take the coffee mug he offers me, slurping the foam off the top as Paul walks in.

'I'll grab one of those too, Jon.' Paul winks at Jonathan and drops a friendly kiss on my head, squeezing my shoulder as he sits.

'Hey Paul,' I offer a tired smile, grateful for the friendship of my workmates. 'Well, now you're both here, I may as well update you.'

Jon finishes making Paul's coffee, grabs his own and joins us at the table, eager to learn what else could have gone wrong for me over the last few days.

I brief them on the note, the sale of Chris's practice, and explain my concerns about Caleb.

'Shit, Steph, I'm so sorry you're having to deal with all this,' Jon says, squeezing my hand.

'I'm happy to have a chat with Caleb if you're worried,' Paul's voice carries a gentle lilt. 'I'm always here for you, too. My friend, Nick, also asked me to pass on his condolences. He's been where you are, Steph. He understands what you're going through if you ever want to speak to someone a little more impartial.'

'Yes, I remember him. He messaged me last week, actually. It was nice of him, but didn't you mention that him and his wife got divorced?' I ask for clarification. 'I mean, it's hardly the same thing. She was the one that stormed out of your wedding. Or am I confusing them with someone else?'

'No, you've got the right person, and yes, Nick and Sarah did get divorced soon after my wedding. When I said he's been in your position, I meant with his first wife. Lee was my best friend from school. I introduced the two of them. She passed away when their two girls were only very young. It was devastating for all of us.'

'Oh Paul, I'm so sorry, that's awful.'

'It was a difficult time,' he nods. 'The offer's there, Steph, from both of us. Any help you need, whether it's for you or the boys, please reach out.'

'Thanks Paul, I appreciate that. I must admit, Chris's admission that he was suffering from depression completely blindsided me. I won't miss the warning signs again.'

'Try not to worry, Steph, we'll get you through this together,' Jonathan chips in.

'Thank you. I'm grateful for you both.'

I muster up an empty smile before dropping my used mug in the sink full of bubbles.

'I guess I should get ready for my first patient.'

'Hi Jayne,' I say when I pick up my desk phone.

'Steph, I have the school on the line. Can I put them through?' Jayne asks.

'Of course, thanks Jayne.'

I dull the expletives that are careening around my head when I hear the call transfer through.

'Stephanie Wilson speaking,' I introduce myself politely. I don't like to use the title of doctor outside of the work environment.

'Mrs Wilson, this is Sue from school. I'm so sorry to bother you at work.'

'Not a problem. Are the boys okay?'

'I'm afraid it's Caleb. There was an altercation in his second period class this morning, and he never turned up for period three. I'm sure there's nothing to worry about, but I wondered if you'd heard from him?' Sue asks.

'I'll check my phone tracker now. Do you know what happened in class?' I hope he's learnt his lesson after fighting with his brother, and not gone down that route again.

'I don't know all the details, I'm afraid, but I'm sure his class teacher will be in touch.'

My phone refreshes and shows that Caleb's phone is at home.

'It looks like he's just gone home, Sue. Thanks for ringing. I'll take it from here.'

I ponder on my next steps. Ever since Chris died, I've doubted my ability as both a mother and a GP. I stare at my phone, dazed, wondering whether to call Caleb or just cancel my day and go home to him.

Maybe I should get Paul's opinion on my current dilemma, I think, and quickly hit the call button.

'Hey Paul, can I just get your opinion real quick?' I say.

'Sure, what is it?' Paul replies.

'I just got a call from school to say Caleb has gone AWOL. I've tracked him and he's at home.'

'You want to know which way to jump?' Paul knows me well.

'Got it in one. Do I go home and deal with it now, or should I just ignore it till tonight?'

'You know your son better than anyone, Steph. What feels right to you?' I know Paul well and I understand that he's sensing my doubt, steering me to my gut.

'I honestly don't know, Paul. He's acting so out of character at the moment, this stuff with Chris has really hit him hard.'

'What's your first instinct?' he tries again.

'To drop everything and drive straight home, storm in there, guns blazing, and ask him what the hell he's playing at.'

'So, maybe think about your second option.' Paul chuckles and recommends a slightly less antagonistic approach.

'How about you call him first and check if he's okay?' he recommends. 'Don't forget he's not only lost his father, he no doubt carries some guilt, too. He's in pain, Steph. The last thing he needs is you going in with guns blazing. It'll just exacerbate the situation.'

'I know. That's why I called you, to talk me down before I did something stupid,' I say.

'It's not stupid, Steph, to act on your instincts. It's just less contentious if you take a breath and pause first. You need to look after your boys, but also yourself. You're all grieving and you don't need to make it any more difficult than it already is. Take care of yourself,' he advises.

'Thank you. Maybe I'll just send a text for now.'

'Good idea, and listen, don't forget I'm here for Caleb anytime, or if he would feel awkward talking to me in that way, Nick will happily see him. He's a psychologist too, and he's great with teenagers.'

'Thanks, Paul, I'll bear that in mind.'

The car journey home has me thinking long and hard. In the end, I neither called nor messaged Caleb, preferring to leave any communication until I get home and can deal with the situation calmly, face to face. I still feel unsure how to approach him, but I know I've composed myself enough to handle it with care.

My phone rings, piercing my thoughts, and the bluetooth picks up.

'Stephanie Wilson speaking,' I frown as I speak, not recognising the number.

'Mrs Wilson, this is Mitch Shaw, Caleb's maths teacher. How are you?'

'Mitch, hello, I heard there was some kind of altercation?'

'To be honest with you, Caleb was provoked, but as you know, we have a strict policy regarding physical violence. He punched a boy in the face.'

I breathe out slowly, pulling my thoughts together before I continue.

'Can I ask who it was?'

'It was Josh. His parents have asked for matters not to be taken any further, in light of your current situation.'

'You mean his best friend, Josh?' I ask, incredulous. 'I can't imagine him saying anything to provoke him. Do you know what he said?'

'I'd rather not repeat that. You should probably ask Caleb,' Mitch says.

'Of course, I'm on my way home now so I'll see if I can get to the bottom of this behaviour. He punched his brother the other day too, split his lip and gave him a black eye.'

'Oh, I saw Levi today and wondered what had happened. I'm sure it will all blow over. Caleb's a good kid, he's just grieving.'

'I hope you're right, Mitch, and thanks for the call.'

I take a deep breath, readying myself as I enter the house, and drop my keys and bag on the kitchen bench-top. As I turn, I catch sight of Levi outside tending to his chickens and I smile at the simplicity. Then I switch my focus to the more complicated situation at hand.

Making my way down the hall towards Caleb's bedroom, trepidation washes over me and I stop dead in my tracks as a familiar but unwelcome fragrance floats through the air. I remind myself of Paul's words of wisdom, to not go in with guns blazing, and inhale deeply the remnants of marijuana into my lungs. I'll need it when I come face to face with my son.

I knock on his door.

'Caleb? I'm coming in.'

There's no reply, so I open the door, peeking my head through the gap. I'm shocked to find Caleb lying on his bed, smoking a joint, making no effort to disguise it. I glare at him in disbelief. His eyes transfix on the ceiling and my anger at Chris's actions rises to the surface once again. I'm furious he's put our family in this position.

'Caleb, please sit up and put that out. We need to talk.' I somehow keep my voice calm but firm.

There's no reaction from Cale. He takes another drag and rests his hand back on his stomach. His lack of response inflames me and I cross the bedroom, peel the joint from his fingers and stub it out on the empty plate sitting on his desk.

'Sit up, Caleb,' I try again. There's still no movement, not even a flicker in his expression. I try a different approach. Sitting precariously on the edge of his bed, I clutch his hand in mine.

'Caleb, sweetheart, please talk to me.'

He blinks and a tear springs from the corner of his

eye. I watch it trickle slowly down his cheek and pool in his ear.

'Oh Cale.' I scoop my arms underneath him, pulling his limp body towards me, hugging him tight. He sags against me for several seconds before I feel the slightest pressure of his arms reaching around my back and squeezing gently.

I rock him back and forth in my arms as though the last sixteen years have been a blur. I don't care that he's six feet tall with a five o'clock shadow. He's still my baby, and he's hurting. Cale eventually pulls back and wipes his sleeve across his face, his head hanging low, unwilling to make eye contact.

'Will you tell me what happened?' I wait until he looks like he might talk. Caleb shrugs, keeping his eyes firmly focused on his hands balled up in his lap.

'Mr Shaw said you punched Josh,' I prompt. 'I know you're hurting Cale, but I thought I'd made it clear that I won't tolerate violent behaviour.'

'He started it,' Caleb argues.

'Mr Shaw also told me that, and he said Terri and Mark don't want to take it further for obvious reasons. You and Josh have been friends since kindy Cale. What did he do?'

'He said I was probably glad Dad was dead because now I can chill out more and not have him on my back all the time. So I hit him.'

'That was insensitive of him, but it still doesn't excuse violence,' I reason.

'I'm just so angry, Mum. I'm pissed at Dad for doing what he did. I wish I'd never seen the letter.'

I bite my tongue, refraining from unleashing a 'told you so' moment. Instead, I step onto the next path I need to venture down. That of the weed.

'So, you're angry at your dad. I guess that explains the weed?' I try to rationalise it. 'Where did you even get it from?'

'There's plenty of people at school who can get whatever you want, Mum.' Caleb rolls his eyes at my apparent naivety.

I ignore his comment and try a different tack, something that might actually make him re-evaluate his actions.

'Smoking weed or anything else is not going to help you achieve your goals, Caleb. Don't let what's happened with Dad steer you away from realising your dreams. There are other ways to deal with your anger. In fact, Paul suggested you talk things through with him. Or if you'd prefer, he can refer you to a friend of his who would be willing to help you process all this.'

'I don't need to see a shrink and I don't have any dreams. Football was always Dad's dream, not mine. I'm not playing anymore,' Caleb argues.

His comment throws me more than all his other behaviours combined. Football has been his dream for as long as I can remember. He lives and breathes it. Playing professionally has been the only career choice on his radar. I tell myself that it's the grief talking, but if I'm honest, I'm not very convincing.

'Well, that's up to you, Cale, but rethink your other choices, because I won't put up with fighting or smoking under my roof. You're grounded. You will stay at the library after school and I'll pick you up after work. And no Xbox for a week.'

This is an alien concept for me. I've never had to punish Caleb before. His constant strive for perfection and the desire to please his father has meant he's very rarely stepped out of line. I clearly make my point by unplugging the Xbox and taking it with me. Half way down the hall, I remember the half-smoked joint I left on the plate and quickly duck back to his room to retrieve it.

Caleb

Dear Dad

I hope you're pleased with yourself. I'm not the perfect little son you tried so hard to get me to be, after all. You gave up on me and chose the easy way out, and now I've been in two fights, smoked weed and quit football. I bet you'd be so proud of me.

Mum's trying to get me to see a shrink to help me sort out my feelings, but what's the point? There's nothing to sort out. Anger is the only feeling I have right now. I'm angry at you, I'm angry at Mum, I'm angry at Levi, I'm angry at Josh. Mostly I'm just angry at myself for spending years of my life working my arse off for someone who bailed on me as soon as things got tough. All that bullshit you used to spout at me. Where was that when you drove into that tree, Dad? All that crap about working hard to achieve your goals and working through the pain. I didn't see you working through the pain. Well, I won't be like you, Dad. I refuse to live my life for you a minute longer. From now on, I'm doing things my way, and if people don't like it, they can get out of my life.

Caleb

Nick

Nick pulled his car into the driveway alongside his middle daughter, Lucy's, car. Jumping to the conclusion that something was wrong, he peeled out of the car and strode to the small hatchback, reaching it as his daughter pushed her door open.

'Is everything okay, Luce?' His breath had quickened, and he panted.

'Yeah, we're fine, Dad. Just thought we'd come and hang out, maybe order a pizza.'

Nick exhaled, slowing his breathing down after the initial panic that something was wrong. He frowned at his behaviour. Why was he so on edge?

'Hey Dad,' Hannah said, climbing from the passenger seat. Nick looked up, surprised to see his eldest daughter there, too. 'Wow, Millie was right, you are in a tizzy.'

Nick shook his head at his youngest daughter's interference.

'I'm fine. What's she been saying?'

'Nothing,' said Lucy. 'She just thought you might want some company, said you were a little down in the dumps.'

'Well, thank you, I appreciate the concern. We may as well go inside and get that pizza ordered then,' he said, the corners of his mouth turning up, grateful for his thoughtful daughters.

'So, what's going on?' Hannah asked, stuffing in a mouthful of meat lovers.

'A close friend of Paul lost her husband a few weeks back and I guess it's shaken me up a little.'

'Do you know her, Paul's friend?' Lucy asked.

'Yeah, I mean, I've met her at Paul and Gerry's parties, but I don't know her well. I've only spoken to her a handful of times, so I'm not sure why I'm feeling so out of sorts. I guess it brought back memories and I feel for her, alone with two kids.'

'That's understandable, Dad,' Lucy said. 'How old are her kids?'

'I've no idea, but there's no easy age to lose a parent.' Nick knew all too well the hardships that such a significant loss brought. He shot his girls a melancholy smile.

The three finished their pizza in comfortable silence, each summoning their own memories of their wife or mother. Lucy had been too young to remember, and Hannah only had vague recollections. The memories both girls had were from stories Nick had told them over the years, showing pictures and video clips to keep her memory alive. He'd given them a part of her they would never have known. It was obvious to them that he'd never loved his second wife in the same way, and after some struggles with jealousy in their teenage years, they'd begun to feel sorry for Millie that she hadn't been born from such a deep love. It hadn't seemed to affect Millie in a negative way. She was the most grounded person they'd ever met, and despite the divorce, had grown to be a wonderful person with a beautiful soul. Millie adored their dad and tolerated her mother with generosity. Not only was she the image of their dad, but she was also kind, like him, and her energy and her genuine nature were inspiring.

'You're a good person, Dad. That's why it's shaken you up,' Hannah said. 'You don't like to see anyone else suffer like you did.'

'Thanks Han. I'm sorry I put you girls through what I did when you'd already endured so much. Having a mother figure in your lives was something I thought would help make up for the loss. Now I see that we'd have been better off alone than me rushing straight into another marriage.'

'No, Dad, please don't think that way. Sarah wasn't all bad,' Lucy argued, and Hannah raised her eyebrows at her sister's pretence.

'You don't have to appease me, Luce. I'm aware of her shortcomings and I've come to terms with the mistakes I made where you two are concerned.' Nick's eyes glistened as he spoke.

'I'm not trying to appease you, Dad. I'm being honest. Okay, parts of our childhood were awful, but if it wasn't for Sarah, we wouldn't have Millie and I can't bear to think about how dull life would be without her in it.'

Nick beamed at Lucy. 'You're right, Luce. I'm so proud of all three of you.'

Nick sat alone that evening, grateful for his three girls. He'd long since accepted that he hadn't got everything right with them, but he'd worked hard on his relationship with each of them and his determination showed. Despite the age gap between Millie and her older sisters, her maturity and easygoing nature meant the siblings had connected at a friendship level. He sipped at his whisky, thinking about where his head was at, figuring out what had him feeling so on edge.

Lucy was right. His empathy with people who were suffering was strong and Steph's story had hit him hard. The loneliness of losing a partner was a tough path to navigate, and he felt sad that she would have to traverse it. He'd jumped into his second marriage, but the loneliness had still haunted him when he lay awake night after night. He'd felt less alone in the last four years than he had during the entirety of his marriage to Millie's mother, but he'd recognised those feelings slowly creeping back in of late, and his sudden awareness of wanting someone to share his life with struck him. It wasn't Steph herself that had him maudlin, it was her situation that had triggered his own sense of loneliness. It was time to think about dating again.

Steph

I toy with the idea of replying to Nick's message to discuss the possibility of him helping Caleb, but I wonder if there's any point at this stage. I can't drag him there and he won't go without force. The only thing I can think to do right now is call Paul. He's always been my voice of reason and his take on the current situation won't go amiss.

'Steph, how did it go?' Paul asks. His voice is a calming influence the second he speaks.

'Not great, if I'm honest, Paul. He was smoking a joint in his bedroom when I got home. He didn't even try to hide the fact, just puffed away until I ripped it from his hand.'

'Shit! Listen Steph, try not to be too hard on him for that. He's had a tremendous shock and his emotions will run high. What did he have to say about the incident at school?'

'He punched his best mate for telling him it was a good thing Chris was dead. He said Caleb would probably chill out more now his dad wouldn't be on his back all the time.'

'Ouch. Can't say as I blame him. I might have

done the same,' Paul muses.

'Yeah, me too, that's why it's difficult. He said he doesn't want to play football anymore either. That was Chris's dream, not his.'

'And what's your take on that?'

'I just don't see it. You should see his face when he's on the field, Paul. He comes alive, and he's so bloody talented, he could make it.' I can feel the brightness in my voice at the mention of Caleb playing football. When he was younger, I used to think I was biased when I watched him play, but as he grew older, his talent shone brighter than his teammates. He's an outstanding player, and I find it hard to believe he's only reached that level for the sake of his dad.

'Maybe a break is all he needs, Steph. If it's in his blood, he won't stay away for long.' I welcome Paul's reassurance.

'Yeah, I think maybe you're right, as usual. Which leads me to why I called you…'

'Oh?' Paul asks.

'I think Cale needs to speak to someone, but I'm wondering if it would be less awkward if it weren't you.' Not that I can see much point to this discussion if he refuses to see anyone.

'Yeah, I'm inclined to agree, Steph. I'll send you Nick's number. He'll be a good fit.'

'He's adamant he won't talk to anyone, so I'm not sure how I'd get him there.'

'Look, speak to Nick. Maybe the two of you could meet up first for a chat, see if maybe you can come up with a strategy. He sees this a lot Steph, few teenagers are eager to see a psych, but he has a way with them. I'll text you his details.'

'Thanks Paul, I appreciate it.' Paul's friendship is exactly what I need today.

'Any time, Steph, you know that. Can I recommend something else?'

'Of course.' Knowing that he's looking out for me warms my heart.

'Take that joint, light it up, and smoke it yourself. A little medicinal marijuana won't hurt.'

I can hear the grin in Paul's voice and contemplate his suggestion.

I take the joint from my bedside drawer where I'd put it out of Caleb's way. It feels mischievous as I roll it around in my fingers, hesitant to light it, but wondering if I should just let myself go, and release all the pent up anger and frustration I've been feeling so I can move forward and begin grieving my husband.

My phone buzzes. It's a message from Paul with Nick's details. I look from my phone to the roll-up in my hand. Paul has never failed to give me good advice in the past, so why not listen to him now? I grab the lighter, which until this moment has been exclusively for lighting fragrant candles, and I light up the joint, pulling it deep into my lungs before coughing and spluttering. I chuckle to myself. It's been a long time since I smoked anything, not since my university days. The next drag comes easier and I soon get back into the swing, the bitterness and resentment drifting away on the cloud of smoke. I lie back on my pillow, puffing away, and I mull over my life with Chris. I loved him. He was a good man, but if I'm honest with myself, the last few years had taken a turn. I'd put it down to the stress of our jobs and raising teenage boys, dismissing it as a consequence of life. If only I'd noticed the cracks appearing in Chris's demeanour. I consider that thought a moment before berating myself. I can't go down that track. There's no place in all of this for blame and guilt. Chris had been a tragic product of his circumstances. It saddens me now that he'd known he needed to talk, but couldn't find the courage. A tear springs a leak from the corner of my eye and I allow it the freedom to run its course. It's the first crack in the dam wall and I sense a flood is imminent.

A knock on my bedroom door startles me.

'Mum, can I come in?' Levi's voice throws me into a panic as I consider how to hide the joint. I don't want him to see me smoking, but it's too late as I watch in horror as the door handle depresses and my younger son's face appears.

Levi's wavering face breaks into laughter when he sees me laid out on my bed, a smoke cloud filling the surrounding air.

'Woah! That's not what I expected to see, Mum.'

Stunned at being caught smoking drugs by my teenage son, I freeze for a second, but the priceless look on his face forces laughter from deep in my belly. The laughter turns to tears as my stark reality swamps me, dragging me down into a deluge of uncertainty. Heavy sobs claw at my chest and I give in to it. I give myself permission to fall apart, right here, in front of my fourteen-year-old son. Maybe not my best parenting moment.

Levi hugs me, shushing me while I allow my sorrow to escape. He removes the joint from my fingers with care and stubs it out in the coffee mug beside my bed. I sniff and wipe my nose on my sleeve, embarrassment battling for position against the sadness.

'It's okay Mum, it's just weed. You probably needed it.'

'This is all so surreal, not a place I ever imagined I would find myself in. The whole situation's messed up.'

Levi smiles. 'It's okay Mum, you're allowed to not be perfect sometimes. You've had a lot to deal with.'

'When did you get so wise?' I study his face. He's handled himself so well throughout this difficult time. I only hope he doesn't follow his brother down the rabbit hole.

'I've always been wise Mum, how did you not know?' Levi jokes with mock horror. 'Where'd you get the weed from, anyway? Is that a perk of the job?'

He has a skewed view of my job. 'Absolutely not. I confiscated it from your brother.'

Levi's mouth almost hits the floor. 'Caleb was smoking? You have to be kidding.'

'Unfortunately, I'm not kidding, Levi, but please don't make this into a big thing. He told me he's quitting football, said it was always Dad's dream, not his.'

'That's bullshit. Caleb lives and breathes football.' Levi rolls his eyes at his brother's falsification. 'I'm sure he doesn't mean it, Mum.'

'I hope not. Listen, Paul gave me a number for a friend of his. He specialises in teen therapy and I want Caleb to go see him. Do you think it would help you too?'

Levi shrugs. 'Honest, Mum, I'm okay. I'm sad

about Dad, but I have my friends to talk to and I spoke to the school counsellor yesterday. She said I can see her anytime, and I promise to let you know if I'm struggling.'

'I love you sweetheart, talk to me any time, okay?'

Sometimes Levi's maturity astonishes me.

'I love you too, Mum. Did you want a cuppa? Or if you'd rather get high instead, I'm down.'

Levi grins and raises his eyebrows at me, sending a bubble of laughter from my throat.

'My rebellious phase was short lived, Levi. I'm going to dispose of this right now.' I shake my head at my unfamiliar behaviour. 'And yes, I'd love a cuppa, thanks.'

Staring at my phone, I contemplate whether to call the new number I have stored on my contact list. A quick online search of Paul's friend produces innumerable five star reviews, not that I'd expected anything different. I tell myself it can't hurt to reach out.

'Nick Salvatore,' a voice answers.

'Oh, er, hi, Nick. This is Stephanie Wilson. I work with Paul. I got your message. Thank you.'

'Stephanie, hey, how are you?' His gravelly voice puts me at ease. 'Paul said you might call. I'm so sorry for your loss.'

'Thank you. Paul said you might be able to help my son. He's been struggling since…' I trail off, unable to say the words out loud.

'Of course. How willing is he to meet with me?' Nick asks.

'He's not willing to see anyone, so I'm not sure why I called you.'

'You called because you want some help. Never apologise for that. Why don't you come and see me tomorrow? We can have a chat and maybe come up with a plan. How does that sound?'

'Thank you, Nick, I appreciate this. It's been a tough few weeks. I don't know how I would've got through it without Paul's support.' My voice fractures under the weight of my emotions.

'He's a good man and any friend of his is a friend of mine. We'll get your son through this together.' Nick's words were soft, his voice resonant with a slight trace of an accent.

My appointments don't start until 10am, so I drop the boys at school early and make my way to the address Nick gave me last night. Once I've parked my SUV in one of the narrow spaces outside his office building, I check my vanity mirror before making my way to the door. There's no sign of life as I squint through the glass into the dark reception area beyond. As my hand reaches for the door handle, the lights flicker on inside and a handsome face with kind eyes strides towards me.

'Sorry, my receptionist isn't in yet. I don't start until ten. Come on in.' He holds the door open, welcoming me inside.

'Thank you. It's nice to see you again. It's been a while.'

Nick locks the door behind me and turns to the counter, picking up two take away coffee cups and passing one to me.

'I took the liberty of guessing your order. I hope a flat white's okay,' Nick says. 'I'm afraid to say I have no idea how to work the fancy machine in the back.'

His honesty is refreshing. 'This is perfect, thank you.'

We settle into the comfortable chairs in Nick's office and I take a much needed sip of coffee. I put the cup on the table and cast my eyes towards Nick. Although we've met numerous times over the years, we've only spoken a handful of times, but he has one of those faces that is familiar, and it feels like we're already friends. He's an attractive man, I muse. His olive skin and dark hair, peppered with grey, give him the look of George Clooney. Eyes that crinkle at the edges draw me in, and his gentle smile makes me want to expose all my secrets.

'I smoked a joint last night.' My nerves stretch tight and the words are out of my mouth before I can think. I flush at my admission and our eyes connect for a beat before I glance out of the window.

Nick laughs. 'I take it that's not normal behaviour for you, Stephanie? You seem guilty.'

'Please call me Steph, Stephanie seems so formal. And no, I haven't smoked since my student days. I found Caleb, that's my son, smoking it in his bedroom last night, so I confiscated it and took Paul's advice and ended up getting high myself.' Despite my embarrassment, I can't seem to stop myself from talking.

'And how did you feel afterwards?' Nick speaks with a complete lack of judgement.

'Fucking fantastic,' I say, and we both laugh, the ice broken.

'So, Steph, tell me a little about yourself and what's been going on so I can get a feel for things.' I'm heartened by his use of my shortened name.

Once I begin talking, I find it difficult to stop. He

gets a rundown of my life, my marriage, my kids and the recent tragedy, and I tell him of Chris's past and the difficulties he suffered as a child with his father. I speak of the guilt I feel having not realised my husband had been suffering in silence for so long, and I tell him of the recent dramatic changes in Caleb's behaviour. Nick listens with unwavering attention. Once I stop talking, I sit back and watch him scribble some notes on a pad.

He puts the pen down and looks up, his eyes fixed on me. The heat simmers between us and I wonder what's running through his mind now. I force a cough to break the tension.

'Thank you for being open with me.' Nick flashes me a smile of encouragement. 'The important thing to remember is, it's very early days, so try not to worry too much. We'll help Caleb get through this. If there's any way you can persuade him to keep playing footy, I think that would be my first suggestion. Both the routine and the exercise would be beneficial right now.'

'I'll try. I just don't want to push him too hard and cause another outburst. It's such unusual behaviour for him.'

'You know, his friend's comment might have been insensitive, but it could've been close to the truth for Caleb. If he's felt pressure from his father, this might just be him flexing his independence. It doesn't mean it'll stick. He might well realise he wasn't doing it for his father after all and figure out it's what he wants. Hang in there, Steph, and stay in touch. I'm happy to chat whenever. Even if Caleb refuses to see me himself, I can still help you help him.'

'Thank you Nick, I appreciate you seeing me like this when you're busy.' I check my watch and make to leave, grateful for the time Nick has given me. Even if nothing comes of him helping Caleb, it's been refreshing to talk to someone neutral, someone removed from my life.

'Any time. I mean that.' Nick shifts in his chair and lowers his voice. 'I'm single, I live alone and I have no life, so don't be afraid to call.'

A rush of adrenalin surges through my veins and tingles scatter to my fingertips. I falter, confused by my reaction to his words.

Nick

Nick's day was long and his focus wavered long after Steph had left his office. Luckily, none of his clients presented with issues that were too taxing. Most were his long-term kids that had become so comfortable with him they talked his ear off and it was just a case of nudging them back on track. He was pleased with their progress, and the sessions flowed. By the end of the day, though, he was shattered, his mind flitting back to Steph with every spare moment. Paul had told him her husband's death had been an accident, and he reeled when she'd delivered the news about his suicide. Maybe Paul hadn't known, or maybe he was keeping counsel. Either way, Nick's heart went out to Steph, his empathy running deep. As a doctor, she felt the same guilt he had when he hadn't picked up on his wife's depression. Their paths had aligned for this reason, and his commitment to helping her solidified.

Nick let himself into his empty townhouse later that evening and prepared dinner for one. With a tray balanced on his lap, he forked the sad-looking omelette around his plate and had never felt so lonely. What was it about Steph that had triggered his loneliness? Every time he thought of her and her situation, he felt like he was reliving his own past and he struggled to get out of his own head enough to contemplate his life.

'Pull yourself together, Nick, you fool,' he said to himself. He wouldn't let himself get swallowed by his memories and sink back into that state of loneliness. Nothing good could come of it. His appetite now lacking, he put down the tray and picked up his phone.

'No time like the present.' It was a sure sign he was doing the right thing, he thought as he talked to himself. He downloaded a dating app and set about creating himself a profile. His fingers tapped away furiously. He wrote about his job, his kids, his likes and dislikes. Nick sat back with a smile, proud of his initiative. He scrolled through his camera roll until he found a good enough photo of himself. It was one Millie had taken at the beach the previous summer. It would do, he decided. After uploading it to his profile, he re-read his paragraph and set about laughing. What on earth had he been thinking? No woman in her right mind would be interested in the tired and banal man he'd just described. He needed some serious help.

'Hey, Nick.'

'Paul, mate, I need your help.'

'What is it this time?' Paul added a dramatic drone to his voice, but Nick knew he'd drop everything in a heartbeat to help his friend.

'I just signed up to a dating app…'

'Nicholas Salvatore! I never thought I'd live to see

the day. What on earth made you do that?'

'An omelette.'

'A what?'

'I was eating an omelette for dinner and decided I don't want to spend the rest of my life cooking miserable meals for one. It's time to get on with my life, Paul.'

'That's music to my ears, my friend. Where do I come in?' Paul asked.

'You need to write my profile. I have nothing going for me according to what I've written. Christ, I sound like a complete loser,' Nick said.

Paul laughed. 'Mate, post a pic and you'll have women swarming. You're hot.'

'Well, thank you. I think.' Nick snickered, 'but I'd rather meet someone who's into more than what I look like. Besides, I'm old and my hair's mostly grey.'

'Hello, that's what women like. I'm pretty sure George Clooney's been voted the sexiest man alive several times over. You've got that vibe going on. Own it,' Paul said.

'Well, thanks for the ego boost. I never knew you were so into me.'

'Nah, you're not my type, but seriously, Nick, you're a catch. You've got way more going for you than just that Italian sex appeal. You're smart, you're kind, you're generous, and you're one amazing dad. I think you should write it yourself, just be honest. The right woman will find that the most attractive trait.'

'You're right. I need to write it myself. Thanks for the pep talk. I appreciate you, Paul.'

'Anytime, mate. Good luck. I'm glad you're

putting yourself out there.'

Nick deleted everything he'd written and thought about what he'd want to read. He wrote honestly, adding a little humour, and kept it short and sweet. His finger touched the submit key before he could chicken out, and he smiled to himself. And with that quick push of a button, he was back in the dating game.

Nick had left the app for a couple of days before he dare look. It was his daughter, Hannah, who persuaded him. She was shocked, as were his other two daughters, when he'd told them he'd signed up.

'You're on Tinder?' Millie had screamed with laughter, bruising his ego a little.

'It's not Tinder, it's a different one aimed at people more my age group,' he said. 'Anyway, what's funny about me being on Tinder?' he asked, his lower lip protruding in mock hurt.

'Just kidding, Dad,' Millie said, taking back her comment. She hadn't meant it hurtfully. It had just come out of the blue.

Once the girls had left him for the evening, he took Hannah's advice and logged on to the app. His mouth hung open in disbelief. There were thirteen replies. Who knew there were so many single women looking for love with someone like him? The reaction buoyed his self-esteem. He scrolled through the profiles of the interested parties and a couple caught his eye. Replying to two straight away, he arranged a dinner date with one and a breakfast date with another. Both were casual, but he was nervous. It had been years since he'd dated, and even then he'd been looking for someone entirely different.

Dinner the following evening was at a low-key tapas bar. His date's name was Victoria, and she was an engineer. She was in her late forties, had never been married, and had no children. By her own admission, she was married to her job.

Nick arrived at the restaurant before her and was seated at a table for two in the courtyard. The air was crisp, but patio heaters dotted the area, keeping a comfortable temperature. He spotted her the moment she arrived and stood as she walked to his table. She offered her hand to shake, introducing herself as Vicky.

'Nice to meet you. I'm Nick.'

She smiled in return and sat down opposite him. Without looking at the menu, she ordered a bottle of Margaret River Sauvignon Blanc with two glasses. He found decisiveness and assertiveness an attractive feature in a woman, but if she'd taken the time to ask, he'd already ordered a beer and he was driving, so that would be his limit. Nick tried not to let it taint his first impression of Vicky and relaxed into conversation. If a monologue could be classed as a conversation. By the end of the evening, he walked away with her entire life history and goals for her future, and she walked away with nothing more than what he'd written in his dating profile.

'Thanks for a lovely evening,' she said when her Uber arrived. 'Call me.'

Nick was polite, but made it clear there would be no call.

He climbed into bed that evening disheartened and thought about cancelling his breakfast date, but a voice in his head told him there must be someone out there for him. It just might take some time to find her.

Steph

The weeks pass by as if I'm in a holding pattern, unsure if I'm making any progress. I can't tell if grounding Caleb taught him a lesson or just drove him deeper into a dark hole. He did what I asked and stayed at school each day until I finished work and could pick him up, but the second we got home, he retreated to his bedroom for the night. Every night has been the same; not eating and not talking.

The exhaustion is draining and I know I've been sweeping my own feelings under the rug, but I can't find it in me to care. My voicemail has picked up several calls from friends that I know in my head I should have taken, but wrapping myself in a cocoon feels like the safest place to be. Reality is too much to handle right now.

Friday night rolls around and I'm in no mood to cook.

'Boys! What pizza would you like?' I hope my voice will reach their bedrooms.

It clearly does, and Levi appears in the kitchen within seconds.

'I'll eat whatever,' he says.

Caleb responds by turning up his music. My mind is not in the right state to deal with this right now, and Levi picks up on my malaise.

'I'm on it.' Levi spins on his heel and heads towards Caleb's room. He bangs on the door.

'Oi muppet.' Levi barges into Caleb's room. There's a pause and Levi changes tack.

'Hey bro, you okay?' His voice has lowered and the antagonistic tone completely gone.

I don't hear a reply from Caleb.

'You know, you can talk to me Cale, I'm probably the only person that understands what you're going through.'

'You don't know shit, Levi, don't pretend you do.'

'I lost him too, Cale. He wasn't just your dad, you know,' Levi responds, hurt in his voice.

'Did he kill himself because of you?' Caleb spits. 'No, I didn't think so. It's me who wasn't good enough for him. You think he ever gave a shit what you did? He never counted on you to be the best at everything. There was no pressure on you to play football professionally just because he wasn't good enough to make it himself. You've always done shit in school and were never any good at sports, but it was always me that was never good enough for him. Me, with the straight A's and playing in the AFL on my radar, but still I wasn't enough for him. Fuck you, Levi.'

The silence from Levi is deafening and I contemplate intervening, but decide to wait a few moments to see where it pans out by itself. My heart is breaking for the pair of them. Their grief is all tied up with a scramble of emotions that their respective relationships with their father have left. The guilt

I've been battling over being blind to Chris's illness rises tenfold whenever I hear my boys talking like this. How did I miss their own internal battles?

'Whatever, Cale, I'm still your brother, and I'm here if you want to talk to me,' Levi says, and I hear the door click shut.

'He's not hungry,' Levi says, unaware I overheard his entire conversation. 'Let's order two and then he can eat the leftovers if he wants them.'

I nod sadly and open up the delivery app.

I had welcomed the weekend with open arms after another stressful week juggling work, Caleb, and my own heartache, but when Saturday morning comes around, once again, there's no football. I face nothing but an endless stretch of emptiness and I can barely breathe. The loneliness grabs at me, dragging me down. At the moment it feels like hard work, but I know I need to accept help from my friends. I haven't even made the effort to see Terri, my closest friend. I know I should. Closing myself off won't help me in the long run, but I'm depleted and I can't summon the energy to explain how I'm feeling. That's why Nick's have been the only messages I've responded to. He seems to understand my withdrawal and hasn't pressed me on it. Maybe it's because he's removed from my situation, or maybe it's because he's been in my position and recognises my state of mind from experience. Likely it's because he's a professional and he's just doing his job. Whatever the reason, his guidance settles me.

I try to relax into the quiet, enjoying my coffee in the morning sunshine, watching Levi's chooks potter around, our two dogs at my feet. I wonder where my life is heading. The next few years were mapped out; work, football matches, driving the boys around until they get their own licenses, and the odd social gathering with friends. Now what? It appears there'll be no more football. Caleb has seen none of his friends. Even since being allowed his freedom again, he has shown no interest in socialising. Maybe taking him out for a driving lesson might help. I make a mental note to suggest it later.

My phone rings, jolting me from my thoughts, and my instinct is to let it ring out. I bite my lip, contemplating whether to pick up. Haven't I just been anxious about spending my weekend alone? What the hell, I think, and answer the call.

'Hey Ali, how are you?' I greet my friend.

'I'm good. How are you doing, sweetie?' Ali replies.

'Oh, I don't know, miserable I guess.' Unwilling to disguise my mood, I laugh without humour.

'Sit tight, I'm on my way over with coffee and cake,' Ali says, not asking if that's what I need.

'Thank you Ali.' I'm surprised to find I'm grateful for not being given a choice.

The car rumbles up the long driveway and pulls to a stop just past the house. Ali hops out and leans back through the door to retrieve coffee cups and a cake tin. Alison is a fabulous baker and the staff at Chris's dental practice enjoyed her homemade goodies every week.

'Hey Ali, I'm surprised you're not working,' I say as she approaches.

'New owner has cut down to one Saturday a month,' Alison explains, 'and I can't say that I'm complaining.'

'I always tried to get Chris to do that, but you know what he was like.'

'I do. It's not the same without him.'

Alison puts the cake tin on the small coffee table and hands me a coffee cup, leaning in for a quick hug before collapsing beside me on the couch, tucking her feet beneath her.

'I'm sorry I've been absent, Al. It's been a lot.'

'Don't apologise, Steph, I can't imagine what you're going through. Just know I'm here for you.'

'I know, thank you.'

I fill Alison in on my drama filled existence that has been developing over the weeks since Chris's death.

'It's like watching dominoes fall. One thing leads to another and I can't seem to catch a break.'

'I know it seems like that, Steph, but I'm sure things will turn around for you. It's been an enormous shock for you all and it'll take time to process everything and readjust,' Alison says.

'I've been chatting with a friend of a friend. He lost his wife under similar circumstances and I think he's kept my head above water these past weeks. I honestly don't know where I'd be without him.' I blush as I think how much I've relied on him of late, not only for his advice, but for his understanding and his friendship.

Alison picks up on my sheepish expression and throws the conversation off balance.

'I've offered to help you too, Steph, but you haven't answered any of my calls or messages. Be careful getting involved with someone you don't even know,' she says.

I stumble over my words, unsure why panic has blanketed me.

'I'm not involved, Ali. He's a psychologist friend of my colleague, that's all,' I splutter.

'Still, I'd be careful of his motives. You're vulnerable right now. I don't want you to be taken advantage of.'

I glare at my friend. 'Not everyone has an ulterior motive Ali, some people are just there to help.'

'Okay, fair enough, you just seem quite taken by this guy, Steph.'

'Alison, my husband just died and Nick understands what I'm going through. What are you implying?'

'Steph, I'm sorry. I didn't mean to imply anything.' Alison tries to salvage her remarks.

I contemplate my friend's comments and, as I think of Nick, his face flashes through my mind. Is it wrong that I find him attractive? Or even that I enjoyed his company? Why do I feel so judged for accepting his help? My line of self-questioning has me doubting my own motives. Am I so lonely that I'm grasping at straws, hunting for a replacement already? It's a ridiculous thought. I'm just overthinking Alison's words. There's no way I'm ready to move on yet.

'Mum,' Levi calls, coming up the garden from his chook pen. 'Oh, hey Ali,' he says, spotting his dad's employee.

'Hi love, how're you doing?' Ali asks.

'I'm okay,' he says politely before turning to me.

'Can we pick up the goat this afternoon?'

Alison frowns at his strange question.

'Sure,' I say, 'where from?'

'I'm not sure exactly,' he says. 'I'll double check. It's not far though.'

Ali looks at me, wondering what on earth is going on.

'He asked me a few weeks back if he could buy one, said it would help with keeping the grass cut. I know he'll look after it. He's a good kid.'

Ali nods. 'He sure is, you lucked out with that one. Well, both of them. Caleb's just going through a tough patch. He'll come back.'

'He will, I know. It's just hard watching him hurt like this.'

There's an underlying frigidity to the conversation and as much as I try to relax, Alison's criticism of Nick's motives has unsettled me. The earlier readiness to return to the company of my friends has drained away, leaving me feeling resentful. Alison appears to pick up on my downturn in mood and takes it as a signal to leave.

'I'm sorry if I offended you, Steph, I didn't mean to. I'm here if you need me,' Alison says, her voice choked. She squeezes my hand while I nod, unable to give her more.

'Caleb, can I come in?' I ask, knocking on his bedroom door. There's no answer, so I push the door open to check on him. I find him laid on his bed with his headphones on, a regular sight these days. Before Chris died, I'd barely caught him in his room before nine o'clock in the evening. He'd be out at football training, practising by himself in the garden, or lifting weights in the home gym his dad had built him. It worries me to see him like this. It isn't just grief, there are signs of depression seeping in. I need to get him out of here and talking to someone.

'Caleb!' I move closer to his bed to get his attention. He removes his headphones and stares at me. His face looks washed out, dark circles developing beneath his hollowed eyes. I sit on the edge of his bed, my hand resting gently on his arm, desperate to connect with my son.

'How are you feeling?' I ask, already knowing what the response will be.

Caleb shrugs, as expected.

'Sweetheart, I'm worried about you.' I don't want to beg, but I feel there's no choice. 'Please tell me what I can do to help.'

'I'm fine.' Caleb dismisses me.

'I'd like you to speak to someone, Cale. It will help you feel better,' I coax.

'No, I don't want to, Mum. Just leave me alone.'

'I'm sorry, Caleb, but I can't do that. If you don't want to see a therapist, that's fine for now, but you need to put some effort into dealing with this yourself. I won't sit back and watch the life drain out of you. I didn't see what was happening with your dad and I sure as hell won't let that happen again.'

Caleb rolls his eyes and puts his headphones back on.

'Caleb!' I yank the headphones off his ears, my volume increasing with my frustration. 'Go get a shower, we're going out.'

'I don't want to.'

'You don't have a choice. Now, get ready.' I turn

and storm out of the room, praying my heavy handed approach won't backfire. I don't hear any movement as I walk down the hall, but just as I reach the kitchen, I hear the shower turn on. My hands are shaking and I steady them on the kitchen bench top, my shoulders hunched over, already wondering what my next battle will be.

'You ready to go Mum?' Levi asks, hesitant about whether he should disturb me.

I take a deep breath before speaking. 'Soon sweetheart, just waiting for Caleb. He's coming with us.'

Levi's eyebrows raise, surprised his brother would want to come.

'I didn't give him a choice.' I flash Levi a grin, but the sadness is simmering just beneath the surface.

'Fair enough,' Levi replies. 'I'll go put this box and some blankets in the car for the goat.'

'Levi, you have researched this, haven't you? You know how to take care of it?' I ask.

'Seriously mum, this is me you're talking to,' he grins and grabs a cardboard box and some blankets. I laugh at his self-assuredness, a tiny fragment of light filtering through the darkness.

Caleb appears, looking a little brighter than earlier, but a far cry from his normal self.

'Hey, sweetheart, you ready?' I'm careful not to antagonise him.

He shrugs in response and I try not to look too deeply into it.

'Do you want to drive? Get your practice hours in?' He'd been enjoying learning to drive, but I haven't made any effort to take him out since the accident. Not that it was an accident, I just can't bring myself to think of it as anything else.

'I guess,' Caleb says, and I toss him the keys. 'Where are we going, anyway?'

'To pick up a goat!'

'A what?' Caleb glares at me like he's heard me wrong.

'Levi is buying a goat, so we're going to pick it up. I have no idea where from. He has the address.'

Caleb smiles for the first time in weeks, and my stomach flutters, hoping this might be the breakthrough he needs.

'Why am I not surprised?'

Steph

Levi is obsessed with his new goat. I'm so proud of the confidence and ease he's shown both dealing with the transaction, and how he cares for the goat, settling her in to the new pen. I can't imagine him ever working in a job that doesn't involve animals.

Caleb doesn't go straight back to his room when we get home, much to my surprise, and sits with me outside, finishing the cakes that Ali had left earlier. I choose to keep the conversation minimal, preferring to leave Cale to initiate it. I don't want to push him too far and cause him to retreat just when I've noticed a flicker of his old self. My phone rings and I frown when I check the caller ID. It's unusual for Paul to call me on a weekend.

'Hey Paul, is everything okay?' I ask.

'Yeah, listen, Gerry and I are having an impromptu dinner party this evening for my birthday and wondered if you'd like to join us?'

I'm gratified by his thoughtful invitation, but the current delicate state of play leaves me dithering.

Paul has a sixth sense for reading people and picks up on my silence.

'Steph, it's just a small gathering. You'll know

everyone. I wouldn't have invited you if I hadn't thought it would be good for you.'

'I appreciate the thought, but I don't know,' I waver, glancing over at Caleb, who is watching me with interest. 'The boys are here, and well, you know how it is.'

'No problem, Steph, I just thought a change of scenery and some adult company would give you a welcome escape from your problems for a couple of hours. If you change your mind, let me know.'

'I will, thanks Paul.'

'What did Paul want?' Caleb probes as soon as I hang up.

'He invited me over for a dinner party tonight. It's his birthday.'

'You should go,' Caleb urges.

'I don't know Cale. I don't want to leave you guys alone after these last few weeks.'

'Mum, we'll be fine, honest,' he pushes, flashing a rare smile.

'Are you sure?' I frown, my suspicious mind wondering if Caleb has an ulterior motive, or if today has marked a turning point.

'Yes! Go!'

I watch him closely. He seems much more like his normal self, so after a few moments of internal deliberation, I decide to take his advice.

'Okay, I think I will,' I say, and text Paul back to let him know my change of plan.

'Boys, I'm leaving.' I grab my bag and check myself in the mirror.

'Okay Mum, have fun,' Levi says, rounding the corner into the kitchen.

'Keep an eye on your brother, will you? Ring me if there're any problems.' I pull him in for a hug.

'We'll be fine, Mum, stop worrying.' Levi assures me as he ushers me out of the house.

I somehow work myself up into a knot worrying about leaving the boys, and by the time I reach Paul's house, I wonder if I should turn around and go home. There's a car in the driveway of the house Paul shares with his husband, Gerry, and as I pull up beside it, I recognise the occupant. Nick beams when he sees me, and my anxieties fade.

'Steph, I didn't realise you were coming. How are you?' He holds my door open, stepping back as I climb out.

'Hi Nick,' I say, pleased to see him. 'My boys talked me into it. I'm still wondering if there was an ulterior motive.'

Nick touches my elbow, a slight gesture that settles my racing thoughts.

'How's Caleb been?' he asks, as we stand face to face, his hand still cradling my elbow.

'It's hard to say. He's been in his room for weeks, barely speaking, but this afternoon I got him to come out with Levi and I to pick up a goat, and he seemed much more himself than he has been since before…' I drift off, not wanting to say the words out loud. I just want to forget everything for one night. 'Sorry, I'd rather talk about something else. I came out to get a break from it all.'

'No problem, but there's one thing I need to know,' Nick grins.

'Oh?'

'Why were you picking up a goat?'

I burst out laughing, grateful that Nick got the

message, and switched to a more lighthearted topic. My laughter feels genuine for the first time in weeks.

'That would be my son, Levi, the animal whisperer. He bought a goat, and I had to drive him to pick it up. With his chickens and pet sheep, too, my house is becoming quite the farm, but he's a good kid and is diligent about looking after them.'

'Sounds like quite a kid,' Nick says. 'You must be very proud.'

'I am, of both of them.' My tears swell and I blink them back, my thoughts once again turning to my boys and all I can see is a long and difficult road ahead.

Nick's hand trails down my arm to my hand, gripping my fingers and squeezing. The gesture surprises me, but it in no way feels uncomfortable.

'Come on, let's go inside. We have a birthday to celebrate.' Nick tugs my hand as I step away from the car. He squeezes again before dropping it, and I startle at the sudden loss of contact. I'm taken aback by the level of comfort that a simple connection could bring, and I question my feelings, trying to justify my reaction to the loss of physical touch. I brush tears from my eyes and smile up at Nick.

'Okay, I'm ready,' I say, walking towards the door.

Gerry welcomes us both with his bright smile, giving me a big hug, and showing us through to the back, where an elaborate table is set for eight.

'Happy birthday, Paul,' I say, handing him a bottle of his favourite Cabernet Sauvignon.

'Thank you, lovely.' Paul flashes a smile before noticing Nick close behind me and raising his eyebrows.

'Happy birthday, mate,' Nick says over my head.

'I just bumped into Nick in the driveway. Well, not literally. We both pulled up together. I mean…' I stop babbling when I see Paul observing me curiously. What is wrong with me? I can barely string a sentence together.

Nick's eyes dart to mine, his forehead raised in question.

'Come, sit down,' Paul says, evading my moment of embarrassment. 'Gerry will get you a drink. You guys both know my sister Lou and her husband Craig, don't you?'

'Of course.' I settle my thoughts and recompose myself. 'How are you both?'

Louise stands and hugs me. 'We were so sorry to hear of your loss, Steph.'

'Thank you,' I say, with the habitual fake smile. It's become second nature by now.

'Hey guys,' Nick says in greeting to them both, before pulling out a chair for me. He sits next to me and engages in conversation with Craig, leaving me and Lou to catch up.

Gerry brings out bottles of red and white wine and fills our glasses.

'Thanks Gerry, I'm driving, so I'll just have the one.' When he's had a few, he gets a little overzealous with the top-ups.

'If you want to have a few drinks, I'm happy to drop you home,' Nick whispers.

Nick's deep voice resonates right through me and for a second I'm tempted to accept his offer.

'Thanks. That's very generous of you, but I'll be fine with just the one.'

'No worries, but the offer stands if you change

your mind.'

I nod silently as two more people arrive.

'Jon, hello, I didn't realise you were coming,' I greet my colleague, and his wife, Julie.

'As if we'd miss out on Gerry's cooking,' Jonathan winks at Paul, who looks aghast at the fact they'd come for the food and not to celebrate his birthday.

'Well, that's charming,' Paul pouts, 'and here's me thinking my birthday was all about me.'

'What made you think that, Paul?' Nick asks. 'Don't you know by now we only come for the food? Mate, if Gerry stops cooking, you'll be losing friends fast.'

Paul flips his friend the bird. My shoulders ease away from my ears as the laughter flows around the table and I relax for the first time in a while. I swallow a large mouthful of wine, followed by another.

'This is good, Paul,' I say, turning the bottle so I can see the label.

'It's my latest discovery. It should pair well with dinner.'

Gerry interrupts Paul as he delivers the starters, and Paul smiles with pride at his husband. Gerry is a carpenter by trade and has recently turned his hand to cabinet making. He enjoys the fine detail and has created some exquisite pieces. After working in the construction industry for years, Paul talked him into moving into the area he had a genuine passion for. It was that or become a chef, his other passion, but that meant retraining. Cooking for friends and teaching himself as he goes nourishes his interest, while making bespoke furniture to order both feeds his creativity and earns him a decent wage.

'Beetroot, goat's cheese and candid walnuts.' Gerry introduces the dish as he delivers a plate to each of his guests. Gerry is vegetarian and has created some mouthwatering, meat-free dishes in the past.

'Oh Gerry, you could start making your own goat's cheese soon,' Nick laughs. 'Steph's son just bought a goat this afternoon.'

Again, Paul's forehead furrows and I blush when he shoots me a look. Unsure if he's querying the goat purchase or the fact that Nick appears well versed in the details of my life, I pick up my wine glass and drain it, reaching for the bottle to top myself up, trying to avoid Paul's gaze.

Nick leans in. 'Are you taking me up on my offer?'

'I think I am.' My thoughts are all over the place and I'm not entirely sure what Paul may have been insinuating, but I feel the need to drink to drown out the confusion in my thoughts.

Nick smiles and takes the bottle from my shaking hand, pouring wine into my glass.

'Thank you,' I say, picking up my fork and diving into the colourful creation on my plate. 'Gerry, this is delicious. You've outdone yourself again.'

'Thanks Steph, wait till you taste the main course. It's to die for,' Gerry says, regretting his choice of words and gasping in horror. The colour drains from his face. 'Shit, I'm sorry.'

His reaction causes me to laugh.

'Gerry, it's just a phrase. Please don't tread on eggshells around me, that will only make me feel bad. I'm fine, honestly, just keep the wine flowing.'

Nick squeezes my hand under the table and I

squeeze back, grateful to him for his support. He recognised my laugh was fake and I'm so thankful for him right now. This evening would be a struggle without him beside me.

The conversation flows around me and I sit back and listen, taking everything in. The main course arrives to rapturous remarks. A wild mushroom wellington with steamed greens and mashed potato. I devour it and when I reach for the wine bottle, it's empty. Realising I've drunk the entire bottle myself, I pour a glass of water instead. I sip slowly as everyone finishes eating, and I feel at peace for the first time since I smoked the joint several weeks earlier. As a GP, I know I can't rely on these vices to get me through my grief, but sometimes it's the only way I can empty my mind.

'Do you want more wine, Steph?' Nick notices the empty bottle.

'No, I'm good, thank you. I think one bottle's enough.' By this time, I'm relaxed and my laughter is sincere.

Dessert is just as wonderful as the rest of the meal, and by the time Gerry brings out the liqueurs, I'm yawning. The bottle of wine has pushed me beyond my limit.

'Nick, I'm going to go, but you stay. I'll order an Uber.'

'No, I'm ready too. I'll drop you home,' he offers.

I push back my chair to stand.

'Thanks for a lovely evening,' I say, stumbling backwards. My cheeks bloom at my inability to stand properly. 'As you can see, it's time I left. Am I okay to collect my car tomorrow?'

'Leave your keys, Paul and I will drop it off for

you in the morning,' Gerry offers, kindly.

'Thank you.' I say my goodbyes to the rest of the party and Paul walks me to the door while Nick says his goodbyes.

'What's going on Steph?' he asks, flashing his eyes towards Nick.

'What do you mean?' I play dumb.

'You and Nick? He's my best friend, Steph, and I love him like a brother, but I wouldn't recommend starting anything in your current position. Be careful.'

I know he's only looking out for me, but he's barking up the wrong tree. There's nothing going on and I don't want people to question our friendship.

'Paul, you're seeing things. He's just being friendly, that's all.' I shake my head, dismissing Paul's ridiculous notion. As I leave the house, a solid weight settles on my chest and I debate the unexpected feelings Nick appears to have stirred up.

Nick switches off the engine as he pulls the car to a stop outside my house. The drive home was quiet, neither of us ready to address the elephant in the room. Nick had seen Paul and me talking, and Paul's eyes had fixed on him with a warning glare as we left.

The air in the car crackles with the resounding silence and my nerves increase tenfold, but I make no move to either say goodbye or get out. To my relief, Nick bites the bullet.

'Did Paul say something to upset you, Steph?' He's direct, but his voice is low, flooded with compassion. 'I felt like there was some kind of underlying message to his parting glance, and you've not said a word all the way home.'

'He thought there was something going on between us. I told him he was delusional,' I say, my voice catching on the last word.

Nick smiles, sympathetic to my concern, his face showing no sign of surprise.

'I'll speak to Paul and make sure he knows he's barking up the wrong tree.' He bites his lip; a gesture that belies his usual confidence. 'If I've overstepped, I apologise. I like you, Steph, and I enjoy your company. I know just how lonely it can be to lose a partner and if I can help ease that burden, then I want to be here for you in whatever capacity you need.'

'Thank you, Nick.' I close my eyes and tip my head back against the headrest, willing the tears to abstain. 'You've been so kind to me.'

A single tear escapes down my cheek and Nick reaches out his thumb to swipe it away. His soft touch unleashes a torrent and I hear the click of his seatbelt, his solid arms folding me into him. Nick's hand caresses my hair as I sob into his chest. His cheek rests on top of my head as he holds me, soothing and hushing, and for the first time in weeks, I feel safe and cared for. My mind skips across my conflicting thoughts. My husband died a matter of weeks ago and my emotions are a constant flood of grief, but as Nick's heart pounds against my cheek, something stirs deep within me and I feel an ever so slight shift. The feeling consumes me for just a moment longer, until the security light blinks on and the dogs bound out of the back door, followed by Levi.

I pull back, my raw emotions exposed. The dried tear stains sting my face as I swipe my thumbs across my cheekbones. My fingers comb my hair, re-establishing a modicum of composure.

'Thank you, Nick.' I squeeze his hand and release the door. 'For everything.'

'Anytime, Steph, take care of yourself,' he whispers, and I step out into the cool night.

Nick spins the car around and disappears out of sight. Levi stands at the back door waiting for the dogs to do their business. He frowns as I draw closer.

'Who was that?' he asks.

'Oh, that was Paul's friend, Nick. He offered to drive me home as I had a bit too much to drink.'

Levi's face scrunches up in deep thought.

'Are you okay, Mum? Do you think you need some help?'

'I'm fine Levi, I promise. Paul bought some expensive wine, and I forgot I was driving for a moment, that's all.'

'If you're sure, it's just you don't usually drink much, and you know, you smoked a joint, which is also not a part of your daily routine,' Levi smiles. He's never going to let me live that down.

'Touché. I promise I'm okay, sweetheart, but thank you for checking up on me.' I drop a kiss on my son's head, thankful for his concern. 'Has Caleb been okay?'

Levi's eyes search for something to fix on and his gaze settles on the dogs.

'Levi, what aren't you telling me?'

'Promise not to tell him I told you?' Levi asks.

I frown at his obvious distress.

'What did he do, Levi?'

'Do you promise? I don't want him thinking I dobbed.' Levi's voice has a serious edge to it I haven't heard before. It's a little unsettling.

'I promise Levi, tell me.'

'I think you both might suffer from hangovers in the morning,' he says.

'Oh no, what did he drink?' I'm sobered by Levi's words.

'Check your bottle of vodka. I don't think there's much left,' Levi mutters.

'Bloody hell, I knew I shouldn't have gone out.' I slump on the couch, annoyed with myself for falling for Caleb's ruse.

'Mum, you can't be with him twenty-four seven. He's sixteen.'

'I know, but he's struggling. I shouldn't have left him. It's too soon.'

I give Levi a hug and make my way to bed, clinging to the hope that maybe he's exaggerating and Caleb hasn't gone too hard on the vodka. Snuggling down under the bedclothes, I replay the evening in my head and a lump forms in my throat. Tonight's reaction to Nick was strong and I wonder what it is about him that sparked such an intensity. No doubt he's attractive and his kindness seems genuine, but it's so much more than that. Nick seems to have the ability to read me and anticipate what I need, as though he's found the end of the thread and knows how much to pull, so I untangle a little, without fully unravelling. I understand why Paul may have sensed some chemistry between us. As much as I alleged his delusion, I feel it. I get the impression Nick does, too.

Caleb

Dear Dad

I just wanted to update you on how my life's progressing without you here to breathe down my neck. I got a bit of a taste for vodka tonight. If I'm honest, it tastes like shit, but fuck if it doesn't make everything feel good. You know, I forgot about you for a while tonight. I forgot what a controlling, overbearing, intimidating bully you were for a while. In fact, I forgot you existed at all. Oh, that's right, you don't, my bad.

It wasn't until I sobered up that I saw things clearly. You were only any of those things because you couldn't stand up to your own dad. The reality was you were insecure and weak as piss. So here's me, standing up to you.

Cheers Dad.
Caleb

Nick

Nick tossed and turned all night. He worried about his developing feelings for Steph and feared Paul's observation had been right on the mark. There was something there, an unmistakable chemistry. Steph had not long lost her husband, so he didn't need to be convinced his romantic feelings were one-sided, but the connection was real. He needed to rein himself in. Steph needed him for support and reassurance, not for him to become gooey eyed over her.

The dawn light pushed through the blinds, and he laid on his bed, staring at his bedroom ceiling. Any feelings of a romantic nature needed to be quashed, and he focused his mind towards more friendly but professional thoughts. A run to clear his head was the distraction he needed.

Nick showered to wake himself up, then dressed in his running shorts and pulled on his Nikes. He scrolled Spotify for an upbeat playlist and pushed his AirPods in his ears. With no idea of the route he would take, he set off running. Concentrating on the beat, he pushed himself to his limits and only realised where he was when he spotted Steph's car still parked in Paul and Gerry's driveway. Paul had been Nick's go to for everything in life since Lee had passed, and his subconscious was telling him this was where he needed to be. He paused at the end of the driveway, catching his breath and checking his watch. They'd be out of bed by now.

'Nick? This is a surprise. Come on in.' Gerry stepped aside, wrapped up in his fluffy dressing gown, coffee in hand.

'Hey, sorry to bother you. I was just out running and… well, here I am.' He rubbed a hand across his face, trying to make sense of the bundle of nerves knotting inside his chest.

'Paul, make another coffee, will you?' Gerry shouted through the house as the pair made their way towards the kitchen. 'We have a visitor.'

'Hey, mate, you look rough this morning.' Nick said when Paul turned to see who had called so early on a Sunday morning.

Paul frowned at Nick.

'Everything okay?' He ignored the teasing jibe.

'I guess so,' he said, scrubbing at his face again. He yawned. The lack of sleep followed by a near eight kilometre run had taken its toll. 'I wasn't coming here, but I ended up at your door, so I figure there's a reason for that.'

Paul smiled, handing him the coffee, fresh from the machine.

'Come sit down, mate, talk to me.'

The three friends sat outside in the winter sunshine and talked over what was on Nick's mind.

'I knew there was something going on between you two last night,' Paul's brows knitted in disappointment.

'There's nothing going on, Paul, I promise. Look, I'm trying to be honest here and I'd be lying if I said I felt nothing for her. I do, but I'm well aware of her situation and I will not put her in a position that might jeopardise her healing.'

Paul held Nick's gaze, nodding at his friend. He knew Nick well; they'd been through hell and back together and he trusted his word.

'I know you won't do that,' he said. 'The thing is, Nick, under different circumstances, I couldn't think of two people more perfect for each other. The two of you are both special to me, you know that, and further down the track I'd be the first person in line to congratulate you, but right now she needs friends. She needs support to get herself and her boys through this, so if you can't be just that, then I'll have to ask you to back away and let me and her other friends provide the solace she needs.'

Nick felt chastised. He hung his head, nodding at Paul's reproach.

'Of course. I want to help. Her grief is so familiar to me; the guilt, the blame, the sadness, all of it.' His eyes fixed on Paul's, letting him know he was aware of the full circumstances of Chris's death.

Paul smiled at his friend. 'That's why I recommended she talk to you. I know you can help with Caleb, too. Please don't blow this.'

Nick drained the remnants from his mug and stood to leave.

'Hey, if you give me Steph's car keys, I'll drop her car off, save you a trip,' he offered, trying for helpful without overstepping.

'That'd be great,' Gerry expressed his gratitude. 'I don't think we're up to driving yet.'

'No worries,' Nick said, hugging his friends goodbye.

Nick adjusted the driver's seat and the rear-view mirror of Steph's X5. As he reversed out of Paul and Gerry's driveway, Siri began barking directions at him from the app on his phone. He had a recollection of where he'd dropped her home, but was doubtful he'd find it without instruction. It was a plush drive; the leather seats and superior sound system a far cry from his old battered truck.

He smiled to himself as he drove, picturing Steph's house in his mind. He'd only seen the outside the previous night, under the muted glow of the solar lanterns that lined her driveway, but from her choice of car and the way she put herself together, he imagined her home would be beautiful with quality furniture and polished wooden floors, lush couches and marble bench tops. Siri directed him to make a left in one hundred metres and he swung her car through the open electric gate, along her winding pea gravel driveway to the side of the house where he'd said goodnight. His mind whirred, retracing last night's chain of events that led to him consoling Steph in the front seat of his car. He knew Steph had said Paul's observations were delusional, and he'd taken on board Paul's warning, but his perception told him Steph had felt something, too. Maybe it was nothing more than missing physical contact, someone to hold her when she needed comfort, but there was a definite attachment, a bond, something that tethered them. He would be whatever she needed him to be, whether that be a friend, a professional, or something more. He vowed to himself right then that helping Steph heal would become his priority.

Steph

I blink awake with the morning sunbeams streaking through the blinds. The hammering inside my skull is incessant, and I squint at the numbers glaring from my alarm clock. It reads 7.00 am and I'm surprised I've slept so late. My body is finely tuned to wake with the birds. Grateful for the forethought to bring a bottle of water to bed, I unscrew the cap and take a long drink, feeling heavy regret over last night's spontaneous decision. I pull on my dressing gown and make my way to the kitchen to fill my stomach and soak up the residual booze in my system.

Levi is up, bright eyed as usual, and I wonder if he'll ever become a normal teenager lounging around in bed all morning. I can't imagine that will ever happen. He loves being up and about, tending to his animals.

'Morning, Mum, you look rough this morning,' he grins.

'Thanks Levi, boost my ego why don't you?' My son, honest to a fault. 'The head's pounding, but I hope my stomach will settle once I've got some bacon in it.'

'I'm up for bacon, if you're cooking,' he says. 'I'm just going back out to check on Billie Eilish.'

I turn my attention to the fridge and I'm thankful

for the pack of bacon staring back at me. I'm just about to light the stove when I hear noises from down the hall. I stop what I'm doing and listen to the unmistakable sound of retching. Caleb is in a much worse state than I am. I sigh, grab some water and a towel, and make my way to the boys' bathroom.

'Caleb, are you okay?' I ask, once there's a lull in proceedings.

'I think I've got gastro.' Caleb retches again. His attempt to hide his actions makes me smile.

'You should hide the evidence before you lie to me,' I say, pushing open the bathroom door.

Caleb sits back against the tiles, pale faced and drained.

'I saw the almost empty vodka bottle you left out, Cale.' I hadn't noticed it last night when I came in, but the evidence of how much he'd drunk was clear to see this morning.

Caleb's ashen cheeks tinge with pink before he hurls forward to expel more contents from his stomach.

'Here, drink this,' I advise, handing him some water. As he sips, I figure now is the time to talk, while he might just be feeling a moment of regret.

'First, drugs, now drinking. Caleb, this is not the way forward. People have offered help. Please take it. It will help you deal with your grief.'

I can't sit back and watch him self-destruct. I could drag him to Nick's office, but I can't make him talk, so I'll try anything to get him to go of his own accord.

'I'm going back to bed,' Caleb responds, pushing up from the tiled floor. His eyes are vacant, void of any awareness.

'Cale. Please just think about it, for me.'

Levi smells the bacon cooking and rushes inside.

'Sauce?' I ask, squirting ketchup on my roll.

'Nah, I'm good,' Levi says, the sandwich already in his mouth. I follow him outside with two mugs of tea.

The grease does its job and my stomach settles. I'd only had a bottle of wine, not a bottle of vodka like Caleb.

The rumble of a car engine breaks the silence and Levi flashes me a questioning look as my car rolls into view.

'It'll be Paul and Gerry bringing my car back. I had to leave it there last night.'

But when the door opens, the figure that strides onto my verandah is neither Paul nor Gerry. It's Nick, with my car keys dangling from one hand and a takeaway coffee cup in the other.

I smile at the sight of him dressed in black running shorts and a grey muscle tee. His legs are lean and tan, his arms shapely and toned. I catch myself as my eyes rove over him appeasingly and quickly restrain myself.

'Hey, I picked your car up for you and I thought you might need this,' he says, almost shyly, handing me the coffee and resting the keys down on the table.

'Thank you,' I say, enjoying a slurp of coffee. 'You didn't have to do that. Gerry said he'd bring it.'

Nick shrugs. 'It was no trouble. Anyway, I don't think Gerry or Paul were in any state to drive this morning. You look to be faring much better.'

I'm conscious that I'm sitting here in my dressing gown, eyes bloodshot, and my face still plastered with last night's make up. And then I notice Levi looking at Nick with curiosity.

'Levi, this is Paul's friend, Nick. He drove me home last night. Nick, this is my youngest son, Levi.'

Levi leans forward and offers Nick a handshake.

'Good to meet you, Levi,' Nick says, accepting the handshake with a heart-warming smile. 'Your mum told me you bought a goat.'

'Yeah, do you want to meet her?' Levi is bursting to introduce Billie to anyone who is interested.

'I'd love to.' Nick grins and Levi leaps from the couch to lead the way.

I watch as the pair of them wander across the lawn towards Billie's pen, then pick up my phone and reverse the camera function to check on my appearance. I've looked worse, I'll admit, but still, it's not my best look. My eyes drift back across the garden to the goat pen where my son and my new friend are deep in conversation, and a heavy knot ties up my stomach. The past month or so has opened my eyes to a life I hadn't even realised I'd been living. Not only had I been blind to my husband's depression and his imperious behaviour towards Caleb, but also Levi's complete lack of fatherly attention. Seeing him now, animated by his exchange with Nick, both breaks my heart and gives me hope. I'm disappointed that my marriage wasn't what I thought it was, and I'm saddened that neither of my boys had an ideal relationship with their father, but I'm hopeful that one day I'll meet someone new, someone who will love not only me but also become important to my sons. What has me so unsettled is that my husband isn't long dead and I think I may have already met that someone new.

Nick and Levi make their way back towards me and the knot tightens in my gut as they approach. Their heads are close, deep in conversation, Levi hanging on Nick's every word. My mind jumps way ahead of itself and I picture a future with this man. I'd thought my attraction was physical, but this, the joy he's just brought to my son in the space of ten minutes, this is a new level of attraction.

'Mum?' Levi breaks me from my fantasy and I stumble as heat surges up my neck, bursting into flames on my cheeks.

'Oh, sorry, I was away with the fairies there for a sec,' I say, trying to hide my internal embarrassment.

'Nick was telling me he's into mountain biking,' Levi says. 'I was just asking him about bikes. I've been thinking of buying one.'

The animation on my son's face makes me smile. I love his enthusiasm, but I'm surprised that this is the first I've heard of the idea of buying a bike. Levi usually talks my ear off about any idea he has.

'Oh, you never said.'

'You've kind of had a lot going on, Mum.' Levi disappears inside to get his phone. Nick perches on the edge of the chair.

'I hope I didn't overstep there. It just came up.'

'Not at all. Thanks for taking the time to go see the goat with him.' My body is a jumble of nervous energy that I hope my voice manages to conceal.

'He's a nice kid,' Nick commends. His eyes meet mine and I struggle to look away. The chemistry between us is palpable. It's no wonder Paul picked up on it last night. It feels intense, raw, like he's stripping away every layer of me bit by bit and exposing every inch of me. Every thought, every secret, every desire, and every painful memory.

'Can I get you a drink of something?' I ask, shattering the tension between us.

'No, I'm good, thanks. I'll get going and leave you to it.'

'How are you getting home? Do you need a lift?' I wonder.

'No, I'll run,' Nick says, getting up and stretching his legs.

'How far away do you live?'

'It's about six k's, not too far.'

'Are you sure? I'm happy to drive you.'

'I'm fine. Tell Levi I said goodbye, and if he wants any help to choose a bike, give him my number.'

'Thank you, Nick,' I say, standing. I reach over and rest my hand on his arm, defying the warnings from my head. 'I appreciate your kindness.'

Heat flares in Nick's eyes, but his lukewarm tone quickly douses it.

'I'll catch you soon, Steph,' he says, turning his back and setting off at a fast pace down my driveway.

As I watch him go, his strength buoys me. I'm not sure I have the fortitude to fight what I'm sure is a mutual attraction.

Steph

After the tiny glimpse of my imaginary future gave me a hint of encouragement, life seems to have extinguished any thoughts I may have had of ever finding happiness again. After Caleb's drinking incident, he's shut down. He won't eat, he won't speak, he just locks himself away in his bedroom with his headphones on. I've somehow got him to go to school every morning, but even that's becoming a struggle. As a GP, I have lots of contacts, not to mention both Paul and Nick eager to help, but I'm at a loss which way to turn.

I don't think Caleb's showered in days and I'm not sure making him attend school is doing him any favours, but I'm too fearful to leave him at home. I've battled the idea of taking some time off work to be with him, but if I'm honest with myself, the routine is the only thing keeping my head above water and I know that if I don't look after myself, I'll be of little benefit to my boys.

Feeling the need to take a moment to gather myself before I drive to work, I swing my car from the drop-off zone into an empty parking space. My knuckles blanch as I grip the steering wheel and a sob tears through my body, unleashing a torrent of tears I have no hope of holding back. A loud knock on my window makes me jump and Terri gasps when she sees me mid-breakdown.

'Steph,' she says, her face exuding sympathy. She leans down to my level and envelops me in a hug and as much as I'm embarrassed to fall apart in the midst of the school car park, I'm grateful it's Terri squeezing me back together.

'Let me come round to the other side and get in,' she offers, once I settle.

'That's better,' she says, climbing into the passenger seat and taking hold of my hand. 'Talk to me, Steph, what can I do for you?'

'I don't know, Terri. I'm so bloody angry at him I can't think straight.' My eyes sting from all the tears I've shed.

'Try not to fuel your anger towards Chris. I know it's a stage of grief, Steph, but it was a tragic accident,' Terri says.

I haven't told her the truth as yet, but she's my best friend and she deserves to know.

'Terri, there's something you should know.' There are no right words under the circumstances, so I blurt it out.

'It wasn't an accident. Chris left a suicide note.'

Terri's face contorts with shock. Her hand smacks her mouth and her throat emits an audible wail.

'Christ, Steph, I had no idea he was in that position. I'm so sorry.'

'Me neither. It was out of the blue. I'm a GP. I deal with depression every single day and I never saw the signs. What does that say about me?' I shake my head, trying to expel those thoughts.

'Steph, all it says is that he did a bloody good job of covering it up. It says nothing about you. Please don't blame yourself. Sometimes life is out of our control.'

'I know, and I don't blame myself. I just feel sad he felt he couldn't talk to me about it.' Terri squeezes my hand. 'You know, I was just going to let everyone think it was an accident, but watching Caleb spiral out of control and refuse the help I've offered him, I've realised I need to talk about it. He needs to understand that getting help doesn't make him weak. It will make him stronger. Chris said it himself in his letter, that he ended his own life to put a stop to the cycle entrenched in him from his own father's behaviour. He constantly pressured Caleb to be the best, but no matter how well Cale did, Chris always pushed for more. He worried he was damaging his son, but didn't know how to ask for help. If something good can come of this, then that cycle needs to end here and now. Caleb needs help and I'll be damned if I let him go down the same track as his father.'

'I didn't realise Caleb was struggling in that way, Steph, and I'm sorry, I should have.'

'It's my fault, Terri. You've called and sent plenty of messages. I just haven't felt up to talking.'

'Still, I should've known Cale wasn't okay after he punched Josh. Although, I'd have decked him too if he'd said that to me.'

I chuckle at her words. Her not judging Cale too harshly means the world to me.

'He's not in a good place, Terri. First, I caught him smoking a joint in his room, then I caught him throwing up from the after effects of drinking nearly an entire bottle of vodka. He's not talking, not eating, not leaving his room, and by the stink of him this morning, he's not showering either. I don't know what to do. There are two psychologists, one of which specialises in teen mental health, both willing to help him, but he just won't go. Medication seems to be his only option at this point. Hopefully, it will just lift him enough to think straight.'

'You're the doctor, Steph, and his mother. You need to do whatever you think is best for him. In the meantime, if there's anything we can do, please tell me. You know that we've always thought of Cale as family. We'll do whatever the hell we can to help him get through this.'

'Thanks Terri, I appreciate that. If Josh could try to get him out of the house, talk him into going back to footy training, that might be a start.'

'I'll do my best,' Terri promises. 'You'd better get to work, but call me anytime, Steph, I mean that. Take care of yourself.'

I check my tear-stained face in the vanity mirror and wipe the mascara stain from underneath my rims. I take a sip of water and start the engine. It's time to go help some other people.

'Hey Steph, are you okay?' I rush into the kitchen and throw my bag into my locker, almost knocking Jonathan over.

'No, not really. It's been a morning. In fact, it's been a shitty couple of months.'

'Come here, take a breath,' Jonathan says, pulling me into his arms for a hug.

'I think my first patient's here.' I try to escape his hold.

'Mrs Johnson's here every bloody day. She can wait. We all know there's nothing wrong with her that a new husband wouldn't fix. You're more important today, Steph. Just breathe for me,' he whispers.

I feel my body sag, relaxing for the first time this morning. In fact, for the first time in a while. I haven't felt relaxed since I drank a bottle of wine at Paul's house several weeks earlier. I've caught myself several times in the last few weeks, drawn to the bottle to escape my thoughts, but I've managed to discipline myself for Caleb's sake.

'Thanks, Jon,' I say when I'm released. 'I needed that.'

'I know you did. Come chat with me at lunch time, Steph. Let me help you.' Both Jonathan and Paul have been watching me and I've declined every offer of help so far, adamant it's Caleb who needs it. But I know as well as anyone that you can't pour from an empty cup, and I can see in Jon's resolute face he won't take no for an answer a day longer.

It's a busy morning, but I get through my patients and I'm only running five minutes over by the time lunch rolls around.

I stumble into the kitchen and Paul tips his head towards the coffee machine in silent question.

'God, yes, I haven't had one yet. I was running late this morning and didn't get the chance.' I pull my lunch from the fridge and grab a fork, slumping at the table just as Jonathan comes in.

Paul finishes up at the coffee machine and I catch a look pass between him and Jon as they sit side by side, across the table from me.

My fork hovers in front of my mouth as their faces

both fix on mine.

'What is this, an intervention?'

'Yes,' Paul says, his face serious.

'Oh,' I'm taken aback. 'I was kidding.'

'Look, Steph, you've been pretending you're okay for weeks now, and we both know you're not. Please let us help you,' Jonathan begins.

I blink back tears, grateful for their concern, but also ready to accept their help. My resolve weakens and my dam bursts for the second time today.

'There's just so much shit surrounding his death that I feel like I can't grieve for Chris. Not to mention that I seem to be losing Caleb. I don't know what to do.'

'Where is Caleb at right now? Mentally I mean,' Paul asks, with compassion.

'He's pretty low, not talking, not eating, not showering. Between school and his bedroom, that's pretty much his entire existence right now.' I feel like a broken record.

'At least he's going to school,' Jonathan acknowledges. 'It could be worse.'

'To be honest, I'm not sure how much longer I can keep him there. Every day's a fight.'

'You need to look after yourself first, Steph, so that you can help Caleb. How about some anti-depressants?'

'I think that's the only option at the moment.' I've resigned myself to the fact that this is what he needs. 'That's if he'll even take them.'

'Not for Caleb, Steph, I mean for you.'

Surprise etches my face when Jonathan catches me off guard.

'Jon, I know you mean well, but honestly, I'm not

depressed. I'm just exhausted and worried about my son.'

'Okay,' Jonathan softens. 'How about you speak to someone instead? If you can't get Caleb to see someone, how about you talk to Paul, or we can refer you to someone else if that's what you'd prefer?'

Paul nods his agreement. 'I'll go along with whatever you want, Steph, just so long as you talk to someone. I know Nick wants to help. Have you seen him since my birthday?' Paul asks, tentatively unleashing the elephant in the room.

'Not since he dropped my car off the following morning. I'm not sure he's the right person.' There's no way I can confess to Paul the real reason I haven't called Nick.

Paul eyes me incredulously. 'Something happened between you two, didn't it?'

I blush at the reprimand from my colleague.

'Nothing happened, Paul, I swear.' My voice is hoarse from the excessive amounts of crying.

'But?' Paul presses, not willing to let it drop.

I glare at him, annoyed that he's making me admit my feelings.

'But…' I start. 'I feel like it could. That thought terrifies me. I just lost my husband.'

Paul reaches across the table and takes my hand.

'Sweetheart, I understand that. You're in a very vulnerable place right now, and Nick would never take advantage of that. He's a good man, and he understands what you're going through. I recommend you speak to him, but if he makes you uncomfortable, then you can talk to me, or like Jon said, we can refer you.'

I stare at my colleague, bewildered by Paul's change of heart about Nick.

'The other week you were warning me off, now you're pushing us together.'

'It wasn't like that, Steph. I just sensed something between the two of you and I was worried you might've been getting yourself into something that you're not ready for. I would hate for either of you to get hurt, but I'd also hate for you to miss out on what could be a valuable friendship. If Caleb's struggling as much as you say he is, then take all the help you're offered.'

He's right. It would be foolish to throw away any opportunity that might help my son. My emotions have been all over the place lately, so it's more than likely that I've confused my feelings. What I'd thought was attraction was probably nothing more than feeling comforted and understood.

'You're right,' I say after thinking things through. 'I need to help Caleb, and fast. I'll call Nick later and see if we can come up with a plan.'

'You're doing the right thing,' Paul says, pushing back from the table. 'I'm sorry, I'm gonna have to leave you. I've got a client due in two minutes. Keep me posted.'

'Thanks Paul, I appreciate you not giving up on me.' He squeezes my shoulder on the way out.

I turn back towards Jonathan and see him studying me, carefully choosing his next words.

'You know, Steph, there are no time limits on grief.'

I frown. 'I know.'

Jonathan hesitates. 'If you meet someone, it doesn't mean you won't still love your husband. The two can be mutually viable.'

I stare at my colleague, unsure what point he's trying to make.

Nick

Nick hadn't heard from Steph in over a week. They'd messaged back and forth a few times after he'd dropped her car off, but then there was radio silence. He knew she'd read his messages, but he'd heard nothing back. There'd been a moment at her house just before he'd left and he couldn't help but wonder if that was why she'd ghosted him. It wasn't like they were close friends, barely more than acquaintances, but he liked her and he wanted to help. He noticed a missed call from her in between patients, and his mood lifted. The voicemail she left was blunt, apologising for her absence and asking him to return her call. Her tone was businesslike, lacking its usual warmth. Nick bit his lip and glanced at the clock. He only had a few minutes before his next patient was due, but he didn't want to leave Steph hanging until he'd finished for the day. His finger hovered over the call button before he chastised himself for being ridiculous.

Steph answered on the first ring.

'Hi Nick.'

'Hey, I'm glad you called Steph. How are you?' His concern for her overwhelmed him, and he tried to keep as much levity as possible in his voice.

'I'm not great, Nick, if I'm honest. Caleb's struggling and I would appreciate a friendly ear.'

'Of course. I have one more patient, then I'm free for the night,' Nick said. 'How are you fixed?'

'I'm just on my way to pick the boys up from school and then I can be free. Or after work tomorrow? I don't want to impose on your time.'

'Steph, you're not imposing. How about you come over around six? I'll cook dinner. You could probably do with a break.'

Steph froze, unsure what the connotations of such an invitation meant. Nick sensed her hesitancy.

'If it makes you feel easier, Steph, come later. But it's just dinner, I promise. I'm cooking anyway,' Nick assured her.

There was another pause and Nick was about to jump in when Steph spoke.

'Thank you, dinner would be great. Send me your address and I'll see you at six.'

'Perfect, and Steph?' he paused. 'We'll find a way to help him, I promise.' Nick ended the call with a smile.

He was eager to finish up with his last patient of the day so he could make a quick dash to the supermarket on his way home. A lasagne and garlic bread would do the trick, but he was short of a few ingredients. There wouldn't be enough time to make his Nonna's traditional sauce, that required several hours simmering in the pot, but he'd do the best he could with his limited timeframe. Italian food was in his blood and was always his staple comfort food. There was nothing quite like the richness of the tomatoes combined with the fresh fragrant flavours of basil and oregano, tossed with pasta cooked al dente, to the bite, or the literal translation, "to the tooth," to soothe the soul.

Nick stirred the beef ragu, along with the bechamel sauce, and carefully constructed the dish. He threw it in the oven and unwrapped a pre-packaged garlic bread before heading to his ensuite for a quick shower. Dressing comfortably in soft heather grey track pants and a fitted white tee, he towel dried his hair and combed it back from his face. Glancing at the kitchen clock, he put the bread in the oven and grabbed cutlery from the drawer, laying the knives and forks in a pile on the breakfast bar, going for a 'casual friends' vibe. He was a psychologist, and she needed help with her son. It was time to stop overthinking and just get on with being her friend.

'Hey, it's good to see you. Come on in.'

'Thanks.' Steph flushed. She'd felt awkward and left him hanging, and now she was barging back into his life.

Nick showed her through to the back, where the rich fragrances hung in the air.

'Oh wow, that smells amazing. What're you cooking?'

'Lasagne, I hope that's okay?' he asked.

'Perfect. I hadn't realised how hungry I was until I smelled that.'

'Grab a seat,' Nick offered. 'It should be ready.'

Steph pulled up a stool at the breakfast bar where the plates were stacked and the cutlery was thrown on top, as though he'd arranged it to look casual.

'Help yourself to a drink.' He pointed to the jug of sparkling water in the middle. Steph filled two glasses and took a sip. Nick set down a salad and some garlic bread, then served the lasagne onto two plates.

'This looks fantastic, thanks Nick.'

'It's probably not to my usual standard. I didn't have time to follow my Nonna's recipe to the letter, but dig in.'

'Your Nonna's recipe? You come from a traditional Italian background, then?'

'I sure do. I spent a month every year in the European summers with my Nonna and Nonno at their olive grove in the Tuscan hills. They were the very best part of my childhood. My brother moved back there when he left school, learnt the business and has since taken over. I try to get back there as often as I can, but it's not the same without my grandparents.' A shadow crossed Nick's face before his smile returned, obviously thinking of his childhood with bittersweet memories.

They ate in silence, not comfortable, but not awkward either. Nick's calm manner removed any stress. He took a sip of his drink and looked at Steph.

'What made you reach out, Steph? How can I help?' he asked.

Steph put down her knife and fork and took a sip herself, clearing her palate.

'I feel like I'm losing him, Nick. I don't know what to do. He barely speaks, and I just fear he's heading for a dark place.'

'And he's still refusing any help?'

'Yes.'

Nick pondered for a few moments while he tucked back into his lasagne. Steph could see him thinking things over, hoping he could find a solution. They finished up their meal, and Nick suggested they move to the lounge room to sit in comfort while they chatted.

'Levi's been talking non-stop about this bike. He even asked if he could come with me tonight,' Steph said, as she kicked off her shoes and tucked one foot beneath her on the couch.

'Really?' Nick asked, surprised.

'Yes, he was quite taken by you. He wants to pick your brain again about which bike he should buy.'

'I'm happy to help,' he said, and his eyes lit up like a beacon as a thought popped into his head. 'Maybe we could kill two birds with one stone, so to speak,' he mused.

'How do you mean?'

'Well, if I spend some time with Levi, I can help him choose a bike, maybe take him out for a ride. If he trusts me, maybe Caleb might too.'

Steph thought about his idea and frowned, wondering how it could work.

'That's a little unorthodox, don't you think? How would we work out your time so I can pay you?' she asked.

'Steph, I don't want your money, I just want your son to get better,' Nick said.

'I can't ask you to do that. You barely know me,' Steph said.

'You didn't ask, I offered. Look, this isn't work for

me, it's helping a friend in need. Paul is my closest friend. I love him like a brother. He cares about you, and we both want to help. I think it's safe to say that we're friends now too, right?'

Steph's heart pounded. He was right. They had become friends, and she regretted her withdrawal over the past few weeks. He was so easy to open up to, and she'd missed his wise words. She'd missed him.

'You're right, we are friends,' Steph flashed him a smile. 'And I'd like to take you up on your offer.'

Nick's eyes flared at the thought of spending more time with her. There was an undeniable chemistry between them and his head was fighting like hell to stop his heart from becoming entangled. Steph wasn't ready for that and possibly wouldn't be for a long time yet.

'You know, I'm surprised we haven't spent more time together in the past, given how close we both are to Paul,' Steph mused.

'Yeah, I guess we've only met previously at Paul and Gerry's larger events, parties and the wedding and such. Paul wasn't a fan of my ex-wife, so it was always a little awkward inviting the pair of us to smaller dinner parties where he'd have to be nice to her.'

'Really? I can't imagine Paul being that way with anyone.'

'He isn't generally. It's a long story.'

'I'm not going anywhere,' Steph said. Her eyes gleamed, unwittingly confusing Nick's feelings.

He studied her, trying to weigh her up, and she flushed at his stare, but held her resolve. She'd shared her deepest feelings with him about her husband, and he felt he owed her the same courtesy. His breath snagged on the lump in his throat, but he kept his eyes fixed on hers as he spoke.

'My first wife, Lee, was Paul's best friend. They met at high school and she was the first person he came out to. After that day, she never left his side, stood by him through all the bullying, the self doubt, the disastrous first dates. Paul and I met at uni and the two of them came as a package deal. To be friends with Paul meant also being friends with Lee, which I was perfectly happy with. She captivated me from day one.' Nick's eyes glazed over as he brought his memories to the surface.

Steph smiled, encouraging him to continue.

'Luckily, she felt the same way, and we were married before long. She was like a butterfly, so vibrant and colourful, always happy. She cared so deeply about other people and brought so much joy to my life. We honeymooned in Tuscany and she won my Nonna over instantly. My heart was so happy. We had a wonderful few years together before our first baby came along. Hannah was an absolute joy; we named her for my Nonna, who had unfortunately passed earlier that year. Lucy came along a couple of years later and she was the image of her mother. We were happy with our little family, or so I thought,' Nick said. 'I woke up one morning, and she was gone. She'd taken a full bottle of sleeping tablets.' Tears filled his eyes.

'I'm sorry,' he choked, swiping at his eyes. 'It still gets me.'

Steph reached out and took his hand.

'Please don't apologise, Nick. I understand your need to help me now. The pain never goes away, does it?'

'It lessens, Steph, please don't think you'll feel this way forever. I fell in love again. Actually, if I'm honest, I'm not sure I did.' Nick sat with his thoughts and contemplated his next words.

'When my second wife, Sarah, and I began having problems, Paul made me talk. After we lost Lee, he hadn't been in a fit state himself to help me through my grief, and we'd just muddled along together the best we could. He'd lost his best friend, his soul mate, and as close as Paul and I were, I wasn't her. My two girls had been my priority and I think I just needed them to have a mum. Paul warned me against marrying Sarah. It was too soon, and I hadn't grieved properly. Although, looking back, I can see it wasn't just that. She wasn't right for us. It wouldn't have mattered if I'd met her two years later. I wasn't in love with her. My friendship with Paul suffered for a while, although he never allowed that to hurt his relationship with my kids; he's godfather to all three. We got back on track and he helped me through my divorce. I'm at the stage where I'm happy again. If I'd had help to deal with my grief in the beginning, I'm sure I wouldn't have married Sarah, but then again, if I hadn't married her, there'd be no Millie. My life wouldn't be complete without her, so I suppose everything happens for a reason.'

Nick stopped talking and Steph's words filled the silence.

'And now? You say you're happy, but aren't you lonely?' she asked, an acute hole in her own life where her husband had been.

'It's funny, I haven't felt lonely on my own until

recently. The loneliness crippled me for years after Lee died, even throughout my second marriage, but after my divorce I felt at peace being by myself. Lately, though, I guess I'm at the stage where I'd like to share my life with someone again.' An awkward grimace spread across his face. 'In fact, I joined a dating app a few weeks back.'

Nick's words were a sucker-punch to Steph. She reeled at the thought of him being with someone else.

'Oh?' she said, the words forced from her lips. 'How's that going?'

'It's a bloody disaster.'

Relief bubbled up through Steph and released itself in a chuckle.

'Have you had many dates?' she asked.

'I've met three different women. All sounded good on paper, but there was no chemistry. Like literally nothing, nil, zero.'

'Maybe that will come later. I mean, can you tell after only one date?' Steph said, without conviction.

Nick eyed her with curiosity.

'I believe you can.' His eyes bored into Steph, heightening the intensity between them. He proved his point, and she was powerless to deny it.

'Maybe you're right,' she conceded. 'I can't imagine having to go through all that again, dating random men trying to find the one. It sounds like hell, but I'm only fifty-two and I can't imagine wanting to be alone forever either.'

'You won't be, Steph.' Nick's thumb caressed hers and she looked down, surprised that she'd been holding his hand the entire time. She dropped it quickly and wrapped her hand in her other one, unsure what was happening.

'But until you're ready to meet someone, please don't be lonely. I'm here for you. Call me anytime you need to talk.' His words said one thing, but the glint in his eye read a different story.

'Thank you, Nick. I appreciate that more than you know. I have lots of people around me, but they're all couples, and I know they mean it when they say they're here for me, but they don't understand how I feel. Their lives are still going on.'

'Ouch, that hurts!'

Steph grinned, the intensity between them broken. 'Sorry, I didn't mean it quite like that, but you said you were single and have no life.'

'You're right, it's true. And I think I'm going to quit the dating app too, so I'll have even more time on my hands,' he says.

'Don't do that on my account,' Steph said, the double meaning apparent.

'Honestly, Steph, I hated it. I think I'll stick to the old-fashioned ways of meeting people from now on.'

'Sounds fair.'

'So, if you're happy with keeping things casual, I'll spend some time with Levi, meet Caleb and take it from there?' Nick steered the subject back to the reason Steph was there.

'I think maybe that's the only way to go, but only if you're sure, Nick. It's a big ask.'

'Like you so generously pointed out, I have no life,' he grinned. 'Other than coaching Millie's football team, I go to work and come home to an empty house, go for the occasional bike ride with a friend, or I run to relieve the boredom. And like you, my friends are all married and they have their own stuff going on.'

'How old's Millie?'

'She's fifteen. She used to split her time between me and her mum, but that became a pain in the arse for a teenager, dragging her stuff around, living out of a suitcase. I would love to have her here full time, but it's easier for her at her mum's, with school and her friends. We're still close, though. I see her at football and we hang out after training. She's a great kid.' Nick's face lit up when he spoke of her.

'Can I ask you a personal question?' Steph asked.

'Of course, you can ask me anything.'

'Do you worry about your older girls being like their mother? With the depression, I mean. It can be hereditary, can't it? I worry about that for Caleb.'

'Absolutely, I worry about them developing PND if they have kids of their own, and I will watch out for it like a hawk. But I've learnt not to allow it to rule my life. It'll drive you crazy, if you let it, Steph.'

'Yeah, I know,' she agreed. 'Well, I should go, but thank you for tonight. It means a lot that you shared your story with me.'

'You're welcome.'

'So, how about you come over this weekend? I know Levi would love to talk bikes with you.'

'Sounds like a plan. We'll take it slow, and see how it goes, okay?' Nick said. 'If I think I'm not getting anywhere with Caleb, we might have to change things up, but we'll play it by ear for now.'

'Thanks Nick, I really am grateful.'

Their friendship felt a little more natural, and Nick pulled Steph into a hug. Her body stiffened against him, but as he held her, she relaxed into him, giving him hope that she just might allow him to be the light she needed to guide her out of the darkness.

Steph

'Hey, Levi,' I say as he sits down for dinner next to Caleb.

'Yeah?'

'Nick said he'd be happy to come over this weekend if you still want his advice on which bike to get?'

My voice betrays my casual words. Levi is oblivious to my strangled lilt.

'Are you serious?'

His eyes brighten and his smile is wide. Levi has always conveyed a spirited enthusiasm for life, and I'm heartened that his father's death hasn't knocked that out of him. He was never close to Chris, just because they didn't have much in common. Chris had no interest in the outdoor activities that Levi enjoyed, preferring football, which Levi has little interest in. Spending time with Nick will give him the attention he's been lacking, but what I want more than anything is for Nick to make inroads with Caleb.

'Yes, I'm not sure when yet. He said he'll let me know when he's free. He coaches his daughter's football team, so he'll have to work around that.'

I detect a vague glimpse of interest from Caleb and hope Nick will connect with him, maybe through football. I'd love to see him playing again, even if it's just for fun. It would be a waste of his talent not to continue on the path he was on, but just to see a smile on his face again would fill my heart.

'How old's his daughter?' Levi asks, shovelling pasta into his mouth.

'Levi, don't talk with your mouth full.' I roll my eyes at his lack of manners.

'Sorry.' He sucks up the last piece of spaghetti. He loves his food and I'm sure he's about ready for a growth spurt. Still, I'd like him to eat in a less animalistic manner.

'She's fifteen, her name's Millie.'

'Is she hot?' Levi grins.

'Levi!'

Caleb is quiet throughout our conversation, but at least he's eating again. I'm thankful for small mercies. He seems to have lost so much weight over the last few weeks. I'm not sure he'd even have the energy to last through a game of football. The second he takes his last bite, he leaves the table without a word and retreats to his room without so much as a second glance.

Sadness fills me once again.

'Do you think he'll get better Mum?' Levi asks.

'I hope so, sweetheart. I spoke to Terri. She said she'll try to get Josh to coax him out of the house and back to footy. I think his lack of routine and exercise is just exacerbating the problem.'

'Kids are talking about him at school,' Levi hesitates, sucking on his bottom lip. 'He's been sitting by himself a lot.'

'Where's Josh and his other friends?' I ask, concerned by this turn of events.

'I don't know,' Levi shrugs. 'On the oval playing footy, I guess, where Caleb would usually be.'

'How long's this been going on?' I quiz, trying to stay calm.

'He hasn't hung out with his mates since Dad died.'

His revelation made me cringe.

'What? Why didn't you say?' I yelp.

'Don't shout at me, Mum, it's not my fault. I didn't notice till people started saying stuff about him,' he huffs.

'Sorry, I know it's not your fault. What are people saying?'

'Just that he's weird and stuff. He's always by himself and looks so miserable. He's gone from being one of the most popular kids in school to being lower down the food chain than me.'

'Don't put yourself down like that, Levi.' I frown at his words. It's unlike him to speak badly of himself.

'I'm not, I'm just saying. I don't care that I'm not popular. In fact, I don't want to be. They all care too much about what people think. I ain't got time for that,' Levi jokes.

He never fails to make me smile. His self-confidence buoys me.

'Never change, sweetheart. You brighten my day.'

'I'll help clean up,' Levi offers, picking up our plates.

'No, you go sort the animals. I'm good here.' Levi scoots out of the door the second I dismiss him, headed across the lawn to tend to Billie and the rest of the menagerie. At least one of my children is happy.

'Mum, can you take me to the bike shop this weekend?' Levi shouts, as he bounds towards me from his growing farmyard. 'Nick's found somewhere that stocks the two bikes I'm trying to decide between.'

Nick follows behind, shaking his head, laughing at Levi's exuberance. He arrived earlier this afternoon and was whisked away by Levi, not even giving me a look in.

'He said he'll take me out for some rides too, when I get it.'

'Only if it's okay with your mum, Levi.' Nick adds his disclaimer and redirects the conversation towards me.

'I'm happy to take him out whenever. The guy I ride with has just had a knee reconstruction, so he'll be out for a while, which is a shame. He'll most likely miss the charity ride we do each year down to the south coast. Anyway, it will be good to have someone to ride with while I train.'

'I'll do the charity ride with you,' Levi says, his eyes almost popping out of his head. 'That would be so cool.'

'Levi, you can't just invite yourself along. That's a huge commitment,' I caution. 'But yes, I can take you to the bike shop, and I'm happy for Nick to take you out riding.'

'Thanks Mum,' Levi says, momentarily appeased.

Nick ponders for a moment, looking between me and Levi, contemplating whether to say something.

I raise my eyebrows, waiting for him to speak.

'How about we see how you go, Levi? Maybe then we can talk about doing part of the trail at some point.'

'Really? That would be awesome, thanks, Nick.' Levi grins. I'm not sure what to make of this developing situation, but I feel the need to allow Levi this connection that he's obviously been craving. He turns to me expectantly, awaiting my approval.

'Okay, as long as you don't pressure Nick into anything he doesn't want to do. I know your moves, Levi, don't wear him down.'

'Thanks Mum, you're the best,' he says with a hug. 'Let me know when you can take me to the bike shop.' Levi picks up a ball and chases across the lawn, calling the dogs after him. He has so much energy, I don't know how to keep up sometimes.

'Thank you.' I voice my appreciation to Nick.

'He's a great kid, Steph, it'll be a pleasure to spend time with him.' Nick perches on the edge of the chair opposite me, elbows resting on his knees. My chest swells at the affection he's shown my son.

'He's what's keeping me going right now, if I'm honest,' I admit. Levi has always been a bright and bubbly kid, full of enthusiasm for life, but I'm not sure I've ever witnessed the absolute look of awe that glowed in his eyes when he was chatting to Nick. He never had that kind of interaction with his dad, and that saddens me. Levi never appeared bothered by his dad's lack of interest. He always seemed content doing things by himself, but seeing this level of elation on his face pulls me up sharp with a kick in the gut. I wonder how I failed to see what was right in front of me. Nick watches my thought process in silent contemplation.

'It gets easier with time, Steph.' He reaches across the table, squeezing my hand, reassuring me he's here for me as much as my boys. My eyes brim with unshed tears and I press my fingertips to my eyelids to prevent them from spilling over.

'Why don't I take Levi to the bike shop? Give you some space for an hour,' Nick proposes.

I offer a smile, unable to find my voice. The awareness he has of my needs blows me away.

I sit and mull over my marriage and the life I'd shared with Chris. There's no doubt in my mind I was happy, but I scrutinise every memory, searching for signs of cracks. Like I'd noticed with Levi earlier, I hadn't missed what I hadn't known, but now I've witnessed the joy in his eyes I realise the lack of fatherly attention was staring me in the face all along, and the way Chris had been with Caleb seems much less trivial than it had at the time.

Nick's car pulls up and an excitable Levi rushes out to regale me with the details of his purchase.

'Where is it then?' I ask. 'Aren't you going to show me?'

'I can't pick it up until tomorrow. They're fixing it up with the wheels I want, and the extras I've bought. Don't worry, Nick said he can take me to pick it up in the morning.' I glance at Nick, who has just joined us on the verandah, confirming Levi's statement.

'What time's dinner, Mum?' Levi asks, his thoughts turning to his belly.

'About an hour.'

Levi turns towards Nick. 'I'll just grab my laptop and you can show me the bike trails you were telling me about.'

'Levi, Nick has a life outside of you.'

Levi looks at Nick for clarification.

'No plans tonight, I'm in no rush,' he shrugs, happy to have some company.

'He can stay for dinner, right Mum?' Levi is desperate to hang on to his new friend a little longer.

I catch Nick's eye and my heart leaps. Not gracefully like a dolphin showing off in the waves, but more like an athlete catching the hurdle with their back foot. Staggering, stumbling, before settling back down with a clumsy rhythm. I'm unsure what it means, but I both like it and feel terrified in equal parts.

'Sure he can. If you want to, Nick, there's plenty of food.'

Nick's eyes widen, never leaving mine, and Levi is unaware of the heat passing between his new friend and his mum.

'Thanks, that'd be great, Steph,' he says, his voice deep, summoning me further into a fluster.

'I'll go make a start on cooking and leave you two to drool over bikes,' I say, and make a hasty escape. I lean on the kitchen bench top, steadying myself and catching my breath. The physical attraction between us sizzles, but the way Nick interacts with my son and the time and effort he's putting in is what's really captivated me. Of course, it's too soon to start a relationship with anyone. I've barely had a chance to grieve. My feelings for my husband won't disappear overnight, but there's something about Nick, something that gives me a glimmer of hope for the future. That maybe in time I'll feel brave enough to open my heart again. I only hope I can keep my feverish thoughts under wraps so the whole situation doesn't blow up in my face.

I've prepared a salad, made up a potato bake, and taken the steak and sausages from the fridge when Caleb appears from his bedroom.

'Hey sweetheart, how are you feeling?' I ask.

Caleb shrugs and runs his fingers through his hair. He's dressed in shorts and a football top, looking like he's just woken up.

'I'm just going to light the barbecue, come out and meet my friend Nick before Levi chews his ear off too much.'

Caleb frowns, but follows me outside.

'Nick, this is my eldest son, Caleb. Cale, this is Nick, he's a friend of Paul's,' I say by way of introduction.

'The shrink?' Caleb asks, a dark cloud crossing his face. 'Is this a set up?' He turns to me, anger spilling from him. 'I'm not talking to a shrink, Mum.'

I'm taken aback, embarrassed by my son's outburst.

'Caleb—' I begin, but Levi beats me to it.

'Cale, don't be a prick. Not everything is about you. He came to see me. I wanted his advice on which mountain bike to buy.'

I appreciate Levi for butting in and giving me a much needed reprieve. Caleb quiets, glaring at me as if waiting for my agreement.

'It's true,' Nick says. 'Levi just bought a bike and now he's trying to rope me into taking him out on some trail rides.' He nudges Levi, teasing. 'Besides, I don't work on weekends.'

Nick stands and offers his hand to Caleb.

'It's good to meet you, Caleb.'

Caleb hesitates before shaking his hand, disconcerted by his own outburst.

'That your team?' Nick inclines his head towards Caleb's blue and yellow football guernsey.

Nick's question is met with a nod.

'I'm sorry mate, even a psych as good as me can't cure you from that,' Nick grins, and there's a ghost of a smirk on Caleb's lips. I smile, praying Nick's friendship will be the answer.

Caleb grabs a Coke from the bar fridge on the verandah and slumps on the couch with the dogs while I go inside to retrieve the meat.

I watch Nick through the fly wire as he continues chatting with Levi, waiting for the right opportunity to make inroads with Cale. I know he won't rush it. He'll want to build mutual trust and respect.

'Hey, let me help with that, Steph,' Nick says when I return with the meat. 'Levi's got a picture of his bike up if you want to have a look.'

'Thanks Nick. Okay, let's have a look then, Levi.'

Levi gets up eagerly, turning his laptop around to show me.

'You paid that much for a bike?' I ask in surprise. I had no idea my fourteen-year-old even had that amount of money.

'Yeah,' Levi grins. 'Don't worry, I can afford it.'

'Good to know. I'll come to you if I'm ever short.'

'Show me, bro,' Caleb mutters. I tense, wondering where the conversation will lead. It's the first time Cale has spoken to Levi in weeks and Levi has given up trying.

Not one to hold a grudge, Levi eases the dog aside

and moves next to Caleb on the couch, showing him pictures of his shiny new toy from a multitude of angles.

'Nice,' he says. It's concise, but it's a damn sight more positive than anything else we've had out of him of late.

'Can you pass the mustard, Cale?' Levi asks, stacking his plate with food. Cale throws the squeezy bottle at his brother and laughs when the cap opens and sprays on Levi's face.

'Caleb!' I flash him a warning glance.

'Sorry, I thought he'd catch it,' Caleb snarks and rolls his eyes. 'I forgot he's a girl.'

'Girls can kick your arse,' Levi spits.

'Whatever, you little brat,' Caleb mutters.

'Boys, can we just eat, please? We have a guest,' I implore.

Nick watches on, his eyes flashing discreetly between the three of us, weighing up the dynamic. There's no sign of tension; he's unruffled by his surroundings as he tucks into his meal.

'Do you play football, Caleb?' he asks, once the boys stop fighting.

'I used to,' he mumbles. 'I quit.'

'Are you any good?' Caleb just shrugs.

'I used to play, but I got injured and it ended my career before it started. I was gutted,' Nick says, to no-one in particular.

'Were you any good?' I ask.

'Yeah, I had a couple of clubs interested, but then I wrecked my shoulder and I was out for a long time.' He taps on his right shoulder. 'This is mostly metal and plastic,' he grins.

This grabs Caleb's attention.

'It messed me up for a long time. I think that's why I went into psychology. Once I realised my football career was over, I went to a pretty dark place, but enough about that, that's not a pleasant conversation.'

'How did your daughter's team go today?' I ask, moving the subject along. I don't want to get bogged down in a depressing tale.

'They lost.' Nick screws his face up with resignation. 'It was a tough match, and they played their best. Millie kicked a few goals, so she was happy.'

Caleb's interest is piqued by the football talk, and I sense he's missing it. If only he would admit to himself that he hadn't played for his dad, but for his own love of the sport. It saddens me he's reached such a low point he would throw away his life's dream. I'm worried about him.

'So what time shall I pick you up tomorrow, Levi?' Nick asks, ready to leave.

'I think they open at eleven, so maybe around 10.40?'

'No worries, be ready mate.'

'Thanks for doing that,' I say as I walk him to his car. 'And thanks for trying with Caleb.'

'You're welcome, Steph, I've had a wonderful afternoon. I've enjoyed spending time with you all.' Nick's eyes flare as he speaks, his voice dropping a level.

My body quivers in response and our eyes hold, taking each other in. Nick's breaths increase speed and I absentmindedly run my tongue along my bottom lip, anticipating what it might mean. If he were to kiss me right now, I'm not even sure I'd want to stop him. Our eyes are dancing as our hearts and heads fight with reason. Nick leans in and brushes his lips to my cheek.

'I'll see you in the morning,' he whispers, and steps back to open his car door.

I sigh, thankful for his restraint, but feeling exposed at the same time.

The lump in my throat swells and my words are strangled.

'Bye Nick.'

Caleb

Dear Dad,

I used to be jealous of Levi for not having to put up with your shit. Why didn't you ever pressure him to do better? His grades were never as good as mine. He can't play sports for shit, but it was always me you came down hard on. I always thought you liked him better, but I could never figure out why. Now I realise that not only did you not put any pressure on him, you gave him no attention at all. He's moved on as if you never existed. Mum has a new friend who's paid more attention to Levi in one day than you have in years. I'm no longer jealous of my little brother. I feel sorry for him. He's never had a father, and seeing him with this new guy, I can see he's desperate for the attention. Maybe Mum is too. Maybe you were a shitty husband to her and this guy's your replacement. It didn't take her long to get over you, did it, Dad?

I wish I could.
Caleb

Nick

Nick was up at the crack of dawn after sleeping soundly for the first night in weeks. He'd enjoyed his afternoon spent with Steph and her boys. That was the thing he missed the most, the family time. He saw his girls on a regular basis, but rarely all together. With Millie still living with her mum and having school, football and a part-time job to fit in, it was hard to collaborate with everyone's busy schedules. It had felt easy at Steph's house. Despite their grief and Caleb's obvious struggles, it was homely, and he didn't feel like he was imposing. Levi had welcomed him into his life with open arms, and if he thought about it, there were some things to unpack there too. He reminded him of Millie in a lot of ways; bright and enthusiastic for life, not beaten down by the way the world viewed him, but content in his own skin. Then there was the moment with Steph. He tried to keep their friendship casual, but he had no control over the way she reacted to him. The temptation was mutual, but he vowed to himself to keep things on the back burner until she was able to reciprocate. He was excited to see her again and took himself off for a run to kill some time and keep his mind from the constant thoughts of her.

His phone lit up with a dozen messages when he arrived back home. They were all from Millie. She didn't like to send just one message, preferring to send one sentence at a time, which made him smile. With her earlier messages going unanswered, she wondered where he was, knowing he never made plans.

'Hey, Mills,' he said when she picked up. 'Sorry, I was just out for a run.'

'Oh, I thought maybe you'd had a date last night, and you were still entertaining,' Millie pushed her luck.

Nick flushed, grateful he wasn't on video call.

'Sorry to disappoint you, Mills,' he said, wishing that had been the case. He'd never felt as lonely as he did now. Having someone he was interested in, who he was sure had similar feelings but wasn't in a position to act on them, was harder than his empty life had been before he'd become friends with Steph.

'Anyway, to answer your message, yes, I am going out today, but you're welcome to tag along.'

'Oh, where are you going?' Millie asked, caught by surprise.

'You remember the friend of Paul's I was telling you about? The one who lost her husband?'

'Yeah…'

'Well, we've kind of become friends and I'm taking her son to pick up a new bike that he bought. He's a nice kid. You're welcome to join us.'

Millie paused, and Nick suspected she was talking herself out of a cheeky comeback. He sensed she wanted to rib him about his crush, but was aware of the difficult situation he'd found himself in.

'Sure, if that'll be okay, Dad.'

Nick flicked a message to Steph, knowing she'd be fine with his daughter tagging along, but wanting to give her a heads up. He swung by Millie's house on the way to collect Levi.

As they got closer to Steph's, Nick started to feel a little jittery. His fingers drummed on the steering wheel.

'You like her, don't you?' Millie picked up on his telling behaviours. She'd always been perceptive, and he could rarely hide anything from her.

'I do, Mills. It's just such bad timing. What I wouldn't give to know her under different circumstances.'

'Hang in there. If it's meant to be, it'll work out in the end,' she said with confidence. 'Just be her friend.'

'Thanks Mills, I'm trying.'

Nick turned off the engine as the car came to a halt behind Steph's X5. The pair hopped out of the car and made their way round the back onto the wide verandah.

Steph's eyes immediately went to Millie and Nick could see the moment she recognised her as his double.

With her athletic build, brown curls and warm chocolate brown eyes, there was no doubt she was Nick's daughter. The genes were strong.

'Hey Nick,' Levi jumped up from his seat on the couch and headed straight towards them. 'Hey, I'm Levi,' he said, offering his hand to Millie.

'Millie.' She shook Levi's hand, smiling at his old-fashioned confidence.

'Hey guys, how are you?' Steph asked, overly chirpy, and Nick caught a look from Levi, as though chastising his mother for her high spirits. He wondered what conversation he and Millie might have walked into.

'Morning, Steph, this is my youngest daughter, Millie. Mills, this is my friend Steph.' Nick got the introductions out of the way, sensing a little awkwardness in the air. He shouldn't have kissed her last night, he thought, but it was just a peck on the cheek, and it hadn't meant anything. He was just caring for a friend who was struggling. Or that's what he'd been trying to convince himself all morning. Volunteering to help Levi had been an excuse to see more of her at first, but now he'd spent time with Levi, he was looking forward to seeing more of him. He'd enjoyed Levi's company the previous day; he was bright and enthusiastic, and appeared dedicated to whatever he put his mind to. Nick knew he'd be a worthy riding buddy.

Nick shot Steph a quick smile before turning to Levi.

'You ready to go, mate?' he asked.

'Sure thing, let's go.' Levi followed Millie to the car while Nick lingered behind for a moment. He wasn't sure what to say to Steph, but felt he should clear the air.

'I'm sorry if I upset you last night, Steph. Are you okay?'

She shook her head. 'You didn't, Nick' she said, and she meant it. He had affected her last night, but she wasn't upset.

Arriving back at Steph's, Nick left Levi and Millie to get the new bike off the rack and made a beeline for the house. He hovered on the verandah as he heard the conversation through the open kitchen window.

'What're you doing, Cale?' Steph asked.

'I want a coffee.'

'Since when do you drink coffee?' This new behaviour puzzled her.

Caleb shrugged and Steph pushed him out of the way, fixing him a coffee. Nick's heart went out to her. It had been hard enough getting his girls through the death of their mother, but they were so young and didn't have any understanding of what was going on. They just knew they missed their mum. This was a whole different ball game. Caleb was almost a grown man with his own thoughts and feelings about his father and what had happened. He dealt with this kind of situation all the time in his professional life, but seeing it first hand from someone he was beginning to care about, shook him.

'Oh, hi, Nick. I didn't realise you were back,' Steph startled, blanketing her face with a fake smile. Caleb followed his mother outside and slumped onto the couch.

'Yeah, Levi's just getting the bike off the rack. How's it going Caleb?'

Caleb mumbled something inaudible as he sipped on his coffee.

Levi wheeled the bike around onto the grass, beaming at his new purchase.

'That looks fancy, Levi. I guess you'll be hanging out to use it now.'

Levi looked over at Nick, who sheepishly replied to Steph.

'I told him I'd take him out one day after school this week if we can find a day that suits us both.'

Steph remained speechless, unsure how to amalgamate her opposing thoughts about how quickly Nick seemed to have implanted himself in her life.

'Hey,' Millie said, stepping away from Levi and onto the verandah, carrying a paper bag in her hands. 'We bought a pie. Levi said it's your favourite.' She directed her comment at Steph.

'Pecan?' Steph asked, grateful to Millie for bringing a sense of normality.

'Yep,' she grinned. 'It's my favourite too.'

Caleb's face brightened, and he couldn't take his eyes off Millie. Nick saw him watching her and smiled to himself. He'd hoped Millie might be able to draw him out of his darkness. He hadn't spoken to her about him, he just knew the effect Millie had on people and was pleased when she'd called him, asking to spend the day with him. She was, in effect, the female version of Levi; bubbly and full of enthusiasm. The pair had chatted incessantly in the car, laughing and bantering with each other. He just hoped she could do the same with Caleb.

'Caleb, this is my daughter, Millie,' Nick said.

'Hey,' Millie said.

'Hey.' Caleb tried to act casual, the twitching of his lip a dead giveaway to the contrary.

'Let's get this pie sliced.' Steph interrupted the strained formalities, taking the pie from Millie's hands. She took it inside and sliced it up, bringing it back out with plates and forks.

Levi and Millie chatted as though they were old friends, both of them easy going and friendly. Caleb watched them, green-eyed at his brother's carefree nature.

'Hey, anyone up for tossing a footy around?' Millie asked, directing her question at both boys.

'Yeah, I will,' Levi jumped up. 'I'll warn you, though, I'm not very good.' He picked up a ball from the basket by the door and Caleb shot after him, tackling it from him.

'You're not wrong, loser,' Caleb ran his hand over Levi's head, ruffling his hair. Both he and Millie towered over Levi's shorter frame.

'Hey, be nice, Cale,' Steph shouted. Levi huffed away from them, heading towards his animals.

'Bro, I'm sorry, come back. You can team up with Millie against me, to make it more fair,' Caleb laughed.

'Oh, you want to get your arse kicked, do you?' Millie stood firm, her hands on her hips. 'Show me what you've got then, tough guy.'

'He's met his match with that one,' Nick said as he cut another piece of pie and sat down closer to Steph. 'She'll run rings around him if he gives her that attitude.'

'It'll do him good,' Steph said, relaxing for the first time all morning. 'I think Levi had that figured out. He's not one to sulk, so my guess is his departure was deliberate.'

'Smooth,' Nick said.

Steph smiled and turned to face Nick. She seemed a little on edge and he couldn't figure out if it was because of Caleb, or because his own presence was making things difficult for her.

'I'm sorry I've been so up and down.'

'Steph, you don't need to apologise. You're going

through a difficult time, I understand.'

'I know, but I feel like it's more than that. I'm having so many conflicting thoughts and I feel like I'm in constant battle.'

'About Caleb? Or Chris? What is it, Steph? You can talk to me.'

'Levi said something this morning just before you arrived and it shook me.'

Nick stayed silent, giving her space to talk in her own time.

'He asked if you were my boyfriend, then he asked me if I would get married again.'

Levi's intuition shocked Nick. He'd picked up on their chemistry, much like Millie had.

'I'm sorry if I've made him think that. That certainly wasn't my intention.'

'I know, and I'm not sure what put the idea in his head, but I need to reiterate my stance on this, Nick. I like you, I enjoy your company, and God knows, when you kissed my cheek last night, I could've taken it further,' she said. Nick's heart soared at her confirmation of his suspicions. 'But it's too soon. I'm not ready, my boys aren't ready, and I still love my husband.'

'Steph,' Nick traced his fingers along her forearm, emitting a warmth that radiated through her. 'I like you too, but I'll never push you for anything more than friendship. I know it's too soon. There's no timeline on grief. You might never feel ready for another relationship, and you'll always love your husband. It's been twenty years since Lee passed away, but I still love her, and I think about her often. Hannah and Lucy are a part of her, so I'll always keep her memory alive for them, if not for me. I would try to encourage that with your boys, too. Talk about Chris, let them know it's okay to speak about him. And Steph, don't put any pressure on yourself. You'll know when you're ready to move on, and if the timing's right down the track, and we become more than friends, then great, but if not, there are no expectations. You've got enough on your plate at the moment without worrying about guarding your emotions around me. If you need to rant or you need a hug, I'm here for you. I promise not to read into anything more than that.'

'Thank you.'

'I appreciate you being so honest with me, Steph. Don't beat yourself up.'

Nick reached for her hand, squeezing tight before releasing it back to her lap.

'And just so you're aware, I won't commit to anything with Levi that I don't want to do, so stop thanking me. I enjoy his company.'

Steph was thankful for him being in her life right now, in whatever capacity that was.

Millie had Caleb pinned to the floor after tackling him hard. At five feet ten inches tall, and solidly built, Caleb had met his match with her. Although he was over six feet and physically stronger, he was out of shape after not playing for a while and he admitted to himself that she was kicking his arse.

'I thought you said you played football? You're not making this very difficult,' Millie goaded.

Caleb laid on the floor and shrugged. 'Yeah, well, I haven't played in a while.'

'Oh?' He intrigued her. She'd known who he was before coming here today, but hadn't let on to her dad that she knew him. Caleb Wilson was one of the best young players in the state and she'd heard on the grapevine that he'd given up after his dad had died. His story saddened her, and once she'd realised who he was, she was keen to find out why someone with his talent would throw it all away.

'I stopped playing when my dad passed away.' Caleb chewed on his lip.

Millie straddled him, watching him with intent, and knew there was more to it than that.

'Why?'

'It was his dream, not mine,' Caleb said.

Millie laughed. 'I call bullshit.'

'What would you know?' Her comment affronted him.

'I've seen you play, Caleb Wilson,' Millie said.

Caleb looked at her in shock, innocent of the fact that she might know who he was.

'Yeah, I know who you are. I've seen your face when you win. You live for football. So what's the real reason you quit?'

Caleb stared at her. He'd known this girl for less than an hour, and she'd already wormed her way under his skin.

He closed his eyes, unwilling to face her.

'It was suicide.'

'That's shitty, I'm so sorry. But you still haven't answered my question.' Millie kept digging.

'He used to put all this pressure on me to be the best, to get straight A's, to be the best footy player. It was constant, and he treated me like crap if I didn't perform. It was hard. His suicide note said he killed himself to stop me from becoming like him. But what if I am like him? What if it's too late? I don't want to be like him. There were times I hated him.' A tear trickled down Caleb's cheek and Millie swiped it away with her thumb.

'I quit football and stopped doing my homework. I smoked pot and drank a bottle of vodka because those are all the exact opposite of what he wanted.'

'And does all that make you feel better?' Millie asked, her voice now filled with kindness, not the antagonistic tone she'd used earlier to get him to talk.

'No, I feel like shit.' Caleb unleashed a torrent of tears, his first since the day of the funeral, before he found his dad's suicide note.

Nick and Steph had listened to the conversation with interest, but when she heard his heartbroken sobs, she jumped up to go to her son. He was obviously in pain. Nick grabbed her hand to pull her back down.

'Steph, leave him. It looks like Millie has a handle on this. Give her a chance. She might be just what he needs right now.' Nick spoke, calm but with an air of authority, and he could see Steph waver, torn between listening to his advice and her motherly instincts.

Nick nodded at her, persuading her to listen to him. She looked back at Caleb and saw that Millie had pulled him into a seated position and was hugging him, consoling him. Steph watched on in anguish, hoping Nick was right. Nick could see how desperate she was to go to her son, but he held on to the hope that she would accept help from other people. Her face had lit up earlier. Seeing Caleb tossing the football around again and having fun like a normal teenager had brought a smile to her face.

'You're quite the double act, you and Millie,' she said to Nick, tears stinging her eyes.

'She's a good kid, tough as boots, with a beautiful soul.'

'She takes after her dad,' Steph whispered, and Nick felt another small chink of resolve shatter.

Caleb

Dear Dad,
I met someone today, someone who opened my eyes and made me look at myself. Football was never about you. I always played for me. You just got in my head there for a while, but you won't control me any longer. You put pressure on me, but it was nothing compared to the pressure I put on myself. I'm gonna make it someday and when I do, it'll be in spite of you, not because of you. I don't want to be like you, but I don't want to be this version of me either. I've tried to be someone else, tried to block everything about myself out, but I don't like the person I've become. The drinking, the drugs, the fights. I hate it. It feels like something alien has taken over me and I just want to be normal, but I don't know how. Millie, the girl I met today, she made me realise how much I miss football. I'm ready to go back, but I don't want to go back to who I was before. I don't want to play for anyone else. I want to be the best for myself.
Caleb

Steph

The crunch of tyres on gravel alerts me to a visitor. I glance at the clock and frown, wondering who it could be. Footsteps sound on the hardwood boards of the verandah and Terri's face appears through the kitchen window.

'Hey, I wasn't expecting you.' I greet her with a hug at the door.

'Hey Terri, I'm ready.' Caleb's voice sounds behind me and I swing round to see him dressed in training gear, his bag slung over his shoulder. The muscles in my jaw go slack. I've been hoping for this for weeks, but now it's here I'm lost for words..

'See you after training, Mum,' Caleb says, grabbing a banana from the fruit bowl on his way past and disappearing outside.

'Hurry, guys,' Josh yells from the car.

I stare at Terri, who just shrugs and flashes a smug grin.

'I'd better go, honey. We'll speak later.'

'Thank you, Terri.' I watch her go, tears of relief flooding my face.

'Mum?' Levi says, coming in from the garden.

'What's wrong? Whose car was that?'

'It was Terri. She came to pick Caleb up for training.'

'Did he go?' Levi's surprise mirrors mine.

I nod, smiling through the tears that are still pouring down my cheeks.

'Whatever Millie said to him the other day seems to have given him a kick up the backside.'

'I'm glad my little plan worked,' Levi grins. 'I knew he couldn't bear to be shown up by a girl.'

'I knew you weren't really sulking.' I laugh at his ingenious idea.

'Nah, I just wanted him to get to know her. She's pretty cool.'

'That was very generous of you, Levi. Caleb seemed quite smitten by her.'

'Well, he won't get far. She's a lesbian,' Levi laughs.

'Levi, that's not for you to share,' I scold.

'Millie won't care, it's not a secret,' he shrugs. 'She's been out since she was thirteen.'

'Well, good for her, but I still don't think it's your place to share.'

It's amazing how a major life trauma can reshape you and change your perspective on life. I've always been pretty grounded, never seduced by flashy cars or glitzy jewellery, five-star hotels and celebrity chefs. The simple things in life make me smile. A coffee with my dogs as the sun rises, the laughter of my boys playing with their friends, a kiss, a look, a warm touch. Now, it seems, something even more mundane has lit me up inside. My son grabbing a banana, choosing to eat without coercion and watching him walk out the door heading to footy training just like he's done hundreds of times before. I can't wait to share my excitement, and there's only one person who will understand the elation I feel.

'Hi Nick, it's me,' I say when he picks up.

He laughs. 'I know, we're not in the eighties, Steph, your name comes up on my phone. How are you?'

'Sorry, I forget sometimes, a sign of my age. I was ringing to say thanks for bringing Millie over at the weekend because what she said to Caleb seems to have had an impact on him.'

'Oh?' Hope radiates from that single word.

'He went to football training tonight. Organised for his friend's mum to pick him up without even mentioning anything to me.'

'That's great news, Steph, a definite step in the right direction. Let's hope things are on the up.'

'Did Millie say anything to you?' I ask. 'I know we heard some of what she said to him. I just wondered if there was anything else, you know, so I can continue to push him in the right direction.'

'She said nothing, but take it easy, Steph. Let him take the lead. Gentle encouragement is fine, but try not to go overboard. The last thing he needs is more pressure.'

'You're right, thanks Nick,' I say, glad of his advice.

'I was going to call Levi tonight to see if he's available for a ride tomorrow after school.'

'I'm sure he will be Nick. You have yourself a new best friend.'

'You sound so much brighter.' I can hear the smile in his voice. I picture the way his mouth turns up at the edges and the way his eyes crinkle in the corners when he laughs. How he radiates compassion and carries a halo of comfort. He's the sole reason I feel brighter; from the kindness and generosity he's shown my boys, to the care and consideration I've come to expect.

'Steph?' My smile slips when his voice penetrates my thoughts. I frown, his concern suddenly stifling my growing feelings as my head and heart go into battle once again. Palms sweaty and heart racing, I choke out a rather curt goodbye, ending the call.

I lie back on the bed, my phone clutched to my chest and my mind clouded by my unexpected reaction to Nick's kindness.

'Mum?' Levi knocks on my door

'Come in, sweetheart.' I prop myself up against the pillows.

'Nick just messaged and said he can pick me up from school tomorrow and bring me home to pick up my bike. Can I go?'

'Yes, but make sure you thank him, Levi. He's being very generous with his time.'

'I know, I will. Did you know he does this charity bike ride every year to raise money for Beyond Blue?' Levi asks.

'No, I didn't know that,' I say.

'Millie said he's disappointed that his friend won't be able to do it with him. It would be hard to do by himself, which is a shame because he raises a lot of money for charity.'

His face is animated, foreshadowing the conversation to garner a sympathetic reaction from me. I'm pretty sure I'm already clued in on his intentions here.

'Get to the point, Levi. What are you suggesting?' I smirk.

Levi laughs at my intuition.

'I was thinking I'd like to do it with him in honour of Dad, since it's kind of personal to us now.'

I forget sometimes that he's lost his dad, too. He's barely skipped a beat.

'Hey, sweetheart,' I say, reaching out my arms for a hug. Levi perches on the edge of my bed and leans in to reciprocate.

'That's a thoughtful idea, but let's just think about it a while before mentioning it to Nick.'

Levi frowns and I can see his wheels turning, trying to understand my reluctance.

'Do you have a problem with me spending time with him?' he asks.

'No Levi, of course not, I just don't want you to get attached to him and then be devastated if he doesn't stick around.'

I chew my lip, refusing to make eye contact with my son. Levi sees right through me, but discussing my apparent attraction to another man so soon after losing my husband isn't a topic I'm planning on getting into with my teenage son.

'Okay,' Levi concedes. 'But Mum, just so you know, he will stick around. I've seen how he looks at you.'

His candid words shock me. Levi's lips curl at the edges when he sees the knowing look on my face.

'Night Mum,' he grins, slinking from the room, confident in his assertion.

My emotions are all over the place, a constant cha-

cha in my gut. Allowing myself to sit with my feelings and not try to suppress them is becoming difficult. Chris's death has given me an insight into mental health that even my experience as a GP hasn't provided. Depression in men can manifest itself in such different ways and nothing is ever text book. Chris functioned at a high level, running a successful dental practice, and being involved in family life, albeit sporadically, now that I look back. There were time periods when he would work solidly, taking on all the late night and Saturday openings, sometimes even working Sundays when the books warranted it. It wasn't constant, but with hindsight I can see a pattern of behaviour, both with work and how hard he came down on Caleb. I see now that it was never about Caleb and everything to do with Chris's mood.

I don't blame myself, I'm practiced enough to know there's nothing I could have done when he'd exhausted himself keeping his own secrets. The person I lay blame with is Chris's father. He's the source of the problem. I didn't know him well, as Chris hadn't wanted him to infiltrate our life together. He'd escaped him as soon as he could, but always carried the guilt of leaving his mum behind, despite his best efforts to make her see sense. When our relationship began, Chris told me countless stories of the things his father had done to his wife, along with the physical abuse and constant belittling and criticism he had engaged in with Chris, but once we got married and created our own family, Chris refused to talk about him. As I ponder on it now, I can see that should have been a warning sign. I made excuses for how he picked at Caleb, knowing he hadn't had a good role model. I tried hard to balance things out, always encouraging Caleb myself, assuming my husband's behaviour was because he didn't know any better. If I'd known how much he was suffering, I would have got him the help he needed, but all I'm left with now is to grieve for the husband I lost.

I loved him with all my heart for much of my life. He was a good husband and I know in my heart he would never have left us behind if he'd thought for one moment his illness was something he could recover from. The decision he made had to have come from his absolute rock bottom and I know he would've dug as deep as he could to find the courage to talk to me. I don't blame him, but I mourn for him, for me, and for our kids.

When I think of Chris now, no tears come. I've cried enough over the last few months, and the tiny glimmer of hope I've been holding onto for Caleb has sparked hope in my heart. I breathe out and allow myself to surrender to the present. I know Nick spoke the truth. Chris will forever hold a place in my heart, but in time, I will have the capacity to love again.

I smile to myself, feeling more at peace with my loss, and I turn my attention to Nick. My attraction to him is strong, something I've never felt towards anyone but Chris and I question why. I'd met Nick several times before and never looked twice, so why does his presence affect me now? I worry that I'm only drawn to him because I'm lonely and he understands my grief, which is fine if we remain friends, but the butterflies that explode in my stomach when I think of him throw me off balance.

I'm not looking for a replacement husband, but nor can I help the growing attraction.

Feeling both love for my husband and attraction to Nick is conflicting, and as much as I speak to my emotions and allow myself to feel both, it's messing with my head more than I can deal with. A door slams and I hear footsteps on the veranda, shelving my thoughts.

I greet Caleb in the kitchen. Noting the advice Nick gave, I don't engage with him on the topic of football and limit conversation to a bare minimum.

He only mutters in response and retreats to the bathroom.

My stomach lurches at the thought it might not have gone well and I hope he's just tired, or even just acting like a normal teenager. The thought of going back to where we were only a few days ago is something I can't let myself dwell on. I need him to move forward. I know the journey won't be a constant forward trajectory and there'll be some troughs along the way, but I'm still clinging to the idea that he's already reached his rock bottom. Anything lower than where he's been doesn't bear thinking about.

Nick

'That was a hard one,' Levi panted, leaning over the handlebars of his bike with mud splattered up his face.

'You rode well, Levi. I'm proud of you.'

'Thanks Nick,' Levi beamed at the praise, something of which he'd had little from his own dad.

'Millie's lucky having a dad like you.'

Nick saw the joy slip from Levi's face.

'I'm sure there are moments when I'm a real pain in the arse. You know the saying, the grass is always greener.'

Levi studied him, his bottom lip curling between his teeth, unsure whether to voice his thoughts.

'What was your dad like?' Nick wanted to get a bigger picture of their family dynamic.

'I dunno.' Levi's eyes cast downwards, and he picked at some dried up mud on his arm. 'He never spent much time with me. Mum and I have always been closer.'

'Was that because Caleb and football took up a lot of his time?' Nick didn't want to probe too much, but wanted to understand how Levi felt about his father.

'I guess so.' Levi reflected on his relationship with his dad and chose his words carefully. 'It never bothered me. Caleb was always under so much pressure to be the best, and he was. He's always been good at everything. Super clever, good at sports, popular, did everything Mum and Dad asked him to, but it still wasn't good enough for Dad. I felt sorry for him, but he thought I was jealous. Caleb's always wanted the glory and loves praise, but the one person he wanted praise from rarely gave it to him. Even when Cale was the best, Dad expected more. He could never live up to his standards, no one could.'

Nick nodded, his throat strangled by Levi's words. It was Chris's illness talking, Nick knew that, but it was still difficult to witness the damage it had caused.

'How do you feel now, Levi?' He appeared to be handling things well, but he didn't know him enough to know just how much he was covering up.

'I'm okay. I know he was my dad, and I'm sad about what happened, but to be honest, I'm more worried about Caleb and my mum.'

'Caleb seems to be a little better though, don't you think?'

'Yeah, I guess so. I mean, he's back at football and he's acting like a prick towards me again, so I guess that's something,' Levi smirked.

'And your mum?' Nick asked, concerned. 'You don't think she's doing okay?'

Levi's smirk became smug. 'I think she's conflicted.'

Nick regretted his line of questioning, but had gone too far to stop now.

'Oh? In what way?' Nick asked, falling short of the nonchalance he was trying for.

Not one to beat around the bush, Levi put it to him straight.

'I think she has a huge crush on you and she's worried how that makes her look, being the grieving widow and all.'

Nick chuckled at Levi's candour, all the while glowing crimson.

'Remind me never to ask you for your honesty again,' Nick said, getting off his bike.

'I'm sorry if I embarrassed you,' Levi said. 'I just want my mum to be happy again.'

They wheeled their bikes to the rack on the back of Nick's ute, securing them in place. Nick was quiet, contemplating Levi's statement. He threw an arm around his shoulder, pulling him in to his side.

'You didn't embarrass me, Levi.'

'You like her too, don't you?' Levi pressed.

'I do, but we're just friends, Levi.'

Steph wasn't home when Nick dropped Levi home and he breathed a sigh of relief. He wasn't sure he could face her after that revelation from her son, although it wasn't something he should keep from her. Nick showered, scrubbing the dried mud from his plastered legs, retracing the conversation he'd had with Levi. He was a great kid, never out to prove anything to anyone but himself. Wise beyond his years, with an enthusiasm for life, Nick enjoyed their rides together. It was never a chore or a hardship spending time with him. He was beginning to feel like family. Nick's breath caught at that thought. His head told him to pull back, but his heart challenged that notion. With his attention now back on Steph, the briefest thoughts of her sent blood rushing through his body, and he hardened at the reminder. He stroked gently as he soaped himself, her face filling his thoughts, wondering what it would be like to kiss her, to touch her. He jerked, coming fast over his hand, and he smiled as he washed himself away, sensitive to his own touch.

Nick stood on the sidelines watching the girls hard at work. They gave everything they had and played with a desire to win, but they didn't have the same depth of talent as some of the other clubs. Millie stood out, head and shoulders above the rest. She had endless opportunities to go play for better teams and he encouraged her to move as often as he could, but his daughter was fiercely loyal to her team and didn't want to let them or her dad down.

As the match wound down, Nick spotted Steph on the other side of the oval, with both Caleb and Levi beside her. Millie had mentioned Caleb was coming to watch her play. The improvements Caleb had made heartened Nick, and seeing Steph there too brightened his day.

'Hey guys, I didn't know you were all coming. What did you think?' he asked, after he'd tied everything up.

'Good game, Millie played well,' Caleb said, still buoyed by the fast pace of the game.

'She did,' Nick said. 'She always does. Millie's the one consistent player on the team. It kills me to say that, her being the coach's daughter, but it's true,' he grinned.

'Yeah, she could do well on a better team,' Caleb said. 'No offence.'

'None taken, but maybe that's something you could talk to her about. She won't listen to me. She just thinks I'm biased.'

'Levi's got his stuff in my car and we brought his bike. Thought we'd save you a trip,' Steph said to Nick.

'That's great, thanks Steph,' Nick said, his eyes fixed on hers. 'We'll drop Millie off and head straight out. I'll bring him home in a couple of hours.' Nick felt the heat rise between them as they spoke, aware of how she affected him.

'Millie could come back to ours if she wants, right Mum?' Caleb asked. 'Nick can pick her up when he drops Levi off.'

'Why don't you ask her?' Nick grinned 'Here she comes now.'

Steph wanted to encourage Caleb's friendship with Millie. She just hoped he wasn't pursuing her romantically. The last thing she wanted was for him to get his heart broken when he was already in such a delicate place.

'Hi Millie, great game. You played well,' Steph congratulated her as she approached.

'Thanks Steph. Hey guys,' she said, turning to the boys.

'Hey,' Caleb said, 'I was just wondering if you wanted to come back to ours while your dad and Levi go for their ride?'

'Sure,' she said. 'Is that okay, Dad?'

'Absolutely. It will save me from dropping you off at home on our way out.'

As the small group reached the car park, Nick was becoming conscious of the fact that these quick pick ups and drop offs weren't enough for him anymore. He wanted to spend some quality time with her, even if friendship was all she could give. It wasn't something he was willing to broach first though, he wouldn't cross that line, so he was thrilled when Steph extended an invitation.

'Hey, why don't you guys stay for dinner?' she asked, before they went their separate ways.

Nick's eyes caught Steph's, and he couldn't suppress the heat that simmered between them.

'That'd be great, thanks Steph. Millie, does that work for you?'

'Yep, beats your cooking.'

'Cheeky. We'll see you soon, then,' Nick said.

'That's a big grin you've got on your face there, Nick.' Levi said on the way to the bike trail. 'I wonder what that could be about.'

'Shut up.' Nick rolled his eyes at the smirk on Levi's face, but appreciated the ease of his friendship with Steph's son.

They drove in a comfortable silence, both reflecting on how their lives had come together, both happy for very different reasons.

'You know, if you want a partner so you can do the charity ride, I'd be happy to do it with you. Millie said you were disappointed your friend had to pull out,' Levi knew his mum had told him to wait, but figured now was as good a time as any to broach the idea with Nick.

'Are you sure you'd be up to it? It's a long ride, day after day, nearly three weeks in total.'

'I'll need to train more, but I reckon I can be ready by then.' Levi gave Nick no doubt he would put enough effort in. 'I'd kinda like to do it in honour of my dad.'

Nick's voice caught on Levi's admission. 'That's a lovely idea, Levi. I'm sure your dad would be proud of you.'

Levi shrugged, noncommittal.

'Listen, run it by your mum and if she's happy with it, then my answer is yes,' Nick said.

'Seriously? Thanks Nick,' Levi beamed.

'She might say no, Levi, you'd have to take some time off school, and I don't want you giving her a hard time about it, okay? Her decision is final,' Nick warned.

'Yeah, I know,' Levi grinned, knowing his mum couldn't say no to him.

Steph

It may be odd, but I love the feel of my hands on raw meat. I stand at the kitchen bench, my fingers massaging the marinade into the chicken. I recommend the therapeutic benefits of this simple ritual. Lost in my thoughts, my mind wanders to the impromptu invitation I extended to Nick and Millie. We've limited our contact to pickups and drop offs and the odd phone call, and I've missed our chats even though I've had conflicted emotions about our friendship. Caleb's been making steady improvements over the last few weeks and, with a little less to worry about, I've been able to find more clarity in my own life. A friendship with Nick won't take anything away from my love for Chris, and in time, who knows? The strongest relationships are based on a solid friendship.

'That smells good,' Millie says, making me jump. 'Sorry, I didn't mean to scare you. I was just coming to ask for a drink.'

'That's okay, I'm making curry. Do you like spicy food?' I hadn't thought to check.

Millie grins. 'I love all food,' she says, and takes the two glasses I offer her.

'Good, you sound like my boys. There's water or soft drink in the fridge.'

'Water's good, thanks,' she says, filling both glasses.

'Millie,' I venture, biting my lip. 'Can I ask you something?'

Millie nods, looking worried.

'I think Caleb might have a crush on you. Does he know you're not interested in him that way?'

Millie laughs. 'He does, and yes, I've made it clear he's not my type.'

Her honesty is refreshing and brings me relief.

'Thank you, I just don't want to add heartbreak on top of everything else he's had going on.'

'It's all good, I promise.'

Animated chatter reaches my ears before Nick and Levi appear on the veranda. I smile at the enthusiasm of my son, pleased it's directed at someone else for a change. I love him, but his incessant energy can be a little overwhelming. Levi opens the fly screen, letting them both in and rushes straight down the hall for a shower. Nick smiles, bemused by Levi's ability to keep going.

'Hey, how was your ride? And how come you're not all muddy like Levi?'

'I called home for a quick shower on the way back,' Nick says. He runs a hand through his freshly washed hair. 'The ride was great. He's a natural and works hard to test his limits. It's a pleasure spending time with him.'

I feel myself glow from his compliment and can't

help but avert my eyes.

'Dinner smells wonderful.' Nick changes the subject and avoids a potentially awkward silence.

'Thanks, I hope you like Indian.'

'It's my favourite.' He winks, causing his eye to crinkle around the edges, and I'm surprised by the flutter it sends to my belly.

'Can I get you a drink? A beer maybe, or a soft drink?' I offer.

'I'd love a beer.'

'They're outside. Come on out. This just needs to simmer for a while.'

I grab a couple of beers from the bar fridge and take the caps off. Nick settles onto the couch next to me.

'How've you been? We haven't talked in a while,' he says.

'I know, I'm sorry. It's my fault. My head has been doing battle with my heart and neither side was winning.'

The need for liquid courage is strong, so I take a long drink of my beer before I make my confession.

'I've been beating myself up about being friends with you.'

'That's the reason I've kept my distance. I guessed that's what was going on when you left me hanging on the phone the other week,' Nick says.

I blush, embarrassed by my hot and cold behaviour.

'Steph, there's no pressure to be anything more than friends. I have no expectations, you know that.' Nick's brow wrinkles, trying to figure me out.

'I know, but maybe I want more.' The beer has loosened my tongue.

Nick's eyes flare, and a burst of crimson tinges his cheeks. He blows out a heavy breath and traces his fingers discreetly along my arm.

'So, if you want more, what conflict are you battling?' His voice is deep and throaty, and I squirm in my seat at the level of desire it brings.

'I want to let myself feel, but I don't want to rush into anything.'

'So, let yourself feel it, and we'll take it slow,' Nick says, still puzzled by my contradictions.

'Nick, if I allow myself to feel everything I'm feeling for you, there'll be nothing slow about this,' I warn.

The atmosphere crackles. Nick's breathing quickens and I can see the lust in his eyes. He wants to kiss me, but he won't. I know he'll never take advantage of my vulnerability.

'I feel it too, Steph, you have no idea.' His voice softens. 'But you're in a vulnerable position and you're still grieving. I don't want you to make the mistakes I made with Millie's mum, so you feel whatever you need to feel and I'll hold the reins until you're ready to take this further.'

'I want to kiss you.'

'Our kids are here, and we don't need that complication.' His laughter breaks the tension. 'But believe me, I want to kiss you too.'

'You're right, that's the last thing we need.' My hand flies to my mouth in horror. I hadn't given a second thought to where we were. 'I'm sorry.'

'Steph, stop saying you're sorry. It's all good. You're not doing anything wrong and I won't let us jump in and ruin this. Relax.'

'Thank you, but just a heads up; every time you

say something nice to me, it makes me want you that bit more.'

'Kids, dinner's ready.' I'm disconcerted about the prospect of us all sitting down to have dinner together. I send a panicked look in Nick's direction and he just winks in reply. If that's his idea of calming me down, he doesn't know me very well. I freeze as that truth hovers around my periphery before slamming hard into my gut. What the hell are we doing? A few months ago, this man was a relative stranger, someone I made small talk with at the odd party. Now he's someone I turn to when I need a shoulder to cry on or when I make progress along my healing journey. He's the person I tell all my deepest secrets to. He's become my person, my go-to, yet he doesn't know me. The only me he knows is the grieving widow, the angsty parent, the woman who is fighting her feelings every step of the way. What he doesn't know is how much I love to watch the sunrise, hold hands when I walk, the snag of breath before a kiss, or the graze of fingertips across my lower back. He doesn't know how a simple wink produces tiny crinkles around his eye that send shockwaves through my lower belly. He doesn't know I'm falling in love with him. I gasp at the realisation that I want him to know all these things. I want him to know me.

'This looks amazing, Steph,' Millie says, pulling out the chair next to Caleb, her eyes popping at the amount of food.

'Dig in, everyone,' I say, recovering myself.

After my initial panic, dinner is a relaxed experience. Levi regales us all with tales of his afternoon ride with Nick, paying special attention to the story of Nick's mishap with a large branch. I struggle to avert my eyes as I watch their interaction, bantering back and forth. Caleb stiffens as he watches his brother connect with Millie's dad, and I can see the envy swallow him as he takes in Levi's simple manner; the way he appears to have moved on from the death of his father. The moment Nick realises what's going on, he flips the conversation around to football in a way that doesn't offend Levi, but also gives no impression that he's trying too hard with Caleb.

'Caleb, I was thinking after Millie's game today of what I could do to help the team play better together. They just don't seem to respond to my strategies. If you had any thoughts while you were watching, I'd love to sit down and hash them out sometime,' Nick says.

The second Cale understands Nick is asking his advice on football and isn't there to give him unwanted counsel. His face lights up and I blink back tears at Nick's thoughtful gesture. I gather plates together to take inside before the dam bursts and I embarrass myself.

'Dad's pretty great, isn't he?' a voice says behind me. I spin around, wiping my tears, and see Millie with a dish in each hand and a big grin on her face.

'He's been so wonderful with my boys since their dad passed.' I swipe at the now constant trickle down my face. 'You're very lucky to have him, Millie.'

'I know. He likes you too, I can tell.'

My cheeks redden at Millie's comment as she spins on her heel and heads back outside. I gather myself a moment, gaining at least a modicum of composure before following her to help clear the rest of the table.

'Can I help?' Nick asks.

'No, I'm all good. You sit and talk football.'

Millie joins me again with more plates and begins stacking the dishwasher.

'Thanks for your help, Millie. It would be nice if the boys offered.'

'Maybe I have an ulterior motive,' she grins. 'Chatting to Dad will be good for Cale, so I wanted to give them some space.'

I'm so touched by her thoughtfulness.

'You're so wise Millie. How did you grow up so fast?' I muse. She seems so mature for fifteen and self-assured.

'I guess it's the perk of growing up with a psych for a dad,' she shrugs. 'He taught us how to talk through our problems. Sometimes I've hated him for it, especially during the divorce, and when I first mentioned my sexuality to him, but I'm grateful now. It's given me an insight into real life, I suppose. No-one's life is ever straightforward, is it? Nothing is ever as it seems. People often act a certain way because of some underlying reason and I think it's always important to understand that.'

Her insight is staggering, and I urge her to carry on.

'When my sisters' mum died, they were only young and I think Dad married my mum because he needed them to have a mother. He'd never admit that to me, but reading between the lines, that's what I've come up with,' she laughs.

'Mum wasn't all that great with Hannah and Lucy

after I came along. Hannah especially took everything out on me. I didn't like her much when I was little, but we're good now. It all changed when Mum and Dad split up. My sisters both spent a lot of time with me at that point, trying to shield me from all the fights.'

'I'm sorry you had to go through that, Millie,' I say, my heart going out to her.

'It turned out for the best in the end. They're much better off apart. Please don't tell him I said this, but I don't think he ever loved her and I think Mum knew she was always a replacement for his first wife. She hasn't said as much, but she's said enough to make me believe that. As much as Mum drives me crazy most of the time, it must have been hard for her. I think that's the only reason I haven't moved in with Dad. I get on so much better with him than I do with her, but I always try to give her the benefit of the doubt. Being married to a man that doesn't love you would have a huge effect on your self-esteem. Anyway, I still see Dad a lot, especially since he's my coach too.'

I watch her as I process her methodical words.

'Is that why you won't move to a better team? Because you fear you wouldn't see him as much if he wasn't your coach,' I ask, curious to understand her reasons.

Millie bites her lip, looking guilty. 'Busted.'

'He'd much prefer for you to challenge yourself and chase your dream, to sticking around in a second rate team for his benefit. You're talented Millie. If it's what you want, you could go far.'

Millie sighs. 'Do you think so?'

'I know so,' I confirm.

'And Dad?' she asks.

'Sweetheart, you'd still see him plenty, even if he wasn't your coach. I can see how close you are. He'd still be at every game watching and cheering you on,' I assure her. 'Can I let you into a secret?'

Millie nods.

'Your dad asked Caleb after your game today if he could persuade you to switch teams. Don't stay for his benefit because he wants you to fly.'

'That would explain why Caleb's been polishing my ego all day,' Millie laughs. 'Thanks Steph.'

'You're welcome.'

There's a kerfuffle at the door and the boys push through the fly screen and into the house.

'I guess we should go, hey Mills?' Nick says, before turning towards me. 'Thanks so much for dinner, Steph, you excelled.'

'Anytime, the pair of you,' I include Millie in the invitation. It was lovely having her to chat to and giving me a different perspective on her dad.

'See you soon, Cale, bye Levi,' Millie says. 'Thanks Steph, dinner was amazing.' She launches at me for a boisterous hug.

Nick holds up his hand and discreetly performs the international telephone signal with his thumb and pinky finger. A contented smile unfurls my lips and I'm powerless to hide it.

'Hi.' Nick's voice is unassuming when he calls later in the evening. The boys are both in their bedrooms and I'm winding down with a glass of wine in my favourite spot outside. The evening holds a chill, but I'm feeling toasty wrapped up in warm blankets with the patio heater glowing red.

'Hi yourself.' Being alone with him, even on the phone, seems so much more intimate after the things we admitted to each other earlier.

'Thank you for dinner. You're an amazing cook. I haven't eaten like that in a long time,' Nick repeats his earlier praise.

'I don't believe that. You're pretty good in the kitchen yourself,' I compliment him in return.

'It's not the same when you have to make it yourself, though,' he says. 'Besides, I'm often on my own, so I cook something quick and easy.'

'I can't imagine how lonely you must get. I'm grateful to have my boys around, even if it's only for dinner some days.'

'It is lonely.' Nick studies me, weighing up how much he should say. 'It wasn't for a long time after the divorce. It felt like such a relief to be away from Sarah. I saw Millie all the time, and Lucy lived with me for the first year until she moved in with Hannah, but now Millie only stays with me on occasional weekends, whenever she's not busy with friends. It's hard sometimes, Steph, I won't lie.'

I contemplate his words. The evenings at home after dinner, when both boys are in their bedrooms, are feeling lonely, and the weekends seem to stretch on forever without Chris. I wonder if that's why I've been so drawn to Nick, craving some adult company. Any of my friends would have been here in a heartbeat had I called them, so I know there's more to it than that. Chris and I had a very healthy sex life and I miss that connection. I'm a very tactile person and crave physical contact in a relationship. Despite his now obvious depression, he always made me feel special.

'Steph?' Nick whispers.

'Sorry, my mind started drifting for a second.' I apologise for my lapse in conversation. 'God, I miss him, Nick.'

'I know.'

'I just want it to stop.'

'It will, I promise,' he chokes. Not only does Nick display his emotions on his face, they are evident in his voice, and I can hear his heart breaking for me.

'You'll get there, Steph, but it takes time. Try not to rush it. I still miss Lee to this day, but now I can think about her and enjoy my memories. Telling my girls stories about her keeps her memory alive for them and that makes me happy.'

'But you know she was happy for most of your marriage. I worry Chris was never happy in all the years I've known him. It seems he had some pretty major issues stemming from his childhood, and now I don't know if our entire marriage was a sham. What if he just put up a front the entire time and was screaming behind the mask?' My voice cracks and the sadness seeps out.

'Steph, listen to me. That's something you'll never know. You can't focus on that or it will tear you apart. Look, I didn't know Chris, but from my experience, I find it difficult to believe that someone could mask such constant depths of despair. There would have been ups and downs along the way, with glimpses of light through the darkness, and I guess the last several months of his life, he just couldn't break through that darkness. Keep your memories sacred, Steph, don't ruin them by overthinking this. You loved him and he loved you. Depression manifests itself in many guises, and it doesn't mean he was never happy. Hang on to the fact that you and your boys brought him happiness.'

I nod, hanging on to his words, desperate to believe him.

'Will you be okay? I can come over,' Nick offers, and as vulnerable as I feel right now, I need to say no.

'Thank you for being so kind, but I'm tired. I think I'll just go to bed.'

'Sleep well, Steph.'

Caleb

Dear Dad,
Today was shit. It's been good being back at football, but I hate going to school. Everyone looks at me like I'm some kind of freak show. Josh always tries to get me to hang out on the oval with our friends, but I hate it now. I don't feel like I fit in anymore. I wish I could just hang with Millie. I had a massive crush on her at first, but once she told me she's into girls, it was a relief. It's good to just be friends with a girl without wondering if she likes me or whatever. She's pretty cool too, loves football as much as I do, and doesn't get caught up in other people. She's not shy in telling me what she thinks either, which is pretty refreshing. It is a good balance for me. I just wish she went to my school, because having to deal with the comments and the stares from everyone by myself is draining. It's overwhelming some days, like I can't deal with people any longer and I just want to curl up by myself and sleep. Is this what it felt like for you, I wonder.
Caleb

Lyndsey Jeminson

Steph

The day has dragged, but the end is in sight. Just one more patient to see before I can get out of here. I hate working later on Wednesdays, as if hump day isn't hard enough to get through without the added inconvenience of finishing at 7 o'clock. We arranged it that way to coincide with Chris's late night openings on Tuesday and Thursday, so there would always be someone home to cook dinner and do the football run. I guess I could change things up now if I wanted to. There's nothing keeping me to Wednesday apart from my receptionist. She might not want to change her hours for no particular reason.

I poke my head into the waiting room and smile at the one remaining patient. My friend Terri has been a registered patient with me since our boys were young and we first met at kindergarten. I can count on one hand the number of visits she's made during that time, so I'm a little concerned about what brings her here.

'Hi Terri, come on through,' I say. Terri gives me

a quick hug and follows me into my office. 'What can I do for you?'

Terri's eyes fill with tears and my concern rises. I hand over a box of tissues and focus as Terri wipes her eyes and blows her nose.

'I almost went somewhere else, Steph. It feels wrong being here after everything you've been going through,' Terri begins.

'Don't be silly, if you need to see a doctor, I'd rather you come see me, Terri, you know that,' I say.

'I know, and that's what got me here in the end,' Terri sniffs.

'Talk to me Terri, what's wrong?' This is so unlike her, and I'm fighting to keep from panicking.

'I found a lump in my breast,' Terri admits, her eyes filling with tears again.

'Oh, Terri.' My doctor's face flies out of the window and I become a concerned friend. 'Let me take a look.'

After checking her over, I print out referrals for scans and a biopsy.

'I want you to get these done as soon as you can. I've marked them as urgent, okay?'

'What are your thoughts, Steph? Be honest,' Terri urges.

I blow out a breath, not wanting to deliver my initial thoughts.

'I don't like the look of it, Terri. But if it is something, I'm hopeful it's still early days.'

'Thank you,' Terri nods. 'How've you been?'

'Oh, you know, plodding on. Caleb seems to be improving since he's been back at football.'

'That's good, you'll all come through this, Steph, I know you will.'

'You too, Terri, but make sure you call these numbers first thing in the morning.'

'I will, I promise,' Terri assures me. 'We'll catch up soon, okay?'

'I'm here for you, Terri,' I say, promising to be in touch soon.

'Levi,' my voice echoes through the bluetooth as I drive home. 'I've just left work. I'll pick up takeout on the way home. What do you fancy? Ask Cale too.'

'Whatever, pizza works for me.' I hear him asking Caleb, but I don't hear a response. 'He's not answering, so just get pizza.'

'Is he okay?' I ask.

'He's in a bad mood, has been since we got on the bus after school, so I just left him alone.'

I hope it's just a minor blip. After seeing Terri, I'm not sure how much more I can handle. In my experience, that lump looked suspicious, but I'm not an expert, so I'm trying to stay positive.

'Okay, I'll be home soon.'

At least I have the day off tomorrow. That's one good thing about my late night on Wednesday. It's followed by my day off. It's always been a time for catching up on everything, but these last few weeks I've twiddled my thumbs with all the extra alone time.

I drop the pizza boxes on the table and fatigue crashes down on me. Levi appears when I call the boys for dinner, but there's no sign of Caleb. With my nervous system already on edge, anxiety grips me as I recall all the times in recent weeks that Caleb didn't show up for dinner. He's still quiet and often retreats inside himself, but he has been much more engaged of late and his fitness regime has almost returned to normal. I make my way down the hall to his room and tap on the door. I nudge it open when there's no reply.

My heart leaps into my mouth. He's laid on his bed, headphones on, gazing at the ceiling. This isn't just a blip.

'Cale,' I say. 'Are you okay?'

'I'm fine,' he mutters. 'I'm not hungry.'

'Did something happen at school?'

'Leave me alone.' Caleb turns over to face the wall, and my stomach churns. I knew we weren't out of the woods, but I'd hoped we were making some progress. Nauseous at the prospect of going backwards, I retreat from the room and close the door behind me. Whatever I say to him right now will not make anything better. Today has taken its toll and I need to get myself in a better headspace before I can think about speaking to Caleb. Tears spring from my eyes and I swipe at my face. The universe appears to be conspiring against me. My appetite has depleted, but I need to stay strong and keep things normal for Levi.

'Is he coming?' Levi asks, ripping into a slice of pepperoni with his teeth as I sit down.

'No, he said he's not hungry.'

'I thought he was getting better, Mum,' Levi's face crumples. It isn't often I see him cry. He's always been such a happy child. I lean over to hug him.

'I thought so too, sweetheart. Maybe he's just had a bad day. Let's see how he is tomorrow.'

Levi nods and tucks in to the rest of his pizza, while I absent-mindedly nibble the edges of mine.

Sapped from the day's events, I retire to my bedroom soon after dinner. My mind whirrs and I'm unable to tame my thoughts into any semblance of order. I scroll aimlessly through my phone, not paying much attention until I notice a message from Nick asking me to call him when I'm free. Not sure that I have the mental capacity to navigate our complicated relationship, I waver a moment. The phone springs to life in my hand and I jump as his name lights up the screen, making the decision for me.

'Hey,' Nick says. 'I just wanted to check in and see how your week's going?'

Nick's soothing voice is all it takes to tip me over the edge and I break down. The dam wall that has teetered on breaking for the last couple of hours crumbles in defeat, my face awash with the deluge.

'I'm here for you, Steph, if you want to talk about it,' Nick whispers. 'I'm a good listener.'

My sobs ease and I smile half-heartedly through my tears.

'I know you are. It's your job after all, but to be honest, it's been a day and I don't have the energy. Take a rain check?'

'Of course,' he says. 'Listen, what time do you finish work tomorrow?'

'I'm not working. Thursday's my day off.'

'Oh, mine too. Do you have any plans?'

'Not really. Why?'

'Well, I was going to suggest maybe catching up after work, but if we're both off, maybe we could go out for lunch?' he asks.

I swallow what he's asking, trying to get my head around going on a date with a man other than my husband for the first time in twenty-five years. It feels too soon, but it also feels right. I enjoy his company and he's easy to talk to, not to mention the way his smile melts my insides.

'Steph, I can hear the cogs turning from here. Don't overthink, it's just lunch,' he says. 'But if you're not comfortable, just say no. You won't offend me.'

'No, no,' I say, 'I'd love to, thank you.'

'Great, I'll pick you up at 11.30.'

'Goodnight, Nick.'

Caleb's mood appears to have lifted a little by the time I drop the boys at school. There's been little in the way of communication, but he's eaten breakfast and showered, so I take that as a win. He even cracked a smile at something on his phone, which elevated my mood, but as soon as my thoughts turn to Terri, concern for my friend runs high.

'You're on the bus this afternoon, boys. I've got some errands to run and I don't know what time I'll be home,' I warn as they climb out of the car.

'No worries Mum, have a good day,' Levi says.

I call Terri the minute I get home, checking she's phoned for an appointment.

'I've got one tomorrow morning,' Terri says.

'That's good. How are you feeling?'

'Worried. Do you fancy coming over for a coffee? I'm taking the day off work.'

'Give me an hour,' I say, glancing at my watch.

Switching up my plans with Nick, I arrange to meet at his house instead.

I deliberate over my clothing choices, wanting to look nice without appearing too eager, and settle on a simple dress. As I put on my make-up, I examine my face in the mirror. My skin looks sallow, my eyes tired, and I'm feeling every one of my fifty-two years. Widowed only months ago, I second guess what the hell I'm doing going out for lunch with a man. I lean in closer to the mirror, then draw back when my reflection becomes blurred. I chuckle at the way I'm scrutinising every tiny thing. It's just lunch with a friend, I tell myself. Stop overthinking Steph, I whisper to my mirror image. My face stares back at me and I can hear her steadfast undertones. 'Go for it, Steph, live your life and enjoy everything this man offers you.'

I dab the dark circles under my eyes with concealer and smear on some foundation. I draw the mascara wand over my lashes and run some gloss across my lips. There, I feel human again. I smile at myself, and with a little more confidence than I had only minutes ago, I grab my purse and leave the house before I can change my mind.

Nick

Nick hoped he hadn't crossed a line. He told Steph not to overthink it, but he was doing the same thing. After the confession she'd made, he feared lunch between friends might be a stretch. The attraction was strong on both sides. They'd both wanted to give in to temptation, but he'd promised to hold the reins. He just wasn't sure he had the strength for the both of them.

He'd tossed and turned for a couple of hours until he got up at just past one in the morning, hoping to calm his nerves with a hot chocolate, courtesy of his Nonna's recipe, with corn flour and a drop of Maraschino liqueur. It was thick and creamy with a hint of cherry and it never failed to hit the spot.

He sat in bed sipping on the warm drink, savouring every mouthful, allowing his mind to wander, trying to make peace with his circulating thoughts. He could call it lunch between friends as much as he wanted, but his internal barometer told him it was more. It felt much heavier than that, and he knew there was only one reason. He was falling for her.

His own acknowledgement eased his mind. If he knew what he was dealing with, he could navigate his way through. He felt his eyes bounce as he drained the last of his mug and slid down under the covers, drifting off into a peaceful slumber.

Nick woke to a flurry of excitement in his belly. He couldn't wait for his date with Steph. Thinking back to the dates he'd met through the dating app, he knew this one would be different. His heart hadn't been in it, and now he understood why. It wasn't natural. He was trying too hard to find someone. Like when he'd met Sarah and was searching for a replacement mother for his kids. He didn't want to find his future wife that way, ticking paper boxes. He wanted the anticipation, the desire, the craving. She didn't need to be right on paper. She needed to give him butterflies when she laughed. Cause his heart to race from a simple brush of her fingers on his skin. Make him breathless from a kiss. He wanted someone to understand the broken parts of him, but love him anyway. He wanted to fall in love. He wanted Steph. The excitement turned to nerves. Messing this up wasn't an option. She was still grieving, and he needed to tread carefully and leave her to call all the shots.

His feet pounded the pavement and his breath evened out into a steady rhythm. He took up running after his divorce, and it had become his go-to stress reliever over the past few years. Nick had been an active participant in sport throughout his life, but nothing had brought him the mental fulfilment that running had.

By the time he got home, he was relaxed and prepared for his date. Although he knew the moment he saw Steph, his preparation would be futile.

Steph

'You look nice. Are you going somewhere?' Terri asks, holding the door open for me.

I blush, embarrassed that my friend has picked up on my efforts.

'Yes, I'm going out for lunch with a friend.' I pause, contemplating whether to fill her in on the details. 'A male friend.'

'Oh?' Terri grins, her face lighting up at the opportunity to think of something other than her impending cancer diagnosis. 'I'll make coffee and you can bring me up to speed.'

I laugh at my friend's enthusiasm and push the door closed behind me.

'So, spill the tea, lady,' Terri says, handing over my coffee and making herself comfortable on the couch, eager to listen to my news.

'His name is Nick.' I feel bashful as his name rolls off my lips. 'He's a psychologist and a very old friend of Paul's from work.'

Terri studies my face and I can tell she's happy to see my spark coming back, but I know she can see right through me. We've been friends for a long time and she can read me like a book, so there's no doubt in my mind that she can sense the hesitancy in my voice.

'You think it's too soon, don't you?' Terri asks, pre-empting my concerns.

'I don't know Terri, it's still early days so who knows if it even is anything, but yes, I'm worried about what people might think. The boys are my primary concern, Caleb, especially. Levi already thinks the sun rises and sets with Nick.'

'But what do you think, Steph? Do you feel ready to take that step?' Terri asks. 'Because it's nobody's business but your own.'

'I know, and again, I have no idea. It seems too fast, but when I'm with him, I'm lighter, happier. I loved Chris, I still do. I'm sure I'll love him until the day I die, but he's gone, and I'm still here. Despite the reasons for his death, we had a happy marriage. Yes, there were moments I would've changed. I wish I'd confronted him about certain things, like the way he was with Caleb, but he was a wonderful husband and I miss that connection. I don't know that I'm ready to jump into something serious, but Nick understands everything I'm going through, he's done so much for Levi, and he's trying to help Caleb the best he can without it being in a professional capacity.'

'He sounds like a good man,' Terri smiles.

'He's so easy to talk to, and there's this crazy chemistry between us.' I shrug. 'I don't know Terri, what the hell am I doing?'

Terri leans forward and rests her hand on my arm.

'Steph, if there's one thing I've learnt from the past

few months, it's that we have no clue what's around the next corner. We have to take life and grab on to it with both hands. Enjoy every single moment, however big or small. If this guy makes you smile, then let him. See where it goes. You've had a few months of shit and you deserve a light at the end of the tunnel.'

'Thank you Terri. What about the boys, though?'

'Do you need to tell them? Can't you just see how it goes first?' Terri frowns.

'Yeah, I guess so,' I concede. 'Anyway, enough about me. How are you?'

Terri's eyes brim with tears and she blows out a harsh breath.

'I'm terrified of what the results will say, but whatever happens, I'm determined to fight it.'

'We'll do it together, Terri. I promise I'll be there for you every step of the way. Both as your doctor and your friend. I'll call you the second I get your results through,' I assure her, and she can only nod through her tears.

Despite Terri's personal situation, she somehow boosts my spirits and assuages the guilt I've been carrying about my date. Nick's already at the door when I get out of my car and he ushers me straight towards his ute.

'Hey, sorry, am I late?' I ask.

'No, I just saw you pull up so thought we may as well leave right away,' he leans in and brushes his lips against my cheek. My insides flare at the chaste contact and the heat scorches my face. I smile shyly as I settle myself in the passenger seat. Nick drives a Toyota Land Cruiser that has seen better days. It's a far cry from the flashy BMW sports car that Chris drove. It makes sense he drives a car that fits his lifestyle. He loves the outdoors, camping and lugging his muddy bike around.

'So, where are we going?' I ask as he backs off the driveway.

'I thought we'd head out to a winery. Is that okay?' Nick smiles.

'Perfect.'

The drive out towards wine country is quiet. The radio's on and Nick sings along to the music, while I relax in my seat and take it all in. Conversation is intermittent, nothing deep, just a casual getting to know each other as and when topics arise.

'Is this one okay?' Nick asks, pulling into the car park next to a small rustic looking building with vineyards stretching back as far as I can see. The front is full of Jacaranda trees, just beginning to bud, and I make a note to come back in a few months' time to see them in full bloom.

'It looks beautiful,' I say. 'I've never been here before.'

'Me neither, but the reviews look good,' he grins, switching off the engine and unbuckling his seat belt.

We enter the restaurant and I look around at the little artisan store in the entrance. There's an array of breads and pickled goods, along with jams and chutneys, and a vast selection of cheese and salami. Colourful macarons and handmade chocolates fill the fridges and my mouth waters at the sight.

'Come on, stop drooling, we can come and buy afterwards.' Nick chuckles at the look of yearning on my face, caught in my little food heaven.

A friendly server shows us to a cosy table tucked away in the corner of a small courtyard and hands us menus while listing off the specials.

'The Barramundi special sounds delicious,' I decide, closing my menu after a quick glance.

'I agree. I think I'll go the same. What about a drink? A glass of wine?' Nick offers.

'Why not? I'll go for the Pinot Gris.' It feels decadent having lunch at a winery in the middle of the week, but I could get used to it.

'Do you want to talk about yesterday, or would you rather forget about it?' Nick asks.

I don't want to ruin the mood by talking about my hellish day, but maybe unleashing will take the edge off.

'I had a full on day with several patients needing a mental health care plan, which to be honest, I find gruelling right now. Then I had a close friend come to see me with a problem that doesn't look good; I think she'll have a hell of a fight ahead of her. To top it off, I went home to find Caleb lying on his bed staring at the ceiling, refusing to either talk or eat. It just felt like I'd gone back in time.' My eyes tear away from Nick and I blink back tears. Nick reaches across the table and takes my hand, gripping it, his thumb tracing lines across my knuckles.

'I'm so sorry you're having to go through this, Steph. Let me be here for you.' His sincerity forces my eyes back to his level and I nod, unable to speak in fear of falling apart.

Nick doesn't remove his hand, instead he leaves it there as a source of comfort as he expresses some ideas he has to help Caleb.

'Millie seems to have been a good influence. How would you feel about spending more family time with us, both you and Millie? Cale seemed to respond well at the weekend.'

'I'm sure that would be beneficial to all of us,' Nick says. A smile ghosts his lips. The intensity of his words washes over me and the lust in his eyes lets me know he's offering whatever I'm ready for. Our server shatters the fervent contact.

'Two Pinot Gris.'

'Thank you,' I say and pick up the glass.

'Cheers.' Nick holds his glass to mine. 'To keeping going and moving forwards.'

We clink glasses. I take a sip of wine, following it with a bigger gulp. It hits me immediately and I feel myself relax into Nick's company. I don't want our friendship to be just about the tough stuff; I enjoy his calm nature and easy humour and I want to know the lighter side of him too.

'What's your favourite movie?' I ask out of the blue, steering the conversation away from the darkness and intensity of the previous topic.

Nick grins. 'I'm not sure I can tell you without you judging me.'

The twinkle in his eye tells me the light-hearted banter has returned

'I can't promise that I won't. How bad is it?'

'Pretty Woman.' Nick's answer is decisive and I find it endearing. 'Twenty-year-old me couldn't get past that Julia Roberts smile.' His eyes twinkle at the memory and I feel the wall around my heart crumble a little more.

'She does have a beautiful smile,' I muse.

Nick lowers his voice. 'Not as beautiful as yours.'

The potency behind his compliment catches me off guard, but for the first time, I don't feel perturbed by his fervour. I flash him a smile, settling in to his gaze.

'Two Barramundi specials.' The server interrupts and we both chuckle at her knack of knowing exactly when to dampen the rising heat between us.

'This is delicious,' I rave, tucking into my lunch. 'What's your favourite food?' I'm going for uncomplicated again.

'No, you can't move on yet. You never told me your favourite movie.'

'Oh, there are so many. Pretty Woman is such a classic, but sticking with the Julia Roberts romance theme, you can't go far wrong with Notting Hill.'

'Oh, so you're a rom-com girl, hey?' Nick asks, the twinkle back in his eyes.

'It depends. Sometimes a good psychological thriller really gets me in the mood.'

Nick raises his eyebrows. 'In the mood for what?'

'That came out wrong,' I blush, 'stop teasing me.' My eyelashes flutter at the mutual flirtation.

Nick beams as he scrapes his plate clean, fully aware of the effect his smile has on me. I wish I could bottle this feeling. This feeling of awareness that has settled inside me, knowing I'm teetering on the precipice of falling. The recognition that I am in the precise moment before I tumble over the edge. I love that feeling. Knowing I'm falling for this man and I am in full control of the situation. I can make that leap whenever I'm ready, safe in the knowledge that he'll be right there falling headlong with me.

'So, favourite food?' Nick ponders for a moment, getting back to my previous question. 'I like most things, but a good curry, or a Sunday roast, would be my top contenders, and Italian, of course, that goes without saying.'

'You'll have to come round for a roast then,' I offer. 'My mother was born in Yorkshire and passed on her family Yorkshire pudding recipe.'

'I'd love that.' Nick's smile is radiant. The air between us crackles, and neither one of us can look away.

We sit in his Land Cruiser, chatting animatedly long after he pulls into his driveway.

'Come inside for a coffee, Steph. I'm not ready to let you go yet. If you have time, that is?'

My eyes fall on his face and his smile lingers, desire pooling in his eyes.

'Okay,' I say, not wanting the day to end, either. I'm not ready to return to my reality when I can live in this dreamworld for a little longer.

Once inside, Nick moves towards the coffee machine and sets about grinding the beans. He doesn't look particularly focused on the task at hand. In fact, he looks edgy, like he's fighting an internal battle. I lean against the bench top, watching his every move, and he turns towards me while the grinder works its magic.

My heart races. The heat in his eyes is discernible. Every one of my senses has heightened tenfold, and my nerve endings are on fire. The energy soars between us, and although I can feel the longing emanating from Nick's body, I know he will never make the first move. He promised me, and I know in my heart he is a man of his word. His eyes burn through my core, giving me confidence. I'm not sure

I'm ready for the next step, but I know I want it. My eyes fix on his and I push back off the bench and drift across the kitchen. My breathing quickens as I draw close and I catch a tremor in Nick's jaw. He's nervous, and that only increases the attraction. I'm powerless to resist him any longer, so with a last second boost of confidence, I reach my hand to the nape of his neck and pull him towards me for a kiss.

Nick moves willingly, his eyes questioning mine before moving his hands swiftly to my waist, pulling me closer. My lips meet his, hesitant at first, then with more fervour as he responds to my advances. His tongue sweeps along my bottom lip, teasing my mouth open, and I groan into him, encouraging him to pick up the pace. My spare hand reaches up to join the other, fingers swirling in his silver strands. He pulls back, breaking the kiss, questioning if I'm with him.

My throat closes over, my words lost in my strangled breath. I don't want him to stop. My hands tremble as they run over his shoulders and down his chest, my fingers fumbling at the buttons on his shirt. My eyes never leave his. I seductively unfasten every button, and running my hands back up his now bare chest, I ease the shirt off his shoulders, letting it fall to the floor. Nick looks torn.

'Steph, we can slow this down.'

'I don't want to,' I choke out.

Nick nods and without a word, he takes my hand and leads me to his bedroom. My eyes widen when I see the bed, a stark reminder of the reality of our situation. Nick is watching my every move, picking up on my unease.

'Steph,' he whispers. 'I promised I'd hold the reins

until you're ready. If you have any doubts about taking this further, please tell me and we'll stop right now.' His fingers brush my cheek. 'There's no pressure, I swear.' He drops a chaste kiss to my lips.

My eyes glisten as he speaks, his words reminding me I'm in charge here. In one swift move, I lift the hem of my dress and pull it over my head. My breaths fragment as my heart roars in my chest. At this moment, I can't think of anywhere I'd rather be.

'Nick, I'm ready.'

Nick groans and lifts me onto his bed, easing me backwards on the soft down quilt. He pulls off my shoes before kicking off his own, then with shaky hands unfastens his belt and pulls off his jeans, searching for signs he should stop.

'Relax, Nick, I want this. I won't change my mind.'

I reach out my hand to him as I take in his almost naked form. He's solidly built, but not excessively so. His years of football, and now mountain biking, have given him a body that is making my mouth water. There's a smattering of hair on his olive chest that I want to run my lips across. I'm panting as he takes my hand and lets me pull him down to the bed.

'You're so beautiful, Steph.' He sweeps his fingers across my belly.

I pull his face to mine and continue the kissing we started in the kitchen. The longer we kiss, the more I need him, and when I arch myself into him, Nick responds with want.

He reaches behind my back, and out of practice, struggles with the fastening on my bra. His palms are sweaty and I smile at his frustration, lending a hand to remove it. His mouth moves to my breasts and I moan at the rush of awareness between my legs. Straddling me, Nick's mouth moves down over my belly, sprinkling soft butterfly kisses as he goes. When he reaches for my underwear, his eyes glance at mine, confirming I'm still on board. A slight nod as I bite my lip in anticipation is the green light Nick needs to make quick work of removing my lace g-string. He sits back and admires my naked form and I can almost hear his heart thrumming in his chest. I smile at his rapturous face and allow my confidence to take over.

'Make love to me, Nick.'

Nick doesn't need to be asked twice. He pushes down his underwear and forages through his drawer. As he hovers over me, a warm sensation creeps over my body. An awareness that this is it, the moment I leap. He immerses himself in me and we fall together, clinging to one another as we tumble over and over into the unknown.

Searching for Sunrise

Steph

I catch my reflection in the rear-view mirror and smile at the warm glow.

'Are you okay, Mum?' Caleb asks, snapping me from my reverie.

'What? Oh, yes, I'm fine,' I startle at being exposed in deep thought about my afternoon tryst.

'I said thanks for the lift and you blanked me with that weird smile on your face,' he smirks.

'Oh sorry, my mind was elsewhere,' I blush. 'Have fun at training. I'll see you later. Bye Josh.'

I laugh at myself being caught out by my son. Thank God he can't read minds. As I queue to exit the car park, my attention drifts to Caleb and his recent state of mind. He seems to have been feeding off Josh's high spirits this evening, which is pleasing to see, but I can't help but worry about the next few weeks when Terri's results come through and there's a high chance that Josh will be dealing with difficult issues of his own. I just hope Caleb will find it in himself to be of support to Josh and not let any bad news about Terri give him cause to relapse.

My day off should give me ample opportunity to prepare dinner, but my time with Nick kept me occupied for most of the day. The smug grin creeps back onto my face as my mind wanders back to his bedroom. We laid together afterwards, cuddled up beneath the sheets, and I waited for the regret to come. Even though I initiated everything that happened between us, I had expected to be sucker-punched with remorse afterwards and faltered when I felt nothing but affection. Nick's actions radiated warmth and tenderness. He was careful of my feelings, and I came away with no misgivings.

'Hey Mum, do you want some help?' Levi asks, picking up a raw carrot from the chopping board and crunching down on it.

'As long as you don't eat it all before it's cooked.' I shoo his hand away. ' You can be on pan duty, here start stirring these.' I scoop the veggies from the board and toss them in the pan to stir-fry with the beef.

'You seem happier today,' Levi says, picking up on my uplift in mood. I guess anything would be an improvement on yesterday. 'Did you do much?'

My face reddens and I veer away from my son. Why are both my boys perceptive today? I'm not ready to share my relationship with them even though I know the idea of me and his new best friend being together would thrill Levi.

'Not really, just had coffee with Terri and grabbed some lunch with Nick. Nothing exciting,' I say, going with a censored version of the truth.

'I'm hoping Nick might take me out for a longer ride on Sunday,' Levi says, losing interest in my day. 'Do you know if he's busy?'

'I wouldn't have a clue, Levi, why don't you ask him?' My heart pounds, unsure whether it's from excitement that I might get to see him again so soon, or nervous about how my body will react to him when we're not alone.

'Levi, I'm off to pick the boys up.' I duck out to avoid the off-chance he might want to tag along.

I need alone time in the car so I can call Terri to wish her luck for tomorrow. I voice my request to Siri, and Terri answers almost immediately, eager to hear about my day.

'Hey, how was it?' Her enthusiasm for my love life makes me laugh.

'I'm calling to wish you luck for tomorrow,' I say, changing my tone to give reassurance.

'Thank you, that's thoughtful. Now spill. Tell me everything. Did he kiss you?' Terri badgers.

I blush, grateful I'm alone in my car and not on a video call. I try to think back to the last time I blushed before I met Nick and I can't. It's never been in my DNA. He makes me feel so many things.

'I've had the best day, Terri. Everything about it was wonderful.'

'Steph, I'm so pleased. You deserve this. So… how was the kiss?'

I chuckle at my friend's insistence, and heat surges through my body at the words working their way to the tip of my tongue.

'The kiss was amazing, Terri, but the sex was out of this world.' I drop the bombshell and leave Terri shell-shocked.

'Stephanie Wilson,' she screams. 'You can't just

drop that on me! Tell me more.'

'We had a lovely lunch at a winery, then we went back to his place for coffee. You should've seen him standing there in the kitchen grinding the coffee beans like a real life George Clooney. I pounced on him.' My voice is giddy at the recollection.

'You go girl, I'm so proud of you.'

'We kissed, and things just ramped up. Before I knew it, we were in his bedroom and the reality of what was about to happen slapped me in the face. I almost crumbled, but God, Terri, I wanted him so much.' My tongue is loose and I can't stop babbling. 'It was so beautiful and it felt natural. I've missed that connection.' Tears well and I'm unsure if they're out of sadness for Chris or the onset of the stronger feelings I'm beginning to feel for Nick.

'Wow,' Terri says. 'I'm speechless.'

'Do you think I've made a mistake?' Her response plants a tiny seed of doubt in my mind.

'Do you have any regrets?'

'None at all.'

'Then no, I don't, Steph. You're the only one who knows how you feel, and your journey has to be negotiated at your own pace. But do it for you and no one else, okay?'

'Thanks Terri, I'll have to go. I've just pulled up at football. I'm keeping my fingers crossed for tomorrow and I'll ring you with the results, okay?'

'Okay.' Her voice breaks and the enormity of her pending situation penetrates the silence.

I hang up before the tears arrive.

My focus is tested the next day at work and a simple morning of straight-forward consultations eases the stress. Terri is at the forefront of my thoughts and worry laces my mind. I'm thankful when lunch time rolls around for the opportunity to regroup.

Paul's in the kitchen when I grab my lunch from the fridge and he spins around to face me. His eyes light up like a Christmas tree.

'Stephanie, is there something you'd like to share with me?' he beams.

My stomach surges, hoping like hell Nick hasn't shared details of yesterday with his friend. I frown, stumbling over my words.

'What? What are you talking about?' I ask, blanketed by fear. If Nick's blabbed to Paul, I'll be disappointed, but Paul smiles at the panicked look on my face.

'Hey, calm down. I was just teasing you.' Paul raises his eyebrows and continues. 'Although I'm guessing from your reaction that my suspicions were correct and you are the reason for the Cheshire Cat grin that was plastered all over Nick's face last night.'

Heat rises from my chest and explodes across my face, tiny beads of perspiration popping on my skin. I'm not happy with my body's sudden betrayal of my inner thoughts. 'He didn't say anything?' I ask.

'Don't worry, Steph, Nick wouldn't do that, I swear. I asked what had him so happy, and he barked at me to mind my business. You don't look as joyful, though. Are you okay?'

I sigh in relief. With everything I'm dealing with right now, I can do without Nick sharing intimate details of my private life. I'm not ready for that. It occurs to me I've shared those details with Terri, and it isn't my place to be mad if Nick wants to share them with Paul. It just feels so exposing when his friend is also my friend.

'Paul, listen, things with Nick are great, but that's all I'm giving you because I need to factor Caleb's mental health into the equation.' Paul nods his understanding. 'But no, I'm not feeling joyful this morning. Terri's having some scans done this morning and I'm ninety per cent sure it's gonna be bad news.'

'Oh Steph, I'm so sorry. How's she holding up?' he asks, concerned for my friend.

I shrug. 'She seemed pretty positive yesterday, but it could be just a front.'

We sit and reflect on our conversation while we eat lunch, and Paul nudges me before he stands to leave.

'I'm pleased for you and Nick, Steph, I mean that. I worry it's too soon, but I hope it works out. You're both very special to me.'

'Thank you, that means a lot.'

By the time I leave for the day, I'm wound up like a spring, anxious for Terri's results. I've still heard nothing. It's going to be a long weekend for Terri, so I'm hoping for news first thing on Monday morning. I arrive at the oval for Caleb's game on Saturday and scan the sidelines for Terri and her husband, Mark.

'Morning, you two,' I say, pulling Terri in for a hug.

'Any news?' she asks, her forehead furrowed in anticipation.

'Sorry.' I shake my head. 'If I haven't heard by Monday afternoon, I promise I'll chase them.'

Terri nods, forcing a bright smile on her face.

'How are you, Mark?' I ask, aware that he is going through the wringer right alongside his wife.

'Pushing through Steph, that's all we can do, right?' he says.

The two teams run on to the pitch as my phone rings.

'Coffee?' Nick asks, instead of a greeting, when I answer.

My lips form a smile, but the heaviness my answer brings weighs it down.

'Sorry, I can't. I'm at Caleb's football game.'

'Yes, I know.' I detect a hint of humour in his voice. 'I'm standing at the coffee van watching you. Millie wanted to come and watch Caleb.'

My eyes zero in on the queue at the van. 'In that case, I'd love one, thank you.'

'I can see you're with friends. Can I get them one too?' he asks, his generosity widening my smile. I turn to Terri and Mark with his offer.

'They'd love one, thanks Nick,' I say, relaying their order.

When the call ends, I can't wipe the grin off my face and Terri pounces.

'If you don't at least attempt to look a little less love-struck, your love affair won't be a secret for much longer,' she whispers.

Although harsh, she delivers her reproach in kindness, and I blush at my lapse in judgement. Mark laughs with a knowing smile.

'You told him?' I ask, horrified.

'Of course, but it won't go any further, I promise. Besides, we're gonna be living vicariously through you for the foreseeable future. I'm guessing whatever way this goes, a mastectomy or chemo, our bedroom's not gonna be seeing much action for a while,' Terri says.

My stomach lurches. I hate that while I'm embarking on something new and exciting, my friend could be about to head into the darkest period of her life.

'Terri,' I say, lost for words.

'Hey, don't give me that face. You've had more than your share of heartache. You deserve some happiness, and I want some enjoyment in my life, so please don't let me down.'

I grasp her hand, willing the tears not to bubble over.

'It looks like George Clooney's on his way with the coffees.' Terri nods her head towards the tall, dark and handsome man with the silver sprinkles in his hair coming our way. His captivating smile turns me to jelly.

'Steph, put your tongue away before you trip over it,' Terri whispers, causing a piercing squawk to slip from my throat. Despite her own troubles, she always brings laughter to my life.

'Hey,' Nick says, approaching with a tray of coffee.

'Hey, where's Millie?'

'Oh, she spotted some friends, so she dumped me,' Nick explains.

'Hi.' Nick turns to Terri and Mark.

'Sorry, this is Terri, and her husband, Mark. Their son, Josh, plays on the team with Cale. This is Nick,' I introduce them all and Nick begins handing out coffee cups.

'Thank you, George,' Terri laughs.

I chuckle as Nick throws us a puzzled look.

'Sorry, I'll explain later about my friend and her warped sense of humour,' I say, and rest my hand for a brief moment on his lower back. It seems the least risky thing I can do to satisfy my craving to touch him.

The game is close, but Caleb's team manages a win, securing their place in the play-offs.

'It was lovely to meet you, Nick,' Terri says as they prepare to leave, 'and thanks again for the coffee.'

I hug Terri with another promise to call her on Monday and watch her leave, sadness flooding my heart.

'Steph? Are you okay?' Nick asks, puncturing my gaze.

'Yeah, I'm fine.' I turn to Nick, studying him, wondering how much I can say. 'You know the friend I was worried about the other day?' I ask. 'Well, that's her.'

Nick's eyes dart back and forth, scanning the surrounding faces, making sure we're alone. He pulls me into a hug and squeezes me for just a moment before releasing me. Though it's short, the contact grounds me.

'I wish I could give you more,' Nick whispers, noticing Caleb and Millie heading towards us.

'Nick, I appreciate you just being here.' I make sure he knows that before I plaster on my neutral mask.

'Well played, Caleb,' Nick greets him with a pat on the back. 'Keep playing like that and you'll be turning professional for sure.'

Caleb's eyes light up and the grin that fans his face makes my heart explode. 'For real?' he asks Nick, surprised.

'It'll take some hard work, but there's no doubt in my mind you can get there, hey Millie?' he looks to his daughter for back up.

'Maybe,' she muses, teasing, 'if he listens to my advice.'

Caleb nudges her. His laughter is like music to my ears and I thank my lucky stars for the day this beautiful man and his daughter burst into our lives.

'Hey Mum, can Millie come back to ours for a bit?' Caleb asks.

'Sure, if that's okay with Nick,' I say.

Nick looks at Millie. 'I can't pick you up later. I'm going to see Paul. He needs a hand with something.'

'I can drop her home later.'

'If you're sure, Steph,' Nick says.

'Of course.'

'I'll see you tomorrow then, when I pick Levi up, about one?'

'Why don't you stay for dinner afterwards? I'm cooking a roast,' I offer, drawing him in.

'That would be great, thanks Steph,' Nick says. His voice is reticent, but his eyes are anything but. I can feel the heat as he fights to keep the conversation on a casual level.

'Can I come too?' Millie interjects.

'Millie! You can't just invite yourself for dinner.' Nick looks horrified, but the fact Millie feels comfortable enough to do that gives me goosebumps.

'Of course you can, Millie.'

Millie grins. 'Mum never cooks a roast.'

'Okay then, dinner for five tomorrow. It's a date,' I say, my wide-eyed gaze flashing to Nick's. He winks and turns towards his car, his smile widening as he walks away.

Searching for Sunrise

Steph

'Hey, Steph, I called Mum. She's picking me up at five.' Millie interrupts the silence.

'Oh okay, I could've dropped you home,' I say.

'I told her that, but she wanted to meet Caleb and make sure he's a sixteen-year-old boy and not some random weirdo.' Millie rolls her eyes. 'She has no faith in me.'

'She's just looking out for you, Millie. I'd be the same.'

Millie nods before heading back to join Caleb in his room, leaving me alone to consider the recent changes in my life. When the police arrived at my door to give me the news about Chris, I felt the air being ripped from my lungs and thought I'd never take a full breath again. My chest was tight and pain razored through me each time I inhaled. I can't remember the week that followed. It passed me by in a daze. Once I found the suicide note and heard about the sale of his dental practice, the anger took over, which, good or bad, gave me the motivation to move forward. My friendship with Nick has done the rest. Without his patience and understanding, his sage advice and his generosity with his time, I don't know where I'd be. And now I've turned another corner, one I never would have imagined. I smile to myself as I think about the tender moments that led us to where we are; shy glances, heated stares, gentle touches, and the raw emotions that were laid bare each time we shared a chapter of our story. The day we spent together formed the first line in a new chapter we were writing together. I'd entered it on impulse, laying my heart on the line, expecting my head to overwrite my joy with guilt and fear. But it hasn't, at least not so far.

Even so, I'm assaulted by nervous energy the moment I hear a car outside. I hadn't given it a second thought earlier when Millie had been talking about her mum, but it strikes me that this woman is Nick's ex and I'm about to meet her. I don't know if Sarah knows the connection between Millie and Caleb, or how they met.

The car comes to a stop, and I wander outside and watch the dainty blonde woman in four-inch heels step out. My eyes rove over her, taking her in, fighting to keep my surprise at bay. She's not what I had been expecting, and it's obvious Millie takes after her dad in every way.

'Hi, you must be Millie's mum, I'm Steph, come on in,' I say in welcome.

'Hi, I hope you don't mind. I just wanted to check out where she was.'

'Not a problem. I'd do the same.' I'm hyperaware of her tumultuous relationship with Nick.

'Millie, your mum's here.'

Sarah stares at me in horror as my voice travels down the hall towards Caleb's bedroom.

'I hope you haven't allowed them in your son's bedroom.' Her tone is snippy. 'I'm not happy about that.'

Millie appears at the door, shaking her head, having caught her mum's comment.

'She thinks my sexuality is just a phase,' she says, rolling her eyes at me.

'Millie, that's not what I'm saying. I just don't think it's appropriate for you to be alone in a boy's bedroom,' Sarah huffs.

'But it's okay for me to be alone in a girl's bedroom?' Millie challenges.

The rising tension between Millie and her mum is becoming uncomfortable as I look from one to the other as they quarrel.

'A girl will not get you pregnant, Millie. Stop being difficult,' Sarah argues. 'Come on, let's go.'

My mouth hangs open at the words Sarah is bleating, and I struggle to comprehend how Nick could ever have been married to her.

'Thanks for having me, Steph,' Millie says, as she follows her mother.

'Anytime, Millie.' I don't want to get involved in a dispute between Millie and her mum, but I want her to know she is welcome here.

'I'll see you tomorrow.' Millie whispers out of earshot of her mum. I can't help but smile at her spirit.

'Hey, how was your afternoon? Millie, okay?' Nick asks on the phone later.

'Yeah, all good. Did you get finished with Paul

and Gerry?' I wonder.

'Yes, Paul caught me off guard, though. You told him?' Nick asks, surprised more than angry.

'No, he put two and two together when he saw the grin on your face the other night and when I saw him at work, he made it sound like you'd told him.'

'I never said a word, I swear.'

'I know, don't worry. It was a guess, and he was digging for dirt. I told him things with you were great and that was all he was getting.'

'Great huh?' Nick teases.

'Pretty great from where I'm standing,' I say, an air of flirtation in my voice.

'You know, it was difficult this morning not being able to kiss you, or touch you,' he whispers.

'It was, you're right, but it's too soon, Nick. I can't go there just yet, not with how Caleb is. He seems to have improved no end, though, and I think Millie's played a huge role in that.'

'That's good news, Steph. Let's hope it's not too long before he's feeling like himself again.'

'Speaking of Millie...' I venture.

'Yes?' Nick draws the word out.

'I met your ex.'

'Sarah?' Nick asks, shocked. 'Where?'

'She came to pick Millie up. Interesting woman,' I grumble.

'Oh hell! What did she do?'

'She berated me for allowing Millie in Caleb's bedroom, but Millie overheard and laid into her.'

'I'm so embarrassed that I was ever married to her,' Nick says. 'Please don't let that change your opinion of me.'

'As if it would ever do that. So she doesn't believe

Millie's a lesbian? Or is she just burying her head in the sand?'

'I don't know, Steph, but Millie's made it very clear to her, and has had several girlfriends, so I'm not sure what else she can do,' Nick says.

'Millie didn't seem too fazed by her, at least she's comfortable standing her ground.'

Nick laughs at my description. 'If there's one thing Millie won't do, it's let anyone walk over her. She will stand her ground till the very end, always has done. I'm proud of the way she came out and stood up to everyone. I couldn't wish for more in a daughter.'

'You're a great dad, Nick. She's had an excellent role model.'

'Thank you, that means a lot.'

I'm surprised to see Millie with Nick when he picks Levi up the following afternoon.

'She said she'd made plans to hang out with Caleb again. I hope that's okay.' Nick is sheepish when he drops her off.

'Of course, you guys have fun. I'll see you back for dinner.'

I watch my son drive away with my… with my what? It's too early to put a name on it, too early to define what's going on. All I know is I'm enjoying the time I get to spend with Nick, whatever is happening between us.

I spend several hours in the kitchen, preparing and cooking the roast while Caleb and Millie hang out in the garden, tossing the football. When Millie breaks off to come inside, I chance a quick chat with her.

'Millie, as much as I'm enjoying seeing Caleb out of his room, you know I don't have a problem with you being in there with him, don't you?'

'Thanks Steph, but we're good outside,' Millie answers.

'Does your mum know I know your dad?'

'I don't think so. I thought it easier not to tell her. She just thinks I know Caleb from school,' Millie shrugs.

'Not that I have an issue with her knowing I'm friends with Nick. It doesn't matter to me either way.' I stumble over my words.

Millie grins as if she has an inkling something is going on, and I blush at the knowing look directed at me by this fifteen-year-old.

'Mum just can't get her head around everything.' Millie directs the conversation back towards herself. 'She allows sleepovers with girls, but I'm not allowed in a boy's room in the middle of the afternoon. From where I'm sitting, that makes no sense. She argues with me about it all the time. I'm sorry if I made you feel uncomfortable yesterday.'

'Millie, do me a favour?' I say. 'Please don't apologise for standing up for what you believe in, and if that makes other people uncomfortable, that's on them.'

Millie tilts her head in contemplation, fixing her gaze on my face.

'You sound like my dad. You'd make a good couple,' she says, whisking two glasses of water away with a grin and heading back to the garden.

I stand and watch her go. Did she just give me permission to date her dad?

Levi arrives home full of beans. He helps Nick get his bike off the rack and takes it straight to rinse off. Nick looks a little bedraggled and sweaty. My mouth waters when he comes closer.

'Fun afternoon?' I ask.

'Great fun, but Levi pushed me hard,' Nick laughs. 'I thought I was pretty fit, but it seems my age is slowing me down.'

'You look pretty fit, to me.' I glance around to make sure no kids are present. Nick raises his eyebrows and gives them a wiggle at my suggestive comment. 'Do you need to take a shower before dinner?' I ask.

'With you?' My inner furnace roars to life and the heat blooms across my face at his suggestion, even though I'm aware he's teasing me. This rosy cheeked look is becoming part of my everyday style.

'Rain check?' I ask, holding his gaze. Nick grins at my seductive side before bringing the conversation back to the present.

'If you don't mind, a shower would be great.'

After showing him to my ensuite, I catch myself lingering, watching him undress. His eyes flash to mine, reading the hunger on my face.

'Steph, you need to go,' he warns, 'but I'm down for a rain check.'

I remember where I am and snap back to reality, slipping out of my bedroom to avoid alerting the kids to our situation.

'Dinner's ready, guys. Come and sit down.' Nick and I lay out the dishes of food for everyone to help themselves.

'Steph, this looks amazing.' Millie's eyes widen,

saliva almost drooling from her mouth. She pulls out the chair next to Caleb, while Levi clinches the seat next to Nick, leaving me on the end. I look around the table and wonder when this little group began to feel like a family.

'Thanks Millie, dig in. I hope you enjoy it.'

Caleb's silence has me on alert throughout dinner. Even Millie's attempts to draw him into the conversation fall on deaf ears and I wonder if he's taken another turn for the worse, or whether I'm just overthinking his mood. It's a tough one to navigate, unsure whether his flat periods are from grief, depression, or the regular stresses that come with being a teenager. He still won't talk to me about his feelings, despite my attempts, and although Millie hasn't told Nick anything Caleb's said to her in confidence, she has said he speaks to her about his thoughts surrounding his dad's death. At least that's a positive and helps settle my mind, if only a little. If he's talking, then he's processing, and Millie seems to have her head screwed on. I'm sure she would talk to me if Caleb told her anything of concern.

After dinner, I tell the kids to go off and leave me and Nick to the washing up. I'm not giving them an easy out. I just want to spend time alone with Nick, even if the only way to get it is by doing the mundane jobs together. The kids don't need to be told twice; Cale and Millie run off to play video games while Levi goes to spend time with his animals.

Nick and I have moved all the dishes into the kitchen in relative silence when he nudges me backwards against the kitchen cupboards. He glances around before dipping his head close to mine.

'I've wanted to do this all weekend,' he whispers, drifting his fingers across my ear and tangling them in my hair. He tugs my head towards his and runs his tongue across my lips, pushing his way inside. I moan and welcome him in. Nick reciprocates with a groan, his other hand brushing my cheek as he works his tongue deeper, kissing me like his life depends on it. And then he freezes. I know we've been sprung and I pray as I turn my head that it will be Levi or Millie. It is. Levi's standing on the other side of the fly screen, watching us with a mix of embarrassment and joy. I tremble in Nick's arms, unable to comprehend what the outcome of this will be. Nick sends Levi a pleading look and Levi grins back, his fingers locking his lips and throwing away the key. He slides the door open and wanders through to his bedroom without a word, a knowing smile plastered across his face.

I look at Nick in horror and he leans in, his lips meeting mine in reassurance.

'Levi's fine, he won't say anything,' he says. 'You don't need to worry, I promise. We had a little chat today.'

'What do you mean? What did you say to him?' I'm a little blindsided by his admission, and, if I'm honest, a little concerned about what he might have said to my son.

'You know, he's been aware there might be something between us for a while, but today he asked if it was more serious. He asked if I "like, like," you.'

'Oh hell.' I bury my head in Nick's chest. 'What

did you say?' My words are muffled by his t-shirt.

'I was honest, or as honest as I needed to be,' he says. 'That, yes, I do "like, like" you, but that the timing isn't right for anything to come of it. You're grieving his dad, because you loved him very much, and you're concerned about Caleb's mental health, but if the circumstances were different, or in time, down the track, then we might look at beginning a relationship.'

Lifting my eyes to meet him, I sigh.

'I hope I didn't speak out of turn, Steph, he kind of sprang it on me and I didn't want to lie, but nor did I want to tell him the whole truth.'

'It's fine. I know how pushy Levi can be, and when you're on the receiving end of his questions, there's not much you can do to avoid it.'

'If it makes you feel any better, he told me he would be cool if we dated,' Nick smirks.

'Oh great, we're getting approval to date from my fourteen-year-old son now,' I snicker. 'I think Millie has picked up on it, too.'

'Yeah, I'm pretty sure she has. She was grilling me on the way here about my dating life, wondering if I would get married again.'

'Would you?' I ask, curious.

His eyes focus in on mine and the edge of his lips quirk upwards.

'I would,' he whispers, dropping a kiss on my forehead. 'Do you have plans for Thursday?'

I still and my panic-stricken face amuses him.

'Not to get married, Steph.' His smirk manages to erase the terror splashed across my face. 'I was thinking more like spending the day together. Relaxing, watching movies, making out, that kind of

thing.'
   'I'd love to,' I say, already counting the hours.

Caleb

Dear Dad,

I don't know why I'm still writing to you. I'm not even sure what to say to you anymore. Everything feels so weird, and it's all your fault. My whole life has changed because of your decision to drive into a tree and kill yourself. You said in your letter that you thought we'd all be better off without you and you did it for our benefit. I don't think you thought about us at all. We have dinner with Nick and Millie and everyone acts like they didn't gatecrash our life just because you're not here. I like hanging with Millie, and even Nick's okay, but it's still weird. It's like we're a family, except we're not. I think Levi wishes we were. Maybe Mum does, too. I wish I could just move on like they have, but I can't because I keep coming back to the fact that I hate you for what you've done to us and how can I be happy when I'm still so fucking angry with you?

Caleb

Nick

'Dad?'

'Yes, Mills?' Nick frowned as Millie turned the volume down on the car radio. She'd been singing along, a little out of tune, he might add, but it still sounded perfect to him.

'You know how earlier I asked if you'd ever get married again?'

'Mmm.'

'If you do, can it please be to Steph?' she grinned.

Nick laughed. 'What are you getting at, Mills?'

'You are so perfect for each other.' Her grin faded and her face turned serious. 'Do you know what she said to me earlier?'

'Go on.' Nick's forehead wrinkled, unsure where this conversation was leading.

'I apologised to her for making her uncomfortable when I went off at Mum in front of her.'

'That was thoughtful of you.'

'And she told me to never apologise for standing up for myself, no matter who it might make feel uncomfortable.'

A lump formed in Nick's throat, tears glistening in his eyes at the support Steph had shown his daughter.

Millie caught her dad's eye and a knowing grin slipped across her face. 'I knew it. You're so into her!' She watched as her dad swiped a tear from his cheek, chewing his lip in contemplation, then realisation hit her and her hand flew to her mouth.

'Oh my God! You're in love with her!' she screamed. 'Does she know?'

Nick shook his head, unable to keep his relationship a secret from his daughter.

'Mills, listen to me. I'm not in love with her.'

'Yeah right,' Millie rolled her eyes.

'It's too soon for that, Millie, but we are together, seeing how things go,' Nick said. 'But you have to keep this to yourself. Steph doesn't want Caleb to know just yet. She's not sure how he would take it.'

'Yeah, I don't know, to be honest. He's improved, but I'm not sure how he'd take something like this,' Millie said. 'Your secret is safe with me.'

'Thanks Mills. Look, things are unknown. It's only a few months since Steph lost her husband, so we're taking it one day at a time.'

'I'm happy for you, Dad,' Millie said, leaning over to give her dad a hug.

'Thank you, me too. And for the record, what Steph said to you about standing up for yourself. She's right, sweetheart, you need to get your mum to understand. But stay calm; yelling at her won't get you anywhere. I speak from experience.'

'I'll try.'

Nick startled awake at the sound of his ringtone. He

blinked, trying to adjust his eyes to read the clock. 11:58PM. He grappled in the dark for the light switch and picked up his phone, knowing there were only three people who could reach him when his phone was in sleep mode. Without looking at which of his girls was calling, he tapped the screen to answer.

'Hello, what's wrong?' he asked.

'Dad, I'm sorry it's so late.' Distressed sounds of sobbing alerted Nick, and he stiffened.

'Millie? Where are you?'

'I'm at home, I'm okay, I just needed to talk to you,' Millie sniffed.

'What's the matter, sweetheart? Did something happen?' Nick pushed himself up against his pillow, his phone to his ear, concerned for his daughter.

'I tried talking to Mum,' Millie said. 'It didn't go well.'

'Oh honey, what happened?'

'I stayed calm, like you said, and I explained how I feel. I even suggested some online resources for her to read.' Millie's heart sank. 'She just wouldn't listen, Dad. She thinks I'm too young to understand what I want. She started ranting about grandchildren and shit. She thinks I'm her own personal baby maker now. It just ended in yelling as usual, and slamming doors, and not by me.'

'Do you want me to talk to her?'

'I doubt she'll listen to you, Dad.' Millie laughed through her tears at her dad's optimism.

'No, maybe not, but it's worth a try, Mills.'

'Can I just come and live with you?' Millie whined.

'Of course you can. You've always had that option, you know that. But think about it, what will that achieve long term? It's better to get your mum on board, not alienate her. Let me see what I can do first and if we exhaust all options, then by all means, come and live with me,' Nick offered.

'But I'll be happier with you, Dad. Isn't that what matters?' She was using her persuasive powers and Nick was tired.

'I'm not saying no, Millie. But I'd rather it be for reasons other than you've fallen out with your mother,' he said.

'Okay, fair enough. You talk to her then. I'm sorry for ringing so late.'

'You can ring me anytime, Millie. You know that. Sleep tight, sweetheart, I love you.'

'Love you too, Dad.'

'What's this all about, Nick?' Sarah said, pushing past him as he held the door open for her. Great, he thought to himself, this will go smoothly.

'Do you want a coffee?' Nick asked in his typical unruffled fashion. Sarah stared at him, unblinking, wondering what his motive for this impromptu meeting was. She knew from experience that she wouldn't be able to rush him, so she may as well go along with him until he was ready to talk to her.

'Yes, coffee would be lovely, thank you.'

Nick ducked his head back out the door to ask his receptionist for two coffees from the fancy machine he didn't know how to use.

'Grab a seat, Sarah, and make yourself comfortable,' he said.

The two made small talk until the coffee arrived,

Sarah growing agitated as they spoke.

'Okay, enough with the intrigue, Nick. Why am I here?' she said.

'I had a phone call at midnight last night from a distraught Millie.' Nick watched for Sarah's reaction.

'Oh, for crying out loud, did she go running to her perfect daddy just because we argued?' Sarah angered.

'She was upset, Sarah, and she asked to come and live with me.'

'What? That's ridiculous.'

'Why is it ridiculous? I'm her father. What is so wrong about her wanting to live with me?' Nick asked, shocked by her comment.

'I didn't mean it like that, you know what I mean. She's just doing it to get back at me,' Sarah said.

'For the record, I told her she's always welcome to come and live with me, but I wanted her to talk to you about this issue you have with her first. It needs resolving. I want her to live with me because she wants to, not because she's lashing out at you.'

'Thank you, I appreciate that,' Sarah expressed genuine gratitude.

'Sarah, you need to sort this out. She's your daughter, and she's hurting.'

'That's why I'm trying to help her. Can't you see that? Her choosing to be a lesbian will only cause her hurt. There are a lot of haters out there, Nick,' Sarah argued.

Nick simmered, pushing his anger down to a place he could keep the lid on.

'Millie hasn't *chosen* to be a lesbian, Sarah. It's who she is. It's something she's known for a long time and she's been honest and open about it. The only person who's hurting her is you. Everyone else in her life accepts her for who she is. Her friends, her team, her sisters, me, everyone but you.' Nick's volume increased, and he clipped his words, fighting to keep from bubbling over. 'Think about this Sarah, you could lose your daughter over this. Then you won't have a daughter, let alone the grandchild that seems to be a top priority for you.'

'I…' Sarah began, her tone defensive.

'Sarah, before you go off at me about this, please just take a minute to think and let this sink in. What's the real problem?' Nick asked.

Sarah stared at him hard. His calm approach to conflict had always riled her when they were married. Her feathers ruffled easily, and attack was always her go to defence mechanism. She took the time to absorb his words this time.

'You have three daughters, Nick. The likelihood of you having grandchildren is high. Millie's all I have.' Her indignation astounded Nick.

'So that's the crux of this? You're upsetting your daughter on the off chance she might not give you a grandchild?' Nick asked, trying his best to keep composed. 'Do you have any idea how that sounds?'

'Well, when you say it like that,' she conceded. 'I don't know Nick, how can she be so sure? She's still so young.'

'Try casting your mind back to nineteen eighty whatever, when you were Millie's age. Were you so sure you were into boys back then? Because I know you had sex with Andrew whatshisface in the back seat of his car when you were only fifteen.' Nick wasn't one for throwing people's actions back at them, but he needed to make his point. 'I'm pretty sure you were old enough to realise you liked boys, not girls. What makes it so different for Millie?'

'I wish I'd never told you that,' Sarah grumbled.

'I'm not trying to be difficult, Sarah. Millie's a lesbian. She may or may not have children. That's her decision, as it would be if she were straight. You need to get your head around this fast.'

Sarah bit her lip, defeated. 'You're right, as usual.' She rolled her eyes as she nodded her agreement. 'It's hard co-parenting with a psychologist, and I'll probably regret saying this, but you're a wonderful dad, Nick.'

Her statement dumbfounded Nick. She'd never given him credit for anything.

'It's not a competition, Sarah. Millie's lucky to have both of us in her life.' Nick swallowed the lump rising in his throat as he thought about his other daughters.

'I know she is,' Sarah acknowledged Nick's remark. 'How are Hannah and Lucy?'

'They're both well. You should call them sometime.' Nick offered her a way in.

'I will,' she said, standing. 'Thank you for coming to me like this, and not just gloating about Millie wanting to live with you. I don't want to lose her.'

'Then don't,' Nick said, offering his arms for a hug.

Sarah hesitated, but accepted his embrace.

'I screwed a lot of things up, with Millie and your girls,' she said, blushing. 'But I want to make amends.'

'I know a good psych if you ever want to talk about it,' Nick grinned as he opened his door to show her out.

Steph

It's Tuesday before I receive the reports from Terri's scans, and just as I'd feared, the news isn't good. I call Terri and hook her up with an oncologist to discuss options. A mastectomy is likely, followed by chemotherapy. It's going to be a long fight, but Terri has the support and determination to do everything in her power to beat it. The news leaves me in a thick fog for the rest of the day and when Caleb comes to me later in the evening in tears, I'm not sure I have the strength to give him what he needs, but I'm damn sure I will give him every drop I have in me.

'Mum?' Tears stream down his face. 'Did you hear the news?'

I look up and wait for clarification, afraid to jump the gun.

'Terri's got cancer,' he cries. 'Josh just called me.'

'Come sit down, sweetheart,' I say, reaching for his hand and pulling him down next to me. I need to be honest with him.

'I spoke to her today with the results and I've referred her to one of the best oncologists who'll explain all the options and they'll come up with the best course of treatment to give her the most positive outcome. She's in excellent hands, Cale, I promise. How's Josh dealing with it?' I ask.

Caleb shrugs. 'He was crying. He's scared she'll die.'

'Josh will need his friends around him Cale, are you up to that? Because if you're not, you need to talk to me. You're my priority, and I need to look out for you first. I need to know if you aren't prepared to handle this.'

'I can't get my head around it all. Why Terri and not Dad? He wanted to die and we wouldn't have been so angry with him if he'd died of cancer.'

'Life doesn't work like that, sweetheart. Is that how you feel? You're still angry with Dad?'

Caleb nods. 'I hate him.'

I pull my son into my arms and let him fall apart on my shoulder. It wrenches at my heart, but I'm glad he's releasing his emotions.

'You know, I was angry with him too.' Caleb brushes his sleeve across his face and slumps back on the couch, taking in my words. 'I was angry that he'd not spoken to me about how he felt. That I hadn't noticed he wasn't well. I hate what he's done to you, to our family. But depression is an illness, and it takes over. He couldn't help how he felt, and he hated himself for putting so much pressure on you. It was the only way that he could see not to turn you into him and perpetuate the cycle. He thought he was doing the best thing for all of us. We can't blame ourselves, Cale. His death had nothing to do with us and everything to do with his illness.'

'You and Levi seem to have moved on. Why can't I forgive him? I just can't get it out of my mind. It's like the crash plays on a loop inside my head, and it won't go away.'

'Sweetheart, there's medication that can help you. I can get Jonathan to prescribe something for you, and you can talk to Paul, or Nick, or if that feels weird, we can find you someone else.'

Caleb frowns, fighting against the help I'm offering him.

'At least give it some thought, Cale. It will help you process what's going on in your head, help you deal with these thoughts you're having. I've spoken to both Paul and Nick a lot these last few months, and they've both helped me work through my feelings. You don't have to feel embarrassed, Cale. That's the last thing Dad wanted. The way his father conditioned his mind prevented him from getting help. He wouldn't want you to suffer in the same way.'

Caleb nods, still not committing to anything, but I'm encouraged that he hasn't outright refused.

A thick fog hung over me all day Wednesday, so by the time I woke up this morning, I was more than ready for the day ahead. Time to think about the more pleasant parts of my life.

'Where are you going, Mum?' Levi asks on the way to school. 'Are you working today?'

His question provides me the excuse I need. 'I'm heading in for a while and then I've got a few loose ends to tie up.' Levi nods, satisfied with my untruth.

The bundle of nerves balled up in my stomach had forced me to skip breakfast, so I swing by my favourite coffee shop to pick up coffee and almond croissants. A deep breath followed by a quick check in the vanity mirror and my nerves have settled long enough to ring Nick's doorbell. The reprieve lasts only until he answers the door with a welcoming smile and anticipation of what lies ahead swarms my belly like bees in a honeypot.

'I didn't know if you'd eaten,' I say, following him inside. 'I brought breakfast in case you hadn't. I got up early and didn't feel like eating and then when I was hungry, I was too nervous, so I picked these up at the coffee shop because I thought you might like a coffee, and now I just can't seem to stop talking.'

Nick puts the coffees down on the kitchen bench. He takes the brown paper bag from my hands and lays it beside them, then in one swift move, my face is in his hands and he presses his lips to mine. It's sweet and wholesome and just what I needed to dissipate my nerves.

'Don't be nervous, Steph, we will not do anything you don't want to do. I want to spend some time with you. More than a few stolen moments. We've got all day to ourselves, so relax.'

I puff out a stream of air from my lungs, soothed by Nick's calming voice.

'Thanks for breakfast, and no, I haven't eaten yet. I just got back from a run and jumped in the shower before you arrived,' he says, handing me a cup and grabbing two plates for the croissants.

'Sit down, make your self comfortable.'

I kick off my shoes and snuggle into the oversized leather couch. The soft chocolate brown cushions embrace my frame, and as I sip my coffee and bite into the flaky pastry, I begin to relax into the day. Nick sits close beside me, his leg hitched and his body angled to face me. We fall into a simple exchange, chatting about our week, skipping the darker parts and keeping things light.

'Millie asked if she can come and live with me,' Nick says.

'What did you say?' I ask.

'I told her the same as I always have. She knows she has the choice to live with me, but I'd prefer it not to be on the back of arguing with her mother.'

'Millie seems so laid back. I can't imagine her not getting along with anyone, but she wasn't happy with her mum that day at my house.'

Nick sighs. 'Millie and Sarah clash. Sarah is fastidious and doesn't like to relinquish control. Millie is easy going, but she'll always stand up for herself. Sarah hasn't been very accepting of Millie's sexuality and although Millie is tough, it must be draining to not feel accepted day after day.'

'I'm sure it would be.'

'I spoke to Sarah and hopefully eased some of her concerns. Millie said they had a big talk and managed to resolve their differences, so we'll see how things go.'

'Millie's such a gorgeous girl. I'm sure Sarah will see that her sexuality doesn't change that.'

'Millie told me what you said to her about standing up for herself and not worrying about making people uncomfortable,' Nick says. 'Thank you for that. It means a lot that you support my daughter.'

Nick's words flame in the pit of my stomach, firing me up from the inside.

'I'll support all your daughters, Nick, like I know you'll support my boys. I don't know what is happening between us, but I do know that you've become very important to me.'

Nick takes the empty plate from me, sliding it onto his own, and with an effortless motion he flips me around so I'm straddling him. My pulse thrums low in my belly and my breathing accelerates. I can feel his breath on my lips, warm from his coffee. His mouth hovers close to mine, but he doesn't make the next move. He waits. I wait. We're in a stalemate. A deep guttural moan emanates from his throat and the sexual tension swells. I ease my body closer to his, trying to relieve some of the pressure, and it's enough to tease him, to release his desire. His tongue runs wild and I grind against him with force, powerless to stop.

'This feels a little reckless.' My words are a whisper on my breath.

'I like reckless.' His eyes flash over my head before they settle back on mine. 'Shall we move it to the bedroom?'

I bite my lip and nod, emboldened by his words. He leans forward and picks me up in one calculated move, carrying me to his bedroom. He lays me on the bed and takes great pleasure in undressing me. My nerve endings twitch in anticipation. Nick wastes no time in removing his own clothes, then he brushes tiny sweeping kisses along every part of my body. His lips devour every curve until they reach my face, and when his tongue meets mine, they dance together, stroking and caressing until I'm moaning for more. Our eyes feast on each other as our bodies come together. I arch my back at the connection and we ride the wave until it crashes down around us.

Panting, I fight to get my breathing under control,

shuddering as my gasps settle. Nick hovers above me, his eyes filled with something I can't identify. They're intense like a full-bodied wine and whatever emotion he's feeling, it floods through me and I want to bottle it.

The morning flies by. Nick stretches out on his back while I curl into his side, tracing lazy circles on his firm abs. A sheet rests over us, skimming Nick's hip bones, and every so often I dip my fingers beneath the sheet, causing Nick to inhale a ragged breath. He reaches his hand across his stomach, interlacing his fingers with mine.

'My whole body is a bundle of nerve endings ready to explode,' Nick whispers into my hair.

'Mine too.'

'Are you okay?'

'I am. Let's not talk about real life and spoil it for me, though. I'm feeling content right now.'

'My lips are sealed.' He presses them together and tosses away an imaginary key. I see the moment he regrets the action, knowing it would remind me of Levi catching us kissing. It does prompt the memory, but it makes me giggle.

'I haven't talked to Levi about what he saw,' I say. 'I hope we didn't traumatise him too much.'

'The grin on his face told me he was ridiculously happy about it. Maybe not the actual kiss part, but what it would mean for him.'

'What does it mean for him, Nick? For all our kids?' My eyebrows crease in thought.

'Steph, it doesn't have to mean anything just yet. We can keep this as meaningful, or meaningless, as you like. You're calling all the shots here. Don't get caught up in putting a label on it.'

I ponder his words. 'Good luck with keeping it meaningless. I'm pretty sure we skipped right over that stage. Or I did at least.'

'Nothing about this is meaningless. I don't know why I said that. But whatever it is, we don't need to label it, not until we're both ready to.'

'You always say the right things. You have a talent.'

'That's good. My job kind of depends on it. If I said the wrong thing all day, I'm pretty sure I'd be out of business in a flash,' Nick grins, his lips brushing through my hair.

'Do you ever just sit and contemplate your future?' I wonder.

'Where are you going with this?'

'Nowhere in particular. I do sometimes, that's all. I picture my kids' partners and my grandchildren. I see myself travelling in my retirement and growing old, but the one thing that's always been absent from my thoughts is Chris.

'Since before he died, you mean?' My comment confuses Nick.

'Yes, always. I've never pictured him in my future and I've never even questioned that until now,' I muse. 'It doesn't upset me. I guess it just makes me wonder.'

Nick contemplates my thoughts. 'I don't think I have an answer to that. What do you see now in your future?'

'You want me to be honest?' I ask.

'Of course.' His voice is unsteady, perhaps worried about what I might say.

'I see lunch,' I grin.

We spend the afternoon snuggled together watching movies, and I have to pinch myself several times to check if this is real. Only a matter of months ago, I faced a very bleak future; one of heartache and sadness, of tragic loss and the struggle of raising two teenage boys alone. Now, here I am, on a random Thursday, lying in the arms of a man who, six months ago, had been nothing more than an acquaintance.

If I put too much thought into my current position, I will raise doubt, so I smile at the absurdity of it and feel grateful for every small sprinkle of happiness that comes my way. Nick's breaths grow slower as he rests his cheek on the side of my face, spooning me from behind, his leg wrapped around me like a cocoon. I allow myself to relax into him and feel the vast expanse of feelings that have cloaked me. My heart warms at the force of my emotions, but I'm not ready to give a name to them just yet.

Caleb

Dear Dad,

I was watching Mum earlier in the kitchen, just before I left to go to a party with Millie. She seemed nervous or worried. I'm not sure why. It's probably about me, though. I know I make this harder for her, although she's been happier lately and I think that's because of all the time she's been spending with Nick. It feels like he and Millie just fell into our lives one day and never left. I know I said it feels weird, and it still does sometimes, but I can also be myself when it's just Millie and me. She doesn't care if I'm in a bad mood and she doesn't try to cheer me up. She's honest with me and calls me out when I'm acting like a dick, but she listens to me and she's the only person I've opened up to. Mum still wants me to see a shrink, but I can't imagine talking to someone like that about all the things I've confided in to Millie.

I've fought so hard to not be like you, Dad, but some days I just don't have the energy to fight. My mind goes deep and I wonder what it would feel like if everything just went black. I hate you for doing it, yet some days the thought of disappearing feels so appealing. I've never told

Millie just how dark my mind gets, although I know she wouldn't judge me. The ironic thing is, I know you wouldn't judge me either. How could you?

Sometimes I feel like I have nothing left. I can feel Mum watching me, her eyes drilling into my head, hoping for a glimpse of my thoughts. I can't talk to her because I could never let her know how dark it gets inside my head. Mum and Levi are the only reason I'm still alive, Dad. They don't deserve to lose me the way we lost you, but on my darkest days, even thinking about them doesn't give me the willpower, when the bleakest thoughts swirl my mind, like a vortex, dragging me down.

I found out that Terri has cancer, and it pisses me off that someone who wants to live has to fight so hard for that. Why couldn't you have had cancer? Then you could've just died and I wouldn't have this monster growing inside me. Since Josh told me about his mum's cancer, I've thought a lot about myself. I feel so guilty for all the darkness inside me, for all the times I've wanted to end it all. I have to be here for Josh now too, and I just don't have the energy for that sometimes.

You thought you were leaving us to give us freedom, Dad, but all you've done is take me down with you.

I'll never forgive you.
Caleb

Steph

There's a comfort in the ordinary that is so powerful. Watching our kids' football games together and hanging out on weekends has been a significant source of healing. Even though we've had to limit our alone time, just being in Nick's company feels cathartic. He gives me a reason to not wallow in my sadness. He's an escape from the lonely, a tangible future I can almost touch, one whose edges are soft and welcoming, not painful and tragic. Even Caleb has warmed up to Nick and has taken small steps forward in his own healing.

'Has Millie decided what she'll do next season?' I ask Caleb, as we watch her game together.

'No, I don't think so. She'd love the challenge of playing for a better team, but she's so loyal and she enjoys her dad coaching her.' He looks wistful. 'I wish my dad had been as excited about me as Nick is about Millie.'

'He was, Cale. Watching you play made him proud. He always wanted the best for you.'

'It never felt that way. He made me feel like I was never good enough.' Caleb's shoulders slump and I wrap an arm around his waist, pulling him towards me.

'I'm sorry you feel that way Cale, it was his illness talking. I know that doesn't change how you feel, but I want you to know he was always proud of you. You're a lot like him; driven and determined. I think he was hard on you and pushed you because he felt that's what drove him to do well.'

'Yeah, maybe,' he says.

'You looked to be talking about something serious with Nick earlier…' I venture, immediately regretting my choice of words.

Caleb frowns. 'We were just talking football.' His walls go straight back up and I kick myself for not biting my tongue and leaving that subject well alone.

We watch the last quarter in frosty silence and the final siren couldn't come soon enough.

'Well played, Millie, you were amazing,' I say once they've wrapped up with the team.

'Thanks, Steph.'

'Hey Cale, I'm going to a party tonight, if you want to come?' Millie offers. 'A girl from the team is throwing it for her birthday.'

'Sure,' Caleb replies. 'If that's okay, Mum?' He's sheepish now, concerned I might say no after he's spent the last twenty minutes giving me the cold shoulder.

'Of course,' I say, forever treading on eggshells around him. I'm just thankful he's speaking to me, even if it is only because he's wants something. The kids walk on ahead back to the car park and I linger behind with Nick, walking slowly to grasp any chance at a fleeting moment alone.

'Hey, Levi's out tonight too if you fancy coming over,' I say in hushed tones.

Nick's grin lights up his face.

'I'd love to,' he beams. 'How about I come pick Caleb up, drop the kids at the party and grab takeout on my way back?'

'Sounds perfect.'

Nerves ambush me from out of nowhere as I pace the floor, waiting for Nick to return. It's not like we haven't spent time alone together, just not in my house where I lived with Chris, where I live with my boys. The more I think about it, the more it seems to worry me.

Nick's spent a lot of time here, on numerous weekends, chatting with Levi, tossing a ball with Cale and Millie, joining us for dinner, and even just the odd quiet coffee with me, but this is different. It feels more intimate, like he's encroaching. I don't want it to feel that way. I'm enjoying our time together, navigating our somewhat secret romance. Terri and Paul are the only ones who know there's something between us, and Levi and Millie have an idea, although I've never addressed it with either of the kids. Terri's been encouraging the relationship from the beginning, I think, to give her a focus other than her illness. With her mastectomy scheduled for next week, and an intense course of chemotherapy to follow, she'll need as much distraction as she can get, and I wouldn't be anywhere else but by her side.

The beam of headlights interrupts my brooding as Nick's Land Cruiser approaches. My belly flutters when I hear the car door slam and I hurry to the door to greet him.

'Hey,' Nick rasps, his husky voice sending a thrill up my spine. He ducks through the sliding door, hands loaded with food, dipping his head for a welcome kiss, his lips lingering before pulling away.

'Hi yourself,' I beam, my recent nerves eliminated.

'What did you get?' I ask, relieving him of one of the bags and taking a peek inside.

'Italian, is that okay?'

'It's wonderful. Thank you, I'm starving. I thought you'd never arrive. My nerves are shot. I've been pacing the house.'

'Yeah?' he frowns.

I shake my head, banishing his concern.

'Honest, I'm fine. We've just never been here alone before. The kids have always been home. It feels like a big step, being alone where I lived with Chris.' I don't know why it feels like such a big deal. 'Ignore me, I'm being ridiculous.'

'Steph, you're not being ridiculous, it's normal. After Lee died, it felt weird having another woman in my house. I felt like I was betraying her memory or something. Your feelings are valid, so don't brush them aside on my account. You know I'm with you every step of the way and if you have any doubts, we'll face them together.'

'I don't know what kind of divine intervention sent you my way, but I am grateful that you appeared in my life.'

Nick's mouth slips into a smirk. 'I think Paul would take the credit for that one, but please don't tell him he's a divine intervention. His ego is big enough. And for the record, I feel the same, Steph.'

His eyes search mine, and the moment catches between us like a polaroid, the moment we both know this has developed into something more. We linger in the weight of it, acknowledging the truth that hangs in the air, knowing neither of us is ready to speak the words aloud.

'Let's eat,' Nick says, releasing the pressure.

'Are you staying over?' I ask, my finger nervously rubbing the rim of the glass as I cradle my merlot.

'Do you want me to?' he whispers, hopefully.

'I do, if the kids are definitely okay to stay over at the party?'

'Yeah, I spoke to Paris's mum. She's got the girls inside and she's set up tents for the boys out the back. I'll pick them up in the morning. What time's Levi due back?' he asks.

'Not till after lunch. He has plans with his friends in the morning.'

Nick removes my glass from my anxious fingers and takes my hands in his. He leans in and brushes his lips against mine, sighing into me.

'Then, yes, I'm staying over,' he confirms.

I retract my hands and bring them to his face, tracing my fingers through the salt and pepper strands at his temples. My thumbs sweep his cheeks and his stubble tickles me. He watches intently, waiting to see what move I'll make next.

I hand him my heart.

'I love you.' My body stills as my mouth hovers over his lips, and my breath floats in the space between us.

Nick's eyes stare at me in disbelief. He said in the

beginning that he would hold on to the reins to keep things steady and not move too fast, but since the first time we slept together, he passed them to me and I've held all the control. I know he won't initiate any developments, but I've felt a shift between us. A shift that gave me the courage to say those words. Now I'm not so sure. The shocked look on his face has me doubting myself, but then his lips twitch and the edges track upwards.

'You do not know how that makes me feel.' His voice trembles as he speaks. 'I love you, too.'

I edge across the tiny fraction of space that separates us, my tongue twirling with his, tickling. Our bodies buckle, breaths shallow, lips and tongues picking up pace in a desperate search for more. I pull him backwards on the couch, pressing him against me, and we make out like horny teenagers.

Nick draws back, propping himself up on one elbow, his other hand on my hip. He peppers tiny kisses over my face as he reclaims his breath.

'You know, I never imagined I'd meet someone else after Lee died. I couldn't imagine anyone could replace her. She was so special. Then Sarah came along, and I guess the idea of having someone to share my girls with consumed me. I think I assumed my love for her would grow.' Nick pauses, his face saddened by the memory.

'Well, we both know how that ended.' He chuckles without humour. 'Meeting someone else after we split was not on my radar for a long time, but from that first day we spoke at my office, I knew you were special. It was way too soon for you to meet someone, but there was this undeniable chemistry and I could tell you felt it, too. Steph, I would have waited as long as it took for you to get on the same page, but I'm so glad I didn't have to wait too long. You make me so happy.'

'I'm happy too, Nick,' I say, my throat swollen with emotion. 'There was a time not all that long ago when I doubted I'd ever be happy again.' I cherish the look of love on Nick's face. 'Thank you for being everything I need. You really are the complete package.'

Nick grins. 'The complete package, huh? What does that include exactly?' he teases.

'Smart, kind, generous, respectful, honest, you know, the usual. Oh, and did I mention very, very sexy?' I bite my lip, going for seductive. It seems to work.

'Maybe you should show me exactly how sexy I am.'

Searching for Sunrise

Steph

I wake early on Sunday morning, limbs entwined with Nick's, his soft breaths humming in the still air. I untangle myself and stare at his face, peaceful in his sleep. A wave of uncertainty rolls through me, thinking about the reality of waking up with a man other than my husband in my bed. I fight my instinct to overthink it. He's here with me, and that's as much as I want to acknowledge. If I get caught up in the finer details, I imagine I will talk myself out of it, and that's somewhere I'm not willing to go.

I ease out of bed so I don't disturb him and pull on his t-shirt for ease, just to cover myself while I go feed all Levi's animals. Nick stirs and I lean over him, pressing a kiss to his lips.

'I'm just going to feed the animals. Don't go anywhere.'

Nick's eyes remain closed, but his smile widens, and he turns over to snuggle under the covers. I watch him a moment from the doorway and my heart lurches at the scene before me.

By the time I've completed the list of chores my son left me with, I'm wide awake and decide there's little chance of going back to sleep. I make coffee and carry the mugs to the bedroom where Nick's propped up on pillows, smiling to himself as he scrolls through his phone.

'Hey,' I say, 'I made coffee. I'm not sure if that's what you drink first thing. You don't have to drink it.' I'm babbling again, nervous that this is another first; waking up together.

'I'd love one, thanks babe,' he says, reaching out for the mug. The pet name makes me smile. I don't think I've ever been called babe before and hadn't expected it to start at my age.

'How did you sleep?' Nick asks, as I slide back under the covers beside him.

'Very well, it was nice not to be alone,' I admit.

'It was. It's been a long time for me. I could get used to this.'

'Me too,' I say, tilting the coffee mug to my mouth. A cheesy grin threatens to sweep my face.

'What time do you have to leave to pick the kids up?' I ask.

'Not for another couple of hours.' He runs his hand under the shirt I'm wearing, tempting me. I discard my coffee cup and reach for the hem of his t-shirt, grinning as I jerk it over my head.

'You're so beautiful.' He trails his lips across my skin.

'You make me feel beautiful.'

Nick blushes at my candour, and the flicker of flames on his cheeks blaze with passion. His lips trail their way to mine and he tastes the coffee on my breath. His fingers sweep a path down my body, brushing over my hip, and reach between my legs. I groan at his sensitive touch and widen my legs in anticipation. The fiery heat overpowers him, giving his libido a sudden boost. He moves between my legs, settling his muscular frame on top of me, bringing me relief. My eyes roll back as he takes me to a limit far beyond my expectations. His rhythm slows as we come down from our joint high and my muscles tense around him, unwilling to break the connection.

A sheen of sweat glistens across Nick's chest, glinting as the sunlight peeks through the blinds. I can't remember seeing anything more beautiful. I press my lips to his and lick off the sweat that has beaded on the stubble over his top lip.

Nick quirks a smile. 'Mmm, sweat and coffee. Tasty,' he says.

'You're very tasty Mr Salvatore, and amazing in bed.'

'Why thank you, Dr Wilson. You are, too.'

I love this playful side that's growing between us. Tragedy and sadness overshadowed the early days, and we spent our time together in deep conversation. Now that things are looking a little brighter, and we're exploring more facets of our relationship, we're both learning new things and his appeal has only strengthened. A smile radiates from my face as we bask in our post-coital bliss.

'Shower?' Nick asks, a tempting smirk forming on his lips.

The boys return, both exhausted for very different reasons. Caleb looks like he's partied hard and had no sleep and mud covers Levi's entire body from a bike ride with his friends. Caleb barely says two words, giving me the odd shrug when I question him about his night. Levi regales me with stories about all the fun he had, and I feel like normal service has resumed. My night of pleasure is nothing but a distant memory. I smile to myself once I'm alone, replaying every moment of my night with Nick. Chances of a repeat are slim, so I feel the need to relish in every single second.

'Hey Terri,' I say, when my phone makes me jump, intruding on the intimate thoughts racing around my head.

'Hey, I'm just trying to keep my mind off Tuesday, so I rang to revel in your raunchy gossip.'

'Well, if you'd been inside my head just then when the phone rang, you'd have got an x-rated video shoot, I can tell you.'

'Oh my, tell me more, you dirty little whore,' Terri teases.

I look around to make sure the boys are well out of earshot.

'The boys were both out last night, so he stayed over,' I begin.

'And?' Terri demands.

'And we had the most amazing night. Terri, he makes me so happy. I love him. Is that crazy?' I ask.

'Oh Steph, of course it's not crazy, it's wonderful. Have you told him?'

'I have, and he feels the same way. It was so nice to wake up with him in my bed. I wasn't sure how I'd feel about that and I'm not sure I was comfortable with the whole situation, but the way he makes me feel just seems to override all the gnawing thoughts in the back of my head. Shit Terri, he has skills.'

Terri laughs before dropping her voice to a more serious tone.

'It's natural that it feels weird, Steph. You were married to Chris for a long time. Nick's very different, but he loves you, and he makes you happy, and it will become more comfortable in time. I'm so pleased you've found him. You deserve to be happy.'

'Thank you for your support, Terri, but it should be the other way around at the moment. How are you feeling?' I switch the conversation back to my friend and her impending surgery.

'I'm okay, resigned to the fact that it's a measure that's needed in order to save my life, so I'm trying to go with the flow,' Terri says.

'That's positive. You'll get through this Terri, I know you will. I'll call Mark on Tuesday night to see if you're up for visitors, otherwise I'll call in on Wednesday to see you. Take care of yourself, won't you? And Josh has my number if he needs anything, right? And I mean anything, Terri, okay?'

'I know, and yes, he does. He said he wouldn't go to footy training on Tuesday, but he might change his mind if I'm okay. He'll let you know if he needs a lift.'

'No worries, whatever he needs,' I assure her. 'I'll see you soon, okay?'

'Thanks Steph, bye.'

It's a tense start to the week with Terri going to the hospital. Nerves are frazzled and Levi seems to be holding both me and Caleb together. Both of us are worried about our friends, and I have no idea when

I'll see Nick again. This feels like the time I need him most. A few stolen moments on the phone each night before we go to sleep is as much as we've managed, but it falls short of a physical hug. I want to feel him breathing, feel the comfort of his arms around me. Keeping our relationship secret is hard, but I don't want to jeopardise Caleb's wellbeing, not when he seems stable. He's a little more down than up, but nothing I'm too concerned about.

I don't get to see Terri until Thursday due to complications from the surgery. It means the one day of the week I get Nick alone is out of the window. I feel selfish for thinking that when my friend is lying in a hospital bed about to start the fight of her life, and I don't mean it that way, I'm just fragile and need a comforting shoulder.

Terri has drifted in and out of sleep several times while I've been sitting at her bed side. She's on strong pain medication that makes her drowsy, but we've managed a few brief conversations in between.

'Steph,' Terri croaks, her throat sore from the intubation.

I look up in surprise, thinking she'd drifted back to sleep.

'What's wrong? Do you need something?' I ask.

Terri puts all her energy into a smile.

'Yes, I need you to go home or see that man of yours. You need to relax and stop worrying about me. The doctors say I'm improving.'

'I know, but I needed to see for myself. I will go, though, and let you get some rest.'

'Give him a hug from me, and tell him I said you need some special loving,' Terri winks and closes her eyes in readiness for another sleep. I lean over and kiss her forehead.

'See you soon.'

Thinking about my next move, I weigh up my options. Taking a moment of self-care is more important than anything I have waiting for me at home.

I ring Nick's doorbell and wait several minutes, hoping he's home. After my second push of the bell, I hesitate before turning to leave, disappointed. The door creaks open, stopping me in my tracks, and when I look back, there he is with wet hair and a towel in his hand.

'Hey, sorry, I just got out of the shower. Come on in.' The kindness brimming in his eyes is all I need to fall apart.

Nick pulls me into the house and kicks the door shut behind me, drawing me into his arms and holding me tight. The weight of his head resting on mine feels comforting as I sob into his chest.

'What's wrong?' he asks once my tears subside.

'Nothing,' I sniffle. 'I'm just exhausted, and I needed a hug.'

'Oh baby, come here.' He tightens his hold until my breathing levels out and then releases me, taking me by the hand and leading me to sit down.

'Can I get you anything?' he asks.

'No, I just needed to see you. Sorry for barging in on you unannounced and having a meltdown.'

'There's nothing to be sorry for. That's what I'm here for. For all of it. I love you, Steph, I'm all in.'

I force a smile and sink into his side. We sit in stillness, his arm around my shoulders tracing patterns on my neck with his fingertips.

'How's Terri? Did you see her?' he asks.

'She's doing okay under the circumstances. Josh has been worried, Cale's been worried about Josh, and I've been worried about all of them. This is the one week I could have done with you in my bed every night. Waking up with you last weekend was incredible, and I want to tell the kids about us soon. I don't know how Cale will react, but I'd rather talk to him about it than he find out some other way.'

'There's no rush, Steph. You need to focus on Terri right now, and take care of you,' Nick says.

'I guess I should go. Thank you for being exactly what I needed.' I lean in and kiss him, my lips lingering on his, needing to breathe him in for a moment.

'Will I see you this weekend?' he asks, before I leave.

'I'll make sure of it.'

Nick

Nick's time alone with Steph seemed to dwindle in the following weeks. Although Terri was recovering well from the operation, her chemotherapy had begun and Steph was determined to be there every step of the way, just like Terri had been for her since she'd lost her husband.

Caleb's football season was coming to a close, and Steph worried about the consequences that would have on him. Football seemed to keep him on an even keel and although there'd still be training in the off season, she knew it was the competitive element of the game where he thrived. With this dark cloud plaguing her, Nick knew she wasn't devoting enough time to herself. He understood her concern for her son and her need to help her friend, but he missed her, and their relationship being secret was becoming a problem. He was running low on excuses to drop by. They still spoke on the phone most nights, but it wasn't the same.

Nick spent as much time as he could with Levi, not only to improve Levi's skills on the harder tracks and increase his fitness, but because he enjoyed his company and it meant he could catch some stolen moments with his mother. Levi had hounded Nick during their rides, asking questions about the seriousness of his relationship with his mum.

'You've been quiet today, Nick. Is everything okay?' Levi asked as they loaded their bikes onto the bike rack. They'd come out early for a quick ride before Caleb's grand final, but Nick's mind had been elsewhere.

'I know, I'm sorry, Levi,' Nick said, humbled by Levi's mature intuition. 'To be honest, I've been thinking about your mum.'

'Is she okay?' Levi frowned.

'Yeah, nothing to worry about. Her focus has been on Terri and Cale and I haven't seen her much. I miss her. It's hard keeping us a secret from Cale and I'm running out of excuses to drop by unannounced.'

'Oh, so I'm your excuse to drop by, am I? I thought we'd been out riding more than usual.'

'It's not like that, Levi. You know I love riding with you,' Nick huffed.

'Just kidding. She misses you, too. I can tell.'

Nick threw a grateful smile at his riding buddy.

Millie's team hadn't made the playoffs, so her season ended a few weeks before Caleb's. It had freed up Nick's time, which only added to the reason he was feeling at a loose end. He'd been looking forward to the final. As a former player, and a football coach himself, Caleb's talent impressed him. Nick's interest in his football appeared to have cracked Caleb's hard shell, and he was opening up more easily. Between him and Millie, Caleb seemed to respond well to their input.

That afternoon, everyone arrived to watch. Nick and Millie sought out Steph, who was on the sidelines with Terri and Mark. Terri was between chemo treatments and wasn't feeling her best, but there was no way she was missing out on her own son's final.

'Hey guys,' Nick said, approaching the group. 'How are you feeling, Terri?' he asked, his concern for her warming Steph's heart. She smiled at the exchange.

'I feel shit, thanks Nick, but I look a million dollars, so that's always a bonus.'

Humour helped Terri handle her illness, and the group joined in with her laughter.

'Hey.' Nick manoeuvred himself to Steph's side. Their relationship was common knowledge among the people here, so they needn't be hypervigilant, but he still didn't want to flaunt their relationship in public.

'Hi,' Steph said, her eyes zoning in on his. 'I've missed you,' she mouthed, and turning to the group, asked, 'who wants coffee?'

'Can I get hot chocolate please, Mum?' Levi asked.

'Oh, me too,' said Millie.

'Sure guys, Nick, do you want to come and help me carry them?' she asked, finding an excuse to get a few moments alone.

'Of course,' Nick grinned.

'I like your style. It feels like I haven't had you to myself in forever,' Nick said, coming to a halt in the queue at the coffee van.

'It was all I could come up with.'

Nick leaned in and dropped a discreet kiss on her lips.

'I thought that maybe if Caleb's team wins today, and he's in high spirits, we should talk to him, tell him we're together.'

Nick's forehead crinkled in thought.

'You don't think we should?' Steph asked, surprised by his hesitation.

'Of course I want to tell him. I want to be with you more than anything, but I don't think basing our decision on Caleb's emotional state is the way to go,' Nick said. 'That's a lot of pressure.'

Steph's eyes brimmed with tears. 'You're right, I don't know what I was thinking.'

'Hey, it's fine. If you feel ready to go public, then we should, just not on the back of Caleb's mood. His depression is internal. It's all tied up in the way he feels about his dad, and the way he died. It isn't about what's happening in your life. I get not wanting to rock the boat when he seems to be improving, but us being together won't change his feelings about his dad. You can't walk on eggshells forever, Steph, he will have to learn to deal with his feelings, and learn to process the things he can't control.'

'You're right, I know. We'll tell them all tonight.'

Caleb and his team fought hard. The result was close, but they came away without the win, and their faces were glum as they watched the winning team celebrate. Steph had invited everyone over for dinner that evening, but Terri had cancelled at the last minute, citing exhaustion.

'Don't even apologise, Terri,' Steph said. 'You

need to take care of yourself and get some rest.' She came off the phone and relayed the news to Nick.

'That's a shame,' Nick said, 'but it's understandable. She did look fatigued earlier.'

Steph's shoulders slumped.

'Hey, are you okay?' he asked.

'I am. It's just hard watching her go through this. I've watched so many of my patients deal with cancer, some with great outcomes, and others not so lucky, but always, it's a long, hard battle.'

'I'm sure, but she's surrounded by love and support. She's got this.'

'I'm worried about Caleb, too,' she said. 'He's been miserable all afternoon.'

'That's only natural Steph, he lost a big match. Don't analyse it.'

'I can't help it. I know he's come a long way these past few months, thanks to you and Millie. You've both done a fantastic job of getting him talking and getting him out of the house. I can't thank you both enough, especially Millie. She's been amazing with him. The two of them meeting couldn't have had a better outcome, so thank you for making that happen.'

'What the hell?' Caleb appeared in the doorway and Steph froze, knowing he had misinterpreted her words.

'Caleb,' she warned, as he turned and punched his fist in to the door. 'Caleb, stop! It's not what you think.'

'You know what I think? I think you set this whole thing up, becoming friends with the psych you wanted me to see and setting me up with his daughter. Was she in on it, too? I can't believe you'd do this to me.'

'That's not how it was, Caleb. I wanted you to see Nick, but you didn't want to and I left it at that. Nick and I became friends, and him and Levi became friends. Millie just happened to be with Nick when he came over. Your friendship with her is between you. We had nothing to do with it.'

'That's bullshit. You set me up.'

'Caleb—' Nick interjected.

'No, you can fuck off, too. I'm not talking to you. You can get the hell out of my house and take your lying bitch of a daughter with you.'

'Caleb!' Steph watched him turn and stalk towards his bedroom, paying her no attention.

She broke down, her shoulders heaving, and Nick enclosed her in his arms, not caring who saw them.

'What was that about?' Millie's voice trembled as she came in from outside. 'I heard all the yelling.'

Steph pulled out of Nick's arms and saw Millie's distraught face. It was obvious she'd heard what Caleb had called her.

'Millie, he didn't mean it,' Steph said. 'He's just angry.' Nick pulled his daughter in for a hug.

'What happened?' she asked, confused.

'Steph was thanking me, and you too, for helping Caleb, and he got the wrong end of the stick thinking we'd engineered the whole friendship between you.'

'And did you?' Millie asked.

'Of course not. I thought I might help him if I could get him to talk to me, and you two becoming friends was just a bonus. But our friendship, and yours, has been natural,' Nick said.

'Let me go talk to him,' Millie said.

'I think you should leave him to calm down, Millie, and speak to him when he's less angry,' Nick said. 'Maybe we should go, Steph.'

Steph nodded. The fight drained out of her. He didn't want to leave her like this, but he had to. She would need to talk to Caleb alone. Nick took her in his arms again and pressed a kiss to her lips. 'Call me if you need me, okay? I love you,' he said. He hadn't told Millie things had progressed that far, but she wasn't stupid. She seemed to know before he did.

Millie smiled, catching Steph's eye as they pulled apart.

'Are you okay with this, sweetheart?' Steph asked.

'Of course, I'm happy for you guys,' Millie said. 'Let me know if I can help.'

Nick draped his arm across Millie's shoulders as they said goodbye.

Caleb

Dear Dad,

Forget everything I ever said about Millie. It turns out she was a lying bitch, after all. I can't believe I trusted her. I told her everything and I bet she's just gone and told her dad everything I've said to her in confidence. She was the only person I could talk to and now I have no one. Is this how you felt, Dad? This never ending pain? I understand you now. I'm sorry, Dad, but I can't do this anymore. Turns out I am like you after all.

Caleb

Steph

I sink to the kitchen floor, feeling like everything good in my life has been ripped from under me. Footsteps sound beside me, and Levi's wiry frame slides down next to me.

'Hey Mum, you okay?' he asks. 'Where did Nick and Millie go?'

I tilt my head sideways and rest it on Levi's shoulder.

'I thought we'd got through the hard stuff, but it seems not.' I shake my head and share the drama with him.

'What does it even matter?' he asks. 'Caleb likes Millie, and if Nick's helped him too, it's not like he's had to sit in a stuffy room and spill his feelings. He's only said what he's wanted to.'

'I know, sweetheart, but he feels like we've coerced him. He thinks his friendship with Millie is fake, and she only spends time with him to help him get better because we wanted her to. That's not the case, but I can see where he's coming from.'

Levi nods and starts putting away all the unprepared food.

'I'm guessing you're not gonna cook this now,' he says.

'I'm not hungry anymore. Do you want me to order you a pizza?' I ask.

'I'll get one later,' he says, reaching up to the cupboard for a wine glass and pouring me a drink from the open bottle on the bench top.

'You're an angel, Levi.'

'I'm gonna go grab a shower, then I'll order pizza. You enjoy your wine.'

'Mum!' Levi's howl rips through my gut and I bolt down the hall towards the pained sounds.

'No, Caleb, no!' A high-pitched squeal pierces through the white noise building in my head as I take in the scene that greets me. This is my worst nightmare. My son lies motionless on the bathroom floor while his brother is kneeling over him, slapping his face, trying to wake him. Several discarded blister packs litter the vanity and a near empty bottle of vodka sits beside them. I freeze. The pressure in my head drowns out everything around me except that guttural yowl. 'No, no, no, no, Cale.'

'Mum! Do something!' A hand grips my shoulder and Levi's panic breaks through my stupor.

Since the very first moment I held Caleb in my arms, being a mother has been the most important role in my life. I've worked hard to provide an exceptional service to my patients, but if my kids have needed me, I've always come running. Being a mum trumps being a doctor every time. Until now. Now I have to push every single maternal instinct aside and be the doctor I'm trained to be.

'Levi,' I bark orders. 'Call triple zero. Ask for an ambulance and tell them your brother has overdosed and is unconscious.'

I speak clearly and calmly, then check Caleb's airways before moving him into the recovery position. His pulse is a little thready, and he's breathing, so I sit and stroke his head, talking to him until the ambulance arrives.

Levi invites the paramedics into the house and shows them where to go. I provide an outline of Caleb's history and the medication he's taken, and leave the bathroom to give them room to help Caleb. In the hall, Levi slouches on the floor, shaking, tears streaming down his face.

'Why did he do it, Mum? Will he die?' he sniffs.

'Oh sweetheart, come here,' I say, pulling him into a hug. 'He's in the best hands. They'll do everything they can for him.'

The paramedics work on him for a while before transferring him to the ambulance.

'Can my son come in the ambulance with us? I don't want to leave him alone,' I ask, dread flooding back through me.

'Of course, hop up son,' the man says.

The journey to the hospital is the single longest thing I've ever endured. In reality, it takes no more than twenty minutes, but fear has gripped me tight and is playing on an endless loop. I feel helpless; a much too common thread in my life. My ashen face turns to Levi, and I watch him bite his lip.

'Mum, I'm gonna need to call someone to come and deal with the animals,' he says, just as the ambulance pulls to a stop outside the emergency department. 'Can I ask Nick? Or is that not a good idea?'

I don't know that it's the best idea under the circumstances, but Levi and I both know he's the only person either of us would choose at a time like this.

'Call him.'

The medical team rushes Caleb through for emergency help, while I'm ushered to a small bay to wait with Levi for news. Nick promised Levi he would sort out the animals and let him know he'd be there for us all, whatever we need. I didn't doubt him for a second.

Levi and I cling to each other in anguish while Caleb undergoes a multitude of tests and treatments. Once he's deemed to be in a stable condition, we're allowed in to see him. I've been a doctor for many years, but never have I felt so distraught at seeing a patient hooked up to machines keeping him alive. I sob at the edge of his bed, guilt and shame riding high as I think about the reasons my son is lying before me, fighting for his life. Just like my initial reaction to Chris's suicide note, I blame myself for this, too. Reason tells me it isn't my fault, but I'm his mother and I should have tried harder.

I close my eyes. My head rests on Caleb's hospital bed while the doctors and nurses come and go, and for once in my life wish I was a lay person with no medical knowledge. I don't want to know what the doctors are saying. Why can't I be oblivious, in my little bubble, unaware of the severity of my son's condition? I have no clue how long I've been sitting here, I don't have my phone with me, and I'm conscious I don't know where Levi is.

My chair scrapes the floor when I jump up, panicked for a second.

'Excuse me, have you seen my other son?' I duck my head through the curtain and ask the closest nurse.

'Levi?' the nurse quizzes. 'Yes, he went out to the waiting room earlier, said your partner was out there.'

I react to the term she uses and wonder if Levi used that description of Nick.

'Thank you,' I say. 'I might just nip out and check. Can I get back in?'

'Of course, just buzz the intercom and I'll open the door for you.' The nurse's smile is filled with compassion.

I stop dead when I walk into the waiting room to see Levi sobbing in Nick's arms. Several scenarios have gone through my mind in the last who knows how many hours and I wonder how much I've missed while my relationship with Nick has preoccupied my mind. I've blamed that for Caleb's current condition and have thought more than once about ending it. But watching him now take care of my son only cements the reason he's in my life. I love him, and his presence has acted as nothing but a positive influence in all our lives. Caleb's condition is separate from my relationship with Nick, and I have to remind myself of that.

Nick pulls back from their embrace and grasps Levi's shoulders with both hands. His voice is low and I'm unable to hear from this distance, but I know he's speaking from his heart, his only goal to settle Levi's mind. My breath stumbles at the power of the moment I'm witnessing between my son and the man I love, and I'm overwhelmed at the depth of the affection that swells inside me.

Levi nods at Nick's words, then looks up and catches my eye. He touches Nick's arm and tilts his head towards me, letting him know I'm here. Nick's eyes fill and he hastens across the room, sweeping me into his arms before my knees buckle and I collapse into him. He clutches me, holding me, soothing.

'How's he doing?' Nick asks, as he leads me to a chair to sit down.

'I don't know, Nick, not good, that's for sure. They're doing what they can.'

'Is there anything I can get for you? Or I can take Levi home? Whatever you need, Steph, I'm here for you,' Nick says.

'What time is it?' I ask, more than a little dazed.

'A little before five o'clock.'.

'In the morning? We've been here all night?'

'Yes, I'm sure Levi will want to get back for his animals, so why don't I take him home and I can grab you a change of clothes, a toothbrush, a decent coffee maybe?'

'Thank you.'

'That's what I'm here for,' he says, his lips brushing my temple. 'You go back and be with Caleb. Is there anything else you need?'

'I don't know.'

'Don't worry, I'll grab a few things for you,' he says. 'I love you.'

I nod, too choked by the situation to speak.

Lyndsey Jeminson

Steph

Had someone asked me a year ago to name the words that best describe me, I would have come up with a list containing words such as honest, loyal, caring, strong, thoughtful, passionate. Right now I would struggle to get past helpless, inadequate, incapable, feeble. Knowing someone you love is in such a dark place that they feel there is no option but to end their life is like something out of a horror movie, but when you find yourself in the middle of that horror movie, you must dig deep and claw your way out. You have to out-think and outsmart the monster.

I've been here before. The days and weeks following Chris's funeral and the discovery of his secret battle were the lowest moments I ever thought I'd see. I survived. I got through it, and never imagined I'd be back there, in the darker, terrifying and chilling sequel. But here I find myself, sitting at Caleb's bedside, watching the monster as it draws my son away. Physically, he's recovering well, but when I look in his eyes, there's no fight left.

He's angry. Angry at me, at Millie and Nick, for coming into his life under the guise of friendship, but mostly he's angry at his father. Millie has begged to visit Cale to explain there was never any ulterior motive in their friendship, but Caleb flat out refused to see anyone. He's refused to see me too, but he has no say in that.

There are two significant differences in this sequel to the horror story of my life. Caleb didn't die and I have Nick. He has been a partner in every sense of the word this week, and his love and support have gone way beyond the level of our relationship. Juggling his own work schedule so he could be there for Levi while I've been at the hospital, cooking dinner and making me eat, and keeping my bed warm every night, caring for me so I can focus on Caleb. The love I have for him has shifted to a place where I can't keep him secret anymore. He deserves a legitimate role in my life, not one where we have to sneak around and pretend. I want to love him on my own terms.

They moved Caleb to the mental health ward as soon as he was physically fit. They've been working with him and he is now deemed fit for discharge under a mental health care plan. I'm trying to be positive for Caleb, but the thought of him coming home terrifies me. He's now on medication, and although we might not see any improvement for some time, I hold out some hope that this might be a turning point. All I can do is watch and wait and trust.

'Okay, Caleb, it's time to go,' the nurse chirps when she enters his room. There's no response from Caleb, just a deadpan face with downcast eyes.

'Thank you,' I say, holding out my hands for the paperwork and medication the nurse offers me.

'Take care of yourself, mate, I look forward to cheering you on when you're wearing the blue and gold,' the nurse says, when Caleb slips off the bed to leave. 'You'll do it. I have faith.'

The tiniest hint of a smile ghosts Caleb's face, and a seed of optimism plants itself in my belly. Football is the only thing in his life that is going to get Caleb through this. It's the only thing that brings him any sense of joy. I just hope we'll be able to keep him motivated to keep training. I have to make that my priority. That will be my fight because there is no way this movie is getting another sequel. I won't allow a franchise to take hold.

I park my car under the carport and switch off the engine. Caleb makes no move to get out, and I know in my heart that I have to do this now. The way I was raised provided me with the ability to think critically and to believe in myself. My career has given me financial independence and the knowledge that I never have to rely on anyone. What this means to many people, myself included, is that we should struggle through difficult times alone. There is no weakness in asking for help, for wanting someone beside you to share the burden. If my family learns nothing else from the tragedy and trauma of the last few months, then I need us all to know that.

'How are you feeling?' I ask.

Caleb shrugs, his eyes concentrated on the dash.

'Are you glad to be home?' I try again.

There isn't even an acknowledgement this time. I blow out a breath, knowing what I have to tell him has no bearing on his depression, but feeling like it could send him spiralling at the same time.

'Cale, there's something I want to talk to you about,' I begin. My voice wavers as I force out the words. Caleb glances at me, a speck of intrigue in his eyes.

'So, I was going to tell you kids after your final, but then… well, it didn't happen.' I bite my lip, angst soaring across my mind. 'I want you to know that Nick and I are together,' I say, 'in a relationship.' Caleb glares at me, his anger rising fast.

'Are you fucking kidding me?' he yells. It's the first time he's spoken anything more than a mumble in days, not that I'm impressed with the words he's chosen.

'Caleb, I don't appreciate you speaking to me like that,' I say, keeping my voice calm under the circumstances. 'I know you think I dreamed up some elaborate scheme with Nick and Millie to trick you into getting help, but that's just not true. Yes, Paul recommended Nick to me, and when I spoke to him, we thought he could help you. But then we became friends and Millie came along and you seemed to improve without Nick getting involved. I promise you, Cale, it didn't happen how you think and you've hurt Millie by jumping to conclusions and not hearing her out.'

Caleb opens his door and gets out without a word,

slamming it behind him and heading towards the house. I let him into the house and slump down on the outdoor couch with my dogs, unleashing a stream of tears I can no longer hold back. My phone buzzes in my pocket, but I don't have the energy to answer it. There's no one I want to speak to right now, not even Nick. I don't even know what will happen between us now that Caleb's home, and that's not a place I'm ready to visit. Nick has been staying here for the last week, helping with Levi and just acting as moral support for the both of us. I've got used to having him in my bed. Of course, I'd known it was only a temporary arrangement, but a part of me hoped he might at least be able to spend more time here on the weekends. Caleb's reaction has brought an abrupt end to that thought.

My phone buzzes again and a voice mail pops up. Nick's recorded voice lets me know he'll pick Levi up from school, and also asks if there's anything I need. Sometimes it's not the unkind people that bring pain, it's the warm-hearted and loving ones. The fear that I could lose him at any moment thrums in my gut.

The sound of tyres crunching on the gravel startles me from sleep. I sit up and brush my fingers through my hair. A glance at my watch alerts me to the fact I've been asleep for a couple of hours. Levi rounds the corner with a bright smile on his face.

'Hey Mum, is Cale home?' he asks.

'He is. He's in his room. Go check if you like,' I say, forcing my lips to curl upwards.

Levi fusses over the dogs before heading inside to see his brother leaving me alone with Nick.

'Hey babe, how are you?' he asks, dropping a kiss on my forehead before taking a seat next to me.

'It's been a day.' I sigh and rest my head on his shoulder.

'Do you want to talk about it?' he offers.

'I told Cale about us.'

'Oh?'

I shake my head. 'I guess it went as well as I expected. He yelled, he swore, he stormed out of the car.'

'I'm sorry,' Nick says, throwing an arm around me and drawing me in. 'He'll come around. Once his medication kicks in, that cloud will lift and he'll have the tools to deal with things rationally.'

'I hope so. I don't want to lose you, Nick.'

'You won't,' he whispers, kissing my ear.

'What's he doing here?' Caleb's voice booms, laced with vitriol.

'Caleb, can we just sit down and talk this through?'

'There's nothing to talk about. I don't want him in my house.' His words are venomous.

'With all due respect, Caleb, it's my house,' I choke.

Caleb grunts. 'Fine. It's not like I want to be here anyway,' he says, storming back inside. Chills travel up my arms, rising from my fingertips. My mouth hangs open and my eyes fill with fear. I jump out of my seat to follow him. 'Steph…' Nick says. 'I don't think that's what he meant.' I ignore him and take off after Caleb, unprepared for what I walk in on.

'Boys!' With entangled limbs and flying fists, I

attempt to pull them apart, but neither will surrender. Seeing my sons' fighting breaks my heart, especially when we've been through so much already. An accidental elbow to my eye pulls me up sharply, and I take a shaky step back. Nick, who had followed me inside in time to witness the incident, yells with a booming voice that contradicts his usual mellow tone.

'Stop!' He grabs both boys by the arm and pulls them apart. He sits Levi on one chair and Caleb on the other, then taking my hand, he examines my face. I wince as he touches the skin that has split at the corner of my eye. Blood is pooling there and I can feel the throb of a lump forming at the edge of my eyebrow. It won't look pretty tomorrow.

'Are you okay?' he whispers, his voice now back to its normal, calming self. I nod in reply, wondering what he's going to say to the boys now he has them captive, or whether he deems his involvement over and he'll leave the rest to me. My eyes drift to where my boys sit, both looking at the floor. Nick pulls up a chair and sits facing them.

'Okay,' he begins, 'I know I am no one to either of you, but I want you to listen to me because your mum is important to all three of us.' Levi jerks his head up to face Nick and the guilt that washes over him is clear. He likes Nick and has a lot of respect for him; he will hate the thought that Nick might think less of him.

'You boys have had a tough ride. You're hurting. I understand that—'

'You don't understand shit,' Caleb interrupts.

'Caleb, I'd like to discuss this like men, so once I've said what I have to say, you'll then get your turn. Now, if you'll please let me finish. You've been through a lot, more than many people go through in a lifetime, but your mum,' he says, his voice snagging on the emotion that's welling up inside him, 'she's been there for you through it all. You boys are her priority and she has done everything in her power to help you get through this difficult time. Your actions have caused her pain. Not just in the damage you have done to her face, but you've caused her mental and emotional anguish. She doesn't deserve that.'

Both boys hang their heads in shame before finding their way to a mumbled apology.

'Caleb, I understand you have misgivings about me being in your mum's life, and your feelings about that are valid. I hope that in time you will accept us being together, because I love her very much.' Caleb's eyes bore into Nick's, not giving an inch. 'As far as Millie's concerned, the only reason she came here at all was because she was with me when I'd arranged to take Levi out, so I can hand on heart say that whatever friendship has developed between the two of you was on your terms and nothing to do with me. Please give her a chance to speak to you.' Nick pauses. 'That's all I have to say. If you have anything you want to add, I'm listening.'

Nick sits back in his chair and I'm dumbfounded by the way he's holding their attention.

'I'm sorry, Mum,' Levi says, more clearly this time. 'I'm sorry I punched Caleb, and I'm sorry you got caught up in it.'

'Thank you Levi, I appreciate that,' I say. The tension in the air crackles as our three expectant faces wait for Caleb to speak. He makes no eye contact with any of us and remains quiet in his seat, not even attempting to leave.

'Alright,' Nick says. 'If that's all there is to say, I'll leave you to have some family time together.'

'I'll walk you out,' I say.

Nick leans against his car and pulls me towards him, enveloping me with his arms. He scatters tender kisses in my hair and breathes me in.

'Thank you.' I pull back to take in his face. 'I don't know what I would've done without you here.'

Nick smiles. 'Let's be honest, if I hadn't been here, that wouldn't have happened. I'm sorry for causing problems, Steph. If you need me to stay away, I can.'

That's the last thing I want, but when life throws us curveballs, we don't always get a choice.

'I don't know, Nick. Emotions are running high and it might be best to cool things a little.'

Nick nods his understanding and his forlorn face breaks my heart. There's no winning scenario here. Whichever way I jump, I will hurt someone I love.

'Maybe we can work around the kids, Nick,' I say, unable to let him go.

'I'll miss you,' he whispers. 'I've loved being in your bed this past week; it's given me a glimpse of a future that I'm very much keen for.'

I'm galvanised by his words and a small glimmer of light shines amid all the pain.

Searching for Sunrise

Steph

'Hey Josh, it's good to see you,' I say, when he opens the door.

'How's Caleb?' Josh asks.

I sigh, unsure if I can answer his question with any modicum of truth. 'I don't know, love. Some days I think he's improving and other days I get nothing from him. Have you spoken to him much since he came home from the hospital?'

Josh shrugs, a guilty look crossing his face.

'We had a fight. I don't know what to say to him anymore.'

'It's okay, Josh. You take care of yourself. You have enough going on. I'll worry about Cale. He'll get better, he has to.'

Josh nods and points to the lounge room. 'Mum's in there.'

'Hi lovely, how are you?' I ask when I'm greeted by my friend sprawled out on the couch. Terri tries to sit up, but I encourage her to stay. 'Don't move, I'll sit here,' I say, perching on a nearby chair.

'I'm so sorry I haven't been here for you through your treatment, Terri.'

Terri's eyes fill. 'Steph, don't you dare apologise to me. I'm so sorry for what you're going through. How's he doing?'

'Not great, if I'm honest. He's on medication and he's seeing a psych at the hospital, but I don't know. I've been hoping for some big breakthrough, but he doesn't seem to get anywhere. There's so much anger inside him. I told him about me and Nick and he just lost it. Levi punched him. For what, I haven't got to the bottom of, and they ended up having to be pulled apart by Nick. I've had to cool things with him a little, which is killing me, but I can't risk losing Caleb.'

'It won't be for long, Steph. I'm sure Caleb will be fine with Nick once he gets better,' Terri says.

'God, I hope so. The thought of having to let him go horrifies me.'

'That won't happen. I won't let it. Nick's been wonderful to us while you were in the hospital with Cale,' Terri gushes.

'How do you mean?' I ask, confused.

'He called round several times to see how he could help, picked Josh up from school when he had Levi, and cooked us some meals. I've only recently met the man, yet he did so much for us because he knew you weren't able to.'

A prickle creeps down my spine. Is there no end to this man's generosity? He seems too good to be true.

'He never even mentioned it,' I say, incredulous.

'You've got yourself a good man there, Steph.'

My afternoon with Terri brings welcome relief from my worries despite Terri's own struggle. It feels good to just be in a different environment, focusing my attention elsewhere for a while. Laughter has been absent in my life for the last few weeks, and it's refreshing to laugh with my friend in the midst of fighting our own battles. I feel encouraged by the time I arrive home.

The house is quiet and there's no sign of Levi in the garden. I call out to the boys, but there's no response. That alone sets my nerves on edge and smashes my jovial mood out of the park. I make my way with a laughable amount of stealth towards the boys' bedrooms, first checking Levi's and finding it empty. The door to Caleb's room is ajar and I can hear voices, happy ones. I peek through the gap and see Caleb and Levi, sitting together on Cale's bed, gaming. They're laughing and joking together and although it tears at my heart to move away, I don't want them to see me. I've longed for this moment for months now, seeing my boys happy in each other's company, and I want nothing to disrupt that. My heart full, I edge away from the door, leaving them to it.

When Monday morning comes around, Caleb has got himself up and is dressed for school. He hasn't mentioned going back to school and I've been tossing up whether I should broach the subject. I was thinking he might need more time, so I've cut my hours at work right back so I can be home for him. The shock of seeing him in his school uniform tucking into breakfast is clear on my face.

'Hey Mum,' Caleb greets me, with a lift in his

voice I haven't heard in a long while.

'Morning sweetheart, you're feeling ready to go back to school?' I ask.

'Yeah, I guess. Isn't that what you want?' he asks, confused.

'Of course, as long as you feel ready,' I say.

I smile at him as Levi bursts through the door in a hurry to go shower.

'Hey Mum, won't be long, I promise. Billie went missing, and I found her next door. I need to fix the fence this afternoon,' he says, running down the hall towards the bathroom.

I laugh at the whirlwind that is my youngest son and raise my eyebrows at Caleb.

'Does he even know how to fix a fence?' I ask.

'No idea!' Caleb laughs. 'But I'm sure he has more of a clue than me.'

A shift has taken place. Caleb's demeanour has changed and the light shines a little brighter in his eyes. It's only small, but I will grab onto it with both hands.

Our receptionist throws me a double take when I say good morning, walking into work with a spring in my step. Paul's already in the kitchen making coffee, and he grins at my smiling face.

'You look happy this morning,' he greets me.

'You know what, Paul? For the first time in a while, I feel it. Cale went to school with a smile on his face and conversed with me in more than grunts or swear words,' I say. 'I know not to get my hopes up, but I'm taking it one day at a time and today is a good day.'

'That's great, Steph. Some good days are better

than no good days,' he says. 'And things with Nick are…?' he prompts.

I laugh at his lack of subtlety.

'It's difficult at the moment, I'll admit. Caleb made it clear he's not on board with us being together, so we've had to take a step back. I just hope Nick has the patience to contend with all the drama I bring to the table.'

'You have nothing to worry about there. Nick wants a relationship with you more than anything. I don't want to speak out of turn, but he is worried he might have pushed you too soon, that he should've given you more time to grieve,' Paul says, with a glare that says, "I told you so."

'He's spoken to you about us?' I say, ignoring his unspoken caution.

'He's my best friend, Steph.'

'I know, and of course he should talk to you, but for the record, he didn't push me at all. It was me that did the pushing. I know it was soon after Chris and I know you were concerned about that. If I'm honest, I struggle to get my head around the idea that I've fallen in love with someone after losing my husband, but it's real, Paul. Nothing about it feels wrong. It's just difficult to give my attention to a relationship with what's going on with Cale.'

Paul nods. 'Caleb will come around, and if it's meant to work out with Nick, it will.'

'Thanks, Paul. It's just a tricky situation to navigate. I know Cale will have to learn to deal with obstacles along his journey, but at the moment he's a little too delicate to have to.'

Paul smiles and kisses my cheek.

'Nick understands that, Steph.' He leaves the

kitchen, whistling all the way to his office, and as I watch him go, my smile is wide, but a bubble of apprehension settles in my belly.

I'm caught by surprise when I arrive at school to pick the boys up and find Josh waiting with them.

'You need a lift home, Josh?' I ask, as they all pile into the car.

'I said he could come home with us for a bit. Is that okay?'

'Sure.' I'm sympathetic to my son's friend, knowing what a tough time he's also having. Their friendship right now is crucial to both of them. I just hope they both realise that. In any case, I will always encourage them to spend time together. They've been friends for a long time and know each other better than most.

'Are you staying for dinner, Josh?' I shout outside to where the boys are tossing a ball around.

'If that's okay?'

'Of course, I'll let your mum know I'll drop you home later.'

'Cheers Steph,' Josh says, going back to honing his footy skills.

I watch them through the window as I make dinner, and my thoughts drift to Nick. I acknowledge that I haven't seen him in a few days. We've spoken every day, but each time he suggests seeing me, I come up with an excuse. Not that I don't want to see him, of course I do, but the way things are going with Caleb, I'm reluctant to tempt fate.

I think about making plans with him on my day off, now that Caleb's back at school. Sneaking around with him in the middle of the day isn't high on my list of options, but I'd rather that than not see him at all. I smile at the possibility of sharing some alone time with him soon and decide I'll call him as soon as I drop Josh home.

I turn my attention back to dinner and take the chopped ingredients over to the pan.

'Hey,' a voice whispers behind me. I startle and turn in panic, wondering what the hell Nick is doing in my house.

'What are you doing here?' My tone is a little harsh, and I wince at myself.

Nick frowns, unsure of the reason behind my frosty reception.

'Is everything okay, Steph?' he asks, concerned. I glare at him, worried about the repercussions of him being here if Caleb sees him.

'Did you not get my message?'

'What message?' I don't mean to snap at him, but I'm blindsided by his impromptu visit.

'Levi called to ask if I could come and help him fix a fence. I left you a message to say I was on my way. If you'd rather I wasn't here, I can leave.' His face falls, and I'm riddled with guilt.

'No, of course I want you here, I'm sorry… I just…' My voice trails away, unable to articulate what I mean without hurting his feelings. 'I'm not sure where Levi is. He's probably outside.'

Nick turns back to the door to do what he came to do.

'Nick, wait…' I call. His sad eyes meet mine and I know I've hurt him, anyway.

'I don't know how Cale will react to you being here.'

He nods sharply and sets off to find Levi.

Embarrassed by the way I reacted, I let him go, but I'm nervous about what might happen when Caleb sees him. I concentrate my attention back on the pan and continue to stir dinner, waiting for the proverbial shit to hit the fan. It's not a long wait. The shouting escalates and I run outside to diffuse the situation, but I am not prepared for what I'm greeted with.

Nick kneels on the grass, his t-shirt lifted to his face to soak up the blood. Caleb is face down on the floor, struggling against both Josh and Levi, who are holding him down.

I feel like I've walked into a movie set. I gasp at the scene, shocked at the outcome of this interaction.

'What the hell?'

'He punched Nick, Mum. I think he broke his nose, go check on him,' Levi screams, tears in his eyes.

My eyes dart from Levi to Nick, and I tend to him. I help him to his feet and take him inside to nurse his injury.

'It doesn't look to be broken.' My eyes brim with tears and the emotion catches in my throat. 'I'm so sorry, Nick.'

'It's my fault. I shouldn't have come.' His eyes flicker away, leaving an awkward tension between us. 'I'll fix the fence and then I'll leave.'

'Don't worry about the fence. I'll get it sorted. Let me clean you up,' I say, grabbing my first aid kit from the kitchen.

'There'll be some bruising,' I say, eyes downcast. 'I can't believe he did that.'

'Don't worry about it,' he says, pushing up off the chair. 'Listen, I promised Levi I'd help him, so I will.' Nick turns and looks me in the eye. 'But I understand if you need to call it quits between us, Steph, I do. Please don't make me renege on my promise to Levi, though. I've promised he can do the charity bike ride with me and I can't let him down. Just because Caleb doesn't want me around doesn't mean Levi should suffer. We enjoy riding together and he's come to mean a lot to me, Steph.'

'Nick, I…' I choke. My heart is in my mouth. 'I don't want things to end between us, but I can't let you keep getting caught up in my family dramas. It's not fair.'

'Steph, listen to me,' he says, pulling me towards him. 'I love you and I want to support you through this, but I don't want to make things any more difficult for you than they already are. Don't pull away from me for my sake, I'm invested in us. Nothing's changed.'

I listen intently and take on board what he says, but the situation with Caleb claws at me and I can't commit to anything.

'I'd better get outside and see what's going on.'

Caleb sits on the grass, his knees bent and his head in his hands. Josh and Levi are muttering to him, but I can't make out what they're saying.

Levi looks up when he hears us approach.

'Is it broken?' he asks Nick, a concerned edge to his voice.

'No, it's fine, Levi. Do you want to come and show me the fence and we can get started?'

Levi jumps up and leads Nick towards the break.

Caleb watches them go, realisation dawning on him that Nick had come over at the request of his brother because he needed help with the fence. I see the guilt flood his face as he bites his lip and his eyes drift to mine. I kneel in front of him, my face stern.

'Caleb, I know you're in a world of pain and I know you have reservations about Nick, but you cannot go around punching people. There are no excuses for this behaviour. We've been through this before,' I warn. 'I didn't know Nick was even coming. Levi needed help and Nick has been a good friend to him. Even if Nick and I weren't in a relationship, him and Levi are training for a bike ride together, so you will be seeing more of him. You'll have to find a way to deal with this, Cale.'

Caleb doesn't answer, but a silent tear rolls down his cheek and drips from his chin.

'You need to apologise to Nick.' I'm resolute about this, and as I walk away, all I can hope is that the happier boy from earlier will return soon. I'm gripped with terror when I think of all the scenarios that might stem from this interaction.

On entering the house, I'm blanketed by smoke and I charge into the kitchen to turn the cooker off. Amid all the drama I'd left the pan on and dinner has well and truly burnt. I fling the pan in the sink and slide to the floor, despair filling me with emptiness. My eyes fill and my throat catches. Every single emotion spills over and I'm laid bare.

Steph

'Steph?' Nick's hands waft through the haze when he enters the house. 'Are you okay?' His eyes scan the room and land on the pan in the sink, taking in the obvious cause of the smoke.

'Steph?' he says again, coming round the units into the kitchen when he hears my sniffling. I'm a huddled up figure on the floor, hunched over, my shoulders shaking, and I watch as his heart breaks before my eyes and he crumbles to the floor before me.

'Baby, let it all out. I'm here for you.' He fingers my hair, soothing my sobs. I'm unsure how long I've been sitting here, but my legs are getting numb and I shuffle around on the floor, trying to get more comfortable.

My sobs subside and Nick wipes my tears with a patch of his t-shirt that isn't bloodstained.

'I forgot to turn the pan off when I went outside to deal with Cale and now dinner's ruined and I nearly burnt the house down,' I wail.

'Hey, don't worry, there's no harm done. Are you okay?'

'I don't know, Nick. I'm at a loss about what to do next. I don't know which is worse, his anger or his complete hopelessness.'

'I can have a chat with him if you like, but I'm probably not the best person right now. Is he speaking to his psych? Have you seen any signs of improvement?'

I shrug. 'I don't know. I thought so, but now I'm not so sure. He seemed to have picked up the last few days and inviting Josh over is a huge positive, but the way he blew up when he saw you…' I shake my head, discouraged. 'How's your nose?'

Nick smirks. 'It's sore,' he says, stroking his fingers across the bridge. 'But please don't let this hang over you, it's fine, I've had worse.'

He stands and pulls me to my feet, wrapping me up in his arms. I nestle my head into his chest, seeking a moment of comfort.

Josh slides the door open and Caleb follows him inside.

'Woah, what happened in here?' Josh asks, his arms waving around to clear the smoke that still hangs heavy in the air.

'Just a minor mishap with dinner,' Nick says over my head. 'Looks like you guys will be having takeout tonight instead.'

Nick's eyes lock on Cale as he speaks and Cale's eyes dart away, embarrassed at seeing the bruising appearing below Nick's eyes. Bruising that he caused.

I step from Nick's embrace and speak to the boys. My face feels puffy and I'm sure I look like hell.

'I'll go pick something up.' All the life has drained out of me and they all stare at me as though I've said something ridiculous.

'Tell me what you want, I'll go pick it up,' Nick offers. Caleb's eyes dart towards Nick, as if in protest, but Josh soon shuts down a conflict with a hard nudge to Caleb's ribs and he retreats.

'Thanks.' He thrusts his hands in his pockets defensively.

'What's going on?' Levi asks, looking around at everyone in confusion when he bursts through the door.

'Dinner's burnt. Nick's going to pick up some takeout, so let him know what you want.'

'I'll get my dad to come pick me up,' Josh mutters, a little awkward to be caught up in all our family dramas. I'm glad he was here. He seems to have curtailed Caleb's impulsive behaviour just now.

'I'm sorry about all this, Josh. You're welcome to stay,' I offer.

'No, honestly, I'll leave you all to it,' he says.

'I'll drop you home when I pick up dinner, Josh. No need to bother your dad,' Nick offers.

'Oh that'd be great, cheers Nick.'

I look around at the kitchen disaster and wonder where to start.

'Mum, we'll do that,' Levi says, including Caleb in the offer. 'You go sit down.'

I pause and look from Levi to Caleb. Cale nods, agreeing with his brother, too shamefaced to do any other.

'Thank you,' I say, and disappear into my bedroom to shower and change my clothes.

I stand under the shower, letting the hot water

needle my skin. Attempting to refresh my puffy eyes and blotchy skin, I blast it on my face. I step out and wrap myself in a towel, then perch on my bed, shoulders hunched in defeat. There's so much going on, with so many implications for everyone I love, and I'm at a loss which direction to take. I'm torn. My boys are my priority, that goes without saying, but whatever choice I make, one of them won't be happy with the outcome. I could end my relationship with Nick in order to satisfy Caleb, until he's healthier and is better equipped to deal with it, but then Levi will miss out because I don't have the strength to see Nick if I can't be with him. It would destroy me. How am I supposed to choose between my kids' happiness? There's no solution that I can come up with and I find myself going round in circles.

I hear the car pull up outside and finish drying myself. I pull on some track pants and an old t-shirt and drag a comb through my wet hair before venturing back to the kitchen to see what progress the boys have made.

The kitchen is immaculate and everything is in its rightful place. They've set the outdoor table with plates and cutlery, and the boys are mid-conversation on the couch. Nick appears at the door holding both hands up with a bag in each.

'Boys, dinner's here,' I say, making my way outside to Nick.

'Thank you,' I say. He puts the bags on the table and removes the containers.

'Well, I'll leave you to it, enjoy.' His fingers discreetly brush my arm, reluctant to cause more drama.

My bottom lip trembles; devastated things have come to this. Levi glares at his brother as though beseeching words from Caleb's mouth. Caleb chews on his cheeks as he watches Nick turn to leave.

'You can stay,' he mutters, not quite loud enough for Nick to hear.

Levi digs his elbow into Cale's ribs, tipping his head towards Nick, who is still making his exit.

Caleb clears his throat.

'Nick.' He speaks more clearly this time. Nick stops and turns around, eyeing Caleb. 'You can stay for dinner. You bought heaps.'

Nick glances at me as I study the interaction. Hope fills my eyes.

'Thanks Cale, I'm starving.'

He sits down with Levi, leaving the spot next to Cale for me. The four of us help ourselves to the food, the conversation proceeding with caution. Caleb is quiet for several minutes, watching and listening to the exchange. He appears to be studying the rapport between his brother and Nick, not in a green-eyed way, more with intrigue.

'Nick.' The conversation lulls and there's a sharp intake of breath as Caleb speaks. 'I'm sorry I hit you.'

Nick listens to his apology.

'Thank you Caleb, that means a lot. I accept your apology.'

Levi beams across the table at me.

'How's Millie?' Caleb asks. 'Do you think she'll forgive me for being a dick?'

Nick laughs. 'I'm sure she will, Cale. You should call her.' He hesitates, deciding whether to proceed. 'Listen, we all go through stuff that makes us act out of character. You've been through a lot. It's normal. The key is to figure out the reason for feeling that way and fix that. You'll get there, Caleb. It may take time, but you've got so many people here to support you. If you can acknowledge that and accept the help, you'll get there much quicker. Don't be ashamed of how you feel.'

Nick pauses and looks at me, seeking my permission to speak freely. I'm not sure what he's about to say, but I put my full trust in him. I nod and Nick huffs out a long breath as though preparing for what he's about to say.

'When my first wife died.' The shock of his words registers on the boys' faces. Nick looks between the two of them, realising I haven't shared his personal story with them.

'She had post-natal depression and took her own life.' My heart breaks for him as he voices those words, aware of how deeply it still affects him. 'I felt everything you've been feeling, Caleb; sadness, anger, guilt, grief, the whole works. I'm a psychologist and I didn't know she was suffering. Paul felt the same. He was her best friend, and he never picked up on it, either. I don't think we'd have got through the loss without each other.'

Caleb nods and throws me a remorseful look, realising he'd read the entire situation so wrong.

After dinner, Nick and Levi are caught up in a conversation about their bike trip and Nick's regaling him with stories of some of the epic falls and injuries he's suffered. I gather the plates and take them into the kitchen. As I turn to go back for more, Caleb appears with the rest stacked in his hands.

'Thanks Cale, just put them on the side.' I'm still treading on eggshells.

'Mum.' I look up, desperate to re-connect with my son. 'I'm sorry I punched Nick, and for the way I've been. I just… I don't even know how to explain it. It's all too much sometimes.' His eyes flood with tears and I reach up and wrap him in my arms, my heart breaking for him.

'I know, sweetheart, but I'm here for you whenever it gets too much. You scared me, Cale. I can't lose you too.' My grip on him tightens.

'I'm sorry for that, too. I didn't mean to do it. I just didn't know what else to do.'

'Caleb, if you ever feel that low again, please talk to me. Or talk to your psych, or Nick. He understands. You have way more in common than you might think. He's a good guy. He wouldn't be here if he wasn't.'

Cale nods. 'I can see he makes you happy, Mum, and Levi, too. You don't have to hide. I'll be okay with it.'

I regard him, wondering how true his words are.

'I promise, Mum, it's all good. I'm gonna call Millie, too.'

'Thank you Cale, I appreciate that.' My heart is full.

Nick sticks around until we can be alone. I turn on the patio heater and grab a blanket, summoning Nick beside me on the outdoor couch, away from prying eyes.

I relax back into the cushions, my head tipped back, eyes closed, and I feel the tension release. Nick sits side on, one leg tucked under him, and he takes my hand.

'How are you, my love?' He focuses his attention on me, aware of the toll the day has taken on me. I open my eyes and roll my head to face him.

'I'm exhausted. It's been a day.'

Nick rubs his thumb in circles on my palm and chuckles.

'I'm not sure it could've been worse.'

'It could. You not being here with me right now would have just about finished me. I'm grateful for where we are right now. There's still a long way to go, but Caleb told me tonight that he'll be okay with us being together.'

Nick's eyes grow bright, a sea of happiness.

'I think he might have turned a corner, Nick. I sensed something different in him. I'm sorry you had to get hurt in the process, but whatever happened in his head after that, I think might have been the breakthrough we've been waiting for.'

'God, I hope so, Steph.' His fingers brush my unruly hair from my eyes and they linger on my cheek. I ease into his touch, tilting my face up to meet his, and when I feel his warm lips on mine, my world somehow rights itself.

Caleb

Dear Dad,
I've been seeing a psych and I'm on this medication that's supposed to help regulate my mood. It's been helping and I've started seeing things a bit more clearly. I'm glad I didn't die, Dad. I've still got a long way to go, but I can see that my life is worth living. I wish you'd been able to speak to Mum about how you felt. She would've helped you. I've caused her so many problems since you died, but she's the one person who is always there to pick me up. I wish you'd given her the chance to do that for you.

Millie's forgiven me. We've only spoken on the phone, but I'm glad she's back in my life. I guess if things work out between Mum and Nick, she might be my sister one day, which is weird to even think about. He's pretty cool, Nick. I think you'd like him. Mum's much happier when they're together.

I've been thinking a lot about my grandfather, wondering about the relationship you had with him.

Maybe if you'd spoken about him, it would've helped you.

I looked him up and he's still alive, but I guess you

knew that. Did you tell Mum he was dead, so you didn't have to deal with it?
What did he do to you, Dad?
Caleb

Steph

I live in constant hope that one day my relationship with Caleb will strengthen, but for now I remain cautious in his company. Although he's making positive steps forward, sometimes he seems to regress and I have to remind myself that this is a lengthy journey and we all need to take it one day at a time.

His seventeenth birthday is looming, and he's had very little driving practise in the months since his father passed.

'Mum, I need to get some driving hours in so I can book my test,' he reminds me on the drive home from school.

'Okay.' I hesitate, nervous about taking him out. Not that he's a poor driver. He picked it up with ease before our lives took a turn. His concentration levels, something he's struggled with throughout his depression, give me concern. That said, I need to encourage any signs of positivity.

'Maybe you can drive to and from school again, and then I'll take you out more on the weekends.'

'Cool, thanks Mum.' He grins at me through the

rear-view mirror. 'I need to practise parking too.'

Conscious of the fact there was a time when I got nothing from him, every trace of positivity is a win and I smile back at him.

'Boys, I'm going out for dinner tonight,' I say, as they throw their school bags down and head straight for the fridge. The weather has heated over the last few weeks as summer approaches, and we all need a cool drink after a long day. 'There's some pasta and sauce. You can cook for yourselves.'

'Where are you going?' Levi asks.

'I'm not sure. Nick's booking somewhere,' I say. While Caleb is upbeat about his driving lessons, I decide to broach the subject of Nick that I've been avoiding. Things between us have been running smoothly for a while now, and both boys have settled into seeing him here more often. I'm not asking permission, but it's their home too, and I want them to be comfortable.

'Listen guys, I have something I want to talk to you about and I want you to be honest, okay?' I say.

'What is it?' Levi asks. Caleb frowns, pensive.

'It's nothing to worry about and if you're not comfortable, you can say so. It won't be a problem,' I iterate. 'I was wondering how you would feel if Nick stayed over sometimes, maybe on weekends, or if I stayed at his place.'

'Sure, I'm cool with it,' Levi shrugs. Nick spent several nights here while Caleb was in the hospital, bringing comfort to both of us, so I knew he'd be fine, but his face contorts in horror when realisation hits and he glares at me, panic-stricken.

'I don't want to hear you having sex.'

'Levi, that's gross,' Caleb protests, pushing his brother in jest. 'Why would you even say that?'

I laugh at their torment. 'Caleb? How would you feel?'

Caleb groans. 'Yeah, whatever Mum, but I don't want to talk about it ever again.'

He makes a face and walks off to his bedroom, followed by Levi, leaving me chuckling at their embarrassment, but filled with contentment.

Buoyed by that encouraging response, I prepare myself for my date. It's the first time Nick's taken me out since our very first sneaky lunch at the winery. With everything going on, we've either met at home or with the kids, so I'm eager for some adult alone time.

I smile to myself as I shower, then smother my body with body cream. Studying my figure in the full-length mirror, I appreciate who I am. I've lost weight, no doubt a result of all the stress, but I'm in pretty good shape for fifty-two. The dark circles under my eyes and the sallow skin have aged me in the last few months and I hope some light in my life will fix that. This evening I don't want to talk about anything sad or difficult, but get to learn more about the man I love and the fun things we can look forward to together.

Leafing through the summer clothes that have been hanging in my wardrobe since the previous summer, I regret not buying something new to wear. I settle on a simple midi dress and pair it with espadrilles that tie around my ankles. Adding earrings and a bracelet, I feel feminine. I flick the mascara wand over my lashes and brush my lips with gloss. Pinching my cheeks to add some colour,

I smile to myself, a long forgotten sparkle in my eyes, and a buzz in my veins that excites me.

Nick comes to the door armed with flowers and I blush at the formality of the occasion.

'They're beautiful, Nick, thank you,' I say, pressing a kiss to his cheek.

'Nowhere near as beautiful as you look,' he whispers. 'You are stunning.'

I dump the flowers in water and grab my purse, and as I walk back to Nick, butterfly wings beat hard against my stomach. Shyness and nerves do battle in my body as I follow Nick outside.

'Oh, I've been wanting to come here for ages. The reviews are amazing.'

Nick is smitten as he takes my hand and leads me inside. Being the object of his affection can often feel overwhelming. The intensity with which his eyes penetrate mine dazzles me. The lightest feather of his touch can sear my skin, and the smooth baritone of his voice in my ear falters my breath. His love is like a love song on repeat.

We're seated near the window overlooking the river, and the view is beautiful as the sun makes its descent.

'Wine?' Nick asks as a server hands us a menu.

'I'll have the pinot please,' I say, pointing to the wine list.

'Make that two, thank you,' Nick says.

I glance through the menu, unable to decide. Everything sounds wonderful and I'm spoilt for choice.

'What are you thinking of?' Nick asks.

'I'm not sure, maybe one of the fish dishes. It all sounds amazing.'

'How about the seafood platter to share?'

'You'd like that?' I ask. Fish was always a no-go for Chris, so I've always avoided seafood share plates.

'I'd love it, if you would,' he says.

'I would! My mouth's watering just thinking about it.'

Once we've ordered and the server has delivered our wine, Nick reaches across the table for my hand.

'Steph, I know you don't want to talk about anything heavy tonight, so I'll make this quick,' Nick says.

I frown, hoping whatever he has to say won't ruin our date. I've looked forward to this all week.

'Don't worry, it's nothing bad,' he assures me. 'I just want to say that the way you've handled everything these last few months with such poise has blown me away. I know we met at a tough time in your life, and I feel like we've skipped a lot of the fun stuff, but I don't think I could love you any more than I do.' Nick reaches into his pocket, pulling out a small box. I gasp and goosebumps prickle my flesh. Sheer panic courses through my body.

Nick laughs at my reaction, visible for the world to see.

'Don't panic, I'm not proposing,' he clarifies for me.

'I wasn't panicking,' I lie.

He passes the box across the table and my shaky fingers release the ribbon. Inside is the most beautiful pair of dragonfly earrings in white gold with a tiny diamond on each.

'Nick, they're gorgeous, but what are they for?' It's not my birthday or a special occasion.

'Dragonflies are a symbol of hope, love, and new beginnings. I feel like this is our first proper date, out in the open, not having to sneak around. We've turned a corner and we can look forward to the future together. I wanted to give you something to celebrate that, and well, these seemed fitting,' he shrugs.

'Thank you,' I say, my eyes filling up. 'I love them.'

'Hey, no tears, there's no crying allowed tonight.'

'They're happy tears for a change.'

Nick picks up his wine glass and encourages me to do the same.

'To us, and to happier times ahead. I love you,' he toasts.

'To us. I love you, too.'

We plough through the seafood platter, which must be the most extravagant and beautiful meal I've ever eaten. It's filled with Barramundi, prawns, lobster tail, scallops and an entire array of other locally caught fresh seafood. Served on a board with three different styles of potato and a whole host of greens, it's as aesthetic as it is delicious. When I can eat no more, I sit back with my hand on my stomach and sigh.

'I think I'm in heaven.' I lick my lips before draining my wine glass.

'More wine?' Nick asks.

'Go on, why not?' I say, hoping to extend the evening for as long as possible.

We laugh and share funny stories about our kids,

and as the evening wears on, I fall a little more in love with him.

'Did you always want to be a doctor?' Nick asks.

'God no! I wanted to be a vet, but didn't get in, so I figured I'd start med and then switch.'

'But you never did.'

'No, I loved med,' I say, excitement bursting from me at the thought of those years. Nick's face lights up as he witnesses a side of me he's only had tiny glimpses of before. He encourages me to continue.

'I loved the hospital environment, but I decided being a GP was more conducive to marriage and motherhood.' My mind revisits the decisions I made early in my career, and I frown.

'Do you regret it?' Nick asks, picking up on the hint of remorse on my face.

'I don't regret it, but I question my reasons for choosing that path.'

'Do you think it would have been easier to make a different decision had you been a man?'

I study his face as I contemplate his question. His thought process intrigues me. He asks both thoughtful and thought-provoking questions and considers the answers. Maybe it's because of his job, or that he's raised three daughters, two of them without a mother.

'Maybe,' I say, honestly. 'I guess back then it still felt like an impossibility.'

'I get that,' Nick says, and the quiet hangs between us.

'Do you fancy a walk?' Nick asks when we leave the restaurant.

'Sure, it would be good to walk this food baby off

a little.'

Nick laces our fingers together and we wander along the riverbank.

'So, do you have any plans this weekend?' I ask, saving my good news.

'No, I don't think so, other than seeing Millie at some point. I'm not sure when she's free. Why?'

'I was wondering if you fancy coming over for dinner,' I ask, 'and maybe spend the night?'

'I'd love to. Are the boys out?' he asks.

'No, they'll both be home.' I can't help teasing him.

Nick tilts his head towards mine, his brow furrowed with uncertainty.

'What aren't you telling me, Steph?' he smirks.

'I spoke to them earlier and asked how they'd feel about you staying over. They were both fine with it. Well, as fine as teenage boys can be when they imagine their mum having sex with her boyfriend.' I squirm at my own words.

'I'm sure they're scarred for life at that thought,' Nick chuckles. 'But that's great news, and tremendous progress on Caleb's part.'

He stops in the middle of the path and swings me around to face him. He takes my face in both hands and finds my lips with his. I'm open to him, receptive to his intimate touch. My hands wind their way around his waist and I pull him closer, wanting to savour every part of him. His tongue dips deeper, exploring my mouth. Desire pools deep inside as he trails his mouth across my cheek to my ear.

'Come home with me for a bit?' His plea is breathless, and I can do nothing but nod.

The fifteen minute drive to Nick's house is the longest journey in the world. He can't keep his hands off me and I feel more needy than I have in years. It's been a while since we've been intimate with each other, since before Caleb was in the hospital, in fact. Excitement and nervous energy battle for position when Nick's car pulls into his driveway.

He swings into his garage and hops out of the car, running round to open my door. I'm far too eager to wait and I'm out well before he reaches me. Grabbing my hand, he leads me into the house, kicking the door closed behind him. I chuckle at the speed we're moving, the desperation in Nick's stride. Once we reach the bedroom, Nick stops and turns to me, slowing the moment down and taking his time now we've arrived at our destination.

The back of his hand brushes my cheek and he winds his fingers through my hair, clutching it at my nape. His assault on my mouth begins again, this time less frenzied, more controlled. He sweeps my mouth with his tongue, running along the edge of my teeth, dipping in and out, tasting me. I groan in delight as my hands grapple with his belt. I fumble over the button on his jeans and undo the zip. My fingers dip inside, stroking under the waistband of his jocks. His moans reverberate right through my body, and I pull at his jeans to give myself better access. Nick steps back and kicks off his shoes, tugging at his jeans to make things quicker. I untie the ribbons from behind my ankles and toe off my shoes. I grab the hem of my dress and pull it in one swoop right over my head. Nick pulls off his shirt and walks me backwards to the bed. Easing me downward, he peppers me with soft kisses until my entire body is writhing beneath him.

'Nick, stop, I need you,' I pant, and his resolve shatters. His mouth moves along my neck to my lips as he pushes inside me. Excited by our spontaneous tryst, and the sheer pleasure it brings, the love I feel gives me a high I feel sure I've never experienced in my life. And judging by the look of pure ecstasy on Nick's face, I'm almost positive he's reached the same place. Our bodies quiver and tremble together as we both tumble from some kind of nirvana. We lie close, wrapped up in our joint state of bliss, whispering our thoughts and sharing sweet kisses.

'I don't remember being as happy as I am right now.' My voice cracks at the enormity of my words.

Nick's eyes brim with tears as I watch him swallow the meaning.

'Me neither,' he says, honestly. I can tell he's surprised by his own words. He never thought he would love someone the way he loved Lee, but somehow, even with all the misery and drama I've brought, I burrowed my way into the part of his heart he'd locked tight so long ago.

'I love you so much, and I can't wait to see what the future has in store for us.'

'Steph… I never imagined I would feel this way. I love you more than I ever thought possible.'

Nick

Nick smiled from the bed as Steph slipped her dress back over her head, his heart still racing. His thoughts had turned to his first wife a lot in the last few days, accepting he'd found a love that lived up to his memories. He'd known Steph was special from the beginning, but he never imagined he'd feel for someone else the way he'd felt about Lee. Tears stung his eyes at the enormity of Steph taking Lee's place in his heart. It was time to let her go, and move forward in a way he'd never been able to with Sarah. She'd never filled the space that Lee had left behind, but Steph had somehow filled it, and then some.

'I can get an Uber home if you want to stay in bed.' Steph's words broke him from his reverie.

'No, I'm coming, I just couldn't take my eyes off you there for a moment,' he said, hopping out of bed and pulling on some track pants and a sleep tee.

The drive home was quiet; each settled in their own thoughts.

'I feel like something shifted for us tonight.' Steph broke the silence as Nick turned into her driveway. 'Something significant.'

Nick swallowed the lump in his throat, waiting to pull up behind her car before speaking.

'I think so, too,' he said, unclicking his seatbelt and turning to face her. 'Can I tell you a story?'

'Of course.' She reached for his hand, the physical touch bringing her contentment.

'When Paul first introduced me to Lee, I was blown away by her. She was beautiful and had that Julia Roberts smile I loved so much. Paul had told both of us we were made for each other, and from that first meeting, I was smitten. She was this bright light in everyone's life, and it took me a while to believe she wanted to be with me. I was so full of insecurities back then and constantly asked for Paul's opinion on our relationship. It took some pretty heavy moments with Lee before I convinced myself she loved me. When I met Sarah, it was such a novel experience. I was a single dad with two small children, and I was grieving. Paul warned me not to get involved, but I didn't listen. I didn't want to be on my own. I missed what I had with Lee and I somehow tried to recreate it. Obviously, that doesn't work. You can't force feelings, and every relationship is different. I thought I could make my marriage work if I treated it the same as my first one, but Sarah was a different person, with different needs, and the dynamic between us was unfamiliar to me. I think I always assumed that no one else would match up to Lee.'

Nick paused, taking in Steph's eyes and the way she listened to his words.

'Then I met you.' His eyes lit up, animated by the mere thought of her. 'Steph, you are nothing like Lee, and yet so perfect for me in every way. Some old insecurities crept in a few weeks back, and I doubted myself, thinking I couldn't be what you needed. I worried I'd pushed you too fast, that I'd taken advantage. When I met Sarah, I knew I wasn't ready for a relationship and yet I ploughed ahead, anyway. I didn't want that to be the same for you. Paul has always been my sounding board; I respect his opinion. I hope you don't mind that I spoke to him, but I think the fact that he's also your friend gave his opinion so much more value. He told me we're perfect for each other, although he had misgivings about it being too soon and us getting hurt, but I think he just cemented everything I already knew.'

Nick steadied his breath before he continued.

'Steph, what we have is immense. I think by accepting I would never again have what I had with Lee, I somehow got more. My love for you is bigger than anything I've ever felt before. You fill me up. You're everything I could ever want, and more.'

Steph's hand trembled in his, astonished by his revelations.

'Wow, I don't know what to say.'

'You don't need to say anything. I just wanted to let you know the depth of my feelings for you. If you felt something shift tonight, maybe that's why. I think I recognised the fact that you've taken Lee's place in my heart. I'll always love her, as you'll always love Chris, but she's gone and you're my future.'

Steph nodded, thinking about everything Nick had said to her.

'He's a wise one, our mate Paul, hey?'

'He sure is.' Nick leaned over to kiss her

goodnight.

Nick smiled to himself the entire drive home. He always felt he put pressure on himself to create a certain relationship that would live up to his experiences, but when he'd least expected it and hadn't been actively looking for a partner, Steph had shown up in his life and thrown him for a loop. She'd given him everything, and he'd had no expectations. There was still a long way to go in terms of her own healing, and that of her boys, but things were finally looking up. There was hope in his heart, which is why he'd bought the earrings. He wanted her to understand that he was all in, for the good times and the bad, that she was his future and he'd be there every step of the way.

Steph

'We should fix the pool up ready for the weekend,' I suggest to the boys over breakfast. 'We're in for a scorcher. Do you have any plans?'

'No, I don't,' Levi says, 'but I'm hoping Nick's free to go for a ride.'

I smile at the mention of his name.

'I thought maybe I'd see what Millie's doing,' Cale says, his face riddled with guilt over the way he treated her.

'Cale, you know she's forgiven you. Stop beating yourself up over it. The past is exactly that, you are allowed to move forward,' I coax.

'I know. We've spoken on the phone. I just haven't seen her yet.'

'How about we invite Millie and Nick over for a barbecue on Saturday?'

'Yeah, sounds cool,' Caleb says.

'Maybe they could stay over and then me and Nick can go out for a ride early Sunday morning?' Levi proposes. I feel myself flush from my chest and turn away to avoid the boys spotting the smitten look on my face.

'Sure.' I force the quiver from my voice. 'I'll ask Nick today.'

'Hey honey, how are you?' I ask when Terri opens the door. She's finished another round of chemo and has perked up a little.

'I'm wearing actual clothes for the first time in weeks, so we'll take that as a positive. Come on in.'

'That's great. You look like you have a little more colour in your cheeks,' I say.

'But not as much as you do. You're positively glowing. Sit down and tell me all about that.' Her face is eager, desperate for an update.

'You have no idea how ridiculously happy I am, Terri. I feel like the bubble's always about to burst, but right now I can't stop smiling.'

'You deserve to be happy, Steph. I'm so thrilled for you. How's Cale doing?'

'Fingers crossed, he's making inroads. He's accepted that me and Nick are together, albeit tentatively, but it's a start. I know he'll warm up to him the more time he spends with him.'

'He won't be punching him again anytime soon, then?' Terri jokes.

'God Terri, I hope not. It was awful. There was blood everywhere, and Josh and Levi had Cale pinned to the floor. Not to mention I almost burnt the house down. It was a low point, that's for sure.' I shudder, remembering that horrible day. 'I think Josh might have had something to do with Cale calming down.'

'He told me he had a chat with him,' Terri says. 'Said he tried to get him to see things from a different perspective. The way Josh has handled everything has been amazing; first with Cale, and then everything going on with me. It's been a lot, but I'm so proud of him.'

'You have every right to be, Terri. Most kids would have dropped the friendship after the way Caleb treated him, but Josh saw through the angry exterior and understood it was his illness talking. I think watching Josh deal with your diagnosis made Cale realise everyone is going through something and he wasn't as alone as he thought,' I say.

'My cancer's had at least one positive.' Terri laughs, despite herself.

'Oh Terri, I hate to see you going through this. How are you coping?' I ask.

'Honestly, Steph, I'm okay. I won't lie, the chemo hits hard, but I'm positive. It's all I can be.'

'And the surgery? How are you feeling about that?' I enquire.

'A little self conscious, but I'm getting there.'

'You know you have options. I'm sure your oncologist would have explained them, but I'm happy to talk through them with you sometime if you're interested.'

'Thanks Steph, I'll see once I've gone through this treatment. It's enough to think about right now,' Terri says.

'Of course.'

'Anyway,' Terri says, brightening the conversation. 'Shouldn't you be off to see your man? Isn't Thursday your sex day?'

I blush at her flagrant description of my life.

'I'm not sure we would call it that, but yes, I am on my way there.'

'Off you go then. One of us may as well get lucky.'

We hug tightly, neither one of us wanting to let go. Our friendship has always been strong; we clicked from day one, but the last six months have brought with it a multitude of challenges that have seen us rely on each other in ways we would never have imagined.

'You know you don't need to wait for me to open the door. You can walk right in,' Nick greets me with a kiss.

'I don't know. It feels weird. It's your house. What if Millie was here?' I say, following him inside.

'Millie wouldn't care, you're always welcome here, Steph. If circumstances were different, I'd be giving you a key and asking you to move in,' Nick admits.

His comment takes me by surprise and I have to catch my bottom jaw.

'Why so surprised? I love you, you're my end game. I'm not doing this again. Besides, you know how that dating app worked out for me.'

His face contorts in humiliation and I chuckle.

'I would love to live with you one day, when the timing's right. But I don't think my kids, dogs, chooks, sheep, and goat would fit into this space, so we might need to rethink our options.'

Nick grins at my openness to his suggestion.

'I'm more than happy to move in with you, if that's what you're suggesting. When the timing's right, obviously,' he proposes.

I grin back and reach up for a kiss.

'So, do you and Millie have any plans this weekend?'

'I don't,' he confirms, 'but I'm not sure what

Millie's up to. Why? What are you asking?'

'Well, it seems summer has arrived, and it's going to be a hot one, so the boys and I wondered if you'd both like to come over on Saturday. Spend the afternoon in the pool, have a barbecue…' I run my finger down his chest, then stand on my tip toes and nibble on his ear lobe. 'And maybe have a sleepover?'

'Seriously? Your boys will be okay with that?' Nick asks, eager to make it happen.

'Well, there might be a catch.' I grin at him. 'Levi expects that you'll want to get up super early on Sunday and take him out for a ride.'

Nick rolls his eyes at my son's enthusiasm for early mornings.

'Do you think he'll compromise and we can go on Saturday morning instead? I'm happy to come and pick him up early and then I can spend Sunday morning snuggling in your bed.'

'Nick, you're his hero. I'm sure he'll go along with whatever you suggest.'

Nick blushes at the description. 'Just happy to help.'

'So what's on the agenda for today?' I ask, already blushing at the name Terri gave to my day.

'I was thinking a little of this,' he whispers, trailing his lips from my ear, along my cheek, and kissing the edge of my mouth. 'Maybe a little of this.' He runs his fingers down my neck and across my chest to cup my breast.

'I like the sound of that,' I pant, already worked up.

'How about some of this?' he asks, reaching for

my backside and scooping me up. My legs instinctively wrap around his waist.

'Mmm.'

'And lots of this.' His lips brush mine once again and then his mouth crashes into me and our tongues dance a sexy samba, backwards and forwards, as he carries me to the bedroom.

'I can't get enough of you,' I whisper as I lie on the bed, Nick snuggled to my side, reeling from the pleasure.

Nick smiles, wallowing in contentment.

'You're so beautiful,' he murmurs. 'I don't want to get up, but knowing I get you all night on Saturday, I'd like to take you out for lunch.'

'Sounds lovely, but just one more kiss first.'

Nick dips his head and presses his lips to mine, the two of us blissful in our little cocoon.

'Where are we going?'

I'm sitting shotgun in Nick's old ute, squinting into the bright midday sun, reluctant to take the smile off my face.

'A little place further up the coast. I can't remember its name. Now I know you love seafood, they do a squid ink linguine you have to try. It's amazing.' He reaches across the centre console for my hand.

'Sounds delicious.' I slide my sunglasses back onto my face to block out the glare and I settle into a stillness I haven't felt in so long. I close my eyes, relishing the feeling. It's been well over six months since my husband passed, but the speed with which I've moved on brings me pause. I loved my husband

and will forever cherish the memories we had together, but I don't want to live with sadness anymore and I know Chris wouldn't want that for me either. In fact, in his last words to me, he gave me his blessing to find love again. He maybe didn't expect me to find it as quick as I have, but sometimes it finds us when we least expect it.

I feel a tear leak from the corner of my eye and I leave it to track down my cheek. I never want to hide the love I had for Chris and even though I've reached a place of peace, there will always be moments when I'll think of him and maybe shed a tear, or remember a happy memory and smile.

'Hey, baby, are you okay?' Nick asks, never missing a beat when it comes to my well-being.

I open my eyes, still smiling, and wipe away the tear as he pulls into a parking spot on the side of the road.

'I was just thinking of Chris. He would've liked you,' I say. 'I don't want to forget him, Nick. He had his struggles, but he was a wonderful husband. We had a happy marriage.'

'Of course you don't want to forget him. I feel that way about Lee.'

I appreciate how much he understands that.

'Speaking of which, I spoke to Hannah and Lucy about you.'

'You did?'

'To be fair, they already knew, Millie was bursting at the seams to tell them. They'd love to meet you.'

'I'd love to meet them, too,' I say.

Nick grins and switches the engine off.

'Come on, we're here.'

The restaurant is light with a rustic beach vibe that's stayed clear of the typical shell and lighthouse decor. It's tasteful, but relaxed, and I love it immediately. We're seated at the open window overlooking the ocean, and the breeze is just enough to keep us cool from the blistering heat without blowing us away.

I peruse the menu but can't get past the seafood linguine that Nick recommended.

'We'll take two linguine, thanks,' Nick says to the server as she brings a bottle of water and glasses.

'I'm looking forward to our sleepover,' he says, once she's out of ear shot. 'I feel like a kid at Christmas.'

'Me too. I'm so happy Cale gave you a chance. I'm not sure how I would've kept my cravings in check otherwise.' My face takes on a crimson hue as my mind casts back to our earlier activity in the bedroom.

'You're so sexy when you blush,' Nick whispers. 'I'm happy too. It feels like a huge step forward. I would've preferred not to suffer a bruised ego and a blood nose to get there, but you win some, you lose some.' He winks at me and I shake my head, embarrassed by my son's behaviour.

'I'm so sorry. I feel so ashamed.'

'Don't be. It's in the past.'

'You know, before Chris passed away, Caleb was the kid you would never have imagined getting into a fight. He lived his life trying to please his dad; worked hard, got excellent grades, put his best effort into his football, never got in trouble at school, or on the footy pitch. Since then, he's punched his brother, his best friend, and you.'

'That makes sense,' Nick says. 'That's a lot of pressure on him to be perfect, whether it came from Chris or it was self-imposed. Finding out about his dad would have sent him into a tailspin. He didn't have anything to live up to anymore, no one he needed to please, and that gave him the release to do whatever he needed to get through his grief. It's tough growing up with a father who puts you on a pedestal with no room to fail.' Nick looks wistful, the smile on his lips not quite reaching his eyes.

'It sounds like you speak from personal experience,' I probe.

Nick sighs. 'I do, unfortunately. My father was a hard man to please, and he held me to ridiculously high standards. I would've loved to have played professionally, but even without my injury, I doubt I'd have made it. Caleb plays in a whole different class than me at the same age. After my injury, I studied psychology, but Dad thought that was for girls. He only ever saw me as a failure after that. I'm not sure why he was like that. He moved here from Italy because he didn't want to take over the family business, so I'd have thought he'd be keen on me pursuing my own path.'

I frown as an unwelcome thought enters my mind.

'You are so very much in tune with my family. Do you think that's why we have such a strong connection?' I worry that death is the root of our love and that can't be the basis of a long term relationship.

'What are you saying, Steph? That we're only together because we have shared experiences?'

'Maybe,' I shrug.

'Where's this coming from?' he asks.

'I don't know. Would we have had the same feelings if we'd met at a different time, or under different circumstances?'

'I can't say we didn't connect because of our experience, but there's way more to it than that, Steph. Do you not feel that?' My sudden doubt confuses Nick.

'Of course I feel it. I guess I wonder what it was about me that attracted you at a time in my life when I was drowning in a sea of doom and gloom.'

'Do you want me to list all your attributes that I find attractive?' Nick asks, nonplussed.

'No! Forget I said anything. Let's just enjoy our lunch.' I regret voicing my thoughts out loud, but I know Nick won't let this drop.

'No, I'm not forgetting it when it's important to you. Steph, I've always found you attractive, even when you were just Paul's friend I bumped into at parties. I know when we met up to chat about Caleb it was more professional than friendly, but even then, even though you were suffering, your warmth drew me in. I took notice of the relationships you had with your friends, your boys, your colleagues, and I knew I wanted to be a part of that circle. You're strong and smart, kind and supportive. The way you are with Millie melts my heart. Each time I saw you, you took another piece of my heart.' Nick reaches across the table and lifts my chin with the tip of his finger, making sure he has my full attention.

'You hold my entire heart in your hands. Never doubt why I'm with you.'

The air in my lungs snags and I blow out a

prolonged breath, unsure why I'd questioned Nick's motives.

'I'm sorry, Nick, I don't doubt you in the least. Things can come crashing down so quickly and I guess I feel vulnerable. I don't want to lose you.'

With impeccable timing, our meals arrive and we both feel grateful for the reprieve.

'I'm not going anywhere, Steph. Let's focus on the future, not the past. In particular, the very near future relating to me getting to spend all night in your bed,' he enthused, lightening the conversation.

Searching for Sunrise

Steph

Saturday can't come around soon enough. I'm more than ready to take some time out and have a little fun. Work has been teeming with patients; they've been backing up due to all the time I've taken off lately. I need to get into a more stable routine. My hours have been a little erratic. Jonathan's taken up a lot of the slack, for which I'm grateful, but he can't keep it up long term. We're past due for a discussion about the future of our practice.

'Hey Jon, do you have a few minutes?' I ask, as we're both getting ready to leave for the night.

'Of course. Is everything okay?'

'Yeah, I just wanted to say thank you for taking on so many of my patients these last few months and basically carrying the load.'

'Not a problem. I know you'd do the same for me.'

'Absolutely, of course I would, but I'm thinking we should maybe look at something a little more long term. You can't keep up with these extra hours and I'm not sure I want to return to my previous hours.' I feel like I need to wind back.

'So what are you suggesting?' Jon asks, unsure where my mind is going.

'I'm thinking of cutting down permanently, to three days a week. How would you feel about bringing someone else on board to pick up the slack?'

'Is that what you want? You'd be happy with only three days?'

'Jon, I've had so much going on. I should have just taken a leave of absence instead of messing you around taking time off here and there. It's time I took care of myself a little more without feeling guilty that I'm leaving you in the lurch.'

'You have no reason to feel guilty, Steph. You've been to hell and back this year, but I understand where you're coming from. I'm happy to put some feelers out, see who's available, and we can go from there.'

'Thanks Jon, I appreciate that,' I say, grateful for my wonderful colleagues.

'So, how are things going?' he asks.

'As of this moment, things are looking positive, but I don't want to count my chickens. We all know how quickly it can all turn to shit.'

'I'm glad things are looking up, Steph. Please know that I'm always here for you, as is Paul,' Jon says.

'I know that, Jon. Thank you.'

No amount of cleaning and preparation for the day ahead is able to curb the excess of nervous energy I wake up with. I leave Caleb in charge of cleaning the pool while I stock up on groceries for the barbecue and I'm restless the whole car ride home, anxious to see what mood I'll return to.

The pool sparkles and Cale is sitting on the lawn playing with the dogs, his face bright. I pause at the scene. These small moments, seeing him relaxed and happy and not suffocating in his own thoughts, are the moments I treasure these days.

'Hey Cale, thanks for doing the pool, it looks great,' I say, my arms ladened with bags.

'It took me a while to figure out how to use everything, but I think I got the chemicals right. The tests looked okay, but don't blame me if your skin falls off.' Caleb laughs at his own remark. The unfamiliar sound is infectious and I laugh along with him. I can't remember the last time we laughed together.

'I'm sure it'll be fine. Can you grab the door for me?'

I slave away in the kitchen, preparing salads for the barbecue and marinating the meat. Veggies are chopped and dips are thrown together for snacks, and I make a stack of sandwiches for lunch.

'Mum, you know there's only five of us, right?' Caleb says, grabbing a couple of carrot sticks from the finished platter.

'I know, but have you seen how much you all eat?'

'Fair point,' Cale agrees, pouring himself a drink.

'So, how are you feeling about seeing Millie?' I venture.

'Yeah, okay. We talk on the phone all the time. It's all good.'

'And everything else? How are you going?' I feel like it's a good time to reach out to him.

Caleb shrugs. He stills struggles to voice his emotions, which is something he's been working on with his therapist.

'You seem happier,' I say.

'I guess so.'

'It's a journey, Cale. There'll be ups and downs along the way, but we'll all get there. Always remember that I love you, okay?'

It's close to lunch time when Nick and Levi return with Millie in tow. Levi's all hyped up and can't stop talking about their ride.

'Mum, it was so good,' he beams. 'Not sure how Nick's gonna keep up over two weeks, though, when we're riding every day.'

'Cheeky,' Nick grins. 'Just you wait, you won't see me for dust.'

I smile at my son's enthusiasm and the easy banter between them and I mouth a 'thank you,' to Nick, who grins back, just as excited as Levi about their morning.

'Hey Millie, it's good to see you. How've you been?' I greet her with a hug. I've missed her smiling face.

'Good, thanks. Better now this idiot's got his head out of his backside.' Millie nods towards Caleb, who stands at the door, his tail between his legs.

'Hey Mills.' Cale is bashful, ashamed of his recent behaviour towards Millie. 'Hope you brought bathers. Mum made me clean the pool out.'

Millie lifts her t-shirt to flash her bikini.

'Sure did,' she says. 'Let's go.'

'I've made lunch if you're all hungry,' I interject. 'Or you can swim first, whatever you like. It'll be here when you're ready.'

'Cool, thanks Steph.'

I can't take my eyes off the kids playing around in the pool, laughing and having fun together. It's like something from another lifetime.

'Such a good sight, hey?' Nick's eyes light up at the scene across the lawn.

'The best.' I smile back. 'It gives me hope.'

Nick's hand takes mine, and he rests them together in my lap.

'I love this, Steph,' he says. 'The five of us here, together, like a family.'

I turn, shading my eyes from the sun, assessing his thoughts.

'It doesn't bother you that this is where Chris and I lived together?'

'No, not at all. Does it bother you?'

'It did, at first. I felt guilty having you here, but it's my home and I love it here. I wouldn't want to be anywhere else.'

'If things work out between us, would you want to stay here long term rather than finding somewhere together?' Nick asks. 'Down the track, Steph, I'm not trying to jump the gun. I know you're not there yet.'

I smile at his eagerness for our future, but also at his insistence that I'm not ready. He would move in with me tomorrow if I gave him the green light. We're in way deeper than I would've thought possible, but that doesn't mean I'm ready to commit to something.

'I love the peace here, off the beaten track. Levi has his animals and Cale's got his gym. Moving wouldn't be on the cards for me unless I had to.'

'Where's the gym? I didn't know Cale had one,'

Nick says.

'Oh, I'll get him to show you. He has it kitted out pretty well,' I say.

Silence takes us as we both contemplate the reality of our conversation.

'What are you thinking?' Nick whispers after a beat.

'That we just talked about moving in together?' I look at him and grin. 'And also the fact that you said *if* things work out between us.'

'Just covering my bases,' he winks. 'But of course I meant when. So, how does it make you feel, talking about moving in together?'

'I love it in theory, but the reality of it scares me.'

'That's understandable,' Nick nods in agreement. 'There's no time frame on it, Steph. I just want to know that we're heading in the same direction, that you see me in your future.'

'Nick, I can't imagine a future without you. Our relationship is without doubt a permanent fixture. I'm just not ready to set it in stone, and Caleb certainly isn't. But, yes, I see us living together, maybe even married.'

Nick's eyes flicker, igniting a flame of anticipation about our future together. He lifts his fingers and tucks a stray curl behind my ear, then pulls my face to his. Our lips brush, tingling with expectation and hope. He runs his tongue delicately along my bottom lip, opening my mouth in search of more. I respond instinctively and my body draws towards him. My mouth invites him in and I feast on him.

'Dad.'

We're pulled apart by the power of that one word. I look up to see Millie standing there with her hands on her hips and a smirk on her face. I blush at being caught making out by my lover's teenage daughter and send a silent apology.

'Pleased to see you've still got it in you, Dad, but maybe pashing his mum in the middle of the afternoon, in full view, is not the best way to win Caleb over,' she says sternly.

'Shit, did he see?' Nick's eyes darken with regret.

'No, he didn't, but just for the record, Levi and I are really happy you're together, and we still don't want to see that.'

Millie draws her finger between the two of us, mildly offended by our public display.

'I'm sorry, Millie, it won't happen again.' I feel severely chastised.

'Just keep it for the bedroom, guys,' Millie says with a wink, and sashays past us towards the kitchen.

I catch Nick's eye and we burst out laughing at the absurdity of the situation.

'Maybe you two should come for a swim and cool off for a bit,' Millie adds on her way back out.

'You want to?' Nick asks.

'What the hell? Why not?' I say. 'I'll go change.'

When I come back outside wearing a bikini, I'm pleased to see Nick had the good sense to be in the pool already. His tongue is almost hanging out of his head, drooling. His eyes are on me from the moment he spots me until the moment Millie also catches on to his fixation and sneaks up beside him, pushing his head down under the water, giving him a well deserved dunk.

He comes up laughing, picking her up and

throwing her as high as he can, which is not that easy when she's five feet ten of pure muscle. Cale and Levi quickly see the fun to be had and join in, ganging up on Nick, three against one. I lower myself to the edge of the pool, sitting away from the frivolity, at the shallow end, my feet on the steps. I watch them play, my heart warmed by the scene playing out before me. They look like a family and I hope before long, the bonds will strengthen and they'll feel like one too.

Caleb already loves Millie like a sister, and Levi thinks the sun rises and sets with Nick. Millie's like the daughter I never had. It's Caleb and Nick who remain the weak link in the group. I know Nick will do everything in his power to gain Caleb's trust, but he'll never force a relationship with him. That goes against everything he preaches. If a relationship is to blossom, it will need to be grown organically.

'Get in, Mum!' Levi calls when he finally spots me on the edge. Nick turns to see me on the steps, smiling at me, watching them. He wades towards me, holding his hand out to me. I ease myself forward off the edge and take his hand as he leads me down the steps and into the cool water. Once I'm past my waist, I take a breath and duck under the water for a quicker entrance. I stand back up and run my fingers through my hair, squeezing the water out before lying back and floating gently. The pool's large enough for us all to have space to enjoy. Chris had it put in when the boys were young, insisting on a pool big enough to swim laps in.

Millie swims towards me as the guys embark on a game of piggy-in-the-middle towards the deep end.

'Thanks for inviting us over,' she says. 'Mum's

house barely has any garden, neither does Dad's. I'd love to have all this space.'

'You're welcome here anytime, Millie. Feel free to come over whenever you like,' I invite.

'Thank you. I don't remember ever seeing Dad like this before. He's so happy.'

'I'm sorry about earlier, Millie. We shouldn't have let that happen.'

Millie laughs. 'It's fine, honestly. I just don't want anything to spoil whatever's going on right now. Cale's actually having fun with my dad.'

'I know what you mean. It's hard not to tread on eggshells around him, but I try not to. I just don't want to go back to the place we were in before.'

'He's so much better. I can see a huge improvement since I last saw him,' Millie offers.

'How's your mum been? Is she okay with you coming here?'

Millie shrugs. 'I haven't told her. I just said I was going to Dad's. It's easier that way.'

'Fair enough. Does she know about your dad and me?' I wonder.

'I haven't said anything. It's none of her business, really,' Millie says.

'No, I guess not, but I'd probably want to know if my kids were going with their dad, but actually staying at some random woman's house with bad parenting skills.'

Millie laughs. 'I'm sure she doesn't think that. Anyway, things have been a lot better at home since Dad spoke to her.'

'You're up, Millie,' Nick says, swimming towards us. 'I need a rest.'

'Okay, old man,' Millie grins, ducking his head as

he comes close.

'Hey, I did my share of exercise this morning. I bet you didn't even get out of bed till eleven.'

'Yeah, you're right,' she concedes, swimming off towards the boys.

Nick

While Steph busied herself in the kitchen, putting the finishing touches to the salads and side dishes, Nick set about cooking the steaks and sausages on the barbecue. The kids raced over, grabbing seats at the table and pouring themselves homemade lemonade from the jug Steph had put out. The lemon tree had been fruitful, and Steph had made an abundance of the old-fashioned drink her grandfather used to make for her when she was a small child.

'Hey Caleb.' Nick leaned over the back of a chair while he left the meat sizzling. Caleb looked up, a concerned expression on his face. Trust was going to be an issue for a while, Nick thought, taking in Caleb's demeanour.

'Your mum said you have a pretty good gym set up. Would you mind showing me after dinner?'

Caleb's face relaxed. 'Sure.'

'I've been thinking of getting some equipment myself, so I thought I'd check out yours first, see what you've got.'

Steph brought out the salads and

accompaniments, and Nick piled the meat onto the serving plate she handed to him.

'This looks amazing, thanks Steph.' Millie's eyes popped as she delved into the food.

'My pleasure Millie, I love feeding people who like to eat.'

'Beer?' Nick asked Steph as he took one out of the fridge he'd filled earlier.

'I'd love one, thanks.'

Three beers later, and a full stomach, Steph leaned back in her chair, rubbing her tummy.

'I'm stuffed. Would everyone mind waiting for dessert? I'm not sure I can fit it in just yet.'

'Sounds good to me,' Nick said. 'How about you take me to see your gym, Caleb?'

'Yeah sure.' Caleb bit his lip as he pushed his chair back to stand. He'd not been alone with Nick before.

Nick smiled at Steph and followed Caleb towards the large shed set back towards the edge of the garden. Caleb punched the code into the door lock and held the door open for Nick. The tension was a little higher now that the two of them were alone, but Nick was keen to make things as comfortable as possible between the two of them.

'Holy shit, Cale, when your mum said you had a gym, I expected a few weights and a bench press. This is on another level.' Nick couldn't believe his eyes as he took in the professional set up, complete with several expensive machines.

'Yeah, I know, it's pretty impressive. Dad always said he wanted me to have the best chance of making it.' Caleb shrugged, as Nick ran his hands over the equipment, speechless that someone would pay this amount of money for a home gym.

'You're welcome to use it whenever you're here.' Several layers of Caleb's wall came down in one fell swoop.

'Thanks mate, that'd be cool.' Nick was touched by Caleb's offer. 'You should get Millie in here. She's been a little lazy since the season finished.'

'Yeah, me too. I need to get back into it. I've let my fitness slide,' Caleb admitted.

'So, Cale, I've got something I want to ask you, but I don't want you to feel any pressure to say yes,' Nick broached. 'I know you have a lot going on.'

Caleb's face slipped, unsure what direction the conversation was going. He waited for him to continue.

'What would you say to helping me out with pre-season training with Millie's team?' he asked Caleb.

Caleb's face registered shock.

'For real?'

'Yeah, I mean, it was hard last year by myself and if I'm honest, I could do with someone to help me right through next season. If that's something you'd be interested in?'

'Yeah, that'd be cool,' Caleb grinned.

'Thanks Cale, I appreciate it.'

Pleased by the way their one on one had turned out, Nick was encouraged when Caleb continued talking on the way back to the house.

'My brother thinks you're pretty dope.'

'Is that right?' Nick was taken aback by the compliment.

'I used to be jealous of him,' Caleb said. 'My dad never expected anything of him. He left him alone to do his own thing.'

'Why was that?' Nick asked, and Caleb shrugged.

'Who knows?' Caleb said. 'Mum thinks it's because I reminded him of himself and he wanted to give me the encouragement he didn't get off his own dad.'

'And you don't agree?' Nick probed.

'I just don't think he'd have got the same reaction from Levi. He doesn't care if he's not the best,' Caleb said.

'I'm not sure that he doesn't care, Cale. He just has different priorities. I think he cares about his animals and that he looks after them to the best of his ability. He cares about putting in his best effort on our bike rides.'

They reached the outdoor table to find it empty. There was no sign of anyone. Caleb slumped down in a chair, mulling over what Nick had said.

'Yeah, I guess,' he said.

'We're all different, Cale. Some people are driven by competition and a need to win, others have their own personal drivers to feel a level of accomplishment that's personal to themselves. Neither way is right or wrong,' Nick said, then used the conversation as a spring board to go deeper. 'It's the same with anything. We all react to things differently. Nobody is right or wrong; we're all individual. Take grief, for example.' Caleb stiffened, but Nick didn't want to let the opportunity slip away. Sizing up the situation, he changed tack.

'When my wife died, I blamed myself, much like you did when you lost your dad. It took me years to accept it wasn't my fault, and if it hadn't been for Paul and my daughters, I honestly don't know that I'd still be here.'

Caleb studied Nick, absorbing everything he said, his eyes widening at his comment.

'Your mum, on the other hand, reacted differently. I'm not saying she didn't feel guilty for not picking up on his illness. Of course she did, but she rationalised it and understood it was something she had no control over.'

'It's funny, I used to be jealous of Levi because he didn't have any pressure from my dad, and then when I started seeing him with you, and seeing his eyes light up, excited to spend time with you, I felt sad that he'd missed out on having that with Dad.'

'And now? How are things between you two now?' Nick asked.

Caleb thought hard for a moment. 'I'm glad he has you.'

Nick was stunned by Caleb's words.

'Thank you. You know, I'm here for you too, Cale, anytime.' He shifted in his chair, leaning forwards towards Caleb. 'Can I say something?'

Caleb nodded, uncertain.

'I know this thing between your mum and me seems fast to you, and that it might take you a while to accept, but I want you to know that there's no pressure on you to do that until you're ready,' he said. 'Without being too weird, I love your mum and I want us to have a future together.'

Caleb glanced away, but listened to what Nick had to say.

'You boys will always be your mum's priority, just like my girls will always be mine. So, we won't move forward until all five of our children are on board. You all have to be ready. But we've all lost someone, and we all deserve happiness.'

Caleb chewed on his lip, letting the magnitude of Nick's words sink in.

Nick pushed back in his chair and clapped Caleb on the shoulder.

'What do you say we go find the others?'

Nick tapped on Steph's bedroom door, but there was no answer, so he eased it open. The shower was running in the ensuite, so he locked the bedroom door and crept into the bathroom. She startled when she saw him, and he pulled off his t-shirt and dropped his board shorts on the floor. Steph grinned widely and invited him in.

'Are we safe?'

'Caleb went to find the other kids, and I locked your bedroom door,' he said, pulling her towards him.

Steph wound her hands up to his hair and framed the back of his head, drawing him in for a kiss. Nick eased her against the wall, pressing his hips into her, his desire evident. His tongue pushed into her mouth, stroking her as his fingers trailed down her body and settled between her legs. Steph writhed against the tiles, burning for him. Nick moved his hands to her backside and pushed her up the wall, settling her on his hips, thrusting inside and making her groan. He moved with her, finding a steady rhythm as the shower rained down above them. Steph panted through her release, biting her lip and resting her head back against the tiles. Nick shuddered inside her and trailed his lips across to her ear.

'That was fucking amazing!'

Steph moved out of her bedroom with a stealthiness that was almost laughable. She rolled her eyes at her own behaviour, not wanting to draw the kids' attention to the fact that she'd been in there with Nick. He had strict instructions to wait five minutes before coming out himself. Nick perched on the edge of Steph's bed, his forearms resting on his thighs, his smile so wide at the direction his life had turned. He watched the clock tick past the minutes and once it passed three, he couldn't wait any longer.

The scene that greeted him was comical. Steph's eyes were roving anywhere but at the kids, her smug grin giving away her secret. Nick smiled as the kids pretended not to know where he had just come from.

'We're having a horror movie marathon. You want to join us?' Levi asked, breaking the tension in the room. Nick brushed his fingers through his wet hair, sweeping it back off his forehead. Dressed in comfortable shorts and a fitted tee, he relaxed onto the arm of the couch, his hand resting on Steph's upper back, fingering the ends of her hair. He watched her eyes drift over him and could see each thought. The moment she took in the tight sleeves clinging to his biceps, the hem skimming his hips. He heard the hitch of her breath as she adored him, then saw the flash in her eyes that told him the enormity of this mundane situation they were in had struck her. Nick kept his eyes focused on hers, trying to will her out of the overwhelm she'd just found herself in. He knew she wanted this as much as he did, but he could also see the internal fight taking place. Her rational mind told her there was no right and wrong for the way she felt, that there was no fixed length of time in which to grieve, and no timeframe in which she should move on, but Nick could always pick up when her brain went into overdrive and doubt deluged her thoughts. His fingers stroked up her back to her neck, and he gave her a gentle squeeze, letting her know he understood where she had just gone.

'Horror movies, huh?' Nick's voice broke her reverie. 'I haven't watched one in years. What do you say, Steph? I'm game if you are.'

'I might not sleep afterwards, but go on, why not?'

'Mum, do we have any popcorn?' Levi asked.

'I can go have a look,' she said, pushing up from the couch.

'Dad makes the best popcorn,' Millie said. 'Will you make some, Dad? Please.'

'Sure, if Steph doesn't mind,' Nick said, darting his eyes to Steph for confirmation.

'Of course, anything that saves me doing it,' she grinned. 'Here you are,' she said, handing him the jar of popcorn seeds.

'Thanks babe, you go sit down and I'll sort this,' he said. 'Go make sure they don't choose a terrible movie.'

Nick handed out bowls to everyone, then sat down on the couch between his daughter and his girlfriend. That term seemed strange to him at fifty-five. They hadn't put a label on their relationship, but she felt like more than a girlfriend, if he were honest. He knew she was still dealing with her feelings about her late husband and all the stresses that brought with it. Even though today had cemented in his mind that this was what he wanted his future to look like, he'd be as patient as Steph needed him to be.

Steph kicked up her feet beneath her and snuggled into Nick's side, resting one hand on his thigh as she picked at her popcorn with the other. Nick balanced his bowl beside him and laced his fingers through hers, giving them a gentle squeeze. Steph nudged him, beaming, and a warm sensation trickled through Nick's body. He knew it was contentment.

Caleb jumped up to flick the light off, the pendants in the kitchen casting an eerie glow, providing a ghostly lighting effect for their movie. Steph squeezed Nick's hand tight in anticipation, while Millie curled up and snuggled into the other side of him. Nick loved the wholesomeness of the scene laid out before him and loved that his daughter was on this journey with him. He knew his older girls would like Steph too, and that Steph would welcome them into her family with open arms, just like she had Millie.

Levi's eyes kept sneaking glances towards his mum, resting on their interlaced hands. Nick met each sneak peek with a content smile. He knew Levi was desperate for them to become a family and they'd talked in depth that morning to make sure Levi didn't get ahead of himself. Nick warned him to give his mum time to catch up.

Caleb directed his vision at the TV screen and kept his conversation to a bare minimum, but he was there with the rest of them, and no doubt he was still processing the chat the two of them had earlier. His acceptance of Nick was growing as his depression lifted. Nick was in no rush. He knew from experience the journey would be a lengthy one, with twists and turns, and ups and downs, but he vowed to be there to support the whole family through it. Their happiness was important to him because there was no other way to love this woman.

Nick felt Steph's body grow heavy, relaxing deeper into him, her breathing slow. He smiled at the serene look on her face as she slept beside him.

'Steph.' Nick roused her. 'Come on, let's get you to bed.'

Steph bolted upright, rubbing her eyes and looking around the room. The two of them were alone.

'How long have I been asleep?' she asked. 'Did the kids go to bed already?'

'You've been out for a while. The kids have just gone. I didn't have the heart to wake you up, but we shouldn't stay here all night.' He kissed her head and flooded Steph with warmth.

'I'm glad the kids have already gone. The idea of setting off to bed with you when they were all still sat here terrified me.'

'I think that's why they all disappeared. It would've been awkward for everyone.'

Steph

I'm woken by a clatter of pans in the kitchen, followed by hushed voices and suppressed laughter. I rub my eyes and squint across at my alarm clock. Eight o'clock glares back at me in its neon glory. My mind casts back to the night before and a joyous smile creeps over my face. I lie on my back and rest my eyes closed, replaying the night in my head. From watching movies with our blended family to the mundanity of brushing my teeth beside Nick and falling asleep in his arms, I can't keep the smile off my face as I think about the tender way in which he makes me feel cherished.

'You look happy this morning,' Nick whispers, his fingers trailing my stomach, inching around to my side. His throaty, sleep-laden voice is close to my ear, and he follows his words with a nibble of my lobe. He tracks his lips along my jaw and alters his position until his mouth is hovering over mine.

'Stop, I've got morning breath.' I fight to turn my head as he dots tiny kisses on my lips.

'I don't care.' He reaches his hand up to tilt my face back to his. Powerless to curb his advances, I open my mouth to allow him access. My self-consciousness soon disappears when his fingers trickle down my neck and stroke my breast. I push my body towards his. A wave of arousal surges through me and I grasp the back of his neck with my hand, my tongue now battling for control. Nick grins into the kiss, his body now on high alert, turned on by my sudden need for him. He pushes up on to one knee and rests back down between my legs, grasping my hands and pinning them to the pillow above my head. His mouth traces a path over my body, and when his lips find their way back to mine, I'm ready for him. Mindful that the kids are only next door in the kitchen, I have to fight my instinct to cry out, keeping Nick's mouth locked on mine to blanket any noise.

'Shower?' he asks when we both return to earth.

'You go. I'm going to lie here a minute and savour the moment before I have to leave my cocoon.'

I tilt my mouth towards his for another kiss before he leaves the warmth and comfort of my bed.

'Morning guys.' I struggle to look casual when I walk into the kitchen to find Levi and Millie up to their elbows in flour and Nick trying to clean up some of their mess.

'Hey Mum, we're making pancakes.' Levi beams with pride.

'Great, I'm starving.' I make a beeline for the coffee machine. 'Coffee anyone?'

'I'd love one,' Nick says, up to his elbows in bubbles.

'Caleb up yet?' I'm concerned about how he'll react to the domesticity happening in the kitchen.

It's hard, but I'm trying not to overthink or predict his response. His depression and his reactions to Nick are separate and I fight against confusing the two. But I want to avoid anything that may trigger him.

'It's not even nine o'clock.' Levi laughs at my optimism.

Millie is busy frying the last of the pancake batter, having already put an enormous stack in the oven to keep warm.

'They smell great, Millie. Who taught you to cook?' I'm hopeful to glean a little more insight into Nick's family life.

'My mum. The savoury stuff at least. But Dad's the dessert guy, so this is his recipe.' My heart surges at the amount of love she shows her dad with just one smile.

'Oh, sweet tooth, hey Nick?'

'Guilty.' He holds up his hands in admission.

'Lucky,' Levi says. 'Dad was always super strict on sugar, being a dentist and all. My main reason for going to sleepovers and birthday parties when I was younger was just so I could eat sugar.'

'Oh my God, try living with a psychologist.' Millie rolls her eyes. 'Sometimes I just want to have a tantrum and slam my door like normal kids, but no, we have to share our feelings and talk everything out rationally.'

Millie adopts her dad's voice and Nick and I both laugh at our kids.

'Well, I think you both turned out pretty well for all the hardships you suffered.' I mean to be lighthearted, but I realise my oversight.

I dwell on the words I used. None of our kids'

lives have been free from pain. They've all faced difficulties. I feel bad for making light of their struggles.

'Hey, I see where your mind just went.' Nick dries his hands and pulls me into a hug.

'I'm sorry, kids,' I say when he releases me. 'I didn't mean to diminish the real hardships in your lives. You've both faced tough times.'

'We know, Mum, we were all just playing around,' Levi says, and Millie nods her agreement beside him.

'Pancakes are ready,' Millie says, lightening the mood. She drops the freshly cooked ones on the warmed plate and carries it outside, followed by Levi with a tray of condiments.

'Hey, stop beating yourself up,' Nick says. 'You're allowed to have feelings and you're allowed to laugh and joke.'

'I know, sometimes I say things and start overthinking,' I say, reaching up to kiss his cheek. 'Let's go eat. I'm starving.'

Caleb

Dear Dad,

When I got up this morning, I saw them out of the window, having breakfast together, laughing and joking. Mum and Nick, Levi and Millie, and for the first time I smiled at the idea of this new family. Instead of feeling angry, I felt relieved. The only thing stopping me from being part of all that is myself, and they've all given me so many opportunities to change that. It was the first time since you died that I've realised things will be okay.

I watched Mum as she ate her pancakes, and I understood her for the first time. How she is around Nick when I'm not there slammed me with guilt. She's always so on edge when I'm around, worried about how I'll react to him. I can see how happy he makes her. She's been so understanding about my depression and it seems so ironic now that you're the one who would've told me to pull myself together and toughen up, yet you're the one who lived your own experience with it. I blamed Mum for a long time for not knowing how much you suffered and not realising what was going on. I blamed you, too, for taking the easy way out, but I know now that there is no easy way out. I tried to do the same, but there was nothing easy about it. I thought you were selfish for not thinking about us when you crashed into the tree that night, but looking at it from my own experience, it wasn't selfish. You thought we'd be better off without you, just like I had. I couldn't bear to keep disappointing Mum and I assumed things would be better for her if I just disappeared and took all my problems with me. I was wrong, and you were, too.

I'm sorry, Dad, that I didn't appreciate you more. Seeing Levi's face light up whenever Nick's around makes me realise just how much he missed out on with you. You were never interested in him. Everything was always about me. I acknowledge that now, but I want Levi to have that too. It's taken me a while to get here, but it's starting to feel good having Nick around.

I know you never had a good family life when you were young, Dad, and I guess your childhood had a big impact on the way you were with me. I wish things had been different, but I know we can't go back and change the past, so I guess it's time to move forward.

I don't blame you, Dad. Since I started feeling like this, I understand you on a whole new level and I know I don't want my story to end like yours.

Watching this family through the window, I knew I wanted to be a part of it. The second I felt the edges of my mouth turning up, my eyes filled with tears. I tried wiping them away, but they just kept coming. I fought to smile through them, but they just turned into sobs.

That's when it hit me.

There are two things I need to do before I can move on.

I need to face my grandfather so that I can close the chapter and let you go.

The other I needed to do right then.

Caleb

Steph

'Cale? What's wrong?' I turn at the slide of the fly screen to see Caleb in the open doorway. His face crumples and I push back my seat to move closer to him, taking his arm and moving him back inside. I wrap my arms around his six foot two frame and hold him tight.

'Shh,' I hush. 'It's okay, sweetheart, just let it all go.'

Clutching him to me, I guide him to sit and hold him until his body calms and his breathing returns to normal. He pulls back when I loosen my grip and I take in the remorse etched on his face.

'Talk to me, Cale. What happened?' Just when things were looking brighter, I'm slammed with the same worry I felt after his trip to hospital. We can't go back there, it's not an option. He's not going anywhere until he talks to me.

Caleb blows out an extended breath, settling himself.

'I don't know where to start,' he mumbles.

'Is this to do with what you just saw outside? About Nick being here?'

'Yeah,' Caleb nods. 'But not how you think.'

'So tell me. Whatever it is, we can work through it.'

'I'm sorry, Mum,' he says.

'For what?' I'm confused by his apology.

'For everything.'

'Cale, listen to me. You have depression. It's not your fault. It's an illness and you're having treatment. You will get better, I promise,' I reason.

'I know, I think I believed that for the first time just now,' he admits. 'I was watching you all together, having breakfast, and you looked like a family.'

'Cale…' I say.

'It's okay, Mum. I get it now. It's like everything became clearer. For the first time, I don't feel angry about it. I guess I kinda feel jealous,' he shrugs.

'Cale, you're my son. You will always be my family, regardless of what happens with Nick,' I assure him.

'I know that, but you're different when you're around me and I don't want you to be. Whenever you're with Nick, I can always feel this tension, and I wondered if it was because of him, but I see now that it's me. When I watched you before and you didn't know I was there, you were different, happier. You can't relax with him when I'm there, can you? Are you worried about what I might do?'

It's refreshing to hear Caleb speaking so candidly to me and it fills me with confidence that he's turned a corner, that he's making progress with his therapist.

'You're right, Cale, I do worry. I worry about what you're thinking or how you'll react. It's been a huge year for us all and I know me being with Nick is a massive adjustment for you.'

'I'm glad he's been here for you, especially having me to deal with.'

'Thank you, sweetheart. That means a lot. I will always love your dad. He was my husband for a long time and he gave me you and Levi, but I love Nick too. It's sudden, I know, but it's just the way things are. We could have met in three years' time and maybe it wouldn't have seemed like such a big deal, but we met when I needed him the most. I don't know how I would've got through the last six months without him, Cale.'

Cale nods his understanding.

'But I want you to listen to me. You and Levi will always be my priority. I will be there for you every step of the way, whenever you need my help, even if you don't want it. Please try not to look at it as, "dealing with you," it isn't like that.'

Caleb studies me as I speak. He's desperate to believe what I'm saying.

'Can I ask you a question?' he says.

'Of course.'

'You know how Dad used to tell me to toughen up and work harder, or do more training and man up?' he says.

'Yes,' I say, wondering where he's going with this.

'I know you always sided with me and stuck up for me, but did you ever call him out on it?'

'I did, often, and he always acknowledged it, blamed it on his own dad, but never changed his behaviour.'

Caleb nods, his mind whirring with questions.

'Cale, I've done nothing but think about my part

in all this since the moment I found the suicide note. Looking back now, it's all so obvious to me. I can't believe I didn't see how he was suffering. Yes, I knew he'd had a tough childhood and his father wasn't a nice man, and I knew that reflected in his own parenting style, but I had no idea that he thought so poorly of himself. I've seen depression in my work, day in day out, and it always manifests itself differently, but I never would have put him in that category.'

He nods, biting his lip.

'I've been thinking a lot about Levi,' he says. 'Until I saw him hanging out with Nick and the way he laughs and jokes around with him, I didn't realise how little attention Dad gave him.'

I nod, sadly. 'Me neither. I've seen a different side to him since he met Nick and it makes me sad that he never had that with your dad.'

'Dad was all about me and my football. I'm glad he has Nick,' Caleb says.

'You know, you can have that too, Cale. Nick loves football. You two have a lot in common. He's not trying to take over, or be your dad.'

'I know.' His face brightens a little as he speaks. 'We talked yesterday. I like him and I'm glad you're happy, so you can stop worrying about how I'm gonna react all the time. It was good yesterday, having them here. It kinda made things feel normal again.'

Caleb pauses, worrying his lip.

'What is it?' I ask.

'Maybe Nick and Millie could come for Christmas? It'll be weird, just the three of us.'

A rush of adrenalin bursts through me at the

sudden turn around in Caleb's attitude and I have to centre myself before I speak, not wanting him to get ahead of himself.

'That's something we can think about, but let's not rush into making hasty decisions.' The last thing I want is for him to dive headfirst into something he'll come to regret. 'I'm glad you're feeling better about things, Cale.'

'Thanks, Mum,' he says. 'Is there any breakfast left?'

'Let's go have a look, shall we?'

I feel such a relief when Caleb and I sit down to finish breakfast with the others. It feels like a physical weight has lifted. Caleb's progress is significant. His mind is much more clear, and he seems to have reached a much more positive outlook regarding the future. I sit back and listen to everyone's chatter, watching their animated faces tell each other funny stories, and I feel at ease in the company of both my son and my partner.

'What are your plans for the day, Millie?' her dad asks.

'I don't have any. What are you guys all doing?'

Eyes dart amongst us, followed by questions and a round of shrugs. No one has anything planned.

'Can we invite some friends over to hang in the pool?' Caleb asks.

'Sure, if you like.' I'd agree to almost any request, happy to see him wanting to socialise.

'Cool, Millie, Levi, you in?' he asks.

Levi's face lights up. Caleb has never included him in plans involving their friends before.

'Yep, I'll go call them,' Levi says, jumping up to

go get his phone.

'Dad, can I?' Millie asks.

'You can for me, as long as your mum's not expecting you home,' he says.

'She's working.' Millie beams, excited to spend more time with the boys.

'Why don't you two go out for lunch or something?'

Nick's eyes sparkle at Caleb's suggestion, while I try not to suspect an ulterior motive.

'Sounds good to me,' he says. 'As long as you don't invite too many people and this thing stays small, okay?' Nick warns.

Caleb's eyes dart to Nick's and the old tension creeps back into my shoulders. I know what Cale said, but old habits die hard.

Nick regrets his words.

'Sorry, it's not my place to tell you that.' He makes light of it. 'It was aimed more at Millie, though. I know how many friends she has.'

'No worries, and it'll just be a few. Don't worry,' Caleb assures him.

I take it as a huge win.

Leaving the kids with a warning to behave and be careful in the pool, we set off in my car for a drive up the coast for lunch, and I feel a certain freedom I haven't felt until now.

'You've released a mountain of tension,' Nick says, as I pull out on to the road. 'What happened with Cale?'

I glance over at Nick in the passenger seat.

'Like you wouldn't believe. He made a massive breakthrough. He needed it.'

'I'm so glad,' he says. 'It feels good when that happens. Was he able to talk to you about it?'

'Yeah, he said things feel much clearer to him and he believes he's getting better. He can see the way through.'

I don't want to pry, but I want Nick to know that Caleb mentioned the talk they had.

'You two talked yesterday?'

'We did. I offered him the job of my assistant with Millie's team and he opened up a little about his dad and Levi.'

'Oh?' I say, taken aback.

'He didn't say much, just that he'd never realised how little Chris and Levi interacted and that he was happy that I was in Levi's life,' Nick says.

'But not in his life?' I'm clutching at straws.

'Steph, try not to force a relationship between me and Caleb. It will happen when it happens. I clarified that I'm here for him too and he knows I want you all in my future. Give him time to adjust. It's a lot.'

'I know, I just want him to feel like he's part of it, part of a family again, you know?'

'We'll get there. He's reached a point of clarity in his healing process, and that makes such a difference. When your head is all fogged up and you can't think straight, it's difficult to see things rationally. As soon as that lifts, it's like you've been short sighted and you put glasses on and everything's so much clearer,' Nick describes.

'He told me he watched us having breakfast through the window and realised how happy I am with you in my life,' I say, my throat thick with emotion.

'Caleb said that?'

'Also that I seemed more relaxed when I didn't know he was watching and he hates that I can't relax with you when he's there. He wants to accept you into our lives, Nick. It's a lot, but he's trying.'

We unwind into a comfortable silence, thinking about what that means for us and for our future together.

I park the car at the marina and we wander towards the boardwalk where the shops and restaurants are, scanning menus as we pass by.

Nick stops abruptly after passing an Italian restaurant. He swings my hand and turns me to face him, threading his other hand through my hair at my nape.

'Thank you for this weekend,' he whispers. 'I've enjoyed every second.'

'Me too. It's been wonderful to just behave like a normal family again.'

'That's exactly what Millie said to me last night before she went to bed,' Nick says. 'She told me she'd had the best day, and she's missed all the family stuff.'

I reach up on my tip-toes and kiss him.

'Things seem to be settling. I hope it stays that way,' I say when I pull back.

'Let's hope so. I'd like you to meet Hannah and Lucy soon,' he says.

'Great, let's organise dinner sometime.'

After a while, we find a restaurant that looks suited to our appetites and choose a table on the waterfront. I order fish tacos and Nick orders gnocchi.

'What do you do at Christmas?' I ask, as we're chatting about his older girls. I'm gearing up for broaching Caleb's suggestion.

'The older girls come to me for the day and Millie splits it between me and her mum. It just depends on Sarah's shifts. She's a nurse,' he clarifies.

'Oh, I don't think I knew that,' I say.

'I guess it's going to be a tricky one for you this year. Have you thought much about it?'

'I hadn't even given it a thought until Cale mentioned it this morning.'

'Oh?'

'Yeah, he said he'd enjoyed this weekend with you and Millie. It made him feel normal again, and he wondered whether it would be an option for Christmas,' I convey.

Nick stares at me in shock.

'I told him there's a lot to factor in, so it might not be possible.'

'Steph, I'd love nothing more than to spend Christmas with you. I just never thought it would be a possibility,' he says. 'I'd have to speak to all my girls, but it's something I'd like to explore.'

I beam at the idea of us all together, one family, cooking together and hanging out in the pool with the kids. It seems too good to be true.

Nick's phone lights up and he frowns.

'Millie? Is everything okay?' he asks. I watch on in anticipation as worry grips his face.

I can overhear Millie's frantic voice.

'Dad, you need to come back. It's crazy and Cale's freaking out,' she cries.

'Millie, slow down and tell me what happened. What's going on?' He's always so calm in a crisis, smothering the flames in an instant.

'We just invited a couple of friends each, I swear, but somebody's spread the word that it's a party and there's so many people here. No one will leave and Cale thinks you're gonna kill him. I'm scared Dad.'

'Okay, Millie, this is what I want you to do, okay? Make sure there's nobody inside the house, and then lock it up. If you feel safer inside, then go inside and lock yourselves in,' Nick instructs his daughter.

'We'll set off now, but we're about forty-five minutes away, so I'll call Paul and Gerry and see if they can get there sooner.'

'Thanks, Dad.'

'Is Josh there? Maybe I can call his dad, too.'

'Yeah, he suggested that, but I wanted to call you first. We're sorry, Dad. Please tell Steph it's not Cale's fault.'

'Of course, Millie, try not to worry. I'll make those calls now and we'll be on our way.'

Nick hangs up and reaches for my hand.

'The guest list got a little out of control,' he says.

'I heard, come on, let's go. You call Paul, I'll call Mark,' I say.

I slide into the driver's seat of my BMW and bang the steering wheel in frustration.

'Fuck!' Disappointment courses through me now the adrenalin's died down.

'Hey, it'll be okay, baby,' Nick says. 'Do you want me to drive?'

'No, I'm good. I was feeling like my head was

above water at last, then along comes a great big hand waiting to duck me under again. I was enjoying our drama-free, grown up lunch date.'

'Steph, we have three teenagers between us,' Nick reminds me. 'There'll be drama for a little while longer.'

We're met by a group of teenagers hanging around at the end of the driveway waiting for rides. I abandon my car behind both Mark and Paul's cars and we jump out, heading around the back to assess the situation.

Paul and Gerry are chatting with Mark on the verandah, while Millie and Levi sit on the couch looking worried. They jump up at the sound of our footsteps and Millie rushes towards me.

'We're so sorry. We didn't mean for this to happen, I promise,' she cries.

I wrap her up in my arms.

'As long as you're all okay, that's all that matters, Millie,' I say.

'Cale's in his room. We couldn't get him to come out.'

'Has everyone left? Even the friends you invited?' Nick asks.

'No, they're still in the pool,' Millie says.

Nick smiles at his daughter and gives her shoulder a squeeze.

'Thanks guys, we owe you one,' he says, turning to our friends who had shown up in our hour of need.

'No worries,' Mark says. 'They left once they saw adults arrive. No harm done.'

I join the guys after a quick chat with Levi to ease

his concerns, and Nick drapes his arm around my shoulders.

'Well, that was a lovely date. We had a wonderful time.' Sarcasm drips from his tongue.

Paul beams at us, his two closest friends, together as a couple.

'There'll be many more, I'm sure,' he says. 'I love you two together.'

I wrap my arms around Nick's waist. Even though the kids panicked and ruined our date, Nick was there beside me. If there are going to be family dramas, then I want him to be a part of my family.

'Cale,' I call, knocking on his bedroom door. 'It's me. Can I come in?'

There's no answer, but I can hear shuffling inside the room and the door opens a crack. I push it further open and venture inside. Cale sits back down on his bed, his eyes red rimmed.

'Hey, sweetheart, are you okay?' I ask, sitting on the bed next to him.

Caleb just shrugs and my stomach drops.

'It's okay, Cale. The other kids have all gone. There's no damage, it's fine,' I assure him.

'I only invited Josh, and Levi and Millie only invited a couple of friends each, I swear. I don't know what happened,' he says.

'I know, Millie explained. The only thing I care about is that you're all okay. Do you feel okay?' I ask.

Caleb nods. 'I just kinda freaked out.'

'Like a panic attack?'

'No, I don't think so, more worried that you were gonna kill me.' Guilt reddens his cheeks. 'I'm sorry we messed up your date.'

'Cale, having you here, saying that means more to me than you'll ever know. I would rather live this day on repeat than go back to where we were only months ago,' I say, hugging my son to me. 'Your friends are still in the pool. Why don't you come back out?'

'Is Nick pissed at me?' Caleb asks, double checking he won't get in trouble.

'Nick's fine, Cale. You never have to worry about him in that way, I promise.'

Nick

'How does dinner sound, Friday night?'

'Erm, yeah, sure. Where?' Steph kicked off her shoes after work and turned her attention to her phone.

'I'll book somewhere. Hannah and Lucy are coming. I'm not sure about Millie, but you're welcome to invite the boys, too,' Nick said.

'Maybe we'll just keep it with your girls for now. I don't want to overwhelm them with all my family drama just yet. I want to make a good impression.'

'You couldn't make any other impression, Steph, they'll love you like I do. Well, maybe not that much.'

'Still, I'd like to get to know them before I get the boys involved,' she said.

'Of course. What are your plans for your day off tomorrow? Can I see you?' Nick asked.

'I'm meeting my lawyer first thing, but I'm free after that. It's my last day with the house to myself before the boys break up for the summer. You're welcome to come over. Or we can do something else if you prefer.'

'I can't think of anything I would prefer than spending the day alone with you. Call me when you've finished with the lawyer,' he said.

'Hey babe.' Nick smiled from behind an enormous bouquet. Steph's face lit up.

She leaned in for a kiss. 'What are these for?'

'Do I need a reason?' he frowned.

'Of course not, thank you.' The scent of the flowers wafted towards her and Steph breathed it in. 'I'll go put them in water.'

'How did it go with your lawyer?' Nick asked, watching her arrange the flowers.

'The business side of things went well…'

'And what other things were there?' Nick frowned, confused by her statement.

Steph paused for a moment, her nose scrunched.

'I think he made a pass at me.'

'Did he touch you?' Nick asked, concerned.

'No, nothing like that.' She shook her head. 'I don't know what happened. One minute we were discussing business, the next his entire body language changed, and he was making these flirty gestures, asking me personal questions.'

'Jesus, Steph, that's off. Are you okay?' Nick asked, dashing round the kitchen bench to give her a hug.

'Yeah, I'm fine. It was a little disconcerting, though. I've never been comfortable alone with Jason, but he's never come on to me before.'

'I guess he's always seen you as someone's wife before. Now you're this hot, single woman.' Nick dropped a kiss to her lips. 'That doesn't excuse his behaviour, though. Has he never heard of professional conduct? Did you say anything to him?'

'I made it clear that I'm with someone.' She kissed him back. 'Not that I should have to. I hate how some men will only accept a rejection if the woman has a partner.'

Steph snuggled into Nick's chest, feeling safe with him.

'Anyway,' Steph said, moving on. 'Caleb's gonna be happy. The reason Jason wanted to see me was because Chris put provision in his will that the boys get money to buy a car when they turn seventeen.'

'Oh, lucky boys,' Nick said, then frowned. 'How does that make you feel?'

'I guess I'm happy for them, but it feels a little calculated. He put so much effort into making everything right for us when he'd gone, instead of putting that effort into making things right for himself,' Steph said.

'Maybe he didn't know how. I don't know, Steph, there's no straightforward answer with depression. Everyone is different, and often their thoughts aren't rational. But you have to take the good things and hold on to the happy memories. It's a lovely gesture for the boys, and probably something he would've enjoyed doing with them. Perhaps it made him feel included somehow,' Nick said.

'Yeah, I guess so,' Steph mused.

Steph was hot lying in the sun. She turned over and asked Nick to rub more sunscreen on her back. The liquid dripped on her shoulders and she groaned at the warm sensation. He smoothed it over her shoulders, then unfastened the clasp of her bikini to give him better access. His hands continued to massage her back, long after the sunscreen had disappeared, and Steph moaned at the sensual feeling. Nick leaned in and brushed her hair away with one hand, while he dropped tiny kisses on her ear before trailing his lips down her neck.

'Oh, I see where this is going.' Steph welcomed the sensation.

'You fancy skinny dipping?' He sucked her ear lobe into his mouth and nibbled.

Steph pushed up with her hands, her top dropping off as she stood. Nick's eyes widened as he took her in. Her eyes locked with his as she teased her bikini bottoms down her legs. Nick's mouth watered and he shed his shorts. Steph twirled and swan-dived into the pool.

'Shit, that's cold!' she squealed when she surfaced. 'You coming in?'

Nick braced himself for the cold and followed Steph's moves with a dive. He surfaced in front of her, and she wrapped her legs around his waist, cupping his face with her hands. Her tongue darted across his lips, licking off the beaded droplets and teasing his tongue.

'This feels naughty.' Steph was breathless when their kiss drew to an end.

'It feels amazing. I haven't been skinny dipping in years.' Nick's mouth smiled into hers, and she drew his tongue back into her mouth, pushing her body closer.

'I never expected to have this again,' she panted. 'The excitement of a new relationship, and the constant need for physical affection. I never want it to end.'

'Then let's make sure it never does. I'll put the work in Steph and always stay present. We know how things work and I'm sure we've both been guilty of letting things slide in our past relationships. Make that promise with me, right now, that we're committed to making this work.'

'I promise, I'm all in.' Steph lost herself in his eyes as they sealed the promise between them.

Nick made himself at home in Steph's kitchen while she took a shower. He moved around with ease, finding his way through her cupboards, chopping vegetables and cooking salmon in the griddle pan. His hands chopped a mango with precision and scraped the pieces into a bowl already containing other ingredients. Turning to rinse his hands at the sink, he caught Steph leaning against the wall, a content smile on her face as she took in the scene playing out before her.

'How long have you been watching me?' he asked.

'Enough to see that you love cooking.'

Nick smiled. 'I do enjoy it,' he said. 'I'd love to cook Christmas dinner with you. We should discuss that more.'

'I'd love that too. Let's ask your girls how they would feel about it. I know Levi would love to have you here, and Caleb was the one to suggest it. I wouldn't want Millie to miss out though, if she's with her mum,' Steph said.

'You're so thoughtful thinking about Millie,' Nick said.

'I'd hate for us all to be together without her.'

'I'll call Sarah later and see if she has her roster yet,' Nick prayed their plan would come together. Now that she'd raised the idea, he couldn't bear to think of spending Christmas without Steph.

He finished his mango salad with some fresh coriander and lime juice, then removed the salmon from the griddle and served up.

'Wow, this looks and smells amazing,' Steph complimented. 'Thank you.'

'You're welcome. I'm happy to cook for you anytime,' he said, carrying both plates outside.

'My day off feels so decadent these days.' Steph popped a piece of salmon in her mouth and savoured the flavour.

'How do you mean?' Nick asked.

'It was a day for catching up on housework and grocery shopping. Now I have romantic lunches and lazy days in bed.'

'And now you can add skinny dipping to the list.'

Steph giggled, her cheeks flaming brighter.

She relayed the conversation she'd had with Jonathan about cutting back her hours.

'We don't have to see each other on Thursdays if you need more time for yourself,' Nick said.

'Are you kidding? This is the single best time of my week. You're not getting rid of me,' she said. 'It's been a tough year and if I'm honest, I'm feeling burnt out.'

'Then I'm happy you've made that decision. You deserve to take care of yourself, Steph, and anything I can do to help take care of you, I'm on board with.'

'Nick, you already take care of me in so many

ways. You're so special to me.'

Nick rested his hand on top of Steph's, his eyes brimming with emotion.

'I feel the same, Steph. I feel so lucky to have met you when I did, and I'm glad I've been able to help you through your grief. Now it's time to look forward to a future we can build together.'

Steph

'Boys, I'm leaving.' I hear Nick's car in the driveway.

There's a vague muttering from Caleb and Levi rushes down the hall to say goodbye.

Nick has just stepped out of the car when I round the corner.

'Oh, hey, I was coming to the door to pick you up properly.' His face drops, and I laugh at his gentlemanly values.

'What, are we in the 1950s? You gonna open the car door too?'

'Okay, okay, get in,' he smirks.

I slide into the passenger seat and lean across the centre console for a kiss.

'Millie's not coming, but Hannah's bringing her boyfriend,' Nick says as we set off.

'Oh, that's nice, have they been together long??' I ask, unsure if Nick's mentioned a boyfriend before.

'A couple of years, I think. They're looking at moving in together next year, which will mean Lucy will have to either find herself somewhere else to live, or find another flat mate. They've shared an apartment for a few years now,' he says.

My belly is flipping somersaults.

'This is terrifying. Is this how you felt when you first met my boys?'

'Well, no, but we weren't together then, and I was there for very different reasons.'

'I forget that sometimes. It feels like we've been together for ages.'

'I know what you mean. Come on, you'll be fine. I've told them you're not at all like Sarah!'

I follow him inside, chuckling.

The girls, and Jack, are already seated when Nick and I are shown to the table. Nick does a round of introductions and I sit down next to Lucy, with Nick on the end. We busy ourselves with the menu, all the while trying not to be awkward. Nick orders a bottle of wine and winks at me. I can read him like a book; he knows the wine will loosen us all up.

Both Nick and Millie have shared some of the difficulties Hannah and Lucy had with their stepmother so I can understand them being a little cautious with me. I feel it's my job to put them at ease.

'So…' I break the ice. 'This is weird, hey?'

Lucy lets her guard down and her laughter is soon followed by Hannah's.

'It's a little terrifying. It kinda feels like we're little again.'

'In what way?' I ask, and Nick frowns.

'I remember when Dad took us to meet Sarah for

the first time and he bought us new dresses to wear. It was like we were auditioning for a part in her life.'

'Oh my God, please don't feel like that.' I don't want to give that impression at all. 'You don't have to dress up for me, or do anything for me, for that matter. All I want is the chance to get to know you both,' I say.

Hannah and Lucy both smile, and I continue.

'I'll lay my cards on the table. I love your Dad.' I glance at Nick and he squeezes my hand, his face beaming. 'We're building a life together, one which will always include all five of our children, no matter how grown up you might be.' I stop talking, embarrassed by my sales pitch.

'Thank you. Millie said you were pretty cool.' Lucy's kind words put me at ease.

Hannah smiles from across the table.

'Thanks Steph, that means a lot. Sarah had no time for us once Millie was born. I don't want to say bad things about her. She's our sister's mum, but it's kind of put us on edge about meeting Dad's girlfriends.'

'Dad's girlfriends?' Nick interrupts. 'I haven't had any girlfriends. Steph's the first woman I've introduced you to since Sarah.'

'I know,' Hannah laughs. 'But we were still worried about the prospect of it.'

'Well, as I've told you, Steph is nothing like Sarah,' Nick says, lacing our fingers together. 'She's been wonderful to me, and to Millie, and I love her very much.'

I blush at his words, not used to someone saying such flattering things about me to others.

'Aww Dad, I've never seen you so mushy,' Lucy

says. 'I'm glad you're happy. You deserve it.'

'Cheers,' Hannah says, holding up her wine, and we all join her.

Once the ice breaks and the food arrives, the wine flows and Nick relaxes. He sits back and watches as I bond with his daughters.

I'm not sure how much Nick has told his girls about my personal situation, so I haven't mentioned anything about Chris, but when the subject arises, I take the opportunity to share my story.

'Lucy, do you look like your mum?'

'Everyone says I'm her double.' Lucy takes out her phone, holding up the lock screen for me to see. It's an old photo of Lucy as a toddler, holding hands with her mum. It must have been taken not long before she died.

'You are her double, Lucy. She was beautiful,' I say, honestly. 'I'm so sorry she didn't get to see you grow up. It must've been hard for you both.'

'It was, still is sometimes,' Hannah joins in. 'Sometimes you just need your mum.'

'Yes, my boys are just experiencing a similar feeling now. I'm not sure if your dad told you my husband passed away earlier this year.'

'Yes, he did. I'm so sorry,' Lucy says.

I blow out a breath before I share more details, ones I know Nick wouldn't have shared.

'He took his own life. It's been hard for us all, but especially for Caleb, my eldest son. He took an overdose a couple of months ago, but he seems to have turned a corner.' Hannah looks at her dad with adoring eyes, tears pooling in the corners.

'Hey,' Nick says, his voice tight. 'This was supposed to be a fun night, not a sharing of misery.'

Hannah's tears spill over and she swipes them away.

'Your dad's right. We're all in a good place, Caleb's doing well, it's supposed to be a fun night for us all,' I say. 'Let's have more wine.'

We order another bottle and the conversation moves away from death and our tragic history.

'I guess we should talk Christmas, seeing as though it's only a few weeks away.'

'Oh, I hadn't thought of that. I assumed we'd be coming to yours, Dad, but I guess you'll want to spend it with Steph too,' Lucy says.

'You're all very welcome to come and spend the day at my house,' I venture. 'But I understand if you guys would rather have your own family Christmas together. I don't want you to feel you have to do anything different. Your dad and I are both happy with whatever you decide.'

'How would your boys feel about that?' Hannah asks.

'To be honest, it was Caleb who mentioned he'd like Nick and Millie to spend Christmas with us because he thought it might be too sad, just the three of us, with it being the first Christmas without their dad. But I don't think he'd factored the two of you into the equation, so I would need to speak to him again. Levi's obsessed with your dad, so as long as he's there, he won't notice anyone else.' Levi's fixation makes me laugh, but I'm humbled by his affection for Nick.

My eye catches Jack, quiet in the corner, looking a little bewildered.

'What about you, Jack? Are you planning on spending Christmas with Hannah?'

'I was planning to, but I don't want to disrupt anyone's plans,' he says.

'You'd be more than welcome to join us, if that's what the girls decide on. You can all spend the night too.'

'Do you have enough room for us all?' Lucy asks.

'We live on ten acres with a huge pool.'

'Not to mention the dogs, the sheep, the chooks and the goat,' Nick laughs.

'There's a spare room and a pull-out in the theatre room. Millie can always bunk up in Cale's room.'

Hannah raises her eyebrows and laughs.

'Do you have a death wish? Sarah would never allow that.'

'I know,' I smirk. 'I've already had a brief run in with her for allowing Millie in Cale's room in the middle of the afternoon.'

'You've met her?' Hannah raises her eyebrows, wondering how that came about.

'Yeah, she came to pick Millie up one day. I'm not even sure Nick and I were together. Anyway, she laid into me. It wasn't fun.'

'Well, I'd love to spend Christmas with you all, if it works for everyone, that is.'

Nick's daughters are so accommodating and they soon agree to a big family Christmas. Their immediate acceptance of me solidifies my love for Nick. I hadn't realised I'd been holding something back, but that final jigsaw piece needed to slot into place. This was never about just the two of us. There are seven people affected by this relationship and we all need to be on board for it to gain strength.

Nick excuses himself to go to the bathroom. He squeezes my hand in solidarity as he stands, knowing full well his ears will burn while he's away from the table.

'I've never seen Dad look so happy.' Lucy gushes as soon as he leaves the table. 'We knew he'd met someone before he even told us, so we asked Millie and she spilled all the tea.'

I laugh at their detective work.

'We kept things quiet for a while, mainly because of Caleb. He wasn't in a good place, and I didn't want to risk upsetting him. I wasn't sure if I was ready either, to be honest. It happened so fast after my husband passed, and I was still grieving. Your dad's been amazing to me, and to my boys, you're very lucky to have him.'

'We are,' Hannah says. 'He's had it tough and we've always worried he wouldn't be happy again. But it's written all over his face. We're so happy for you both.'

'Thank you, I appreciate you saying that. I was terrified of coming here tonight.' Nervous laughter fills the air. 'Your dad and Millie have both mentioned how bad things were between you two and Sarah, and I didn't want for that to happen. I see the difference in the way Nick speaks about Sarah and how he speaks of your mum. She was the love of his life, and I'm glad he felt that way about her. I think we bonded over that same shared experience before we even fell in love.'

Hannah and Lucy are both in tears by the time I finish speaking and Nick wavers when he sits back down.

'Everything okay?' he asks.

'Yeah,' Jack pipes up. 'They've all had too much wine and have started on all the mushy stuff.'

Nick looks down at me and smiles, then his eyes roam the table and fall on his girls. The evening started a little awkwardly, but has turned into something special. The love shared between Nick and his daughters is tangible, and the more I learn about his life from other people's perspectives, the more brightly he shines from mine.

Steph

'Are you sure you won't stay over?' I ask Nick as he gets up to leave.

'No, honestly, I think you should spend Christmas morning with just your boys. It's going to be difficult enough for you all. I don't want to make things awkward for anyone,' he says.

'You're so thoughtful, but the boys have both said it's fine.'

'I know, but you do your thing and I'll be here right after breakfast,' he says.

'I don't like the thought of you waking up all alone on Christmas,' I pout.

'Hey, I get to spend the rest of the day with all the people I love,' Nick points out. 'I'm so excited about that.'

'Me too. Goodnight, Nick. I'll miss you in my bed tonight.'

'I'll make it up to you tomorrow, I promise.' His throaty growl in my ear travels to every nerve ending.

'Stop teasing me, that's not fair.'

Nick leans down and kisses me with a hint of desperation before heading to the door to spend the rest of the night alone. He brought a car full of Christmas presents earlier, adding them to the pile already under our tree, ready for when his whole family descends on us tomorrow for our first big shared Christmas. We have a fridge full of food and the older girls are bringing drinks and mixers for cocktails. I know it will be a tough day to navigate for all of us, but I hope it will be one that's filled with laughter and love, and a promise of a new tradition between our families.

Levi's the first one up on Christmas morning, just like any other day. I stir when I hear him leave the house to go feed the animals and I lie in bed thinking about the previous Christmas and how we hadn't known it was the last one we'd share as a family. Would I have done anything differently if I'd known? We've always had a small, quiet celebration, just the four of us, but this year will be quite the opposite. There'll be eight of us altogether and I'm looking forward to a lazy day in the pool with a huge buffet of seafood, ham, and salads.

I was unsettled about Nick not staying last night. I didn't want him to be alone, but he was adamant I should spend time alone with my boys. Chris was never invested in Christmas. I was always the instigator of traditions, the organiser of presents and food, so other than his physical presence, nothing would be different for me. I take my time before getting up to cast my mind over Christmases past, remembering the happy times when the boys were little and Santa was the main event. The memories of their big smiling faces bring me hope that I'll get to see them again today.

There's no sign of Caleb by the time I've made my coffee, so I take it outside and enjoy the peaceful morning.

'Merry Christmas, Mum,' Levi says, when he treks back across the lawn in his PJs and a Santa hat.

'Merry Christmas, sweetheart. Animals all good?' I ask.

'Yeah, are you okay, Mum?' He's always such a thoughtful boy, and the role he's played in my healing has been pivotal. He's been such a tower of strength to me this year.

'I am. Thank you for asking, Levi. How are you doing?'

'I'm okay, but it's weird. It's just another day and I'm used to him not being here, but it's Christmas and it kinda feels like something's missing.'

'Yeah, I know what you mean. I think Nick was right, though. I'm glad it's just us this morning, but I'm also glad everyone else is coming later. It's good to remember Dad with our own traditions, but I want to make something new too.'

Levi pulls Sully, the chocolate lab, up onto the couch between us, stroking his fur. Mike, the kelpie, is curled up at my feet. Levi named the dogs after characters in his favourite movie when we got them about eight years ago.

'Do you still miss him, Mum?' he asks.

I frown at his question.

'Yeah, of course, don't you?'

Levi shrugs.

'No, not really,' he says, and I raise my eyebrows in surprise.

'I'm sad he died, and sometimes it feels there's

something missing, like today, but I don't miss him. It's not like he ever took an interest in my life.' Levi pauses. 'Not like Nick does.'

I focus on his words. He's so mature sometimes, way ahead of his years.

'You've changed recently, Levi, and I think maybe Nick might have had something to do with that.'

'I like him, Mum. Do you think you'll ever get married again?'

I shake my head at his persistence.

'Maybe one day.' I consider what that would look like and grin at the prospect.

Levi's smile is wide, his eyes shining at the prospect.

'What did you mean when you said I've changed?' he asks, thinking about my comment.

'I don't think I ever realised how little attention Dad gave you, and I'm sorry for that. You've always been such a happy and content kid, doing your own thing. I guess I just never thought about what you might have missed out on. Your face brightens whenever Nick's around and seeing the two of you together brings me so much joy, but I also feel a little sad that your dad didn't have that. He missed out on so much because he fought his illness alone.' We sit in silent reflection and I think about what was and what could have been. If only Chris would have spoken to me.

'Levi,' I say, breaking our silence. 'Thank you for talking to me. It means a lot that you don't hide your feelings, especially with what's happened with Dad and Cale. It's important to me we keep communicating. You can talk to Nick, too, about anything. He'll always listen. He loves you, you

know.'
Levi smiles.
'I know, Mum.'

Caleb drags himself out of bed and the three of us gather around the Christmas tree. Levi hands out our presents before ripping into his own gifts. It's a quiet affair, and the atmosphere is more subdued than jolly, but we get through it the best we can. We all breathe a sigh of relief when Nick arrives after breakfast, bringing respite from our low spirits. His presence provides a normality that we've relied on of late, even Caleb.

'Merry Christmas, beautiful,' Nick whispers from behind when the boys have gone to inspect their presents in more detail.

'Merry Christmas to you too.' I turn in his arms for a kiss.

'Would you like your gift now, or when the girls arrive?' he asks.

'Why don't we exchange ours now and then later can be all about the girls,' I suggest, wanting a moment alone with him before we're surrounded by all our kids.

The two of us sink to the floor in front of the Christmas tree and I dig through the unopened presents to find the gift box I wrapped for him.

'I hope you like it. I had help from Millie.'

'Thank you, I'm sure I'll love it, whatever it is,' he says. I watch him read the tag and smile at my words before untying the ribbon and opening the box. His eyes widen at the Apple watch inside and his face contorts in horror.

'Steph! You shouldn't have bought me this,' he

says.

'You can exchange it if you don't like it,' I say, 'but just so you know, Millie told me you wanted one. She said you're just too tight to buy one for yourself.'

Nick laughs.

'Yeah, she's right about that, but that doesn't mean you should've spent so much on me.'

'So you do like it?'

'Of course I do. I love it. Thank you, Steph. I should've led with that.' He leans over to kiss me. 'But you shouldn't have.'

'I wanted to. You're worth it. Besides, I got Levi the same one and I can't wait to see the look on his face when he realises you match.'

Nick hands me a small box and bites his lip. Just as I pull off the paper, he grabs my hand and stops me.

'Steph, before you open it, I want you to know that I spent a lot of time agonising over this gift. If I'm being honest, I'm still not sure it's the right thing to do, or if it's the right time, but I want you to know that however you receive it, it comes from my heart.'

The size of the box, his little speech, and the anxious way he's looking at me all tell me there's only one thing inside this gift. I'm not ready. I want to be, and I will be one day, but not right now, not today.

'Steph,' he whispers. 'That's the second time I've seen that look on your face. I hope when I do propose, you'll be much happier about it.'

My eyes dart to his and I blush.

'Relax, it's not a ring.'

I grin as I pull off the last strip of paper to reveal the robin egg blue Tiffany box. My heart leaps in my chest when I remove the lid and see the delicate necklace with two love hearts, one silver, the other rose gold.

'Nick, it's beautiful, thank you. Why the worry? I love it.'

'There's a meaning behind it,' Nick says. 'I chose the two hearts, one to represent me and one to represent Chris. I want there to be a place in your heart for both of us.'

My eyes fill, spilling down my cheeks in torrents.

'Nick…' The ability to form words has gone, my empty mouth dry. I swallow several times, trying to rid myself of the lump forming in my throat. Nobody has ever done something so special for me before and I'm unable to express my gratitude. I stare at him and shake my head.

Nick smiles at my incompetence and cups my face in his hands, wiping away the tears with his thumbs.

'I'm glad you like it,' he says. 'Merry Christmas, my love.'

'They look happy,' Hannah says.

We're lying on sun loungers, sipping on margaritas, watching an impromptu game of water polo taking place in the pool. The smiles and laughter emanating from both of my boys is heart warming.

'They do. I couldn't have asked for a happier Christmas after the year we've had. Those smiles mean the world to me. It could've turned out so differently.'

'It must've been so hard for you all,' Hannah says. 'When Mum died, I guess it was different for us. Lucy and I were too young to understand. I can't imagine going through that as a teenager.'

'When did you know?' I ask. 'About her depression, I mean.'

Hannah pauses, considering my question.

'I would've been around fourteen, I guess. I was having a difficult time with Sarah and I was very jealous of Millie. Dad thought I was depressed, so he sat me down and explained Mum's illness to me. It was a shock. My memories of her were all so happy. I never remember her being unhappy. Dad worries about us. He's terrified of us having kids and I know he'll be unbearable, but I wouldn't change him for the world.'

The love Nick's girls have for him flips my stomach.

'Me neither,' I say, sipping on my straw. 'He's pretty special.'

'Do you like your necklace? He was so nervous buying it for you.'

'Hannah, it's so beautiful. I can't describe how much it means to me that he wanted to include Chris in my gift.' The two love hearts rest on my chest, and I think fondly of my husband and the new love in my life.

'I think it's time for more cocktails,' Hannah says, while I slurp down the last dregs and hand over my glass.

'Thanks Hannah, I'll have one more, and then I'd better start on dinner, or I'll be too wasted and the kids will be in charge.'

Hannah giggles and takes off to the kitchen to make another round, while I lie back and think about what my answer would have been if this necklace had been a ring.

I'm frying up a pile of prawns in garlic while Nick's arranging all the salads and cold meats on the breakfast bar. The hairs on the back of my neck stand on end and goose pimples erupt down both arms when I feel his warm lips brush my jaw. He wraps his arms around me and I rest the wooden spoon against the side of the pan, switching off the pan so I can reciprocate. My head tips back to rest on his chest and he drops kisses from my ear, across my cheek, to my lips.

'How's your day going?' he asks.

'Getting better by the minute.'

'Oh, I'll have a lot to live up to later.' I can feel his jaw tense as he grins into my neck.

'You better be bringing your A game.'

'You better believe it,' he whispers, kissing my cheek with a loud pop.

'Get a room guys,' Lucy says, filling her glass from the cocktail jug in the fridge.

'Sorry,' I blush and duck out from Nick's hold, throwing Lucy an apologetic smile.

'Hey, I'm just happy my dad's happy,' she says. 'Thanks for having us all, Steph, this is the best Christmas we've had in years.'

'You're welcome, sweetheart. We're about to serve up.'

'This spread looks amazing, Steph,' Nick says, as Lucy goes off to round up the masses. 'You've outdone yourself.'

'It was a joint effort, but I think we pulled it off.'

Our blended family overindulge on the delicious feast until we're stuffed, then spend the evening playing the card games we had gifted each other. Caleb eyes the girls throughout the night, trying to get a read on the newcomers in his life. It's a lot to come to terms with after everything he's been through, and he's still a little wary and cautious about the speed and direction his life is travelling.

It was nice to see him having fun in the pool earlier. Even though Millie's mum wasn't working this year, she allowed her to spend the afternoon with her dad, which made the day more comfortable for Cale. I have no idea if Sarah knows Millie is spending Christmas with us, or even if she's aware of our relationship, but it's none of my business and I'm not asking about Nick's ex when the day is running like clockwork.

'Well, guys,' I yawn. 'I think I'm gonna call it a night. Please feel at home, help yourselves to whatever you need, and we'll see you in the morning for breakfast. Nick and Millie are on pancake duty.' I wink at Millie.

'You coming babe?' I take Nick's hand and he grins and follows, wishing everyone a good night as we leave.

Nick

'You're ready, Cale,' Nick said as Cale pulled his brand new car up the driveway.

'Are you sure?' Caleb asked.

'Your parking is great. Just watch your speed in the fifty zones and you'll nail it.'

Caleb had his practical driving test the following morning, and Nick had given up a lot of time to help him log all the hours he needed.

'Hey you two, how did it go?' Steph asked as they made their way into the house.

'Yeah, not bad,' Caleb shrugged.

'He'll be fine, just a few nerves, but he can do it all.'

'Thank you for taking him out. I appreciate it.'

'You can thank me by making me a coffee.'

Steph smirked and turned the machine on.

The minute Caleb passed his driving test, Nick barely saw Millie. She was out constantly with Caleb, in his car, and although he trusted Cale's driving, he was still on edge until they got home.

'I feel the same, Nick,' Steph said one morning

when Caleb headed off to pick Millie up. 'It scares me, him driving.'

Nick looked at Steph, surprised that she'd picked up on his nerves.

'It's not that I don't trust him, Steph,' Nick defended.

'I know, but it's still scary. Our kids are out together in a car. I know Caleb seems to have come through the worst of it, but I still worry. Just a lapse in concentration and…' Steph's eyes filled, and she looked away.

'Hey, come here,' Nick said, his arms always ready to catch her in these moments of doubt. He kissed the top of her head, breathing her in, finding his centre. 'We'll always worry, Steph, they're our kids, but I'm glad we get to worry together. It takes the edge off.'

'Do you want to get out of here? Let's go do something fun.' Steph needed to take her mind off the worry.

'Sure, what do you have in mind?'

'I have no idea. Let's just drive somewhere and see where the mood takes us.'

'Come on then, let's go.' Nick grabbed his car keys off the counter.

'We'll take my car, but you can still drive,' Steph said, taking his keys and handing hers over.

'You're letting me drive the beamer at last? I feel honoured.'

'You've driven it before.'

'When?'

'When I was too drunk to drive home from Paul and Gerry's, you dropped it off the next morning.'

'You're right, I did. I needed an excuse to see you

again,' Nick grinned.

'This has been the best day,' Nick said, as he lapped up the ice cream dripping down his cone. 'I can't remember the last time I laughed like that.'

'Me neither,' Steph grinned, nudging her shoulder against his. They went bowling, ice skating, and ate fish and chips on the beach, behaving like a couple of kids, without a care in the world. The waves crashed in front of them, the sun beat down on their backs.

They were in love.
They were happy.
Until they weren't.

Nick's ring tone blared from his pocket and he frowned at the unknown number.

'This is Nick Salvatore.'

'Mr Salvatore, this is Detective Andrew Price. I'm at the scene of an accident. Your daughter, Millie, has been injured and is on her way to the hospital in an ambulance.'

Nick's heart sank as their earlier fears came true. He listened for further details before hanging up and turning to Steph.

'What's happened?' Steph asked, her voice breaking, knowing it was something bad.

'There was a car accident and Millie's unconscious. We have to go.'

'Oh my God, is Cale hurt too?'

'He's fine.' Nick's words dripped off his tongue in bitter disgust, and Steph felt the punch to her gut.

They dumped their half eaten ice creams in a nearby bin and ran as fast as they could towards the car. Nick hopped into the driving seat and slammed it in reverse before Steph had even closed her door.

'Nick, wait!' she yelled. 'Calm the hell down or we'll be needing an ambulance, too.'

Nick was stone faced, angry, more than upset. The voice of reason, the person everyone turned to when they needed clarity, was far from rational right now. Images of Caleb driving at high speed into a tree, taking his little girl with him, filled his head. He couldn't speak, couldn't answer the questions Steph fired at him. The only thing he could think of was the harm he would do to Caleb if his baby died because of him. Never in his life had he felt this amount of rage. His hands shook on the steering wheel, his jaw locked, his lips fixed in a solid line.

He swung the car in front of the emergency department and leapt out, leaving the engine running and Steph watching after him. Her mouth hung open at the vision in front of her. Nick pushed open the door and ran to the desk, begging for news. The nurse guided him to sit while she found out what was happening. He looked up to see Caleb on a nearby seat, practically unscathed, and he lurched forwards.

'Mr Salvatore,' a voice stopped him as he raised his arm. He jerked his fist back, glaring at Caleb. 'Mr Salvatore,' the voice behind him repeated. 'Please follow me. The doctors can speak to you now.'

Nick turned to see the nurse waiting patiently for him to follow. He looked back at Caleb, his eyes drilling into him in a warning, then followed the nurse.

He couldn't see Millie, she needed emergency surgery. The doctor explained the procedure as he signed forms of consent. She had taken the full impact of the crash, hit side on by another vehicle, and had suffered several broken ribs, a broken arm, and a head injury.

'Once we've stemmed the bleeding and got her stable, you'll be able to see her. She's in excellent hands Mr Salvatore.' The doctor spoke softly and Nick felt reassured. His anger at Caleb, however, had not subsided.

Caleb

Dear Dad,
I wish I'd never gone to see him.
Fuck. Fuck. Fuck.
Millie might die, and it's all my fault.
What have I done?
I should've just accepted things and moved on, but I couldn't. I kept pushing. I needed to see for myself who made you the way you were. I get it now, Dad. I wish you'd been stronger, but I understand why you weren't.
If Millie dies, I'll never forgive myself.
Caleb

Steph

'Cale!' I see him as soon as I run into the waiting room. Caleb stands as I rush towards him, but his knees crumple the second he's in my arms. He sobs on my shoulder like a small child as I rub small circles on his back, soothing his cries. We sit, his hand gripped in mine, both of us terrified of what the next few hours will bring.

'What happened, Cale?' I ask, coaxing him to speak.

'I don't know, this car just came out of nowhere and ploughed into the side of us. We rolled and rolled. It seemed like forever. Everything was in slow motion. I couldn't wake her up, Mum. Is she gonna die?' Caleb wails.

'I don't know, sweetheart. Let me go see what I can find out,' I say.

As I stand, I notice Millie's mum hovering in the entrance, looking dazed.

'Sarah?' I say, moving closer. Sarah frowns, recognition in her eyes, but unable to place me.

'I'm Caleb's mum. We met once when you picked

Millie up from my house.'

'Why are you here?' she asks, confused.

'I was with Nick when he got the call.' My voice is thick and I don't want to get into details. 'My son was driving when the accident happened. A car ran into them.'

Sarah nods her understanding. 'Are they okay?'

'I was just going to see what I could find out about Millie. Nick ran inside while I parked the car. I'm not sure where he is.'

Sarah's eyes widen and I follow her eyes to see Nick standing several metres behind me, desolate.

'Nick!' Sarah charges forward into his arms and they hold each other, clinging on in their shared despair.

I watch on as tears sting my eyes. Nick pushes back from Sarah's grip and he holds her, arms outstretched, while he speaks, filling her in on Millie's condition. I can't hear what's being said, but the moment between the two parents seems so intimate. I ease backward to give them some privacy. Nick's eyes catch mine as I turn. Cold and hard as steel. He glares at me, sending a shiver through my body. I feel sick. Does he blame me for this? I blink away tears and make my way back to Caleb.

Nick and Sarah disappear through the double doors, further into the hospital, and my heart breaks. For Millie, for Nick, and for myself and Caleb. How could a day that had begun with such joy turn so terrible?

'Nick's pissed at me, Mum. I think he was going to hit me when he came in.' Caleb's voice wobbles as he speaks.

'What? When did you see him?' Caleb shocks me from my thoughts.

'When he came in, he saw me and charged at me. If the nurse hadn't called his name when she did, I think he would've decked me.'

'He's just upset, Cale. I'm sure he didn't mean it,' I say, unsure if I even believe my own words. 'Let's just think about Millie and worry about everything else later.'

'Caleb Wilson?'

We look up to see two police officers standing in front of us. Cale nods.

'Can we speak somewhere private?'

We both stand and follow the officers to a quieter area of the waiting room. Cale and I sit in numbed silence, waiting for the officers to speak.

'How's your girlfriend?' the officer asks.

'Oh, she's not my…' Cale begins, then sighs. 'I don't know. Nobody will tell us anything.' His eyes fill and he scrubs them away. I worry for him, terrified that he'll blame himself for this.

'I'll see what I can find out for you,' the officer says, leaving us with her partner.

'Can you tell me what happened, Caleb?' the remaining officer asks.

'I don't know,' Caleb mumbles. 'We were driving along and the next thing I knew, there was a bang and my car flipped over. I was so scared. I tried to talk to Millie, but she wouldn't wake up.'

Caleb's eyes brim again and I pull him to me, brushing a hand over his cheek, to soothe him.

'We've spoken to several witnesses; the three men in the car that hit you, and others who were near the scene. One witness had a dash cam, so that is under review to see if we can gain a visual of the accident. What I can tell you is that from our primary investigations, it doesn't appear that you were at fault. The other vehicle appears to have run a stop sign, and the driver tested three times over the legal alcohol limit. I'll be in touch once we've assessed the video footage and we've spoken to Millie.' The officer clapped Caleb on the shoulder. 'I hope your friend's okay.'

'Thank you, officer,' I say, relief pooling in my belly.

'Hey guys,' the officer says when she returns. 'So, Millie is undergoing surgery to stem some bleeding in her brain. The next twenty-four hours are critical, but the prognosis is hopeful. Why don't you two go home and get some rest?'

Caleb shakes his head.

'I'm not leaving, Mum.'

'Okay sweetheart, we'll stay a little longer.'

Once I'm convinced that Cale's okay, I leave in search of coffee. We could be in for a long night. The relief that Caleb isn't at fault lifts my spirits, but my mind soon returns to Millie's injuries and the icy glare from Nick that I just can't shake.

I approach the vending machine with caution when I see him there, right in front of me, leaning against the machine, his forehead resting against his hand.

'Hey.' I stroke my hand down his back. Nick flinches and steps back, away from me, his eyes grey and tired.

'How is she?' I try to push aside my own feelings

and focus on Millie.

'I can't, Steph.' Nick backs away further, his hands up in defence.

'Please, Nick. I just want to know if she's okay.'

'No, Steph, she's far from okay. She's lying through there hooked up to God knows what machines, while your son walked away without a scratch. Tell me what fucking part of that is okay.'

His body stiffens and his nostrils flare. I flinch at the fury he unleashes on me. Hatred spews from him like a caged animal and I can't equate this vitriol with the man who showed such sympathy and understanding when my son was suffering.

'It wasn't Caleb's fault, Nick. The police said the other driver was drunk,' I reason. I see a flicker of remorse before his face clouds again, shutting himself off from me.

'I'm going to go, Nick. Please give my love to Millie when she wakes up and know that I'm thinking of you. I know this is difficult and I understand you don't want me here, but if there's anything at all that I can do, please call me.'

I reach out to him, wanting to give him the same comfort I needed when I was in danger of losing my child. His arm flinches at my touch and I ache right through my core.

'I love you,' I choke, turning on my heel and running back along the corridor, all thoughts of coffee gone.

I persuade Caleb to leave the hospital and as we head through the car park, Hannah and Lucy are heading in our direction.

'Steph, how's Millie?' Lucy asks, concern

blanketing her face.

My lip trembles as I try to force words out of my mouth.

'The police said she was in surgery to stop some bleeding, but that's as much as I know,' I whimper.

Lucy and Hannah exchange a worried glance, then direct their question to Caleb.

'What about Dad? Doesn't he know what's going on?' Hannah frowns.

Caleb shakes his head.

'He won't speak to us. He thinks it was my fault.'

'That doesn't sound like Dad,' Lucy says, confused by the situation. 'What happened, Cale? Are you okay?'

Caleb shrugs.

'A drunk driver ran a stop sign and hit us.'

'Oh my God, Cale,' Lucy gasps, flinging herself towards him and wrapping her arms around him. Caleb welcomes the comfort from Millie's family. At least her sisters don't blame him. He has no idea if Millie will when she wakes up.

I watch the exchange, taking everything in, unsure of what to say to Nick's daughters.

'Steph, he doesn't mean it,' Hannah says. 'He'll come round.'

I nod, mute. My entire world has come crashing in for the third time in less than twelve months, and I'm not sure how many more times I can take a hit.

Both girls hug me tight before saying their goodbyes.

'I'll call you, Steph, and let you know how Millie is,' Lucy whispers.

'Cale?' I break the silence of the tense car journey.

He looks across at me, chewing on his lip, reading my mind.

'Why were you all the way out in the hills today?'

'Can I tell you when we get home?' he asks.

'Why? Were you somewhere you shouldn't have been?'

'Mum, I promise I'll tell you.'

I drop the subject, trusting he has good reason to wait, but I can't help the sense of dread I'm filled with. This feels big, but I can't for the life of me think what he could've been doing that's serious enough to warrant us getting home to discuss.

I pull the car to a halt under the car port and turn in my seat.

'Okay, talk to me. We're not leaving the car until you tell me what's going on.'

Cale puffs out his chest and takes a deep breath, steadying himself for the onslaught he seems to expect. I vow to remain calm, whatever he's about to throw at me.

'So, I've been doing some research on Dad's family,' he ventures.

'Research? What kind of research?' I don't know what I was expecting, but it wasn't this.

'I've never even questioned that I didn't have grandparents on Dad's side. He just always said they'd died when we were little. It wasn't something I ever paid any attention to until I read Dad's suicide note.'

His casual use of the word makes me flinch.

'I guess I just wanted to understand what drove Dad to do what he did, and maybe understand myself a little better, too.'

'But how does that explain where you were

today?'

Caleb hangs his head and picks at his fingernails.

'My grandad is alive. I joined some websites and researched some family history.'

Goosebumps creep along my flesh, causing a shiver to sweep through me. My skin feels clammy and I think I'm going to vomit. I don't know how many more surprises I can take.

'What do you mean, he's alive? Your dad went to his funeral.'

'Well, he must've lied, Mum. His mum died right around the time he said she did and his dad sold their house and moved to the hills. He's been there ever since.' Caleb pauses, allowing me to put two and two together.

'You went to see your grandad?' I ask.

Caleb nods.

'Why would your dad lie about something like that?'

'I don't know, Mum, but having met the old man, I can think of a few reasons of my own,' Cale justifies. 'He's not a nice man.'

'I know. I met him a few times many years ago. So, what happened? Did you speak to him?'

'Yeah, Millie and I knocked on his door, and when he opened it, he did a double take. He knew who I was.'

'That's no surprise, you're the image of Dad.'

Cale continues his story.

'He asked what I wanted, so I told him what happened, to Dad, and to me. I told him what Dad wrote in his letter.'

'What did he say to that?' I can't believe what I'm hearing. All these years, I thought my father-in-law was dead.

'He called him a sook, a mama's boy. Said he was always worthless, and he deserved what he got. He told me I'd probably end up the same way.'

Cale holds his head up and looks me in the eye.

'Mum, I want you to know that I'm determined to beat this and get better. That man won't take anything else from this family, I promise.'

The admiration I feel for my son brings me at least a little joy after the day's turn of events.

'I'm so proud of you, Cale. What did you say to him?'

'I didn't. Millie dragged me away before I could punch him,' Cale laughs. 'But she gave him a mouthful as we left.'

The mental picture I've conjured up of Millie standing up for Cale makes me chuckle, but my laughter soon turns to tears when I picture Millie lying in her hospital bed fighting for her life.

'She'll make it, Mum. She's so tough,' he says.

'I know, sweetheart. I just wish someone would tell us what's going on.'

'Hannah was right. Nick will come round once Mills wakes up, and he can think straight.' Caleb's reassurance falls on deaf ears.

'I don't know, Cale, the way he looked at me…' I shake my head to clear my own thoughts. I can't let myself walk that path. 'Come on, let's go find Levi and fill him in.'

Searching for Sunrise

Nick

Nick and Sarah hadn't left the hospital in two days. The doctors were confident Millie was over the worst and she just needed time to wake up. Hannah and Lucy had called in several times, bringing a change of clothes and food. Steph had sent a string of messages, all of which had gone unanswered. He didn't know how to talk to her. If Millie never woke up, how could Nick continue a relationship with the mother of the boy who killed her? And if Cale wasn't at fault, how could he ever forgive himself for the way he treated them? He'd reacted in a way he'd never imagined was in his nature. His heart ached for her, but he just couldn't get his head to go past that huge hurdle. Better to distance himself now than later.

'Nick, can I ask you something?' Sarah asked with a tenderness that surprised him. They'd spoken on and off over the last few days, reminiscing about happier times with Millie. Nick never looked up from his coffee cup.

'Sure.' His vacant expression matched his monotone voice.

'Caleb's mum, Steph, is it?' Nick jerked his head up and frowned.

'What about her?'

'Is there something going on between you two? I sensed tension the other day.' He didn't recognise this side of Sarah, she didn't appear to be judging him. Her question was out of concern.

Nick sighed and brushed his hand over his face, sitting up and taking a large swig of coffee.

'There was,' he said. 'We were together.'

'What happened?'

Nick looked at her as if she'd gone mad.

'You realise Caleb was driving the car that put Millie right here in this bed, fighting for her life?'

'Nick, you heard the police. They have cleared him of any wrongdoing. The other driver was drunk and ran a stop sign. You watched the video footage yourself,' Sarah said.

Nick's reaction confused her. His propensity to rationalise situations and listen to all sides of the story was something that drove Sarah mad when she was married to him, but it was a wonderful trait and seeing Nick behave this way concerned her.

Nick shrugged.

'Do you love her?'

Nick's eyes filled, and a stream of tears unleashed down his cheeks. Anger had been his primary emotion for the last two days. He hadn't allowed himself to feel anything else because he if let the dam burst, he wasn't sure he'd ever stop. Sarah's hand rested on his shoulder before she leaned forward and took him in her arms, comforting him as he fell apart.

There was a stifled cough behind them and they

leapt apart to see Millie moaning, fighting against the tube in her throat.

Sarah leapt up and pressed the call button, tending to her daughter to keep her comfortable and calm until the nurse came to check on her, torn between taking charge and waiting for the staff on duty. Sarah and Nick stood back when the room filled with medical staff, all checking Millie's vitals. They tended to her with care, checking her over before advising her to rest.

'Welcome back, Millie,' her doctor said when she arrived. 'You gave us quite a scare there for a while. How are you feeling?'

Millie nodded and tried to speak.

'Sore.' Her voice was croaky and dry and she winced in pain.

'You just take your time and rest. I'll be back to see you later when you're a bit more awake, and we'll go from there, okay?'

Nick and Sarah pulled their chairs close to Millie's bed and, after a gentle hug, they sat and held on to her hands.

'Caleb?' she croaked, remembering what had happened to them.

Nick's jaw tensed and his eyes darkened. Millie frowned at her dad.

'He's fine, Mills,' her mother said. 'He just had a few scratches. A drunk driver hit you.'

Millie's eyes widened and then looked at Nick, confused by his reaction to Caleb's name.

'What's wrong?' Nick shook his head, dismissing Millie's concern.

She turned to her mum to see if she would be more forthcoming, but she stayed silent.

'What's going on?' She gripped her throat at the pain she felt.

'Millie, it's nothing to worry about. You need to rest your voice, get some sleep. We'll be here when you wake up, I promise,' Sarah said.

'Mum, tell me.' Her eyes filled with tears, and Nick hung his head low, not wanting to be party to this conversation.

Sarah sighed, knowing her daughter wouldn't give in until she heard the truth.

'Your dad blames Caleb for the accident and he broke up with Steph in the process. That about covers it, right Nick?' Sarah said, not wanting to involve herself in her ex-husband's love life, but after all the grief he'd thrown at her about not listening to both sides of a story, she felt a little aggrieved.

'I'll go ring Hannah and Lucy and let them know you're awake, and I'll leave you two to talk.'

'Thanks Mum, can you ask them to let Steph know I'm okay?' Millie said, her throat easing after sipping some water.

'Of course, sweetheart.'

Millie glared at her dad, waiting for an explanation, but Nick kept quiet, deliberating what to say.

'Dad, this wasn't Cale's fault. He was careful,' Millie said. 'Please don't blame him, that's not fair.' Millie's eyes filled. 'What happened between you and Steph?'

'I don't know, Mills. I was so angry. All I could think was, if you died, and Cale survived, I could never reconcile myself with that.'

'He wasn't responsible, Dad, and I'm very much

alive, so get your arse round to Steph's right now and apologise for behaving like a dick. Now if you'll excuse me, I need to rest.' Millie closed her eyes, a tear escaping the corner as she thought about the way her dad had tossed away his happiness and his future.

Searching for Sunrise

Steph

I haven't heard from Nick since I saw him at the vending machine in the emergency department. He hasn't even bothered to read my messages, let alone respond. His behaviour is so out of character from the Nick I know. I can't get my head around why he won't talk to me. Luckily, Hannah and Lucy have been keeping me updated with news of Millie, not that there's been much change. I've kept a close eye on Caleb over the last couple of days, but he's handled things surprisingly well. In fact, he's stepped up and has been a significant source of comfort for me.

I hold my phone in my hand, contemplating whether to call Nick, when an unknown number lights up my screen.

'Hello?'

'Hello Steph, it's Sarah, Millie's mum. Hannah gave me your number. I hope you don't mind me calling.'

'Of course not. How's Millie doing?' I ask. Caleb's attention piques at the mention of Millie's name.

'She's awake and talking.' Sarah's relief shows in

her voice.

'Oh, thank God. That's fantastic news, Sarah. Thank you so much for letting us know. We've been going out of our minds with worry.'

'You're welcome.' She takes a breath and directs the conversation towards Nick. 'Listen, can I say something?'

'Go on.'

'I know it's none of my business, but Nick told me you and he were together.'

'Were?' I pray she doesn't mean past tense.

'Don't give up on him. He knows the accident wasn't Caleb's fault. He'll come round.'

'I'm not sure, Sarah. You didn't see his eyes when he looked at me. He looked so cold. I've never seen him like that.'

'To be honest, neither have I. Even throughout our divorce, he was amicable and accommodating, to the point of being annoying. I don't know what's going on in his head, but his girls have lavished praise on you. My experience of Nick tells me he won't throw that away.'

'I hope you're right, Sarah. I'm not sure I can survive any more heartache right now.'

'Hannah told me you've had a tough year.' Sarah's kindness belies all descriptions of her.

'I don't know how we'd have got through it without Nick and Millie. You have a wonderful daughter, Sarah.'

'Thank you, I appreciate that. Nick's wonderful too, Steph. I didn't appreciate what I had when I had it, although I didn't get the best of him. His first wife got that, and from what Hannah said, you have it too. He loves you, he'll be back.'

'Thank you, Sarah. I appreciate your call. Please give our love to Millie.'

'Of course, but please visit her. I know she'd love to see Caleb. His name was the first word from her lips when she woke up.'

I hang up the phone, startled by the conversation with Nick's ex-wife. She sure doesn't fit the horror story Nick and his girls had written her into.

'Well, that was weird,' I say to no one in particular.

'Mum? Is Millie awake?' Cale asks, appearing before my bemused face.

I snap from my trance and smile at my son.

'That was her mum. She just woke up and your name was the first word she spoke. I think we should visit tomorrow. Let her see for herself that you're okay.'

'Will Nick be there?' Cale asks, drawing away from me.

'I don't know, sweetheart, but let me deal with that, okay? Sarah said he's aware the accident wasn't your fault.'

'That doesn't mean he won't still blame me,' Cale mumbles.

Millie's sitting up in bed when we knock on her door and her face lights up when she sees us.

'Hey guys,' she greets us. 'It's so good to see you.' She holds her good arm open for a hug and Cale takes it as a sign that she's not angry with him.

'Hey Mills,' he says as he hugs her. 'You okay?'

'I will be. Did you hear it was a drunk driver?'

'Yeah, the police told me. I'm not sure your dad's accepting that, though. He blames me.'

Millie turns to me in surprise.

'He still hasn't called you?'

'No, but don't you worry about it, Millie. We're here to see you, sweetheart,' I say, leaning in for a hug. 'I'm just so glad you're okay.'

'I'm not sure how you walked away from it, Cale. The police said the car was a wreck. Apparently, we rolled and ended up smashed into a tree,' Millie says.

'You don't remember?' Cale asks.

'I remember seeing the car coming straight at us, then everything goes blank.'

'It was so scary, Mills. I didn't even see him coming. I heard a bang and then we started rolling, over and over. Then we hit the tree and I couldn't get you to wake up. I'm so lucky there were heaps of witnesses or they'd have blamed me for sure.'

'What about your car?'

'It's trashed, so I'll have to get a new one, I guess,' Cale shrugs.

Millie catches Cale's eye as if trying to ask him something.

'Mum knows, Mills. I told her everything.'

Millie looks at me with remorse.

'It's fine Millie. Cale told me how you stopped him from punching the old fool.'

'God, I did too. I'd forgotten about that. I gave him a bit of a mouthful. He was horrible.'

Movement at the door catches my attention and I turn to see Nick, standing stock still, unsure of his next move. My eyes lock on his, waiting to see which way he'll go.

'Hey, Dad, come in,' Millie says, as though everything is fine.

He looks away from me, to Millie, and back to me. Then he flees the room. My eyes fill and I touch my hand to my jaw to stop the tremble.

'Steph, go after him,' Millie urges. 'Don't let him do this.'

I scrape my chair back and follow Nick out of the door.

'Nick, wait!' I call, and he stops in his tracks, not turning to face me.

I catch him up and reach out my hand to his shoulder. He tenses at my touch, and a wave of emotion surges through me. I'm no longer upset. I'm fucking furious.

'How dare you treat me like this? After all the promises you've made. I thought you loved me,' I say.

Nick's eyes wash over me, taking me in. He remains tight lipped and I can't get a read on him.

'I can't believe I fell for your charm and let you into my life when I was in such a vulnerable position. Nick, I'm so disappointed in you.'

With my head held high, I turn and walk away as though my world didn't just come crumbling down.

Caleb

Dear Nick,

I know you blame me for the accident, and I get that, but I can assure you it's nothing compared to the blame I put on myself. I love Millie. She's like a sister to me, and I would never hurt her.

I know I've been difficult, and I'm sorry for all the ways I've lashed out at you and made things hard for you and my mum, but I also want to say thank you, because without you, I don't think I'd still be here.

You've changed my life, Nick, and my brother's, but most of all, you've changed my mum's life. We've had the toughest year, but you and Millie have held us all together.

I don't know if you can ever forgive me for the way I've treated you, and the way I put Millie's life at risk, but please don't take this out on my mum. She loves you, and I know you love her. Whatever you're going through right now, speak to her about it. Talking things through helps, you taught me that.

I know a good psych, if you need one!
I am sorry for all the harm I've caused.
Caleb

Nick

'What the fuck, Nick?' Paul pushed past his friend and through the front door.

'Hello Paul, nice to see a friendly face in my hour of need. Come on in.' The sarcasm dripped from Nick's tongue as he closed the front door behind his friend.

'You look like shit, mind telling me what the hell's going on?' Paul asked.

'Oh, I'm sorry if you didn't hear, my daughter's in hospital.'

'Cut the bullshit, Nick. I've just been to see Millie. She's fine. I also saw Sarah, and she's behaving more like an adult than you are right now. Guess who else I've spoken to? That's right, your girlfriend.'

Nick's anger disappeared at the mention of Steph and he slumped to the floor, his body hunched, the fight drained out of him. Paul crouched down in front of him, his hand on his shoulder, bringing comfort.

'Talk to me, Nick. This is not like you. What am I missing here?'

Nick's eyes filled with tears and he looked everywhere but at Paul, unable to meet his gaze. A myriad of emotions churned within him, and for the first time in his adult life, he didn't know how to unlock them.

'Nick, I know you had a shock, and I know you might have laid blame on Caleb. I get that. But where are you now? Millie's okay and Caleb's not at fault.'

Nick's silence was something Paul hadn't experienced, so he changed tack.

'I warned you when you started this thing with Steph that she was vulnerable. You promised you'd take things slow, but you didn't.'

Nick's head jerked towards his friend.

'I relented because I thought it was real, Nick. You looked so bloody right together, and I was so fucking happy for you, man, my two best friends, together. I couldn't imagine that you'd ever hurt her. How could you when you love someone that much? You have shared trauma and you understand every thought process she goes through every day. She doesn't deserve this, Nick.'

Nick's breath quickened. He didn't need Paul to tell him what he'd done. The one thing he'd promised he would never do. He'd hurt her in a way there was no coming back from.

'I hurt her, Paul. Do you think I don't know that? Do you think I don't loathe myself for the way I've treated her?'

'Then why are you sat here wallowing in self pity? Go talk to her. Apologise. Explain. Do whatever you need to do to stop that woman's heart from breaking for the third time in a year.' Nick had never heard

Paul raise his voice before.

'Because I don't deserve her. I don't even know who I am anymore. The second I got that call, I blamed Caleb, and I was angry at Steph. That's not me, you know that, Paul.' Nick said.

'It's not you, no, but Steph understands you were in shock. She even questioned herself if Caleb was to blame. It's natural, Nick.'

'We were building a life together, Paul, blending our families. I wanted to marry her. How can I marry a woman whose son I blamed the first chance I got? That same son that tried to take his own life? My doing that could have sent him spiralling. I can't forgive myself for that.'

'So, this is your own guilt and fear driving this?' Paul nodded as he unravelled Nick's behaviour.

Nick's shoulders heaved and Paul grabbed him in a tight embrace, holding him while he fell apart.

'We can work with this, Nick. I've got you.'

Nick sat at his desk, staring at his computer, drained from his impromptu session with Paul. His thoughts were clearer, but he still didn't know how to rebuild the bridges he'd burnt. It had been a week since his run in with Steph at the hospital and her communications had gone silent since then. She'd given up on him, and he couldn't blame her. Millie was mad, he'd disappointed Hannah and Lucy, even his ex-wife thought he was behaving like a fool. He agreed with them all, but he just hadn't been able to get past his initial reaction to the accident. The way he'd laid blame before he knew what had happened was such an alien concept to him, something he'd never done before. But his daughter's life was hanging in the balance and he and Steph had both had their concerns about Caleb driving. His reaction to Steph had nothing to do with her or Caleb. It was the self-loathing at the way he'd reacted that had caused him to back off. His first thought was to blame her son. What kind of partner did that make him? She didn't deserve the way he'd treated her when he got that call, nor did she deserve his silence now.

He re-read Caleb's letter. The maturity he'd shown in writing it showed Nick how far he'd come, and he was right, Steph deserved an explanation. He just prayed it wouldn't be too late.

Nick had never been so nervous in all his life. He didn't know what Steph's reaction to seeing him would be, but he knew he had to do this, whatever the consequences. He switched off the engine and took a deep breath before making his way onto the verandah at the back of Steph's house. This place was so peaceful. He loved the feeling he got every time he came here. There was a time, not too long ago, that he thought it would become his home. Now, he didn't know what the future held for him, but he feared he'd ruined it.

Nick caught Steph's eye when he approached the fly screen door and she stopped still inside, staring at him with a look he didn't recognise on her. The lump in his throat almost choked him. He'd caused this.

'Steph, is Caleb home?' He'd decided Caleb might be the most receptive person with whom to begin his apologies.

'What do you want with Caleb?' Steph wasn't

giving him an inch.

'I just want to talk to him,' he assured her.

'Not if you still blame him for the accident. It was a drunk driver, Nick. There's video footage. I'm not having you blame my son. He's been through enough.' Nick couldn't blame Steph for being protective of her son.

'Mum, it's okay.' Caleb slid the door open and squeezed past his mum. 'I'll speak to him.'

'Thanks Cale, I got your email,' Nick said. Caleb pushed open the fly screen and wandered outside to join him. Steph watched on in surprise.

'Hey,' Caleb said, his hands in his pockets, leaning back against the timber pillar.

Nick stood face on, eye to eye with Caleb as he spoke.

'It took a lot of guts to write that letter, Cale. I'm proud of how far you've come.' Caleb nodded in response, wondering where the conversation was heading. 'But you were wrong about me. You've done it all yourself. I hope you're proud of that.'

Caleb frowned.

'You were wrong about something else, too. I don't blame you for the accident. My initial reaction was to blame you, and for that, I'm sorry. I'm angry with myself for having those thoughts. Sometimes we do things we're not proud of, and I've done a lot in the last week that I'm not proud of, but the biggest thing is I've gone against all my own teachings and values. I pushed you all away without talking to you about how I was feeling. When I needed your mum the most, I didn't allow her to be there for me, but starting right now, I will do everything in my power to earn her trust back. Cale, she means the world to me, and I'm sorry I've treated her poorly. I hope you and Levi can forgive me too, because I love you guys and I want nothing more than for us to be a family.' Nick's voice broke on the last word, and Caleb pulled him into a hug. The two men gripped each other, only breaking apart when the fly screen door slid open and Steph stood watching.

Nick turned to her, wiping a stray tear from his eye.

'Steph, can we talk?' he whispered.

No words formed on her lips. She was confused by the physical display of affection she'd just witnessed.

'Mum, please listen to him,' Caleb said, before slapping Nick on the back and heading back inside to give them some privacy.

'Did you hear any of that?' Nick asked, referring to his conversation with Caleb.

'Only that he sent you an email,' Steph hovered in the doorway, unsure whether to hear him out.

'Can we sit?' Nick's jaw trembered. He was terrified she wouldn't forgive him.

Steph nodded and followed him to the outdoor seating, curling herself up on a chair to keep away from him. It killed him that she didn't want him to touch her, but he understood how much he'd hurt her.

'I'm so sorry, Steph. There's no excuse for the way I've treated you, I know that, but I would appreciate the chance to explain what was going on inside my head.'

'Okay, go ahead,' Steph said. Her words were flippant, but her face told a different story. She was hurting. From the way he'd treated her, but also because she missed him. Her eyes were still full of love for him.

Nick took a breath, steadying himself to tell her what he'd just told Caleb.

'When I got the phone call about the accident, my first thoughts went to the conversation we'd had that morning about Caleb. We were both worried about him driving. I told you I trusted him, and I did, but my daughter's life was threatened and I lashed out. I know you understand how that feels, Steph. All I could think of was Millie and if she was going to die. I didn't allow myself the time to process my thoughts, and for that, I'm sorry.'

'Nick—' Steph began.

'Steph, please let me finish. I need to get this out.' Steph nodded in reply.

'I know Caleb wasn't to blame. I was angry with myself more than anything. If I'm honest, I'm still angry with myself. I've been beating myself up about the way I reacted, telling myself I don't deserve you for even having that thought to begin with. How can I be with you when my first reaction is to blame your son? You don't deserve that, Steph, and neither does Caleb. So I backed off, distanced myself so I couldn't hurt you any more.'

'Nick, you hurt me. I wanted to be there for you, to support you. I know what it's like to have my child's life under threat, and I'm aware I pushed you away when Caleb was in a delicate state. My children will always come first, Nick, just like your children will always come first with you. I wouldn't have it any other way. I also wouldn't have blamed you for thinking Caleb was at fault. We'd talked about our fears that same morning. I even understood you withdrawing from me while you had Millie to think of, but for you not to reach out and let us know how she was doing, that she was awake? That's where you went too far, Nick. I love Millie, and Caleb was desperate to find out she was okay. Can you imagine how he felt having that hanging over him after everything he's been through this year? I had to hear the news from your ex-wife. How do you think that made me feel?'

Nick hung his head in shame. His eyes stung, but no more tears would come. He'd cried more in the last week than he had since his first wife had died. His actions had devastated Steph, and he wasn't sure she would forgive him, but he was going to do whatever he could to make things right.

He moved from his seat on the couch and perched on the edge of the table in front of her. He reached for her hands, unsure if she would allow him to touch her. She bit her lip as he took her hands in his.

'Steph, I love you. I haven't felt this way in a long, long time. Caleb wrote me a letter asking that even if I couldn't forgive him, then to at least not take my anger out on you and Levi. He also advised me to talk about whatever was going on in my head. So, here I am, talking to you. I'm so proud of him for reaching out, Steph.'

Steph squeezed Nick's hand, and a slither of hope slid into his heart.

'Please let me make this right, Steph. I know I've hurt you, but you still love me. I can see it in your eyes.'

Steph slipped her hands from his and reached forward, grasping his face.

'Of course I still love you, Nick. That's not even under question right now.'

She tipped her head towards his and brushed her lips against his. He responded with hunger, but she pulled back.

'I'm still hurting, Nick.'

Nick nodded, embarrassed by his actions.

'Sarah said she never saw you react in this way to anything the entire time you were together. She also said she never got the best version of you, that Lee had got that, and maybe me too.' It shocked Nick to hear his ex-wife's words.

'Ten days ago I would've agreed with her, but right now I'm so angry with this version of you that's just blindsided me. Openness and honesty were my stipulations for a relationship, Nick, and you withdrew from me. I'm not sure I can reconcile that at the moment.'

Steph's words were harsh to his ears. It felt like a tremendous blow and the tears he thought had dried up gushed like a cloudburst, a wordless plea to change her mind.

'I'm not ending this, Nick. I'm just not ready to forgive you.'

Steph

I watch from the sidelines as Nick weaves his way back into my family. Once Millie was home and healing, he started taking Levi out for bike rides again. When Caleb's insurance money came through, Nick was the one he took with him to find a new car. The two of them have become great friends, training Millie's team together and working out in Cale's gym. It's everything I've dreamed of, except it's all going on around me and I'm just a spectator.

No one blames me for taking a step back from Nick. Everyone's aware just how much he hurt me, but our children and my friends are becoming fatigued by my lack of forgiveness.

Terri's the first one to push me into resolving my mess.

'Everyone makes mistakes, Steph, and you can't deny the fact that the thing you love most about him is how he puts his kids first,' she says. 'I know he should've spoken to you, but he didn't and you can't change that. Move on. Don't throw away a beautiful future over one mistake. You put up with way more than that in your marriage to Chris. I know you did. Nobody's perfect, Steph, it's time to forgive him.'

Paul tried to stay neutral throughout the whole situation, but it's become difficult for him to watch his two closest friends in misery.

'Steph, it's time to either forgive him and let him back in your life, or end it and move on. You're not being fair keeping him hanging like this.' He pulls me to one side at the end of our workday and lays it on the line. 'I know what he did, and I know it was wrong. He hurt you, he did, but you're hurting him now, too. If you can't forgive him, then let him go so that I can at least begin putting him back together. I can't watch any longer while you destroy him like this, and yourself, if I'm honest. You're both miserable. Sort it out.' He walks out of the practice, furious with me. It's the shove I need. I can't go on like this either. My heart aches for him.

'Mum, can I have a word with you?' Cale asks. It's the morning of his first game of the season and his tone worries me.

'Of course, sweetheart. Is everything okay?'

'Yep, but I need you to know that Nick will be at my game today,' Caleb warns, 'and I don't want there to be an atmosphere between you two. I need to know that I can put all my energy and focus into my game, without worrying about you two not speaking.'

I feel the edges of my mouth curl up, so proud of the way my son now speaks whatever's on his mind.

'You don't have to worry, Cale, I promise. In fact, I'm going over to Nick's this morning to talk with him. I'll see you at the game, okay?'

'You're gonna take him back?' Caleb's eyes flash with hope.

'If he'll have me.'

Cale hugs me, happier than I've seen him in such a long time. Things are looking up.

'Are you kidding? He's been hanging out for this, Mum.'

I arrive at Nick's house, butterflies beating in my belly. I knock on the door with trembling hands, balancing two coffees and a couple of muffins as I wait for my future to unfold.

Nick's expecting me, and he answers the door, his face more alive than I've seen it in weeks. Each time he's been at my house seeing the boys, he's looked lost. It must have been torture for him seeing me, desperate for my forgiveness, but he still showed up for them and put all his energy into being there for them. That's what's driven me to forgive him the most. His continued love for my boys.

'Hey, Steph, come in,' he says, his voice tinged with nerves.

I follow him through to the lounge room and put the goodies on the coffee table. Not wanting to waste time with small talk, I get straight to the point. I take his hands in mine and look up at him.

'Sorry it's taken me so long to get here. I forgive you, now I hope you can forgive me too.'

'God, I've missed you.' Nick wraps me in his arms, breathing me in. I burrow into him, resting my ear against his chest, listening for his heartbeat. 'I never want to be without you again.'

Our hearts beat in sync and I settle into the steady

rhythm, allowing myself to feel at peace with him again.

'Thank you for showing up for my boys these past weeks. It's meant so much to me.'

'Of course.'

We drink our coffee and eat our cakes, side by side, neither of us wanting to let go. We talk, we kiss, and we make up for all the time we've missed. By the time we leave for Caleb's match together, it feels like we've never been apart.

Nick hurries to my door when we park at the football oval. He takes my hand in his and we walk together to where our kids, and Terri and Mark, are standing waiting for the game to begin. Our faces are beaming, both of us happy we're reunited.

A cheer erupts from the small group when they lay eyes on us, and Millie comes bounding over to pull us into a group hug, excited that I've forgiven her dad.

'Guys, I'm so happy,' she cries.

'Me too, Millie.' My heart is filled with everyone's joy.

Terri's smile is rapturous when she hugs me.

'I'm so bloody happy for you both. Life's too short for you two not to be together. You deserve every happiness.'

Mark slaps Nick on the back.

'Pleased for you, mate,' he says. Mark and Nick have become close over the months they've known each other, and I know from Terri that our falling out hit Mark hard. Nick helped out a lot while Terri was going through her treatment, especially while I needed to focus on Caleb. He flashes me a grin and sends me a wink, happy we've sorted out our differences.

Levi doesn't say a word, but the smile never leaves his face throughout the entire game.

Searching for Sunrise

Steph

'Mum? I've been thinking,' Caleb says one night after training.

My heart leaps into my mouth at the tone of his voice. I know his mental health is stable, but I still worry whenever he sounds serious.

'What is it, Cale?' I try to hide the panic in my voice.

'Do you think we could scatter Dad's ashes? I think it's time to say goodbye.'

Surprised by his words, I breathe a tremendous sigh of relief at the direction his thoughts are travelling. We haven't spoken of Chris's ashes in a long time, and I've been wondering whether we'll ever reach the point we're all ready to give him a proper send-off.

'That's a nice idea, Cale. Did you have somewhere in mind?'

'Yeah, I was thinking when we drive down south to pick up Levi and Nick after they finish the charity ride, we might head to Bluff and scatter them from the top. I know Dad grew up around there and I think his mum's grave is nearby.'

My face blanks in response to the unexpected proposal. I hadn't imagined Cale would come up with something like this, but I warm to the idea. It seems like a fitting goodbye and I'm sure Chris would love the idea of being close to his mother, especially now we know his father moved away from the area.

'That sounds like a lovely farewell, Cale. Are you sure you feel ready for that?'

'Yeah, I think it's time. We have a new life now and I'm pretty sure Dad would be happy for us. He'd like Nick too, how he always includes Dad and never tries to pretend he didn't exist. I'm glad you're together, Mum.'

My arms open, inviting my son for a hug, and I reach up on my tiptoes to hold him.

'Thanks Cale, you don't know how much that means to me. I'm so proud of you.'

Caleb nods, embarrassed by my praise.

Nick spends all his weekends with me and the boys and whenever he has Millie, they stay at my house. Millie often comes over by herself too, if Nick and Levi are out training. We've settled into family life together with ease.

'Hey Millie, do you have a sec?' I call one Sunday evening as Nick is getting ready to take her back to her mum's house.

'Sure, what is it?' Millie asks, hoisting her overnight bag over her shoulder.

'I was wondering if you can spare some time to go shopping with me?' I ask.

Nick looks at me, confused.

'Erm, I can do late night on Thursday, or Saturday

after footy. What is it you need to get?' Millie asks, unsure why I need her to tag along.

'I was thinking we might pick out some things for your bedroom here to make it your own. It's not very inviting in there at the moment. Maybe we could even look at some new furniture?' I offer.

I want her to feel included, like this is her home too, even though she's not here full time.

'You want me to have my own room here?' Millie's surprise is clear.

'Of course, you're part of the family. Besides, you spend more time here than you do at your dad's.'

'Thanks Steph,' she says, giving me a hug. 'You're the best. But maybe just new bedding and stuff. I love the furniture.'

'Great, Thursday night, then. We can grab dinner out too, just the two of us. It'll be fun.'

Nick grabs my hand and spins me around for a hug before he leaves.

'She's right, you know, you are the best,' he whispers. 'That's generous of you, Steph, thank you. Maybe I'll get takeout and come over and watch a movie with the boys while you're out shopping.'

My eyes glaze over when I think about how much I love him and what we could have lost. Some weekends, he spends more time with my boys than he does with me, but I wouldn't have it any other way. My boys are thriving once again and I credit Nick with a huge part in that. I'm sure it won't be too long before we're ready to make the leap and move in together, and that thought fills me with joy.

'So, what kind of style are you thinking?' I ask Millie, as we wander around the soft furnishing store.

'Like a boho kind of theme, maybe a Moroccan vibe. Bright rugs and plants. Although maybe the plants will have to be fake, I won't be there often enough to look after them.'

'You're there most weekends now, Millie. I'm sure it'll be fine,' I say. 'We'll call at the garden centre on the way home.'

Our trolley fills fast once we've made a plan of what to buy and it's all coming together. We stop off for dinner at an Italian on the way back to Millie's house and both order gnocchi.

'So, I hear you've been having coffee with my mum,' Millie delves. 'Is that not weird? She's your boyfriend's ex-wife.'

'I guess it seems a little odd when you put it like that,' I laugh. 'It's only been twice and I'm sure it won't become a habit, but she was very kind to me when you were in the hospital, Millie. If it wasn't for her ringing me, who knows when we'd have found out you'd woken up?'

'I still can't believe Dad behaved like that. None of us could.'

'I know, sweetheart, I find it difficult to get my head around too, but I know he's full of remorse for the way he acted. You don't have to worry about us. Everything's good between us now, I promise.'

'Yeah, I know. It's nice to see both my parents happy at last. Has Mum told you about her boyfriend?'

'Yes, she seems smitten. I'm pleased for her.'

Sarah has opened up to me about her marriage to Nick, and how different things are with the new man in her life. I wouldn't call us friends, but she's given me perspective and I think I've done the same for her.

We drive to Millie's house in silence, listening to the radio.

'Do you want me to unpack everything or would you rather organise it all yourself at the weekend?' I ask when I pull up on the street outside.

'Do you mind if I do it?'

'Of course not, I'll just strip everything out and you can have a blank canvas. Did you want to paint the walls?'

'No, I like the white. The pictures will brighten up the walls.'

'We'll see you at the weekend then, yes?'

'You will, thanks Steph.' Millie leans over to hug me.

'Oh, before I forget,' I say, reaching into my bag and pulling out a key. 'I had you a key cut so you can come and go when you want. I want you to feel at home.'

Millie stares at me with a blank expression.

'I don't even have a key to Dad's house,' she says.

I drive away with a smile on my face, buoyed by my life and the closer I'm getting to my future happiness.

A year ago, my world came crashing down around me, and the road since then has been an uphill battle to keep from losing my son, my best friend, and my new relationship. It feels incredible to me how much my life has changed. Caleb's still on medication and will be for some time to come, but he's cut down his psych appointments to once a month, and chats with Nick in between. He's on an even keel; happier and more vibrant than I've seen him in a very long time. His grades have picked up again and his football is going from strength to strength. His coaches and Nick all think he has a genuine shot at turning professional, barring injury. Terri's in remission and her oncologist has given her a positive prognosis. I'm feeling ready to move on and as I drive home, I reach an unforeseen decision. Once we've scattered Chris's ashes and said goodbye to that chapter of my life, I'm going to speak to Nick about the possibility of him moving in with me. I grin at myself in the rearview mirror, butterflies fluttering in my stomach at the thought.

Caleb

Dear Dad,

It's time to say goodbye. This last year has been so hard on us. You underestimated how much losing you would affect us, and you underestimated just how much we loved you. I'm sorry for all the anger I had towards you. I wish I'd known more about your past, about what you must've suffered at the hands of your father. It's easy to imagine the way you were treated, having met my grandfather.

Dad, you weren't like him. I hope you know that. Of course, there are things I would've changed about the way you were, but nobody's perfect and we all have our own struggles to battle. I forgive you for the pressure you always put on me, but I also thank you for that. You gave me a drive to succeed and I will always be grateful that you were my dad.

I learnt a lot this year, about life and death, about the struggles that other people face. That depression isn't a weakness, but an illness that can be so crippling it takes away all rational thought. I learnt that help is available. Even if it's not professional, just talking to people can lessen the pain. Depression manifests itself differently in *everyone, and it's not always obvious.*

It's time to move on. I have a new family now. Nick will never replace you, Dad, but he's brought a different dynamic to our lives. He's not just here for Mum, he's made space for both me and Levi in his life. I hope you're happy for us all and you can rest in peace.

I love you, Dad.
Caleb

Nick and Steph

Nick and Levi had left on their mountain biking trip a few weeks earlier, and Steph, Caleb and Millie had had their own adventure travelling to various spots to meet them en route with extra supplies. They were due to arrive at the finish line the following day, where Steph would pick them up with their bikes and drive them to the Airbnb she'd booked. The plan was to let the boys have a few days' rest at the house before the five of them embarked upon Bluff Knoll for a sunrise hike. Chris had grown up in the foothills of the mountain and Steph thought scattering her husband's ashes from the peak was a fitting farewell. Not only was it an opportunity to say goodbye to Chris. It was a chance to open her heart to her future. She'd organised it as a personal journey with just her boys, but they'd both been insistent that Nick and Millie be there too, as they'd played such a big part in getting their family to where it was now. Steph had been dubious when Levi had first suggested it, more concerned for the boys than herself. Having Nick there for comfort and support would mean the world to her, but she was wary about how the boys would feel when it came down to saying their goodbyes. She thought they might prefer a more personal and private moment. They were adamant, however, and she gave in to their wishes.

When Nick and Levi came into view, Steph and the kids gave a cheer and clapped them over the finish line. They looked exhausted and filthy, but alive with an energy that seemed to bounce off each other. The two bikes came to a stop, and Nick leaned across to hug Levi.

'I'm so proud of you, kiddo.'

Steph watched on, happy at the scene that played out before her.

'Well done, both of you. You look knackered.'

Steph hugged them both, lingering on Nick, overjoyed to see him, despite the stink of dried sweat and mud.

Nick hauled their gear into the boot and fastened the bikes onto the rack before sinking into the passenger seat.

'I bet you can't wait for a shower and a soak in the hot tub.'

'There's a hot tub?'

'Sure is,' she grinned.

The time at the holiday house was a real family occasion, and it cemented Steph's thoughts about asking Nick to move in. She'd already spoken to the boys and had noticed a look pass between them, which had unsettled her a little, but they'd convinced her they were both happy with the situation. He was there three or four nights a week anyway, so they didn't see any difference. Spending the last few days together gave her a security that she'd been wavering over. It was the best thing for all of them, she was sure now.

On the morning of the hike, they woke early and dressed, layering for all weather. It was a fair drive to the base and then a good few hours' hike to the top, and they wanted to make it before daybreak.

'Are you okay, sweetheart?' Nick asked, sensing Steph's unease. She nodded, a fake smile crossing her lips.

'If you'd rather do this by yourself, Millie and I can stay behind,' he said.

'No, Nick, I want you there. I'm fine, it just seems so final, that's all.'

'I know.' He dropped a kiss on her forehead. 'He'll always be there in your memories, I promise you that.'

The kids were all excited as they arrived at the trail, and their fitness showed as they took off ahead, with Steph and Nick lagging behind. Nick carried the box of Chris's ashes in his back pack, and he reached for Steph's hand under the moonlight, giving her an extra boost to keep going.

By the time they made it to the top, the three kids were sitting around on rocks, chatting amongst themselves, giving a little cheer when their parents came into view.

'Wow!' Steph gazed around and admired the view from the top. 'It's so beautiful.'

Daylight was breaking through as the sun began its ascent on the horizon.

'Okay guys, are you ready to do this?' Steph

asked, gripping the hands of her boys. Caleb and Levi both looked at Nick, their eyes questioning him. Steph turned to him in confusion.

He returned the silent look, and they both nodded. Steph saw Millie smiling to herself and it dawned on her there was something happening that she was unaware of. She searched their faces, waiting for someone to tell her what was going on, and then she clasped her hand over her mouth, everything falling into place. Millie held her phone, filming, as Nick fell to one knee, producing a small box from his jacket pocket. The sun radiated above his head and a shimmery glow shone around him. Her eyes filled with tears and she looked at her boys, questioning their involvement and their acceptance of what was happening. They both grinned and nodded before she turned back to Nick, who waited for her to look at him.

'Steph.' Nick cleared his throat, and he ran through the words he'd practised in his head. 'Caleb, Levi and I have discussed this moment at length and we all agreed we wanted Chris to be here with us for this, but if you feel even a tiny bit like I've hijacked your special moment, then please say so now, and I'll stand up.'

Steph again looked at each one of them and they beamed back at her. She shook her head.

'No, carry on,' she said, shellshocked.

'Like I said, I know this is unorthodox, but it's important to me, and the boys, that Chris always be a part of your life. We didn't feel it was right for you all to move on without him, so we came up with this as a plan for him to be involved in the only way possible by sharing this moment with us before you say your goodbyes.'

'Nick...'

'I love you, Steph, and the way you've welcomed me and my girls into your family has made us realise that we never want to be apart from you. We want to share our life with you and for you to share your life with us. We want to be a family, to be there together for all the ups and downs.' Nick's voice choked on his words as his emotions overwhelmed him. 'Will you marry me?'

This was so much more than a proposal. It was an emotional goodbye too, and Nick had worried about bringing the two moments together, but the boys had given him all the encouragement he needed. They'd thought it was fitting, a perfect way to close one chapter and open another.

Steph looked around at all three kids, needing reassurance from them. They all nodded in support, eager for her response. She smiled at them, the tears flooding over and trailing down her cheeks.

'Yes,' she said, nodding. 'Yes, I'll marry you.'

He leapt up from his kneeling position and pulled out the ring, a simple white gold band with a princess cut diamond. His hands were shaking as he slid it on her finger, a perfect fit after Levi had done some detective work on his behalf. Steph held up her hand and admired the ring.

'I love you, Nick. This means so much to me. Thank you for putting my boys' feelings first.'

Nick beamed as he hugged her, then stepped back and took her hands, the moment turning a little more sombre.

Steph nodded. It was time to say goodbye. Nick picked up the container where he'd placed it before he got down on one knee and handed it to Steph. The boys came forward to join their mum as Nick and Millie moved to the side, giving them space to do this alone.

Steph unscrewed the lid, and with a deep breath, released her husband's ashes across the landscape.

'Bye Chris, I hope you're at peace now. I will always love you, and I'll always carry you in my heart.' Her words carried across the breeze as her fingers grazed the two entwined hearts hanging around her neck.

'Bye Dad, we love you,' Caleb said, followed by his brother's words, 'rest in peace, Dad.'

Steph put down the container and wrapped her arms around her sons' waists.

'Are you guys okay?' she asked.

'Yeah,' they both said. 'Are you okay, Mum?'

'I feel at peace. You know I'll always love your dad, but I love Nick now, too. We have a new family, but Dad will always be a part of us. We won't forget him,' she said.

The three separated and Steph turned to where Nick and Millie watched on, empathy and kindness flooding their faces.

'Come join us,' Steph said. 'Let's not waste this sunrise. It's beautiful.'

The five of them stood, arms wrapped around each other, as the sun rose on their new chapter.

reached out sooner and asked for the help they needed.

There is a number of organisations working to break the taboo and provide access to much needed services. Talking about our thoughts and feelings is an important step in seeking help - whether it be a call to lifeline, a visit to a GP, a chat with a loved one, or even a stranger, that initial contact can make a world of difference.

As always, I thank my family for their love and support, and their daily anecdotes that bring joy and laughter to my life.

Acknowledgements

I couldn't have written this book without the very specific insights into living with depression from the men willing to share their stories with me. I respect the wishes of certain sources to remain anonymous and thank them wholeheartedly for their brave contribution.

One source has given me a personal insight into high-functioning depression. Very few people know of my husband's battle with depression as it can be difficult to read the signs, and like many men he felt trapped by the taboo surrounding mental health. His courage to embrace his illness and adopt a transparent approach to his recovery has been inspiring and I thank him for stepping out of his comfort zone to help break down the stigma for others.

Although it has improved in recent years, the stigma surrounding mental illness is still very real, more so for men than women - an estimated 72% of men don't seek help. The overriding message I got from my research is that people wish they had

About The Author

Lyndsey Jeminson grew up in Bingley, West Yorkshire, a stone's throw from Brontë Country. She moved to Perth, Western Australia with her husband and two daughters, where they live with their British Short Hair silver tabbies, Aspen and Blizzard, and their spoodle pup, Ralph. She has a Bachelor degree in History and Australian Indigenous Studies and loves nothing more than a walk on the beach and an oat latte.

Printed in Great Britain
by Amazon